THE DAVE BLISS QUINTET

Also by James Hawkins

INSPECTOR BLISS MYSTERIES

Missing: Presumed Dead
The Fish Kisser
No Cherubs for Melanie
A Year Less a Day

NON-FICTION

The Canadian Private Investigator's Manual
1001 Fundraising Ideas and Strategies for Charities and
Not-for-profit Groups

THE DAVE BLISS QUINTET

An Inspector Bliss Mystery

James Hawkins

A Castle Street Mystery

THE DUNDURN GROUP
TORONTO

Editor: Barry Jowett
Copy-editor: Jennifer Bergeron
Design: Jennifer Scott
Printer: Webcom

Canadian Cataloguing in Publication Data

Hawkins, D. James (Derek James), 1947-
    The Dave Bliss Quintet / James Hawkins.

ISBN 1-55002-495-7

I. Title.

PS8565.A848D39 2004   C813'.6   C2004-901390-4

1   2   3   4   5   08   07   06   05   04

We acknowledge the support of the **Canada Council for the Arts** and the **Ontario Arts Council** for our publishing program. We also acknowledge the financial support of the **Government of Canada** through the **Book Publishing Industry Development Program** and **The Association for the Export of Canadian Books**, and the **Government of Ontario** through the **Ontario Book Publishers Tax Credit** program.

Care has been taken to trace the ownership of copyright material used in this book. The author and the publisher welcome any information enabling them to rectify any references or credit in subsequent editions.

J. Kirk Howard, President

Printed and bound in Canada.♻
Printed on recycled paper.
www.dundurn.com

Dundurn Press	Gazelle Book Services Limited	Dundurn Press
8 Market Street	White Cross Mills	2250 Military Road
Suite 200	Hightown, Lancaster, England	Tonawanda NY
Toronto, Ontario, Canada	LA1 4X5	U.S.A. 14150
M5E 1M6		

*To my son, Captain Ian Hawkins, one of the
many brave mariners who have navigated the
Mediterranean Sea, at the mercy of its unpredictable
winds, since time immemorial.*

North

La Tramontane

Mistral

Gargali

Pounant

La Levantade

Sirocco

La Bech

Lou Marin

The Winds of the Mediterranean Sea

chapter one

"A m I interrupting? What are you writing?"
*The blade of a dagger sliced between her ribs,
nicking her bikini strap. A pair of perfectly moulded
breasts perked upwards in momentary relief, her back
arched in agony, then she slumped to the sand with her
attacker's name on her lips.*

"Sorry," he says, glancing up at the slender woman
silhouetted against the Mediterranean sun, her plentiful
breasts still safely clasped in her bikini's hold.

"I asked you what you were writing," she repeats,
sliding closer to him along on the seawall while casually dusting sand from her naked feet.

"A novel," he answers, pumping himself up, getting
a lift from the words. Nothing wimpish — not a short
story or a newspaper article. Nothing egotistical, either
— like poetry or memoirs. "A novel," he repeats, immediately realizing the allure the simple phrase could have.

"Can I read it?" she asks.

That's allure, he thinks, saying, "No. Sorry, it's not finished yet." And, folding his journal with emphasis, he gazes out over the blue bay, seemingly seeking inspiration.

"*Pardonnez-moi*," she mumbles, edging away, then pauses quizzically. "Are you known? I mean ... famous, perhaps. Should I recognize you?" Her narrowed, questioning eyes corner him.

"Dave," he says, tentatively extending a hand, peering into her eyes with the slowly developing realization that she may be the one he is seeking.

"Dave?" she queries, then hesitates. And ...? her eyes demand. Do I have to ask? Do you expect me to drag it out of you? Maybe your mother stitched it to your underpants — should I look? "Dave?" she queries again.

"Dave ..." He wavers, still undecided. "Dave Burbeck." Shit! he thinks, why did I say that? Maybe because that poster over there says: "*Festival de Jazz de la Côte d'Azur — avec Dave Brubeck.*"

With a curious eye on the poster she inches closer to him. "Not ...?"

"Oh, good Lord ... no. Not *Bru*beck," he replies a touch hastily. "It's *Bur*beck, Dave Burbeck."

Now she eyes him skeptically and queries, "Burbeck?" as she checks out the poster again. "Bit of a coincidence, isn't it?"

Bugger — I've only just started and she's blown my cover already.

"I said," she continues, like a poodle with a bone, "it's a bit of a coincidence — Brubeck; Burbeck."

"Sorry," Detective Inspector David Bliss of London's Metropolitan Police replies, hoping to move on. "I was miles away ... thinking of the next line for my book."

"It must be very exciting being a writer," she says, putting on her high beams in admiration and letting go of the bone. "What's it about?"

"Life."

"Romance?" she queries with a mischievous smirk.

"Death."

"Oh," she shudders, "I'm not keen on death."

"I'm not sure many people are."

"I'm Marcia, by the way," she says, finally reciprocating and offering a hand, deliberately holding back her surname, waiting for him to be straight with her.

"Dave Burbeck," he starts, still holding her hand, still wondering how to break the ice. "Oh. You know that already."

"Yes," she says, critically eyeing the poster on the billboard. "That is what you told me." Then, catching Bliss by surprise, she jumps onto the sand and strides off along the beach towards the centre of St-Juan-sur-Mer. "See you again, Mr. Brubeck," she calls over her shoulder with a knowing lilt in her voice.

"It's Burbeck," he calls after her, adding, "Wait, I need to talk to you." But she doesn't.

"Nice looking woman; could she be the one?" he muses, watching as she heads towards the centre of town. "Who would want to stick a knife in her?" And he picks up his pad and starts again.

A gunshot rang out ...

"I think I've made contact," Bliss says a few hours later, telephoning his office in London from a pay phone a few miles along the coast, in the ancient Provençal port of Antibes, strictly according to his handler's instructions. ("Christ, that's taking it a bit far," he said originally. "Can't be too careful, Dave," the senior officer insisted.)

"You *think* you've made contact," his handler queries now, impatience adding a critical edge. "Didn't she ID herself positively — give the code word?"

"Not exactly, Guv, though I didn't expect her to immediately. She'll probably be a bit cagey for awhile ... want to check me out. She's probably got a lot at stake." He pauses, thinking: Her neck, probably. "But she's English, thirty-five-ish, short black hair, mouth-watering breasts, eyes like pools of liquid ebony ..."

"What the hell?" exclaims the voice on the phone.

"Oh. Sorry, Guv. I got carried away. Anyway, she obviously made a beeline for me when no one else was about. The beach was almost deserted — everyone still sleeping it off or jostling for a croissant and *chocolat chaud*. The bloody beaches are packed by nine in the morning, and Noel Coward was wrong — mad dogs and Englishmen aren't the only ones baking in the midday sun — and no one leaves 'til five."

"Hardly a day in the office, though," snorts the sarcastic voice at the other end with the weariness of a wet Thursday in London.

"Tougher, if you ask me. Have you any idea what it's like to be a professional sunbather?"

"Stop whining. You're getting paid. By the way, what's your cover?"

Bliss tells him, and the phone explodes. "Dave Burbeck!" yells his contact.

"I know what you're thinking, Guv. But the name just slipped out. Anyway, it matches my initials. Dave Bliss, Dave Burbeck."

"Detective Inspector Bliss," starts the voice, a mixture of officialdom and royally pissed-offedness. "You've had two weeks swanning about on the poxin' beach in the South of France to come up with a plausible cover, and the best you do is a bleedin' rock star."

"Jazz, actually. But it's Burbeck, not Brubeck."

"Don't push it, Bliss. So what bloody creative occupation did you conjure up for Mr. Burbeck? Astronaut, perhaps?"

"I'm an author, working on my first novel — a historical mystery."

The line goes silent while his contact thinks for a few seconds. "That's actually a bloody good cover," he says, taking his hand off the mouthpiece, Bliss's inappropriate choice of name temporarily forgotten or forgiven. "But what about the informant?" The crustiness is back. "Where is she? Who is she? Why the bloody hell did you let her go?"

Leaving the pay phone, nestled coolly under a fruit-laden fig tree in the shade of the stone ramparts of the fifteenth-century fortifications, Bliss flinches under the stark glare of the midday sun and scuttles into the shade of a clump of eucalyptus trees edging a dustbowl. A group of serious-faced *pétanque* players momentarily take their eyes off their *boules* and critically inspect him as he flops onto a convenient bench, flicks away a hostile wasp, opens his writing pad, scrubs out his previous words, and begins again.

The pink and white blossoms of oleanders, together with the trumpets of hibiscus, paint the hedgerows and scent the air with a sweetness that transcends the derision and bitterness of everyday existence.

The *pétanque* players pick up where they left off, like a small grazing herd that was only momentarily alarmed by the presence of a predator. Typically French, thinks Bliss, perplexed by the indifference of the seemingly earnest players as their *boules* ricochet off stray pebbles on the bumpy ground and veer off course. Why don't they play on a proper court? he wonders, his desire for competitive precision honed on the billiard-table bowling greens and fiercely rolled cricket pitches of England, and his mind leads him home and to the reason for his presence on the Côte d'Azur.

"We want you to take it easy for awhile, Inspector," Commander Richards, his contact, declared a few weeks earlier, immediately raising Bliss's suspicions. Richards was a stranger. An admin man from headquarters with half-rimmed reading glasses, a no-nonsense moustache, and a seriously sympathetic mien. He had been brought in for the occasion, Bliss assumed. Bad news, like a solicitation for a charitable donation, was always easier delivered by, and received from, a stranger, and Bliss saw through the ploy, and the words, immediately. Take it easy *permanently*, the commander meant, hoping Bliss might take the hint.

"You probably need a bit of help from the trick-cyclist after what you've been through," he suggested, and Bliss knew what that meant as well. Seeking help from a psychiatrist was an easy route to an untimely discharge, his record of service indelibly embossed "Unfit for duty." Funny that, he thought. Get a bullet in the leg in the line of duty and the force can't do enough for you ... but a wounded brain can be more damning than bubonic plague.

"Have a stiff drink, old chap. Do you a world of good," was about all the sympathy you might expect following a traumatic event — and Bliss had certainly suffered that. Of course, he might wangle a spell of light duties — as if regular police work were particularly heavy — frittering away a few months, even years, flying a desk at New Scotland Yard, churning out irksome directives with Richards and the rest of the sore backside brigade, muttering: "My life's bloody boring; why should you be enjoying yourself?" Or quit. Wasn't that what they really wanted? A tasty pension was being dangled — his twenty-two years of service would be rounded up to thirty, and they'd throw in a disability bonus — then he could follow the common path down to a little country pub where he would enthrall his patrons with wildly exaggerated tales of heroic adventures. Not likely, he'd decided unhesitatingly, perplexed by coppers who'd spent half their careers chucking inebriates out of pubs, and their retirements dragging them back in. There was, in any case, a more self-serving reason for him not to ride off quietly into the sunset: retribution. He still had a score to settle. However, there was an alternative on the table: a covert assignment on the French Riviera under the guise of protracted convalescent leave.

"This is absolutely hush-hush," Richards whispered, leaning menacingly across his desk, his tone as sharp as his moustache. "Not a word to anyone — understand?"

Bliss recoiled into his chair, ducking a waft of whisky-laden breath, and Richards took it as a rejection. "It's OK, Inspector," he said, relaxing. "I quite understand. I don't suppose you want another foreign assignment just yet."

"It wasn't an assignment ..." Bliss started, then tried to let it drop, knowing he was still under a cloud for attacking his senior officer and then flying halfway around the world in pursuit of a multiple murderer on his own initiative. The fact that the officer, Superintendent Edwards, had been promoted while facing disciplinary charges arising from the incident gave Bliss a fairly good idea of the direction of the wind.

"It's entirely up to you," Richards said with an encouraging half-smile, "but I would have thought a few months in the South of France, full pay plus all expenses — and I mean *all* expenses — would get you back on track."

"Have you any idea ...?" Bliss scoffed, knowing the usual stinginess of the force.

But Richards knew the cost. "It's an important case, Inspector. The sky's pretty much the limit."

If this was an olive branch, it was hung with juicy fruit. Or would it turn out to be just a carrot to lure him out of the way while a certain senior officer was given a slap on the wrist?

"I can't," Bliss replied, easing himself forward. "I'm a witness against Edwards. He nearly got me killed trying to cover his backside."

"Chief Superintendent Edwards to you," Richards admonished, his tone immediately souring. "Innocent until proved guilty, Inspector, as I'm sure you're aware. And you needn't worry — you'll be notified of the disciplinary hearing in plenty of time to return."

"Your mission," Richards told him, "is simply to locate this person, positively identify him, and report his whereabouts."

The apparent simplicity of the task left Bliss skeptical. They didn't need an inspector for this. A grunt with six months' service could do this — even a civvy could do it — at a fraction of the cost.

"Is that it?" he asked, certain he was being sidelined.

"That's it, Inspector. In fact, you are specifically ordered not to take it further. This is very delicate, as I'm sure you appreciate."

Bliss nodded appropriately, none the wiser.

"Precipitous action on your part could prove fatal," Richards continued, his face saying he was well aware of Bliss's proclivity for taking matters into his own hands when he believed the situation demanded it.

But what about me? wondered Bliss. Could it prove fatal to me as well? He didn't ask, suspecting the unreliability of any possible answer.

"Just find him, and enjoy yourself while you're at it," Richards concluded, asking, "Is that a problem?"

"What's he wanted for?" Bliss asked, but the senior officer's blank expression and vague explanation left him hanging.

"Worldwide crackdown on the big boys. Someone upstairs pissed off with prisons full of petty criminals when the real villains are laughing all the way to the Caribbean and the Côtes du filthy rich."

"Don't we have special people for this?" asked Bliss.

"Yeah — you."

"Give me a break, Guv. You need someone who can mingle with the hoi polloi. Why not pick someone with an aristocratic background?"

"Yeah — like they're lining up to join the force, Dave. I can just see it: Lord Fotheringale hyphen Smythe the poxing third turning up at training school in a Ferrari, with his butler, valet, and personal chef dragging behind in a Range Rover."

"I knew a cop who had a Ferrari once."

"I remember his case," Richards said. "Didn't he go down for three years for extortion? Wasn't he rolling over pimps for twenty percent of their takings and showing the new girls the ropes?"

"That's him," Bliss laughed, "but what about MI5, or whatever they call themselves these days?"

"Not their bag. This has nothing to do with national security. This guy's just a crook."

"Interpol then?"

"Waste of time, unless we know for sure where he is."

The heady scent of oleanders, writes Bliss, restarting his journal as he strolls around the bay towards the lighthouse that dominates the town from its lofty outcrop, *and the bouquet of mimosa and hibiscus fills the motionless parched air, already laden with the perfume of lavender and rosemary, and sweetens the stench of decaying seaweed and overburdened sewers.*

He pauses, scrubs out the whole lot, and starts again. *Oleanders,* he writes, stops, and slams the book shut — his concentration sabotaged by the heat, the beauty, and a degree of apprehension. Worrisome thoughts of Chief Superintendent Edwards weigh him down as he struggles up the Chemin du Calvaire towards the Cap D'Antibes lighthouse. Rough stone steps, grooved by the feet of pilgrims since 981, according to the sign, lead him past the

Stations of the Cross let into wayside niches, and he tags onto a group of straight-faced novitiates under the tutelage of a wimpled nun. They may be following the footsteps of a millennium of Christians, but he can't help feeling they've been led to the Côte d'Azur as a warning against the sins of the flesh.

"Christ is condemned to die," he translates, using the bas-relief carving as a guide at the first of the tableaux. The figures of Pontius Pilate's court, assembled to pronounce the verdict with Judas skulking in the wings, are carved into the background, with the thorn-crowned head of Christ taking centre stage. Turning away, he smiles at the ironic thought that were it today, Chief Superintendent Edwards would undoubtedly be the one in the middle with the toga and laurel wreath.

The walk back to his apartment should only take fifteen minutes along the narrow laneways fringed with oleander, mimosa, and grapevines, but his eyes and mind wander to the barely covered nymphs sashaying to and from the beach. Where are all the fat women? he is wondering, when a couple of grandes dames, with two hours of makeup and more glitz than a mirror ball, light up as they hobble by on four-inch stilettos. Their string thongs bite deeply into flabby behinds. He returns their smiles — just for a second. *Oh, their agony and their ecstasy.*

The afternoon drips by as he soaks up the sun on the apartment's balcony.

Bollocks to Richards and the lot of them, he thinks to himself. Why should I put myself out? I think I'll just stay here and write my book. It might even turn out to be a best-seller — *Six months in Provence,* or something similar.

Seeking inspiration, he peers over the balcony. Fifty feet below, a lemon tree straddles an unmarked fence line between the garden of the ground-floor apartment and the park beyond. Ripe lemons dot the tree like Christmas decorations, and he watches as one, fatigued by the heat, lets go of its branch and falls to the grass.

"Wow!" He laughs, startled by the synchronicity of the event, feeling that, in some way, he had been drawn to watch — as if the lemon were a gift to him. It is a Hollywood moment, he decides — lights, cameras … action! — but isn't everything here a movie set?

The lemon, starkly yellow in the bright afternoon sun, shines like a beacon, and, pulling on shorts, he plops a fresh ice cube into his Perrier and heads for the elevator.

The click of a door latch catches his attention as he emerges on the ground floor. He spins — too late, the door has closed, but he knows which one — and stands in frustration as he feels the stare of the occupant through the spyhole. Now what? he wonders, knowing the apartment is the one that backs onto the garden bordered by the lemon tree. Returning to the elevator in disappointment, he is struck by a feeling of déjà vu and casts his mind over similar occasions during the previous week. The same door latch had clicked more than once. The same eye had spied.

"Weird," he mumbles, sloughs off the temptation to squint through the spyhole, and takes the stairs up to his apartment, the climb giving him thinking time.

I'll phone Samantha, he thinks, realizing he hasn't spoken to his daughter since a brief call from the airport in Nice to report a terror-free flight. And tell her what? *There's a lemon on the grass and I want to pick it up.*

What did Richards say? "No personal calls, Dave." Though he pulled back at the sight of concern on Bliss's face. "Except in emergencies, of course."

This is an emergency, Bliss lies to himself, and calls.

Listening to the *brrring* of her phone, he works out how long it has been since he spoke to her. Two weeks, he realizes. What to tell?

I'm writing a book.

Great — what's it about?

OK. Better not mention the book, but what else? Two weeks walking the streets and quays clutching a photograph of the wanted man. But what was he wanted for? Who wanted him? What would happen to him?

Two weeks and absolutely nothing has happened — apart from the woman on the beach this morning, and the lemon falling — hardly notable. Though maybe it is some sort of portent, signalling the start — but of what?

Samantha's recorded voice breaks into his thoughts and invites him to leave a message. He puts the phone down. What could he have said? *Love you — miss you.*

And what would she think?

OK, so I'm a bit lonely. Lonely and bored, he admits to himself, wondering why he hadn't given her his cellphone or apartment number for a return call. He would have to talk to her soon, though. It wasn't as if she didn't know where he was or what he was doing.

"This could take months, even years," he explained to her before leaving, despite Richards's admonition that he shouldn't tell anyone. Samantha wasn't just "anyone," and a disquieting internal voice urged him to make sure someone knew — another reason he didn't want her to call. Just in case *they*, whoever *they* were, had tapped the phone at either of their apartments.

"They are asking me to live in the South of France, all expenses paid, for gawd knows how long, just to catch one villain," he told her as they meandered along the back lanes of the South Downs.

"Dad. Where's this leading?" Samantha asked, puzzled by a church that appeared to be identical to one she'd seen ten minutes earlier.

"I'm not sure," he replied, missing her point, preoccupied with thoughts of Edwards and Richards. "That's the problem. I can't decide if this is a put-up job just to get me out of the way —"

"No, I meant where does this road go?" she cut in. "I thought you were taking me to lunch, not on an expedition to the farthest flung corner of the British Empire."

"This is Kent," he started, then caught on. "Oh. I see what you mean."

A mock-Tudor pub appeared around the bend ahead, and Bliss gave the impression he'd been aiming for it all along as he swung into the parking lot. Minutes later, they were at the bar, waiting for their table.

"Drugs," suggested Samantha, sipping her gin and tonic.

"No thanks," he joked.

"Be serious, Dad. You know what I mean."

It was the obvious conclusion, though it offered no explanation for the secrecy. The faces of drug barons regularly filled the pages of *The Police Gazette*.

"Is it common to be given a assignment without being given the reasons?" Samantha enquired.

The correct answer would have been: "Yes, if there's a risk someone will tip off the target." Although that answer left him questioning what the hierarchy really thought of him. "All they told me was that he's a really big fish," he said, skirting the question.

"Well," she laughed, "the Med's only a small pond. It shouldn't be too difficult to find him."

"It's still a bit fishy," Bliss said, making her laugh again.

"What do you know about him?" Samantha enquired, switching on her courtroom voice.

"Not a lot," he confessed, though he was reluctant to admit Richards had fobbed him off with a "need-to-know basis" excuse. "I've got a photo and a description, and I'm supposed to get the rest from an informant when I get there."

"Informant?"

He nodded, a handful of peanuts poised. "Someone tipped off the Yard to his location — possibly his wife. Apparently he did a bunk with a bimbo."

"Hell hath no fury ..." Samantha started, and then urged him to take the case as she screwed up her nose at the dog-eared menu. "It sounds like a doddle to me. Can I come and visit? The food there is fabulous."

"Might have known you had an ulterior motive. The trouble is that people have a habit of getting killed when I get involved."

"And you blame yourself?" she asked, her voice lifting in surprise.

"No," he began, though he was beginning to wonder.

During Bliss's evening promenade, which has become a daily ritual, he checks out the quayside restaurants and packed bars of St-Juan-sur-Mer, Johnson's photograph tucked inside his writing pad. Two weeks' eyestrain has left everyone looking pretty much the same, and every day he's spotted at least one dead cert whom he has eliminated one way or another, but he still searches diligently, and still waits for the informant to leap out of the shadows and announce herself with the codeword.

The ancient port and faded resort of St-Juan-sur-Mer, squeezed out of the travel brochures by the pushy hoteliers of Cannes and Nice, has kept a grip on its narrow beach and clientele of loyal tourists only by fighting off the invasion of casinos, nightclubs, and amusement arcades that have swamped its neighbours. The one concession to modernity lies at the foot of the main street, where once upon a time Napoleon, escaping from exile on Elba, landed to form an army. Now a modern marina, with cosmopolitan quayside restaurants and bars, accommodates the overflow of yachts escaping from the snobbery of the long-established harbours that dot the coast.

The bar L'Escale is one of the old brigade, with its smoke-stained ceiling, twenty-year-old Pernod posters, and a flickering 1960s neon sign. It still stands sentinel over the old port, although it is cut off from the wide promenade — and its customers, sheltering under shady plane trees and parasols — by the racetrack of the coast road. What's the life expectancy of a staff member? wonders Bliss, watching the slender, olive-skinned waitress zigzagging between speeding cars, buses, and motorbikes as she spies him approaching his regular table.

"*Vin rouge,*" he orders with a smile as he pulls up his chair.

"*Vous parlez français comme une vache espagnole,*" laughs Jacques, the table's other occupant, as Angeline,

the waitress, streaks back across the roadway to fetch
his drink from the bar.

Why would Spanish cows speak French? Bliss
wonders, but doesn't ask for fear of further exposing
his linguistic shortcomings as he greets the weather-
tanned Frenchman.

"*Bonsoir*, Jacques, you smooth talker. Are you
well? *Ça va?*" asks Bliss.

"*Oui*. I am absolutely perfect," responds Jacques,
but then his face falls as he casts a jaundiced eye out
over the sea, complaining, "But zhe fishing ... *merde!*"

"No sardines today then, I guess," says Bliss in
English, mindful that while his ability to speak French
may get him a decent meal and a good bed for the
night, it doesn't stretch very much further — a point
that came into question during his briefing by
Commander Richards.

"You do speak the language, don't you?" the officer
asked, and while the words "not much" might have got
him off the case, his service record lay open in front of
Richards. The answer was there — he'd put it down as
an attribute when applying for promotion to inspector,
never thinking anyone would ask for proof or expect a
conversation — and this was not the time to give anyone a reason to call him a liar.

Angeline rushes the traffic with the determination
of a frog heading for spawning grounds and delivers
Bliss's wine as two couples swoop on a nearby table and
vie for seats overlooking the harbour. The men win; the
women's faces fall; the men relent; the women smile —
everybody feels victorious.

"Zhey are Engleesh," says Jacques, nodding to the
newcomers as he lights a cigarette. "Zhe anorak brigade,"

he adds with a sneer, and his words sink home with Bliss as they tuck plastic raincoats and rolled umbrellas under their seats, while pulling sweaters and jackets tight against the balmy night air.

"Warm evening," Bliss calls to break the ice.

"Too bloody hot if you ask me," answers one, taking a handkerchief from his jacket pocket to dab his forehead.

War babies, thinks Bliss, putting them in their late fifties or early sixties, and he wanders over to introduce himself.

"Hugh Mason and my landlubbers, Mavis, John, and Jennifer," pronounces Hugh, the sweaty one, the fit of his navy blazer marking him as a man whose seafaring experience has been largely honed in the bar of the Admiral Nelson or Rover's Return. Bliss is still wondering how long it has been since he was able to button it up when Jennifer pipes up and asks his name.

"Dave Burbeck, author," he responds.

"Ooh, what d'ye write?" she gushes.

"Books," he begins, but the start of a frown warns him against humour. "I'm working on a historical mystery," he continues.

"The old skulduggery —" starts Mavis.

"There's plenty of that here," butts in Jennifer, and Bliss is on the point of asking if anyone can place Johnson's face when Jennifer lets slip that she is referring to the local entrepreneurs. "Do you know what they charge for a cuppa?" she demands.

"Cheaper to drink wine, if you ask me," says Hugh, clearly speaking from experience.

"First day?" asks Bliss, their pallidness marking them out as new arrivals, and is surprised to learn they're starting their second week.

"They're going to the beach tomorrow," Bliss explains, returning to his wine and Jacques, as if apologizing for the tardy behaviour of his countrymen.

"Not tomorrow," says Jacques forebodingly, after a thoughtful inspection of the star-filled sky.

"*Pourquoi pas?*"

"Why not?" he repeats in English, castigating Bliss for daring to ask. "The wind, *naturellement. Le mistral*," he declares, as if he has the power to summon the fearsome wind that will strike a chill into the hearts of *les patrons* of the beach restaurants, sweeping with little warning down the valley of the Rhône to toss beach mattresses and umbrellas into the sea, leaving near-naked sun worshippers sand-blasted and wind-sore.

The skepticism on Bliss's face is palpable — this is not the first time Jacques has forecast an ill wind. And, despite the fact that the local man loftily declared, "I am a fisherman — *un pêcheur*," at their first meeting some two weeks earlier, most of his meteorological predictions have been way off course.

"*Bof*," says Jacques, shrugging. "You will see."

The squeal of tires signals a narrow escape, and turns a few heads, as Angeline cheats death to deliver a tray of drinks to a sombre group assembling a few tables into a huddle. "What's happening?" Bliss whispers to her as she passes.

"It is zhe meeting of *les hôteliers* — zhey are crazy. Zhe *potier* makes zhem crazy," she explains. And it's significant that in an area renowned for potters — the pottery capital of France, if not the world — Bliss immediately knows which potter she is talking about. It can only be the bearded man, his battered straw hat perched on a bush of grey hair, throwing small vases and candle holders for a fascinated crowd at the other end of the promenade.

Bliss has paused most evenings, watching the man's deep-set, piercingly blue eyes constantly sweep the crowd as he moulds the revolving clay, noticing the way he works the crowd as he works the piece, watching the girls and women entranced by his powerful, yet tender, fingers sensuously massaging the malleable paste into pretty pots just for them.

Spellbound by his eyes and hands, the women hang back to watch; their menfolk, uneasy at the potter's power, try unsuccessfully to pull away, heading for the bar. The adroit fingers mesmerize and the eyes ensnare as he works pot after pot. Two pots a minute — two hearts a second. Who could not fall in love with this gentle man with the blue eyes? And the women make themselves tall in the crowd as they try to catch his eye with a smile.

"*Combien?* How much?" they ask, as he singles out a recipient and tenderly hands her a pot balanced on a little cardboard tray.

"*Gratuit.* Nothing — it is free," he answers softly, speaking French or English as appropriate, but his begging bowl overflows with notes and coins.

Beaming, they walk away with a little masterpiece forged in wet clay. Who would not leave a large tip for such an exquisite pot? And, pot in hand, they parade their delicate prize along the promenade until they tire. Then, "*Papa,*" or "*Mon chéri,*" they snivel, "please carry my pot." If they are lucky it will still be in shape when they return to their hotel room. "He made it just for me," they imagine boasting to their friends back home in England or America — but how to get it home?

The monthly meeting of L'association des hôteliers de St-Juan (founded 1903, according to the bronze plaque on the wall of the Hôtel Napoléon) is about to address that issue, as the last of the twelve members mutters an apology for his tardiness and pulls up a chair.

"*C'est un emmerdement,*" mumbles the *président,* before calling on the local priest to say a few solemn words at the commencement of the meeting.

"He says it is a shitty mess," explains Jacques, seeing the confused look on Bliss's face.

"What is?"

"*Merde* — zhe pottery, of course," Jacques says, as if Bliss could have worked that out by himself. "Zhey say zhat since zhe potter started giving away his little pots, zheir toilets are always stuffed up."

It is a full turnout, the first in years. Not since the government tried to introduce a uniform and understandable rating system for hotels have they been so united — *no snobby suit from Paris is going to tell us how many stars we can put on our signs — mon dieu!*

Ten men and two women, faces and voices taut with determination, are deliberating the problem of blocked plumbing with more passion than jurors in a contentious homicide. No one seriously articulates a murderous suggestion, though a few moments of solemn consideration are given to ramming a wet pot down the bothersome artisan's throat — a taste of his own medicine. "*Salaud,*" mutters one, and the black-robed priest tactfully withdraws to commune with Bacchus at the bar as he decides on the penance for calling someone a bastard.

"I have asked, begged, and pleaded," explains the *président.* "But no — he will not stop."

"I even offered him free dinners for a month in my hotel," says one, a dustbin-bellied man.

"What did he say?" asks another.

"Zhat he would rather eat his own pots," he mutters weightily as he forks most of an onion and anchovy pie into his mouth, adding as he chomps, "He said ... my food ... tastes like *la ragougnasse* — pigswill — but what does he know? ... He is *Anglais, n'est-ce pas?*"

"The potter is English?" Bliss queries of Jacques, surprised. "Is that true?"

Jacques shrugs. "Perhaps."

The meeting disintegrates into animated discussion groups as the *président*, lacking answers, loses control, and a few passers-by become embroiled, most in defence of the popular artisan.

"What harm is he doing?" complains a young woman carrying a pot. "He makes me smile."

"You'd think differently if you had to dig the shit out of the toilets every morning," replies one of the hoteliers, although the look on the woman's face suggests otherwise.

The answer appears simple to Bliss. "Just put a notice on each toilet," he mumbles, unaware Jacques is listening.

"Do you zhink zhey haven't tried?" he demands, one ear tuned to the proceedings. "*Autant pisser dans un violon.* How you say? It is as much use as pissing into a violin."

"We don't say that," protests Bliss, but he gets the drift.

The raised voices dwindle to an angry murmur as a pretty teenager walks by with two freshly minted pots. "Look what I've got," she calls, beaming, balancing a pot in each hand as she rushes to show her prize to her father.

"Someone's gonna have a bunged-up toilet tomorrow," mutters one of the hoteliers in French, and no one smiles.

"Oh-oh! Here comes another pot headed for zhe toilet," says Jacques, giving Bliss a nudge. Bliss turns, spotting another outstretched hand heading their way, but then his eye is caught by a familiar face hovering in the mid-distance.

"*Excusez-moi*," he says to Jacques, tosses a handful of coins on the table, and takes off.

She's gone by the time he gets there; Marcia, he's certain, was standing alone looking thoughtfully in his direction, but she has been swept into the wash of late-night promenaders, leaving him perplexed.

chapter two

Bliss wakes to another postcard day and wanders, coffee in hand, onto the balcony. Short flecks of cloud, like fleece, turn puce in the first rays of the sun, then shift through red to pink before evaporating in the day's gathering warmth. Ahead, the blue waters of the Mediterranean sparkle with sun diamonds as the gentlest of breezes tickles the surface, and the mistral, foretold so forcefully by Jacques, is stillborn in the mountains.

"This isn't real," he breathes, taking in the sweep of the bay, thinking: It's a setting for a movie, a scene of perfection even Hollywood would have difficulty matching. All that's missing is some mood music, he thinks, and, putting on his Walkman headphones, he flips through the small stack of Brubeck CDs he's picked up at a second-hand mart and stretches out on the padded lounger with "Summer Song" tinkling in his ears.

The top-floor apartment, arranged by Commander Richards, was found for him by Daisy, a bouncy real estate agent with a smile almost as broad as her hips.

"*C'est pas donné*," she explained, expressively rubbing forefinger and thumb together under her nose as she ushered him in. But he didn't expect it to be cheap; didn't want it to be cheap. If this was an olive branch, he intended to squeeze it for all it was worth.

"It would be less expensive in winter," she added, making him wonder what she had been told about his visit.

"It is very comfortable, *n'est-ce pas?*" she gushed, bouncing enthusiastically from room to room as she presented the stainless steel kitchen, pink marble bathroom, and beige leather study complete with computer. Then, with more than a twinkle in her eye, she led him from the lounge to the bedroom and trampolined her ample bottom on the king-size bed, giving him the distinct impression that, with very little encouragement, she could probably be induced to be included in the comforts.

"Very comfortable," he parroted, leaving her testing the bed as he opened the shutters with a touch of a button. "A room with a view" was an understatement, he realized, as he stepped onto the balcony and found a scene culled from *South Pacific* — blue waters, palm trees, white sand beaches, and a cluster of verdant islands in the hazy distance.

Now, two weeks later, the beauty of the vista still stops him every time he gazes out from the balcony. This really could be Hollywood, he thinks, watching yachts in full sail glide silently across the horizon as if pulled on tracks, and he picks up his journal and makes an earnest start.

The shiny façade of the Côte d'Azur is painted gaily across the skyline, and the set is finished with a spectacular backdrop of snow-capped peaks. Across the bay, a cluster of green islands swim in the perfectly blue sea. Sardines and snorkellers dance together in underwater ballet, seagulls share sandwiches with sunbathers, and —

However, the veneer of respectability is thinly spread. Behind the front of Provençal knick-knack stores, pricey fish restaurants, and snotty perfumeries, the stockaded villas of gangland thugs, corporate raiders, stock market fraudsters, smugglers, tax evaders, and tax exiles take cover in the wooded hillsides. The sun, so sharp and welcoming on the beach, barely penetrates the thick cover of eucalyptus and pineapple palms. Heavy-set men loiter in the deep shade near fortified gateways, their bulky jackets singling them out from tourists and tradesmen alike. Powerful cars with deeply tinted windows glide almost soundlessly around contorted laneways, and spiked gates whirr open in recognition of electronic commands. The cars, and their equally shady occupants, slip out of sight as if they had never existed.

Putting down his pen, Bliss picks up his binoculars at the sight of an interloper in the peaceful bay. "It's huge," he breathes, scanning the length of the five-decked yacht, guessing it to be at least forty metres. Must be worth a fortune, he is thinking, when the throaty sound of diesels bobbles across the water as the captain kicks up the power. The sleek vessel lifts her bow and takes off. "Wow!" he murmurs, guessing the mini-cruise liner capable of twenty knots or more as the bow wave rips a white scar across the blue silk sea.

With his concentration broken, he checks his watch and decides on another visit to the beach — maybe Marcia will resurface.

The elevator hums to a halt on the ground floor, and as he steps out the click of the door lock reminds him of the lemon. Damn — I forgot to check if it's still there, he is thinking, when he has an idea and steps back into the elevator. Thirty seconds later, the elevator, empty now, hums to a halt again, and as the door starts to open Bliss, out of breath, bursts out of the doorway from the emergency staircase further along the ground floor corridor.

The apartment door slams with enough force to shake the walls, but not fast enough to prevent him from glimpsing a long-haired woman. Youngish, he thinks, and blond; it's more an impression than an accurate assessment, but it's a start, and he resolves to try again later when she's lost her jumpiness.

The early morning beach still tingles with the freshness of dawn, and the lazy swell gently sighs as it falls onto the shore. Parallel lines pattern the sand where students have earned their croissants and coffee, raking away all trace of the previous day's fun in the sun before taking up their posts as mattress purveyors and beach waiters. A serious-faced couple wearing headphones swing metal detectors ahead of them as they search sightlessly for yesterday's pocket change.

Bliss has hardly taken in the scene when his quarry rushes breathlessly along the beach. "He's gone. He's gone," screeches Marcia, her silk scarf still flying.

"Slow down — slow down," he implores. "Who's gone? Why are you telling me?"

"Aren't you …?" she begins, her eyes questing deeply.

"Aren't I whom?" he demands, determined to force her hand, mindful of Richards's warning to give away nothing without the password.

Marcia, looking confused, starts to turn away. "Sorry, I —"

"Hang on," says Bliss, and the expectancy in his look gives her a clue.

"Bingo," she explodes, almost shouting the pre-arranged codeword.

The meeting is brief, leaving Bliss with more questions than answers. Marcia will say little beyond the fact that the man he seeks has suddenly upped anchor. "He'll kill me," she repeats several times, her eyes as skittish as a doe's on a freeway verge.

"Let me help," he starts, taking a firm grip on her arm to stop her from running.

"Tonight," she says, pulling free. "Go to the same bar tonight and if it's safe I'll talk to you."

"It was you!" he exclaims, but she's gone, walking purposefully away.

A couple of sixty-year-olds skip along the promenade with the agility of teens, rejuvenated by the newly risen sun, their years whisked away on the sea breeze, and Bliss smiles. But his smile is in relief that, after two weeks of soaking up the sun and ridiculously cheap *vin rouge* at the taxpayers' expense, there is finally some substance to the case.

His customary morning stroll to the *boulangerie* for *un petit pain au raisins secs* — a sticky bun shaped like an escargot and stuffed with soft raisins — takes him along the beach road, and he walks in a daze, meditating over his meeting with Marcia. She's scared shitless, he is thinking, when a car skims by, close and fast, and startles him. "That's Edwards," he breathes in disbelief, instantly recognizing the driver. Or was it? The car, speeding like all others, has rounded the bend before he's pulled himself together sufficiently to take the number. Disorientated by concern, he passes the bakery and heads directly for the supermarket.

The cart finds it own way as he idly plucks groceries from shelf and bin. Three jars of salted anchovies end up exchanged for a tub of caramel ice cream, and four varieties of Camembert all make it to the cart when he can't choose between them. Several inviting packets with unknown contents seem to select themselves, but he's careful to pick a twelve-pack of fat-free yogourts. His mind should be on Johnson, but what is Edwards doing here? This is serious, he thinks, putting back the yogourts and taking the crème brûlée instead. Was it him? he wonders, adding a second pack.

Why didn't Richards warn me that Edwards was here? he worries, and, searching for something sweet, he wanders away from his buggy. Later, reaching the cash desk, he comes to his senses when the young assistant gives him a quizzical look as she scans a pack of incontinence pads.

"What the —" he starts, catches on, grabs the package, buries it deep in the cart, and scurries out of the lineup.

Further back in the store, an elderly spinster stands next to Bliss's cartload of comfort food with a tube of hemorrhoid cream in her hand and a lost look on her face. Bliss rounds the corner of the pharmacy aisle, sees her, and scoots off. Try explaining that in Safeway let alone *Le Supermarché Géant*, he reasons, dumping her buggy in the wine department, and, empty handed, he hurriedly makes for the bar next door.

The possible presence of Chief Superintendent Edwards is enough to drive him to order a double Scotch as he deliberates on the suspended officer's motives.

He could be on holiday, says his inner voice.

He's suspended, facing dismissal — for what? Abuse of authority and neglect of duty. Doesn't sound like much, but he nearly got me killed trying to protect his own backside.

So ... he could be on holiday.

He'd only be happy if I were dead. Perhaps that's the plan. That's why I'm here on my own — no backup, no witnesses.

"You are not to tell anyone of this mission. Do you understand? Not anyone." Richards repeated, his face saying he meant it. "As far as everyone is concerned you are on indefinite convalescent leave and no one else will know — not even the force admin officer. If anyone enquires they'll be told — honestly — that you are sick," he said, before adding forcefully, "This is very big case."

Big or dodgy, Bliss thinks, downing the Scotch, seeing Edwards's fingerprints everywhere. *Set Bliss loose on some risky adventure where the best possible outcome is an anchor around his neck ten miles out in the Med.*

He might just be on holiday! screams his inner voice again, desperately wanting him to believe it. Then, with a sudden realization that he has absolutely no idea what is going on in the rest of the world, he finds a pay phone and calls Samantha.

"How are you? Have you found him yet?" she blurts out as soon as she hears his voice.

"Shhh — you're not supposed to know."

"What's up? Do you think my phone is tapped? Dad you're just a cop, not James Bond."

What to say? *My last will and testament is under the mattress in the spare bedroom. You can keep the car.*

"I'm OK, love. Just thought I'd give you a call," he says. There is little point in burdening her with worries of Edwards. Particularly as he may be mistaken — hopes he is mistaken.

"There is something you can do, though," he says, realizing that now the informant has surfaced, Morgan Johnson is a huge step closer to being real. "Maybe you could ask a few discreet questions — who wants him and why. Make sure I'm not chasing a wild goose."

Samantha senses there is something else. "And ...?" she queries.

Warning himself he is getting paranoid, he tasks her to phone Edwards on a pretext. "Just to make sure he is home," he says. "Tell him you're doing a survey on the police suppression of free speech. That should get him going."

"OK. If I've got time."

"Please, Samantha," he begs, then warns in afterthought, "Make sure you use a pay phone."

But what if he's not at home? Bliss sets himself puzzling as he puts down the phone, wanders across the road to the seawall, removes his shirt, and painfully plucks a few grey hairs from his chest as he ponders, What if he is here in the South of France? What does that prove?

He could be working on his defence.

He could be, but surely his best defence would be the mysterious disappearance of the prime witness — a certain detective inspector of close acquaintance.

He wouldn't risk that.

Not personally, maybe, but I bet he'd like to. Not only did you uncover an inconvenient murder that he'd swept under the rug for his own benefit, you also screwed up his restaurant business and broke his wrist.

That's all in the past, he tries telling himself, but knows that Edwards has a long memory.

The morning drags with frustrating slowness, and Bliss spends much of the time tugging at a recalcitrant hair as he lounges in the warmth of the mid-morning sun, cogitating on the Edwards problem while listening to Brubeck playing "Black and Blue" on the radio of the beach café behind him.

Given a choice, Bliss might simply kick back and golf away the rest of his life, but he fears that "out of sight" will certainly leave him "out of mind," and the disciplinary board will let Edwards off the hook. Even with his evidence, Edwards is still capable of squirming his way out of the dung heap he's piled up for himself. Not that he needs to. He has enough names, dates, and places in his little black book to finger most of his colleagues into throwing him lifelines.

That is Edwards's MO, and has been from the day he joined up. Every indiscretion by a fellow officer, every game of golf or glass of beer on company time, every insurrection, however slight, has been meticulously recorded as a hedge. And, like Napoleon, he has never forgotten or forgiven a single transgression.

Turning anxiety into action, Bliss heads along the beach with his journal in hand and a picture of

Edwards in his mind. It is nearing Sunday lunchtime, and memories of Saturday night still haunt some of the faces on the beach. After an hour of diligently searching every prone figure for either Edwards, Johnson, or Marcia, he gives up when he realizes he is starting to have naughty thoughts about near-naked fifteen-year-old schoolgirls. This should be illegal, he thinks, constantly shocked by his inability to judge the age of sun worshippers from more than a few yards, and, plonking himself under a striped umbrella of a beach café, he writes:

The chaud-froid of life stuns with the sharpness of a blisteringly hot sun reflecting off a glacier. The very young and extremely old stand apart, but there is no place for middle age. The middle-aged either pretend to be young or are forced to be old. Nothing in the middle. Seventy-year-olds party the night away. At home they'd be in bed by ten, wrapped in a flannelette nightie, complaining of bunions and biliousness.

Mothers, even grannies, dress with more daring than their offspring. "Mum," the kids complain. "You're not going to the beach in that. I can see your thingies."

"Why not? I can see yours."

"Yeah, but I'm only sixteen. You're old enough to know better."

"Who's the parent in this relationship?"

This place is all about sex, he realizes, and is not disillusioned when a lone woman under the next umbrella peels a purple fig with impossibly long fingernails and exposes the swollen pink interior.

"Witch," he mutters, as she runs her tongue sensuously around the bulbous fruit before taking it, whole, into her mouth.

Back on the beach, a gaudily overdressed Senegalese salesman wearing a coolie hat wilts under the weight of watches, bracelets, and necklaces and is mobbed by a bunch of faithful come to worship at the shrine of glittering possessions.

Twenty watches, stamped Rolex or Cartier according to the whim of the man whose hat he has borrowed, clinch his forearms — ten on each arm, like slave-master's irons — and a hundred other tacky trinkets with expensive names weigh him to the sand. Women and children swamp him as he sinks, and he spreads his wares as best he can. A young girl buys a shell necklace. The string snaps as she puts it on, showering shells onto the sand where other children scrabble for them. *Look, Mum. I've found a shell on the beach.*

Bliss arrives earlier than usual at L'Escale and sees Angeline dodge a speeding motor scooter only to be nailed by a rollerblader as she jumps the curb to the sidewalk. The two English couples, still clutching plastic raincoats, have played musical chairs again, the women having realized that staring out over gently bobbing boats in the serene harbour all evening loses its appeal faster than a shocking pink woolly hat with a spinning plastic rotor blade. Now they can watch the passing hordes and toxic traffic while their partners crick their necks.

Bliss returns their nods of greeting. "Beautiful day again. Did you enjoy the beach?"

"Not on Sunday, old boy," says Hugh, adding in a reverent whisper, "It doesn't seem right, somehow."

"The churches here are so beautiful, aren't they?" responds Bliss, having had plenty of time to study the stack of tourist magazines left in the apartment by previous tenants. "Do you attend regularly?"

"No," Hugh says vaguely, "not particularly — but it just doesn't seem right to go to the beach. Not on a Sunday."

"Not on Sunday," echoes Mavis, though John and Jennifer keep out of the discussion, heads in the menu with an unspoken air of insurrection.

"Tomorrow then," suggests Bliss, but Hugh is ahead of him.

"Monday — washday — always do our washing on Mondays, don't we Mavis?"

"Even on holiday?" exclaims Bliss.

"Especially on holiday," says Hugh.

"Got to keep a sense of proportion, keep a routine," chimes in Mavis forcefully. "You could lose your sanity if you don't keep to some sort of routine."

John and Jennifer look ready to take the risk when Hugh appears to offer a compromise. "We'll probably go Tuesday, if the weather holds."

"It's held perfectly for the past two weeks," Bliss explains.

"Exactly. That's what I'm afraid of," scoffs Hugh, searching the cloudless sky. "Must be about time for it to break. I think I'll wait to see what the BBC forecasts tomorrow evening. No sense in getting our hopes up."

"Wouldn't it be easier just to look out the window in the morning?"

"I think I'd rather rely on the professionals, if you don't mind, old boy," says Hugh huffily.

The squeal of a train's hooter announces the arrival, or departure, of another crowd of tourists, and Hugh laughs, "Mavis says the train whistles here sound like strangled ducks."

Bliss smiles at the image of the driver in his cab throttling a duck into a microphone, then John breaks into his comical thoughts. "Personally, I think it sounds more like an elephant," he says, but Hugh slaps him down.

"Don't be silly, old boy. You couldn't get an elephant in one of those."

As Bliss sits apprehensively on the promenade, checking every face for Edwards or Marcia, an American tourist, foolishly assuming that red traffic lights at a pedestrian crossing will bring traffic to a standstill, is clipped by a flashy Italian bird-puller as he steps onto the crossing.

"Where are you from?" asks Bliss, as he drags the man from the brink and guides him to a chair on the promenade.

"New Jersey," replies the stranger. "Say, thanks bud — that Ferrari nearly got me. It's like a racetrack out there."

"Traffic lights are only advisory here," Bliss explains. "Mainly decoration, in fact."

"Let me get you a drink," says the Yank, summoning Angeline. "You take dollars?" he asks her.

"Sure," she counters. "When you take euros."

A couple of street musicians set up in front of the pre-assembled audience. "Pinky and Perky," Bliss christened them the first night they showed up — two animated little pot-bellied creatures with a piano accordion and a set of pan pipes whom he quite enjoyed, until he realized they played the same four tunes every evening, always culminating in "Guantanamera, gua-ji-ra Guantanamera."

But it isn't just Pinky and Perky — every pianist in every bar, and every busker on the beach and quayside constantly belt out "Guantanamera." It is as if they wait for him as he strolls along the boulevards. He can hear them warming up, timing his arrival. "Guantanamera, gua-ji-ra Guantanamera."

Jacques, the fisherman, isn't at the bar — too embarrassed to admit his weather forecast was off track again, perhaps — or is he out hooking a bigger fish? But the potter is at his wheel. At least a dozen delicately thrown pots are paraded past Bliss by beaming young women and girls, and another half-dozen carried by men, their feelings clearly signalled on their faces: "*Merde!* This one's going straight down the toilet."

"So what was your name before?" Marcia startles him, sliding into an adjacent chair.

"What d'ye mean?"

"Look, one of us is going to have to lay our cards on the table, starting with your name. I mean — Dave Burbeck?"

"It could be," he says, giving nothing away, offering her a drink.

"A cocktail, if you're paying," she says, then refuses to be drawn until Angeline has taken the order and is waltzing her way through the wall of death towards the bar.

"How did you know it was me?" he asks.

"You've been wandering around like a lost Japanese tourist for the past two weeks."

"You've been spying on me!" he exclaims.

"I had to be sure," she starts, but Pinky and Perky, sensing the possibility of a burgeoning romance, appear out of nowhere and jump in with "Autumn Leaves."

"It's July, for gawd's sake," mutters Bliss, hoping to deter them, but they switch to "Strangers in the Night." He tosses them ten euros, which they mistake as a sign of approbation and delve into "Guantanamera" with gusto. Bliss puts his head in his hands, complaining, "Oh God, Perky's singing," then pleads through his fingers, "Please don't sing."

Marcia buries herself in her handbag as heads turn in their direction, and Bliss, worrying she may bolt again, angrily waves the musicians away.

"Please be careful. And make sure you're not followed," Marcia says, sliding a fiercely twisted scrap of paper into his palm, then she slips smoothly into the crowd.

"Bloody woman," Bliss mouths after her, and Pinky and Perky, finally getting the message, seek their next victim as the waitress returns with a giant goblet sprouting vegetables.

"Oh! Your friend, she has gone," Angeline says, her disappointment evident. "She is very pretty."

"She didn't like the orchestra," he says, giving the departing performers a poisonous stare. Then he stops momentarily as he gives Marcia's appearance some thought: shortish — petite, even — with all her lumps and bumps developed in the right places. However, the tautness of concern in her face has left a cloud. He assumes her to be about forty, but is totally confused by the compression of ages, having decided that virtually all women between fifteen and

fifty somehow manage to look twenty-five in this
never-never land. "Yes," he agrees, "I suppose she is
fairly pretty."

Pinky and Perky strike up "Guantanamera" at the
next table, and Bliss pointedly puts on his headphones
as he debates whether or not to run after Marcia. Dave
Brubeck's quartet, playing *"Por Que No? (Why Not?)"*,
reminds him that he is still clutching the paper twist.
"Watch the potter," says the message, and he realizes
that was why she was scrabbling in her handbag —
scribbling a note. But what does it mean?

"Are you Engleesh?" asks a woman with more than
a mouthful of teeth and a nose-in-the-air sneer that says,
"I detect smelly armpits and skid-marked underpants."

"Yes," he starts, removing his headphones, then
switches to French, thinking: I'm supposed to be blend-
ing in. *"Oui. Je suis Anglais."*

Apparently undeterred by his admission she invites
herself into Marcia's seat. *"Cigarette?"* she queries, but
it's an offer, not a request, and, as she delves into her
Louis Vuitton bag for a packet of Gauloises, he wonders
if she is somehow connected to the case. Quickly pulling
his thoughts together he realizes that after two weeks of
inactivity, concerned he is chasing his tail, he is suspicious of everyone.

"Excuse me," he says, guessing her game and rising
to leave. Her face falls. "Please, have this on me," he
says, offering her Marcia's cocktail in consolation, and
she beams.

"Zhanks, Engleesh," she sings out. "Maybe next
time."

I doubt it, he thinks, heading off along the promenade, though he concedes that without the cigarette

she'd be reasonably attractive, despite the teeth — although upsetting her during a bout of *soixante-neuf* could be a painful mistake.

Bliss, trying to work out the meaning of Marcia's note, hurries along the promenade, upstream against a tide of outstretched hands balancing little pots, and finds a semi-circle of admirers around the maker. The women remain transfixed as Bliss pushes his way deeper into the crowd — seeking what? He has no idea. "Watch the potter," the note says, and he watches as the strong hands, caked with creamy clay, cup around the brownish red mound as it rises under the pressure of his fingers. The electric wheel, spinning fast, shoots off droplets of water as the potter teases the rising lump, and Bliss turns his attention to the women in the crowd as they are drawn closer.

What's going on here? he wonders, studying the fascinated faces of the women, as the mound of clay rises like a swelling phallus in the potter's soft, moist hands, his penetrating blue eyes holding the gaze of each woman in turn — just for a second — just long enough to send a message.

Bliss is looking around the mesmerized crowd of women, wondering how many of them will be rinsing out their underpants when they get back to their hotels, when, almost magically, a perfectly proportioned candle holder complete with crenulated drip tray seems to form itself from the ductile material. Seemingly without taking his eyes off the crowd, the potter lifts the work onto a cardboard disk and stands — teasingly.

"Me, me, me," call the younger girls who've elbowed their way to the front — but he is seeking a bigger catch, and locks eyes with a dark-haired teenager hanging onto her mesmerized mother. With the faintest of nods, he signals that she is the chosen one. Blushing fiercely, she forges a path through the crowd and beams with the bashful joy of a supplicant dragged out of the congregation in St. Peter's to kiss the Pope's hem.

For a second the crowd deflates and a few disappointed souls trail away. Others take their place and gravitate towards the wheel as it starts to spin once more.

Over and over the spinning wheel draws the crowd in, until they are glued by the potter's eyes and hands. Two pots a minute spin off his wheel — vases, mugs, candle holders, egg cups, ashtrays — each as perfect and elaborate as the next, each one warming the heart of the recipient. There's going to be a lot of blocked toilets tomorrow, Bliss is thinking, when Marcia catches his eye — she is hovering outside the circle and immediately turns her back as he moves to extricate himself from the throng.

"Do you see the way the women watch him?" she hisses, grabbing his arm and steering him away, marching staunchly from the brightly lit quayside towards the moonlit beach. "Doesn't it make you sick," she spits, "the way they grovel? He gives them a lump of clay that'll dry and crack in a few hours, and they treat him like some sort of god."

"He is giving them more than a pot," starts Bliss defensively. "He is giving them expectation — that they will be the chosen one. He gives them hope."

"Huh! And I know what they're hoping for," she counters angrily.

"What's your problem?" he asks, pulling her up sharply. "You don't own a hotel, do you?"

"Oh, I know all about the hoteliers and their toilets." She laughs dryly. "No, no hotel."

"So why do you care?"

"He's my husband."

chapter three

Away from the boisterous promenade and the rapt throng surrounding her husband, Marcia drags her feet on the beach. Every attempt on Bliss's part to get her talking is rebuffed as, head down, she scuffs along the edge of the gently fizzing surf away from the lights of the town.

Be patient, he tells himself as he drags behind, knowing only too well the vexations of dealing with informants, remembering the hours he's spent doing a dance of a thousand veils with smelly stool pigeons in smoke-filled back rooms of seedy bars, as he pried off each shroud with promises, threats, and rewards. Many proved to be time-wasters, with nothing of substance to offer, holding onto useless snippets with the desperation of a superspy, while others were nothing more than publicity-seeking nutcases. Then there were the altruists, divulging information out of a sense of public duty, throwing off veil after veil with the enthusiasm of a nymphomaniac playing strip poker.

But he also knows, only too well, of the blind alleys, false leads, unwarranted conjecture, and score settling that might turn any informant into a slippery eel, one who could end up writhing around and giving its handler a nasty nip. So it isn't just the information he seeks — it is the motive behind its disclosure. And there is always a motive. Without a clear knowledge of the motive the information is useless.

Marcia, whatever her information and motive, strings him along until he finally digs in his heals.

"Where are we going?" he demands eventually, and she stops and sits decisively.

"Here."

She tests his patience for nearly an hour as they sit on the shadowy beach — using the darkness as another veil, making it impossible for him to read her as she dances back and forth between disclosure and concealment. Eventually, stumbling through tears — pain or fear? he wonders, knowing that almost every informant has fear: the fear of exposure and retribution — she twists a rambling trail out of broken promises and wrecked dreams.

Through her tears, Bliss pieces an image of a charismatic young artist barely out of art college, with his young wife and newborn daughter, fêted by the community and the bank, setting up a pottery in a quaint Cotswold backwater — but the idyllic lifestyle they envisioned gradually soured over the years as the bills repeatedly outweighed the receipts.

Working harder, faster, and longer each day, Greg, her potter husband, tried to outrun a tide of cheap imports and domestic oversupply. Slaving sixteen hours or more a day he turned out pots that, together, they painted, glazed, and fired, but he barely kept their heads above water.

"Ooh! Isn't that lovely," visitors to the studio would coo, watching with fascination as he threw another masterpiece out of a dull mound of clay, but in the showroom their enthusiasm would quickly wane as they pored over the price tag.

Marcia breaks down completely as she reveals the torture of disenchantment with life — the years of struggling to make ends meet.

"Your husband is so clever. I love his work," potential clients would enthuse.

"Why don't you buy it then?" she'd scream inside, knowing that was unfair, knowing her husband's work was so much more valuable than the mass-market products stamped "Hand painted" by some barefoot kid in a sub-Saharan mud hut.

Marcia's snivelling continues as she explains how the stack of bills grew over the years, and the banks, initially so enthusiastic in support of such potential, gradually lost confidence and closed in. The cost of heating a kiln, expensive paints and glazes, rent, taxes, gas, advertising, and the expense of driving around the country with an old Volkswagen van full of pots visiting stores, craft markets, and fairs swallowed everything they ever made. There was never enough, until finally she hit on an answer — a way out of the hole they'd slowly sunk into.

The promenade at St-Juan-sur-Mer. No studio to rent, no light and heat to pay for, none of the expensive materials — only clay, costing little more than the price of digging it out of the ground, and each tiny pot used only a few ounces. No breakages in the kiln — no kiln. No shelves of unsold stock in the showroom — no showroom, and no sticker shock at the exorbitant prices, for there were no prices. "It's absolutely free," he would declare with a sly smile, yet everyone paid.

However, there is obviously something amiss in nirvana. Marcia's attitude towards her husband tells Bliss that the apparently flawless resolution of their problems somehow backfired. Is she jealous? he wonders, his mind on the fawning horde of females wilting under her husband's spell on the promenade. Isn't jealousy so often the spur that finally forces an informant's hand? But if that's the case, what is she trying to tell him? What information can she have that would interest the upholders of Her Britannic Majesty's Law? That her husband isn't paying income tax? Of course he isn't — who would? Bliss thinks, doing a quick mental calculation. Three euros a pot, two pots a minute, he estimates conservatively — all cash, coins, and untraceable bills. No tell-tale receipts or embarrassing credit card slips. That's nearly four hundred euros an hour, he is staggered to realize, not counting the hundreds of tips dropped into the craftsman's begging bowl by the hopeful and grateful whose hearts he touched with a glance or a smile.

But what has this to do with Johnson? he wonders, realizing that, in their three brief meetings, Marcia has never mentioned his target by name. Suddenly, concerned that he may have duped himself into singling her out as the informant when she is just a disenchanted expatriate looking for a convenient shoulder, he catches her arm and demands, "So precisely who is Morgan Johnson? And what's he got to do with you?"

Wrenching her arm free, she covers her face with her hands and scrunches herself into a sobbing ball. "He'll kill me. He'll kill me. He'll kill me," she repeats constantly through the tears, leaving Bliss searching his memory for clues in his briefing with Commander Richards as he tries to figure out what Johnson could possibly be wanted for that would so terrify her.

"Morgan Johnson has our daughter," Marcia finally concedes, her knees protectively clasped to her chest as she sits on the sand staring straight out over the bay, making Bliss gulp at the thought that the girl has been kidnapped.

"And he's demanding a ransom?" he opines, trying to forward the conversation while immediately understanding the reason for so much reticence and secrecy.

"Ransom," she echoes, clearly lost. "What makes you think he wants a ransom?"

The sudden clarity with which he's seen the situation has blinded him to other possibilities, and he finds himself stranded. "I ... I thought you meant she'd been kidnapped," he stammers, but she cuts him off.

"Kidnapped.... No. She's eighteen. Technically old enough to do what she wants."

"So she's not a hostage?"

The answer seems stuck in her throat as she queries, "Hostage?" before admitting in afterthought, "In a way, I suppose she is a hostage," then sheepishly adding, "Hostage to the big H. If you understand me."

"Heroin," he breathes. So, Samantha was right. It is drugs.

But what is he doing here? What has this to do with Scotland Yard? So Johnson is a dealer — even a major player. So what? The back streets, even high streets and executive boardrooms, of London are awash with enough drug barons to keep half the force busy. Why would the Yard push out the boat for this one? There must be more to Morgan Johnson, but Marcia clams up and sits sobbing quietly as she stares out to sea.

With nothing to offer, none of the usual incentives — immunity from prosecution, reduced sentence, money, protection — he can only ask her what she expects of him. What is her motive — revenge?

"Revenge?" she asks vaguely, as if it has never occurred to her.

Bliss has taken two weeks to pin her down and now she's playing a guessing game. As an informant she is as much use as an anonymous tipster. What is in it for her? The return of her daughter? She might get her daughter back physically, but Bliss knows from previous experience that she'll probably end up regretting it.

"Perhaps I should talk to your husband," he suggests finally, realizing he is getting nowhere.

A slap across her face might have brought a less violent reaction. "Don't you dare!" she screeches. "You leave that pig out of this."

"So where is Johnson?" he asks. It is the only question open to him.

"He's gone," she cries, tears streaming down her face and glistening on her cheeks in the moonlight. "I told you this morning. Didn't you see his boat leave?"

"The big one?"

"Yes — the big one," she spits.

"Well, where is he going?"

"Treasure hunting, he reckons."

"But where? How can I find him if you don't tell me where?"

She shakes her head. "I don't know. The only thing I know is that he said he was following the winds."

"Going to see a man about a dog," Bliss muses, recalling the expression his father always used whenever he was being secretive about his destination. "And what about your daughter?"

"Haven't you been listening to anything? I told you — Morgan's got her."

The glow of the waning moon lights a path across the Mediterranean and greets the rising sun as Bliss is drawn to the balcony. Caught in the half-light between the celestial bodies, the lemon, on the grass beneath his apartment, is illuminated by both, and beckons.

With Marcia finally out in the open, though hardly out of mind, he seeks a distraction, and the temptation to seize the fallen lemon re-engages him. Not that he needs a lemon — it's the principle, he tells himself, knowing it is probably bloody-mindedness — but the thought that the only lemons he's previously picked were neatly stacked in a supermarket gondola spurs him on. Who will know or care? he thinks, his determination strengthening as he takes the stairs.

The fallen lemon glints golden in the early morning sun and lures him across the park until he closes in on the tree. Bending, arm outstretched, he is startled upright by the sight of a woman with straggly blond hair and baggy pants, hunching as she shuffles from the ground-floor apartment to the garden, carrying a bundle in her arms.

Caught in the open, only yards from her garden and the tree, Bliss bluffs it out. "*Excusez-moi,*" he says, pointing to the lemon, hoping she may tell him to help himself, but she spins on him in such alarm that he jumps. "It's a man," he breathes, and the certainty of the gender surprises him. It is definitely the person he had glimpsed through the crack in the apartment door — the same hair and eyes — but he's stunned to find a man — a fairly young man at that — twenty-five, he guesses — and in his arms a small spaniel, being cradled face upwards like a baby.

With a shriek of terror the man brings the dog up as a shield in front of his face and scurries across the lawn back to the apartment.

"Sorry — *pardon,*" Bliss calls after him, but the door slams. Sorry for what? he wonders.

Slinking back to his apartment, still lemon-less, he pauses briefly before entering the elevator and has difficulty resisting the temptation to knock on the young man's door to tender a proper apology. If it was a woman, he thinks, I could buy her flowers, even offer a meal — but what to say to a guy?

The weirdness of the young man's appearance and curious behaviour still absorb him, but only as a diversion from deeper thoughts, as he picks up a couple of croissants from the *boulangerie* and heads to the promenade for a morning stroll.

The whisper of a dawn breeze gently wakes the yachts in the marina and sets halyards against masts as he swings his legs over the quayside, bites into a croissant, mulls over his meeting with Marcia the previous evening, and wonders why he has been sent here.

"All you have to do is find him and positively ID him. That's it," Commander Richards instructed. "We'll take out an international warrant and the French can lift him."

Lift him for what? Bliss wondered, skeptically suggesting, "It sounds like you're sending me on a taxpayer-funded holiday."

If Richards had similar thoughts he wasn't sharing. "You happen to be the right man for the job."

"So what are my qualifications?" Bliss pushed, determined to find out what was really behind such an apparently cushy posting.

"You're well travelled."

"That wasn't my fault," he responded, thinking of his previous escapade, which ended disastrously in Canada.

"You're intelligent — got smarts," Richards said, trying flattery, but making Bliss laugh.

"What's funny?" queried Richards.

"Nothing, Guv," lied Bliss, knowing he was laughing at himself for all the times in his life he'd thought everyone else knew more than he and worried about the day he might be found out.

"You look the part," Richards continued, as if reciting a prepared list. "Distinguished, mid-forties — old enough to be wealthy, young enough to be a playboy."

"Plus the fact that it will keep me nicely out of the way while that bastard Edwards does his Houdini impersonation."

"Chief Superintendent Edwards will get what he deserves," Richards replied calmly. No outburst of refutation; no denunciation of Bliss for insubordination; no pulling of rank.

With the realization that Richards was bending over backwards, and figuring he had little to lose, Bliss lounged back in his chair and tried a hot button. "He'll probably get promoted again — but isn't that the way he always gets on? Stirs up enough shit to be a pain in the ass until someone recommends him for promotion, then he climbs on someone else's back and bites their bum."

"And finally — you're single," Richards said, pretending not to have heard, sticking to his script.

"That's not an achievement, Guv."

"I didn't say it was, but for an operation of this kind it's a definite advantage."

This is a misuse of police resources, Bliss thinks, as he dangles his legs over the harbour wall. Cracking down on drug dealers in suburban Surrey might make sense, but sending him to stake out a high-rolling renegade in the South of France only confirms his suspicions that they want him out of the country while Edwards slips his noose.

I bet Edwards orchestrated this whole thing, he reasons, knowing that where other people pull strings, Edwards twists testicles. He must have his hooks into somebody close to the top of the tree for a commander to get the authority to approve this, he is thinking, when he is struck with a mind-blowing realization. What if Richards hasn't got anyone's authority? What if I am actually on convalescent leave? Maybe this important and totally secret undercover job is just a cover; maybe no one really wants Morgan Johnson and no one is going to swear out a warrant for his arrest and extradition; maybe his name has simply been picked out of a hat of international villains for no other reason than he's known to be out of the country.

No wonder Richards was so adamant that no one else should know what I was doing. It had nothing to do with security or the possibility that someone might tip off the suspect; Richards's only concern was that someone might tip off the commissioner — the Grand Vizier of London's metropolitan police force — that one of his most senior commanders was playing hide and seek with a lowly detective inspector.

In that case, who's paying for all this? he asks himself. At the briefing, Richards gave him a shiny American Express card with an unlimited credit balance in the name of John Smith. And the apartment he is staying in is already paid for.

So, how far will Edwards and his cronies go to keep me out the way — assuming that is the plan? he wonders, and considers sticking a hundred-thousand-euro motor yacht on the card as a tester. He could always sell it if the balloon went up.

Wake up, he tells himself. It would be cheaper to have you bumped off.

Would Edwards do that?

He might.

The certainty of the realization stings with the sharpness of a paper cut, then he shakes his head. No, he wouldn't ... I don't think.

With many more questions than answers, he strolls the town streets half-heartedly seeking Johnson, though concentrating more on gathering ideas for his book. It's the contrasts here that make it interesting, he realizes, seeing a shrivelled grey crone, cross-legged on the pavement, with her hand out to an expensively designed woman whose lipstick allowance would feed her for a year. Though it's not just the disparity between rich and poor, he decides, it's the beauty and the beast.

Everything and everyone has a front, he is thinking, as he tours a smelly, garbage-littered back alley and sees a sleek-haired Madonna, sporting breast implants and slinky leather, emerge from a house with peeling paint and sagging brickwork. Then the clack of her Italian stilettos on cracked flagstones echo off the abandoned dust-filled stores where the faded signs of *boulangers*, *traiteurs*, and *charcutiers* are epitaphs to their stolen dreams. Hurrying past abandoned cars with smashed windows and bicycle wheels chained to posts, she turns onto the glitzy shopping street and picks up her head as she passes the storefronts of purveyors and designers whose names and logos fill the glossies of the world.

"It's not exactly Hollywood," Bliss muses, looking around and realizing the streets and stores are filled with local people going about their daily chores. How confusing it must be for them, he thinks, living out their lives in a land of vice-versa, where international villains are lauded and pampered while the odd unemployed bum, unfortunate enough to be of no fixed abode, is roughly rounded up and thrown in jail; where giant yachts, costing more than the Madonna girl could earn in ten lifetimes, sit idle in the harbour, their owners preferring the comfort of their villas after a night at the casino, club, or *bordel*, while the crews busy themselves preparing for another day of idleness.

Rich and poor, good and evil, beauty and ugliness, greed and compassion, all co-exist here in equilibrium, but overall it's the obsession with possession that strikes him most. Flashy yachts, cars, motorbikes, and jewellery may be the preserve of the rich, but even the poorest shop workers and student waiters race around on motor scooters; the girls, with their skirts and hair flying, sit boldly upright for all to see, while the young men, revving their aggressively black 50 cc machines up to 250, crouch low over the puny fuel tanks and dream.

Trapped by indecision, absent-mindedly plucking at his nose hairs, Bliss spends the afternoon on his balcony picking up and putting down the phone. But whom to call? Who would not only know the truth about his assignment, but be prepared to put him in the picture? Any of his regular colleagues at HQ will know only the official line. "You're on convalescent leave, you lucky devil," they'll chirp, and if he pushes them to check in his personal file he'll get the same reply. "Yup. You're on leave all right."

He could try Commander Richards, but to what end? "I thought I made myself clear, Inspector …"

Only the commissioner himself might be privy to his true status, and he smiles at the thought of calling the Yard and demanding to be put through to him — a man commanding a force of thirty thousand, with an entire division of administrators and lackeys whose sole purpose is to isolate him from the riff-raff on the front line.

OK. Just supposing he takes your call — then what? *You probably don't remember me, Sir,* he mentally practises, *but I just wondered if you happen to know that I'm in the South of France chasing a drug smuggler.*

And what if the case is genuine? What if his suspicions are totally unfounded and the commissioner is not only well aware of his mandate, but receives a daily progress report from Commander Richards in person?

"Weren't you specifically ordered that under no circumstances were you to reveal your involvement in this case, Inspector?" the commissioner will bark and slam down the phone. Fifteen minutes later he'd be relieved of duty and ordered home pending disciplinary charges for disobeying a lawful order, breach of confidence, and jeopardizing a major investigation. Not to mention the fact that Edwards's defence team will make mincemeat of him on the witness stand at the upcoming hearing.

"Isn't it correct, Mr. Bliss," Edwards's smarmy lawyer will jab, pointedly refraining from using his rank, "that you yourself are currently facing numerous disciplinary charges?"

Then what?

Though, if Edwards's defence team is as devious as their client, they'll apply for a deferment of the charges against their man, pending the outcome of the trial against the key witness. By which time the civilian address of "Mr." might be entirely appropriate.

Picking up the phone eventually, he decides the only person he can safely call is Samantha.

"I haven't had much chance —" she starts defensively.

"It's OK. Don't bother. I know who he is," he says, adding, "But I'm pretty sure they're trying to buy my silence on the Edwards case."

"It sounds like a pretty fair price to me," says Samantha, well aware of the situation.

"But Edwards might get off the hook."

"So what?"

"Do you know what he did to me?"

"Dad, as far as I remember you broke his wrist," she says, recalling his violent reaction as Edwards tried to save his own skin by taking Bliss off a controversial case.

"Trust you to bring that up. I was provoked. He was trying to save his neck — you know that."

"OK. But it didn't help his wrist, did it? So, if you want my professional advice, I'd say take it — a few months in the sun will do you good."

"Don't you want to know what Johnson's been up to?"

"Not particularly," she says.

"You were right — drugs."

"Did I say drugs?" she asks, confused. "That isn't what I was told."

"I thought you said you haven't had much chance."

"I haven't — but rumour is he may have done a runner with a fair wad of investments."

"How big a wad?"

"About a hundred million quid or so. Though it's just a whisper — pure speculation. He's probably innocent."

"Innocent!" scoffs Bliss. "You're telling me that this guy may have scarpered with more than one hundred million pounds in investments — a hundred million! — and you say he's innocent. What did they think they were investing in — a gold mine?"

"Sunken treasure," she tells him.

"Sunken dreams, more like it."

"Humph," she snorts. "And just where did these investors get that sort of money in the first place?"

"I don't know. Maybe they worked hard — life savings, that sort of thing."

"Don't be naive, Dad. People who knock their guts out for fifty years to keep themselves in dentures and diapers in their dotage don't usually risk it on a dubious treasure hunt. I bet most of it was dodgy lolly. Serves them right."

"That's your trouble. You're a defence lawyer."

"Don't blame me. You sent me to law school."

"My fault again," he says, thinking: You're beginning to sound more and more like your mother every day. Then he asks, "What about Edwards?"

"Dad. I've got a lot on …"

It's an excuse; he can tell from the drag in her tone.

"Why not call him yourself?"

Telling her he is concerned about phone taps won't wash. "Use a pay phone," she'd say, but the truth is that he doesn't know how far Edwards is prepared to go, and imagines his lawyer lodging a counter-complaint of making nuisance calls.

"Maybe you could try for me, Samantha."

"Maybe."

"Please."

The parade of pots has taken on a new significance as Bliss strolls the promenade to the bar L'Escale after dinner.

Despite Marcia's admonition against it, he is tempted to confront her husband, and stands amid the throng of beguiled women watching the genial potter spinning off tiny ceramic heartwarmers. Many of the faces in the crowd are familiar — groupies, he guesses, and figures he would find them there most evenings.

On the edge of the crowd is another familiar face: one of the hoteliers, scowling at the procession of little wet pots headed off along the promenade towards his hotel.

Jacques is back, though he seems to be keeping a distance.

"So — what happened to the mistral yesterday?" Bliss grunts with phony chilliness.

Jacques shrugs as he lights a cigarette, then blows out his answer with an accompanying cloud. "*Putain —* we were so lucky. It was just ten kilometres away."

"Not here, though, was it," Bliss continues to grumble, as if he had been looking forward to the refreshing blast of mountain air in place of the smoke.

"*Ah, vous enculez les mouches,*" Jacques spits. "You are parting zhe hairs."

"It's splitting hairs, Jacques. Not parting hairs. We say: splitting hairs."

"Zhere — you are parting zhe hairs again."

Bliss turns in frustration and finds four pasty-faced individuals shuffling seats.

"So — no beach today?" greets Bliss, tongue in cheek, as they finally sit.

"No. Not today," pipes up Jennifer with a mutinous edge to her voice. "We had to do the laundry today, didn't we. We're going to the beach tomorrow."

Hugh shakes his head sadly. "Probably not — they spoke of rain."

"Who spoke of rain?" cuts in Jennifer in outright insurrection.

"The BBC World service last night," he ripostes authoritatively. "They say there's a big depression headed this way."

Jennifer's scowl suggests it has just arrived.

"What do they know?" Bliss puts forward conciliatorily, his mind still on Edwards as he searches the moonlit sky for trace of a cloud. "They're a thousand miles away."

"Well we never watch the French telly," whines Mavis. "The weather forecast's never very accurate, is it Hugh?"

"*Les Anglais sont complètement dingues,*" scoffs Jacques, tapping his temple suggestively.

Hey, we're not all crazy, thinks Bliss, though has no intention of defending the mental state of Hugh and Mavis. "Don't worry," he says, turning to Jennifer, "I'm sure the weather will be perfect for the beach tomorrow."

"*Non, non, non,*" says Jacques. "Not tomorrow."

"What is this — a bloody conspiracy?" Bliss mumbles angrily to the sky. "What has everybody got against the weather? There hasn't been a bloody cloud in more than two weeks."

"It is not zhe cloud of which I speak," explains Jacques. "It is zhe wind."

"Not the damn mistral again," spits Bliss, sitting resignedly.

"*Non, Monsieur. Le mistral* was a *pet de lapin.* Tomorrow *la tramontane* will give you zhe wind up."

Notwithstanding Jacques's indecorous assessment of the mistral as nothing more than a rabbit's fart, Bliss has to agree with him. "*La tramontane?*" he queries.

"*Oui, Monsieur,*" says Jacques, then explains in lurid detail how the icy blast is already gathering its battalions and winding itself up, ready to sweep down from the permanently snow-capped Alps of Switzerland and Austria.

"That's it then," says Hugh, in apparently cheerful resignation.

However, memories of the misplaced mistral spur Bliss to lean across to a glum Jennifer and whisper a message of hope. "I should wait and see if I were you."

Leaving L'Escale, Bliss wanders homeward along the promenade weighed with concern — worrying that he may be the reason for Morgan Johnson's sudden departure. If Marcia had smoked him out so easily, could not Johnson or one of his people? But there is a difference — Marcia had been expecting him. Was Johnson?

chapter four

Three days of heightened awareness since his first meeting with Marcia has got Bliss no further forward, other than confirming his suspicion that he is a very small fish in a very large cesspool. Still jumpy at the sight of anyone vaguely resembling Edwards, he wanders the jetties and quays of the port with a warm baguette under his arm, journal in hand, and his thoughts on the ranks of flashy yachts, trying to calculate how many mainline junkies it takes to keep each afloat.

With his eye on two especially well-appointed craft, each bristling with a helicopter, a deck load of expensive marine toys, and enough communications hardware to out-manoeuvre an average frigate, he drops onto a convenient bench and watches the frenzy of activity as deckhands and day-workers scrub and polish the already immaculate vessels.

A flotilla of drab harbour ducks, a drake and his harem, spot Bliss taking a meditative bite from his bread, quickly leap the quay wall, and mob him noisily for tit-bits. The crumbly French loaf showers flakes onto the quayside, which are swooped on by the male, leaving his wives squabbling over thin air. After three failed attempts to reach the smaller birds, Bliss christens the aggressive drake "Edwards" and decides he might as well let him pig out until he is stuffed.

Ten minutes later, with half the baguette inside him, Edwards's head suddenly flops to one side, and he waddles to the edge of the quay, his gut scuffing the ground. With an ungainly belly flop the large drake drops with a noisy "plop" into the harbour and promptly sinks.

"Bloody hell," utters Bliss, rushing to the edge, but other than a thin trail of bubbles there is no trace of the bird. The words "serves you right" die on Bliss's lips and he slouches away from the rest of the family, head down, facing yet another restless day.

In an effort to clear his mind he isolates himself at the end of a jetty and opens his journal for another serious start.

I am an author writing about a man who sits alone on a jetty gazing at the ocean. Who am I? Why am I here? What do I think? What am I waiting for?

Like the breathing of a somnolent giant, the gentle swish of the tide rises and falls under the jetty with such power. I feel my spirit being carried away across the ocean to some distant paradise where all is revealed.

Footsteps on the wooden planking bring his head up as a young woman throws out a towel suggestively close to him, then does a striptease with her dress, revealing a bikini thong that offers virtually no protection against the elements.

"Look at me!" screams the tiny triangle of strategically arranged material.

"What are you looking at?" says her face as she catches him, "and what are you writing about?"

Paradise is not all it's cracked up to be, he writes, sensing that the woman is somehow annoyed that he may be writing about her. That, like the naked *indigènes* of other less civilized cultures, she is concerned his writing will steal her soul, or will expose her to her enemies.

Feeling the weight of her stare he keeps his head down, writing gobbledegook, and debates whether or not she wants him to pay her attention. Should I approach her? he wonders. Let her know I'm not a nutter. But what to say — flattery? I am writing about a beautiful woman …

What does she expect? he questions, trying to read her expressions and feel her vibes as she swings from inquisitiveness through interest to concern, then annoyance, and eventually outright fury, as she snatches up her towel and storms off along the jetty, the naked cheeks of her bottom clenched in fierce anger.

What did I do wrong? he wonders, feeling even more dejected as he puts away his pen and turns his thoughts to the malignancy of Superintendent Edwards. The possibility that an old rattan beach mat would solve his dilemmas does not occur to him as he sits on the jetty and winds himself up with worry.

Watching as the beach quickly fills with the day's visitors, his eye is caught by a noticeable void in the carefully arranged mosaic of basking flesh. A frayed beach mat lies abandoned on the sand, like an empty raft amid a sea of floating bodies, yet is accorded more reverence than any sun worshipper.

"Mind the mat!" shout worried parents, as playing children blindly rush across the sand in pursuit of balls, kites, and each other, and newcomers give the space a wide berth as they scout for a vacant spot. Near-naked sun seekers, shining with oil, can fend for themselves, but the unoccupied mat obviously demands protection from all.

"Gosh — did that swimsuit shrink?" muses Bliss, spotting a V-shaped man whose skinny legs seem incapable of supporting his pumped torso. His chest still bears the breadth of an active youth, but the rest of his body is retreating into old age as he spends his days patrolling the shoreline with the arrogance of an elephant seal beachmaster. The sunbathing beauties instinctively know the trophy he seeks, and at his approach they quickly turn onto their stomachs or grab a towel.

The beach prowler takes on the question of the vacated mat, standing overly close as he scours the beach, hoping his intrusion on the mat's personal space will induce the owner to claim possession — hoping the owner may turn into a trophy.

"See. I was guarding your mat for you," he will insist, but only if she is worthy; otherwise he will snort loudly and grumble about the inconsiderateness of people leaving unattended mats.

After five minutes of posturing, the pariah becomes restless at his lack of magnetism and draws upon the strength of surrounding bodies, gathering a small group to infringe upon the mat with him as he leads a deliberation on its fate.

"I zhink we should move it," he suggests, taking command. "*Ça vous défrise?*" he enquires — any objections?

The crowd backs away from the edge. "It is nearly midday," one quickly explains. "He could be having an early lunch."

"He?" the beach-master queries, with more than a trace of disappointment.

"*Mais oui*," says the other, "it seems most logical to me. *Regarde* — zhere is no bag, no towel, no dress, and no sunscreen. What woman would go to zhe beach without sunscreen?"

The realization hits the old beach bum like a cold shower. His chest deflates as he loses interest and wanders off.

Then the French veneration for lunch — *déjeuner* — from midday until mid-afternoon, wins the rattan mat a breathing space. The halyards and shrouds of yachts sing in the early afternoon breeze like a giant musical extravaganza, then the *vent de midi* picks up a notch and sends parasols, plastic chairs, and small children on skateboards skidding along the harbour wall. The rattan mat lies unruffled until three o'clock, precisely when an inquest is convened by a holidaying Berliner.

"Is zhis beach mat kaput?" sniggers Bliss to himself from his vantage point on the jetty as the German gathers a small group to surround the antisocial item.

"It has been here since zhis morning," explains one in English.

"Yes — but precisely when?" the German demands to know.

"Does that matter?"

"Certainly. It is essential."

"But why would anyone abandon such a beautiful mat?" asks another in French, leaving the German out of the loop.

"*Beau?*" questions another native. "It is *crevé* — dead. See, it is limp — not even rigor mortis."

"But we must know if it was here before nine this morning," insists the German, attempting to restore his authority by precision. "Then we might assume it is abandoned."

"Why?"

Because, though nobody will express it, the early morning bathers are a breed apart. Misfits, misshapes, and those burdened with an unruly metabolic system who take the waters before the high achievers arrive in the spotlight of the sun and further batter their bruised egos.

The momentary awkwardness is broken by a young Englishman, with a beer bottle in each hand and a couple of illuminated plastic ducks on his head, making a fool of himself by dancing around the mat, turning the funeral into a wake.

"Get away," they shout, maddened by his apparent irreverence. Then one utters the unthinkable. "Maybe we should just move it."

No one will take the risk, so search parties form to scour the beach, and a swimming team volunteers to check the sea. "But what are we to look for?" asks one.

"*Un homme,* of course. A man."

"Why not *une femme?*" pipes up a woman, thrusting her bronzed chest forward, unwilling to allow her gender to be so lightly dismissed simply because of the lack of sunscreen.

"OK. Half will keep a look out for a man, and half will search for a woman," decides the German, and the meeting breaks as constituents return to their sunbathing with an eye to every potential aberrant mat owner.

Bliss's amusement is suddenly dimmed with the thought that recently drowned bodies usually float just below the surface, and he worriedly scans the bay for a few minutes, but the bright sun clouds his vision. He considers calling the authorities. But what would he say? *Officer — someone's left a mat on the beach!*

The weary sun starts to fade, heading lower towards the craggy red peaks of L'Esterel in the west, and dinner beckons the beach lovers — but they spare a respectful moment as they pass the rattan mat, and take one final look around for its soul mate. Finally, picking up a cue from the mountains, the sun blushes as it sets. The beach is completely deserted and the cerulean sea is perfectly clear. With no possibility of a claimant challenging him, Bliss gathers up the mat and bundles it under his arm, thinking he has had such an enjoyable interlude he might bring it back one day, and on his way home to the apartment he laughs inwardly at the thought that everybody has spent the day searching for someone who had simply discarded an old mat. Then he stops with the realization that the situation offers an ideal solution to his dilemma.

What if he, like the mat's owner, were to disappear, buying a yacht and simply sailing away? But where to? That might be tricky, he admits, realizing his only previous nautical experience involved a rowing boat on the Serpentine in Hyde Park. But he wouldn't need to sail anywhere, that is the crux of the plan — just like the rattan mat, the yacht would be crewless — a modern-day *Mary Celeste*.

However, by the time he reaches the apartment he has all but given up on the idea, having realized both the limitations and complications, and, wineglass in hand, he leans over the balcony to watch the moon rising from the sea at the start of yet another spotless evening.

The lemon, catching the first rays of moonlight, is still there, still sitting on the grass, ownerless and neglected just like the rattan mat. But — Bliss brightens as his germ of an idea undergoes a resurgence of growth — there is a crucial difference: everyone on the beach saw the mat, but, as far as he is aware, no one but him knows the lemon is there. And if no one knows it's there — does it exist?

I don't need a yacht, he tells himself, seeing his plan beginning to blossom. I only need certain people to believe I have a yacht — a yacht that, like me, has disappeared.

The logic of the plan is so simple that he questions its viability. "What a stir it'll cause," he muses, envisioning Commander Richards and Chief Superintendent Edwards scrambling to find him and his yacht before Richards is forced to lay out some sort of explanation to the commissioner and the press. And in the meantime he can quietly continue his enquiries into Morgan Johnson.

The plan seems flawless as he runs and reruns it in his mind. If this doesn't flush out the bad guys nothing will, he realizes, judging his disappearance cannot be entirely ignored — even convalescent leave has its limitations. But, in order for it to have any effect, he will need to draw attention to his apparent disappearance. No one has contacted him during his first two weeks — but isn't that their plan? Out of sight ...

What if he closes his bank account so his monthly transfer is returned to the admin office? he thinks, then shakes his head. No, they'll assume it's an error and contact Commander Richards. He will assure them there is no problem. It could be months before someone starts asking questions and demanding answers — unless Samantha were to warm them up by putting a worried call in to the administration department. "I haven't been able to get hold of my dad since he told me he was going sailing," she can say, with all the innocence of a defence lawyer asking a deviously loaded question in a major trial. And someone in admin will be on the phone to Richards wanting to know what's going on. "According to our records this man's off sick. How come his daughter doesn't know? And what's this about a yacht?"

That would work, he thinks, but what's the downside? An international search and rescue operation, perhaps. It'll be a good training exercise for someone, he reasons, then seriously considers the possible repercussions such an escapade could have on his career.

There are two possible scenarios, and both see him coming out ahead. If the Morgan Johnson case turns out to be genuine, he pops up and says, "What's all the fuss about? Of course you couldn't find me, I was working undercover — what did you expect?" But if the malfeasance of Morgan Johnson is a put-up job, then he surfaces and drops everyone in the shit — Edwards, Richards, and anyone else he can put the finger on.

But what about Commander Richards? Knowing the truth, what possible recourse could he have?

"You specifically ordered me not to tell anyone where I was, Guv," Bliss can say, like butter wouldn't melt, and watch Richards seethe as he realizes he's been end-run.

With the perfection of the plan exposed, Bliss spends a few moments considering the possibility of taking it one stage further, and seriously contemplates actually disappearing completely, opening a bistro or a bar on some remote Aegean island *à la* Shirley Valentine, but stops himself — I'm not going down that road again — the quaint English pub scenario. The only difference would be the climate and the prices. "How much?" they'd screech in disbelief, though it wouldn't stop them from getting plastered.

Marcia is waiting for Bliss at the bar L'Escale and can barely conceal her excitement.

"He's back," she whispers as he sits.

"Where?" he asks, his eyes roving the harbour and not finding the large yacht.

"No, he's not here," she explains. "He sailed into Cannes this afternoon. I couldn't find you. I looked everywhere."

"I was dealing with a death on the beach." He laughs, but doesn't elaborate. But what now?

All his plans have been thrown into turmoil. With Johnson uncovered he can go home — as soon as he is sure the Morgan Johnson on the yacht is the Morgan Johnson in the photograph. But what then? Case closed. *Bon voyage, Monsieur Burbeck.* But the detective in him wants more — wants answers. If this isn't a put-up job, then who wants Johnson, and what for? What about the information Samantha has gleaned regarding the huge investments? And where is Edwards in all this?

Maybe it is time to disappear after all, he decides, as he plans to visit Cannes the following morning. "Richards has no way of knowing I've tracked Johnson down so quickly," he mutters, "so he can wait for a few days while I dig a little deeper."

Hugh and Mavis seem a little out of sorts as they sit alone staring silently out over the harbour as Marcia leaves.

"So," says Bliss, going over and taking a seat. "How was the beach today?"

"Never made it, old boy," says Hugh, clearly prepared for the enquiry. "Surprised you even asked after what happened."

"Sorry," Bliss says, concerned that his dalliance with an old mat has caused him to miss news of a global catastrophe. "What's happened?"

"Storms, of course. Didn't you watch the news?"

"I try not to."

"Don't know what you're missing."

"Storms, apparently."

"Half of France got washed away last night," says Hugh, with a disaster-monger's delight. "Thunder and lightning like you wouldn't believe — dozens dead and missing."

Bliss casually inspects their surroundings. "Seems to have missed us though," he says, heavy with sarcasm.

"Luck if you ask me, dear boy. Mavis was petrified, weren't you dear?"

Mavis nods on cue. "Petrified."

"Wouldn't risk the beach today, would you, old dear?"

"Not likely — not with all those storms about. But there's always tomorrow."

Hugh shakes his head solemnly. "Not tomorrow, dear — you're getting your hair done."

But what of Jennifer and John? Bliss looks along the promenade. "Are you expecting the others?"

"Wouldn't know," says Mavis, with unconcealed chagrin. "They can do what they want. They don't have to ask us. Do they, Hugh?"

"Of course not, dear."

I guess they went to the beach, then, Bliss figures, but sees no point in asking.

Jacques is also conspicuous by his absence, just like his wind — *la tramontane*. What a day, thinks Bliss, wondering if any other relationships have been destroyed by contrary meteorological conditions, and he sets off along the promenade, determined to extract some information from Marcia's husband in the first stage of his plan to uncover the truth — the whole truth.

The evening's breeze dies, and the moon — another full moon — picks its way across the harbour, highlighting the masts of yachts while perfectly mirroring the vessels in the still water. Bliss sits in a comfortable canvas chair opposite L'Offshore Club readying himself to ambush Greg the potter when he has finished his work for the day.

Midnight on the quayside and the families start thinning, leaving little gangs of girls flaunting their sexuality like gaudy fluorescent signs while fending off those attracted with a nasty glare. The body allures — face repels. This is the game — this is not a game — this is war. If you don't know the rules of engagement — you're dead.

Will I ever learn the rules? wonders Bliss, his mind returning to the sensual woman on the jetty.

The crowds may be winding down, but the pots keep coming; Greg is having a heavy night. How can you not be busy when you have nothing to sell? thinks

Bliss, realizing the prospect of receiving something for nothing, even something as useless as a wet clay pot, turns almost everyone into a child.

The menfolk, standing back, or wandering to a nearby bar, scowl at the delicate pots won by their womenfolk, and laugh, mockingly. "And just how much did you pay for that?"

"Absolutely nothing — the nice man just gave it to me."

"Yeah. Right."

"Well, I did tip him a few euros," they admit under continued scorn.

"A few euros' tip for two cents worth of cheap clay — *une merde!*"

"But you don't understand ..." they complain, and they're right.

"Want a beer?" asks Bliss, apparently catching Greg's eye by chance. "Burbeck," he adds, holding out a hand at the passing man. "Dave Burbeck."

"Greg Grimes," the potter replies, but waves off the handshake, his hands still caked in clay.

Promenaders still toting their pots nudge each other as if they've spotted a film star as they pass. "That's him — that's the potter," they whisper, just loud enough for him to hear.

"You're something of a celebrity around here," says Bliss, grateful for an opening gambit.

But celebrity is not on the potter's mind as he mocks the stupidity of gullible foreigners. "There are a thousand potters better than me up there," he says, giving a nod to the wooded hillsides shrouded in darkness above the port. "Picasso himself lived up there — did you know that?"

"I saw a sign," admits Bliss, "but I thought he was a painter, not a potter."

"He was an artist," screams Grimes, his hands clenched in passion. "Painters slap whitewash on walls — artists create masterpieces."

Bliss drops the temptation to say he'd visited the Picasso exhibition in Antibes at which he personally thought whitewash slapped on walls would have been an improvement.

"Picasso was a master in ceramic art," continues Grimes, winding down. "He lived and worked up there in the hills after the first war."

"Oh ..."

"And did you know," he goes on with reverence, "that he used to eat just over there — in Le Bistro?"

"Imagine that," replies Bliss, turning to seem interested as he tries to come up with a way of levering the man away from the Master.

Playing him along until he can throw in the hard questions, while fearing Marcia might show up any minute and put a spoke in his wheel, Bliss chats of England, beer, football, and the monarchy, without comment or dissent from Grimes, although the mention of marriage clouds his face, and the question of children only makes things worse. "I used to have a daughter," he grieves, staring out over the harbour to the distant bay.

"Odd reply," suggests Bliss, knowing it isn't at all odd, considering the plight of so many parents whose children's lives have been stolen by drugs, but Grimes catches him unawares with his response.

"Yeah.... She ran off with an asshole."

That's interesting, thinks Bliss, as he takes a few seconds over his drink and notices that the wayward

Jacques has been blown off course and is having a night-cap in the next bar. The fisherman looks away as Bliss tries to connect; too embarrassed, assumes Bliss, and he turns back to the potter, wondering why he'd not mentioned the heroin. "Asshole?" he queries, opening a chink, and Grimes heads for it full throttle.

"Morgan fuckin' Johnson," he spits, asking, "Have you heard of him?"

"No." Bliss lies, but Grimes isn't listening as he rants.

"Big-shot fuckin' bastard. He'd pinch the scum off a cesspit if he thought he could make it smell sweet enough to flog."

So what about this Johnson? Who is he? What is he? Where is he? Bliss desperately wants to ask, but doesn't dare for fear of alerting Grimes to his mission. When Marcia told him she'd lost her daughter to Johnson, he assumed she meant through drugs, not physically. Now he has to string her husband along for the rest of the information. "So — how old?" he asks, showing a glimmer of interest.

"Eighteen."

"No — Johnson."

"Buggered if I know. Fifty-something, probably — slimebag."

"I can see why you'd be upset," sympathizes Bliss, but it backfires as Grimes lets off a broadside.

"You have absolutely no idea. You don't know the half of it — not a fraction of it." Then he clams up.

"What about you — what are you doing?" Grimes asks when he's calmed.

"Holiday," says Bliss, adding, "I write a bit." It is a shot in the dark — based on what Samantha told him — but he carries on: "Actually, I'm researching for a book about expatriate villains who rip off British investors and bunk off to Shangri-la."

Grimes's face lights up knowingly. "You've come to the right place then," he says. "This joint is full of them."

"You think so?" asks Bliss, then he enquires with the innocence of an incognizant, "And Johnson — is he one of them?"

The potter's watchful stare probes Bliss's eyes inquisitively as the mind behind them seeks to connect — telling him what? Bliss wonders, maintaining the stare. An opportunity to get something out in the open, perhaps? Marcia had that same look, leaving Bliss with the feeling that both husband and wife were ready to explode with information, but for some reason were keeping it in.

"You'd have to ask him yourself," says Grimes, as the moment is lost.

It's two o'clock in the morning by the time Bliss leaves L'Offshore Club. Finally fed up with "Guantanamera" and his lack of progress with Grimes, he puts on his CD player and listens to Brubeck's "Look for the Silver Lining" as he strolls the deserted quayside, thinking that he may as well positively confirm Johnson's identity, and whereabouts, before he puts his disappearing act into gear. He will take the train to Cannes in the morning. The yacht, the *Sea-Quester*, according to Marcia, should be easy enough to spot.

With the apartment in sight, and Johnson virtually in the bag, Bliss decides the time is ripe to pick up the fallen lemon, and, with the full moon to light his path, he creeps around the back of the building and sneaks up on the tree. With one eye on the door to the ground floor, he bends and picks up the fruit, but a faint glow from the apartment window draws him like a magnet as he goes to pocket the lemon. Nothing could have prepared him for what he sees, and he drops his prize as he inches closer and peers into the apartment's kitchen. The long-haired young man is there, naked, together with his dog, curled as one in sleep, in a large steel cage in the corner of the room.

chapter five

Wednesday blossoms as sharp and bright as a sunflower and rouses Bliss from his sleep on the balcony's lounger. The temptation to rush to the ground floor, batter down the apartment's door, and release the young man is almost overwhelming, and has kept him out of bed since the early hours. The risk of blowing his cover holds him back, but so does the fact that he saw the young man in the garden the previous morning, and has felt his prying eyes for the past two weeks — although that isn't strictly true, since he's only seen the boy once — the click of the door on prior occasions might have been the jailer, whoever the jailer may be. Furthermore — notwithstanding the fact he can't get his mind past the large brass padlock on the cage door — there seemed to be an air of warm innocence about the scene.

What to do? He could call the police, but finds himself drawn back to the unoccupied mat problem: *There's a boy in a cage with his dog, you say? So?*

Nothing harmful is going to happen to the kid for a day or so, he concludes eventually. So, why not complete the current case and keep tabs on him until the French legions show up with an extradition warrant for Johnson, then put them in the picture? In the meantime, identify Johnson as soon as possible and let Grimes and his wife worry about their daughter. Once Johnson is in custody and on his way to the U.K., it shouldn't be too difficult to rescue her.

With his plan formulated, Bliss slips on his swimming trunks and grabs a towel. Might as well take advantage of my last few days, he is thinking as he heads for the elevator.

Cannes is already awake when Bliss arrives to look for Johnson. The window displays of butchers, bakers, and candle-stick makers of the Rue Meynadier have been plumped up and the staff outfitted in stiffly starched uniforms with clinically white aprons. Fifty varieties of cheese, most coated in mould, overflow onto a sidewalk display outside a *fromagèrie*, and a surprised American voice pipes up, "Wow! And I thought all cheese came from Wisconsin."

Stopping to eat his morning croissant on the beach, Bliss is struck by the constant hum of excitement as adverplanes buzz the beaches trailing billboards, Jet Skis and Sea-Doos bother the big yachts in the harbour, and rust-streaked passenger ferries zoom back and forth to the offshore islands. Behind him, a three-mile wall of hotels, restaurants, and casinos stretch around the bay and stolidly keep watch on the exuberance from behind the curtains of their daunting Victorian facades.

An Englishman with rolled-up trousers paddles in the gently lapping wavelets and says, "No trace of the storm," with the conversational ease of someone who's just arrived at the office.

"What storm?" starts Bliss, taken by surprise, then freezes, concerned he's been discovered by a neighbour or colleague. "How did you know I spoke English?"

"Doesn't everyone here?" says the man rhetorically, then exclaims, "Oh dear God!" as a woman in translucent pants strolls by. "That girl's mother should really make her wear knickers."

"You've just arrived?" chuckles Bliss knowingly.

"Yes — overnight train from Paris. How did you know?"

"Lucky guess." He laughs and goes in search of Morgan Johnson.

Johnson's yacht, stern first against the harbour's inner wall, snuggles tightly between two similar behemoths. The *Sea-Quester*, while not the largest privateer in the world, dwarfs many of the others owned by winners in life's lottery, and distinguishes its moniker by the two-man mini-sub lashed to its aft deck.

Strolling along the quay with the nonchalant inquisitiveness of a well-travelled sightseer, Bliss takes a mental snapshot of his quarry's yacht and senses a laissez-faire attitude amongst the deck crew, who are playfully dousing each other while scrubbing the deck. Adding to the casual air, a CD player indiscreetly pumps disco music over the surrounding vessels, where demure stewardesses in fresh white shirts are trying not to walk with a dance as they serve deck breakfasts to their guests with the solemnity of royal household staff.

Wait a minute, he thinks, looking along the lines of multi-million dollar yachts. Many of them probably *are* royal households.

With Johnson's yacht identified, Bliss settles himself into an observation point in the shade of the Palais des Festivals, clicks on his walkman, and listens to Brubeck playing "All By Myself" as he watches the sun rising high over the islands of Sainte-Marguerite and Saint-Honorat in the bay. Then, realizing his shelter on the wide quay is quickly disappearing, and figuring that the lackadaisical attitude of the *Sea-Quester*'s crew suggests the owner is not aboard, he seeks a better surveillance spot.

The Suquet, like a castle, with its château and fortified ramparts, sits in ancient grandeur overseeing the port from its perch on a rocky outcrop at the west end of the bay. Binoculars in hand, Bliss struggles up its steeply winding stone staircases until he has a grandstand view of the entire bay, with the old harbour lying at his feet. "Typical," he moans to himself, checking out the binoculars. "They send me out to search for a major drug dealer who's done a bunk with a hundred million quid, and all they give me is a crappy pair of binoculars."

So? What else do you need? he asks, playing devil's advocate.

That's not the point ...

You've got the credit card — buy what you want.

OK. Valid argument.

The force-issue binoculars pick out the *Sea-Quester* with ease, and, reassured that nothing aboard has changed, he settles down in the partial shade of a spindly tree to direct his glasses on the town's cramped thoroughfares. The maze of streets, designed for peasants' donkey carts, coil tightly around the Suquet before relaxing as they stretch around the bay and follow the railway line that once brought trainloads of Edwardian Brits escaping their northern summers and intolerable food.

"God — that's Edwards," he murmurs, spotting a suspect as he peers intently at the crowds, but gives up when he realizes he sees him everywhere. He'll wait to hear from Samantha, he decides, and spends his time enjoying the view.

A masked mime, dressed like a seventeenth-century *mousquetaire* in a flambouyant purple robe, complete with French falls boots and feathered hat, creates an instant stage on the Suquet's quadrangle with an old beer crate and pulls a fluffy tabby cat from each of his coat's capacious pockets. Motionless, with his arms set like tree branches, he stands as the cats mime a duet in perfect tandem, and Bliss is so rapt in the performance he misses the arrival of a chauffeured limousine at Johnson's yacht. Joining the applause for the musketeer, Bliss rises to donate a few coins, when his eye is caught by movement on the quay below and he grabs his binoculars in time to catch two ant-like figures scurrying across the *passerelle* to the aft deck of the *Sea-Quester*.

"Shit," he shouts, takes off, and races headlong down the awkwardly spaced steps, praying no one will suddenly step out of a doorway or side street. Stopping for breath after the third flight, he swigs a mouthful of spring water from one of the gargoyle-faced fountains, then rushes on — but he has taken the wrong path and has to fight his way through the narrow lanes, thronged with holidaymakers rooting through the bric-a-brac of tourist trash in the expensively named emporiums.

Cutting across the *pétanque* courts of the Pantiero he kicks up a dust cloud.

"*Merde,*" shouts an irate player, slapping his crooked arm in anger as he rants, "*Va te faire foutre!*" Bliss misses the foul-mouthed insult as he plays car drivers at their own game and forces three lanes of traffic to a halt by dashing erratically across the busy seafront road.

The long run along the harbour wall, constantly leaping mooring ropes, bollards, and abandoned chandlery, leaves him breathless as he nears the *Sea-Quester*'s berth — but he's too late. The gangway has been slid aboard, the moorings cast, and the vessel has edged off her berth, turned hard to port, and is heading for the open sea.

"*Putain,*" swears Bliss, as he focuses his binoculars on the departing vessel, but he's foiled by the tinted bridge windows. He shrugs. Oh well, at least it gives me time to do something about the boy in the cage, and maybe I'll make some more enquiries about Marcia's daughter.

The boy in the cage plays on his mind as he edges his way through the tight laneways crammed with a potpourri of tourists. Every English voice turns him, until he decides to act and, finding a pay phone, fishes out his Amex card to call Samantha.

Chief Superintendent Michael Edwards was not only home, Samantha tells her father, but cheerfully answered her "absolutely confidential" phone survey and was more than happy to spend a few minutes outlining his opinions on gays in public service. "Thanks so much. Your views are very valuable to us," she cooed, thinking: very valuable, indeed, especially to a defence lawyer with a difficult police discrimination case in the wings.

"Then who was in the car?" Bliss muses aloud, and his mind rambles on in answer: I s'pose it could have been anybody. The speed they drive here, you never get more than a glimpse. They're crazy. Driving like maniacs from A to B, then they spend an hour in a traffic jam. Everyone's the same — rush, rush, rush. Why? So they have more time to do nothing, of course. Or more time to do it again.

"So," says Samantha, "is that it, or do you think you're being followed by someone else?"

"That's it," he answers, then, with no sign of a quick resolution to the Johnson case, tells her about his encounter with the prisoner in the ground-floor apartment. Samantha, still on the defensive, suggests the boy might be happy in the cage.

"You can't be serious."

"What about that kidnapped American girl who'd spent years in a box under the bed in a trailer?"

"I remember," he says. "She escaped, but missed her box and went back — weird."

"And you're not in a cage — not weird?"

"No," he starts, then rounds on her. "What do you mean?"

"Dad. Face it. Edwards has barricaded you in. You escaped to the South of France, but you're still in his box. Still worrying he's stitched you up or is traipsing around Europe following you."

Trapped, he tries worming his way out. "That's different —" but she cuts in to let him off the hook. "Dad ... we all have our cages."

"We do?"

"Sure — most people make their own. They pen themselves in and never stop bleating about it. Half my colleagues are lumbered with a husband, two cars, three kids, and four beds. And they're locked into jobs they hate. And what about all the poor schmucks holed up with partners they despise but are too scared to escape from? Yeah — we all have cages."

"So what are you suggesting? That I just leave him there?"

"Find out first — don't assume that because you wouldn't want to live in his cage neither does he. He probably wouldn't want to live in your cage."

"I don't live in —" he starts angrily, but she laughs it off.

"All right, Dad."

"Kids," he moans as he puts the phone down. "Find out," she said. How the hell am I supposed to do that? Creep up to him when he's taking his dog for a crap in the garden and say, "Excuse me. Do you like living in a cage?" And he says, "Of course I do."

Then what? he questions himself. But isn't that always the problem with abuse — all abuse: children, spouses, elderly? Nine out of ten they'll say there's nothing going on.

Walking the coast road back to St-Juan-sur-Mer, Bliss flips through his Brubeck CD to find "Prisoner's Song," then finds himself thinking in circles as he tries to come up with an answer, realizing he's suddenly confronting the same dilemma as so many people he's interviewed in a career-spanning basket of abuse and neglect cases.

"Such nice people," they say, adding disbelievingly, "I never would have thought it. Quiet, mind you, kept themselves to themselves."

But wouldn't you keep your head down if were up to something like that? he thinks.

"He is Engleesh," explains the concierge, when Bliss returns to the apartments and makes an off-hand remark about the "nice young man with the little dog" on the ground floor. There's a certain guardedness — evidence of a tacit awareness, perhaps — in the old man's manner as he keeps his head down over a drain in the parking lot, angling for a tenant's lost set of car's keys with a bent wire coat hanger.

"English," echoes Bliss, trying to see over the big man's shoulder, but, with Samantha's words still in his ear, doesn't take it further.

"*Le mollusque* lives zhere wiz his mother," sneers the concierge in answer to Bliss's silence, leaving little doubt as to his feelings. The fact isn't particularly startling to Bliss — he has assumed it is a close family member; it usually is. Although an alternative has crossed his mind, that the young man was involved in some sort of bizarre sexual tryst — a *ménage à deux et demi* — if a dog could be considered a "half."

"Let me help," says Bliss, gently nudging the concierge aside as he simply lifts the drain cover and picks out the keys.

"*Merci,*" he says, taking the keys grudgingly, as if he'd been enjoying the fishing, and in return agrees to open the tenant's register.

"I think they may be friends of my mother," Bliss prattles on. "I'm sure I'll recognize the name ... embarrassing not being able to remember ... sure you understand ..."

"*C'est bizarre,*" exclaims the concierge a minute later, pointing to the fact that no current entry exists for apartment 101. "*Ce n'est pas possible*," he carries on, furiously scratching his forehead, then shouts, "*Merde*," in comprehension of the situation. He was on holiday, he explains, at the time the English arrived, and made no entry.

"So what is their name?"

"*Bof*." He shrugs, making it clear it is of no interest to him.

"But who pays the rent?"

He shrugs again. It's not his problem — he is only there to keep the place clean. A sore point, apparently, as he takes off in complaint about the young man's dog fouling his garden. "Zhe leetle sheet machine," he explodes, "*chie partout dans le jardin*," then rants on about the inordinate quantity of "sheets" from one small dog: "*Merde*!"

Bliss heads to the town centre in search of Daisy, his bouncy estate agent.

"She'll know the tenants," the concierge told him, explaining it was her agency that handled all the leasing arrangements for the building.

Ten minutes later he's outside her office, pretending to peer at the properties for sale, still trying to come up with a devious pretext to get her to open her books.

"Hello," she drools, as she spots him, and, taking his hand, guides him in. "What can I do you with?"

"What can I do *for you*," he corrects, but she misunderstands.

"No. I asked to do you first," she says, and Bliss drops the devious pretext, realizing from her expression that there is little she would hold back, if asked.

"This isn't possible," he breathes a few minutes later, his eye on the building's tenant register.

"Is zhis a problem?" she asks, sliding an arm around his waist as she leans over his shoulder.

"Could this be a mistake?" he asks, his finger firmly on the entry.

"No," she replies. "No mistake. The apartment belongs to Mr. Morgan Johnson.... Why — you know him?"

"Do you?" he enquires with an innocent mask.

"Oh, yes. He was here zhis morning."

"What for?" he asks, barely containing his eagerness.

"He collects the rent. He owns many of zhe apartments in zhat building," she explains, running her finger down a column. "Yes, I thought so," she adds. "He owns the one zhat you have — 401."

I bet Richards would love to know that, he thinks, but he's filled with confusion and consternation as he tries to construct a jigsaw puzzle out of a handful of mismatched pieces. Although, it is something of a relief to know Johnson leased out the apartments — he was beginning to think that, in addition to dealing in drugs, scamming investors, and seducing schoolgirls, he was also keeping a boy in a cage.

"But," he wants to know, "who is the tenant in 101?"

"Zhere is no rent for 101," she says, closing the book. "Morgan Johnson's wife lives there."

Bliss jumps at the news. "His wife?"

"Yes. He wanted her to have zhat apartment because it has a garden. I remember him saying to me zhat all English women like it in zhe garden. Would you have dinner with me zhis evening?"

The request, coming out of nowhere and tacked on

to an intriguing piece of information, catches him by surprise and leaves him stumbling. "I ... I don't ..."

"It is all right," she says, turning away. "I understand. Your wife would not like. Yes."

"Yes ... No ... I mean, yes. Sorry, no ... OK," he says, finally getting his brain and mouth working in unison. "I would like to have dinner tonight, but I've already got plans. What about lunch — tomorrow, perhaps?"

It is partially true, he tells himself. He does want to get hold of Marcia as soon as he can, hoping she may know where Johnson and her daughter might have gone, and hoping she will show up at L'Escale. He also has it in mind to have another bash at the husband — there are too many unanswered questions, like: How come he's not trying harder to get his daughter away from Johnson?

In any case, there is another problem with dinner, a problem he is determined to avoid: the unspoken innuendos between two singles spending an evening together, and the inevitability of the momentary awkwardness afterwards when either, or both, will have their minds on etchings.

Having agreed on the lunch — something special, she promises him, not just *un sandwich dans le Snack-Bar self-service* — Bliss wanders thoughtfully along the harbour wall and stands watching the fishermen unravelling nets as he tries to puzzle out the situation. What on earth is Johnson's wife doing in the apartment? he wonders, but cautions himself of the need to seriously re-evaluate his situation. If the Johnson case is as secret, and potentially dangerous, as Richards made it appear, the last thing he should do is bust in on the target's wife; even living in the same building might be risky.

But who is the boy? No, he stops himself — that's where you're going wrong. It's a man — not a boy. What if Mrs. Johnson is having a little S&M tryst in retaliation for her husband having it away with young Miss Grimes? Good job he hadn't just rushed in, he thinks, realizing Samantha might have been right. The Johnsons have big money; she could be paying the guy to live naked in a cage and lets him out a couple of times a day to service her. This is France, after all — although she's English ... or is she? I'll have to ask Daisy.

No wonder Johnson's taken a bimbo, he laughs to himself. He probably didn't fancy living in a cage.

But why did the young man shield his face and run? he questions, thinking about the lemon tree incident.

Wouldn't you, if you were doing that? he thinks, then swallows hard as he realizes it isn't only the spaniel fouling the garden — no wonder the concierge complained about the amount of mess from one small dog.

There is no sign of Marcia as he takes his usual seat at L'Escale, a point quickly seized on by Angeline, the waitress.

"Your beautiful friend — she did not come today?" she says, as she scoots off across the bustling road with a heavy tray.

"I can't watch," Bliss mutters, seeing her play French roulette with a slew of fast-moving cars and motorbikes. But, despite the occasional screech of brakes from a startled motorist, her timing is impeccable as she braves the racetrack — thirty times an hour, back and forth with trays heaped with drinks and elaborate sundaes and other *glace* concoctions, some sprouting fizzing sparklers that light her path across the road.

"You should not be alone," she says, returning to Bliss with his customary *vin rouge* — no longer bothering to ask for his order. "Zhis is zhe Côte d'Azur, even zhe statues make zhe love here."

He's seen some of the statues in the galleries and has to concur, but, taking a sip of wine, he reassures her, "I'm fine."

"But every night zhe same, you sit all alone. It is not possible. See — zhere are many beautiful women," she says, sweeping a hand to encompass a dozen.

"I don't want a woman," protests Bliss, and Angeline thinks she catches on. "Zhere are some very nice boys here too," she says, and he looks up in time to see one.

Pinky and Perky are back, but where is Marcia? "Strangers in the Night" again — wait for it, he thinks, "Guantanamera's" coming up, and it does, on cue. What's the life expectancy of a waitress? he wonders, as Angeline skirts death again by inches. What's the life expectancy of Pinky and Perky if they play "Guantanamera" one more time?

Mavis has her hair scraped under a headscarf as she and Hugh arrive. They have been reunited with their erstwhile friends now that the laundry, the weather, and the *coiffeur* have all been settled. The usual fuss over the seating has also seemingly been resolved as Hugh waves John and Jennifer into the best seats, while he slips over to Bliss. "Don't mention the hair, old chap — bit of a balls-up," he whispers.

"No problem, Hugh." Bliss smiles, thinking he's inadvertently stumbled into a Jacques Tatti movie.

"We're going to the beach tomorrow," announces Mavis triumphantly, as if they've been practising seaside celibacy to increase the ultimate gratification — a kind of sand-free foreplay — leaving Bliss laughing at the mental image of Mavis on the beach in her modest one-piece, lying flat on her back in the sun, whimpering, "Oh God ... Yes! Yes! Yes!"

"Good for you," he says, fervently hoping Jacques won't show up and dampen their ardour with news of another ill wind.

Where the hell is Marcia? he worries as he sits on the promenade, and is aggravated by the fact he is forced to rely on someone as unreliable as her. Maybe it's time Mohammed went to the mountain, he thinks, and resolves to find out where the Grimeses are living. Even if Marcia shows up there will be little point in asking her, considering her reluctance even to be seen with him. The last thing she would want is him knocking on the door. I bet Greg Grimes hasn't the faintest idea who I am, or that she has grassed on Johnson, he thinks, guessing the potter, being a man, has taken the loss of his daughter to Johnson more phlegmatically than his wife — "At least he's got some money," Bliss imagines him protesting. "She could have hooked up with some long-haired bum with a ring up his nose and fewer prospects than a capon."

Skulking in the shadow of a schooner that has been drawn up on a dolly onto the quayside, Bliss spies Grimes wrapping up his wheel and stowing it into a storage locker tacked onto the side of one of the harbour-front bars. Rented for the purpose, he assumes, as the potter pockets the key and saunters off along the promenade.

Where are the crowds when you need them? he wonders, being forced into the open more often than he would like as he takes off in pursuit, but he doesn't push his luck, knowing the likelihood of a successful surveillance at the first attempt is remote without having some idea of where or how his quarry is going. Grimes need only jump in a car or hop a late-night bus to leave Bliss standing. He'll make a start, and tomorrow night he'll pick him up where he leaves off and be ready with a car if needed.

The prospect of a car or bus fades the further Grimes strolls along the promenade, passing bus stops and car parks without stopping, but his dawdling sends Bliss scurrying into darkened doorway after doorway.

Deceived by the slow pace into suspecting that Grimes has spotted him, Bliss is compelled to hang back further than he would prefer and, when Grimes takes a side turning, he's forced to risk exposing himself by running. Heart pounding, eyes glued on the intersection, he makes up the distance in seconds and cautiously peers around the corner. Grimes is still there — plodding unconcernedly on.

The decorative lamp standards of the promenade and the lights of the dock disappear in the shadow of eucalyptus and palms as they start up the steeply winding road on the edge of town, but invisible infrared surveillance cameras pick them up as if it is still daylight, and shadowy hulks appear out of concealed corners to stand warningly in front of gates. Apprehension creeps in as the gloomy atmosphere darkens. The narrow road, overhung with rampant vegetation and soaring walls, is silent apart from the soft thud of Grimes's footfalls somewhere ahead — no people; no cars. Just the occasional goon stepping menacingly out of the shadows and staring unmannerly at Bliss until he is out of sight around the next bend. His hackles rise at the weight of stares and his adrenalin clicks up a notch as he worries one of the goons might finger him as a threat and decide to neutralize him.

They wouldn't, he says to himself, but the black look on the next face tells him differently.

Another three bends, he decides, then he'll call it a night and come back in the daylight to scout the place out, so at least he'll have a better idea of the extent of the threat.

The tight twists and hairpin bends have ruined his chance of staying close to Grimes, and he's dropped back and relied on the measured footfalls in the dead night air.

Grimes's disappearance, when it happens, is so unexpected that Bliss has rounded another tight bend before catching on to the fact the footsteps have stopped. Kicking off his shoes, he lightly runs barefoot round the next bend, and the next, and next, but Grimes has vanished in the darkness.

Which villa? Which doorway? Which fortified gateway? wonders Bliss, as he quickly backtracks. But there are none. Despite the dim light, no matter how many times he searches, there are no entrances — no guarded portcullises or wooden gates built to take a battering ram, and no heavy-set men staring him down. Fearful of drawing fire from one or another of the men farther down the road, Bliss stops and gives thought to the situation.

What if Grimes has latched on to the fact he is being followed and pulled the trick of diving into the shadow of a building or a boulevard tree and freezing? No, there are no trees on the sidewalk, and one side of the road is an impregnably high stone wall, while a viciously spiked iron fence, backing onto a densely wooded estate, holds the other side. There is no escape route, and Bliss has passed no entrances, other than a ghostly portico with colossal stone columns and impenetrable iron gates. Retracing his steps to the enormous gateway, he quickly dismisses it. Grimes was well beyond the entranceway before his footsteps ground to a standstill, and the noise of such huge metal gates in motion would have easily reached Bliss's ears.

Perplexed and a little annoyed, he has no choice but to follow the road back into town and suffer the hostile stares of the guards as he passes. He considers staring back, but quickly changes his mind under the ferocious glare of the first gorilla.

Returning to the scene early the next morning Bliss catches several of the heavies dozing in little sentry boxes niched into gate pillars, but he is just as baffled as before — even more so. The only gate Grimes could possibly have entered is the imposing portico that looks more like the entrance to a palace than a mansion. Even in the shadowy light of the morning, it is apparent that the ornate ormolu gates have not been opened for years. Spindly seedlings have lodged themselves into crevices in the spalled stone columns; the iron gates are welded shut with rust; tattered ribbons of gold and black paint hang like peeling birch bark; and a forest of eucalyptus tress behind the gates form an unyielding barricade.

The name "Château Roger, (MDCLXXXVII)," inscribed deeply into a foundation stone of one of the columns, has survived, and stands out well as Bliss kicks away the scrub in his search for clues, but otherwise he learns nothing of interest. The high stone wall on one side of the road and the barbed iron palisade surrounding the château's grounds are just as impenetrable in the daylight as they were in the dark.

"Can you afford zhis?" questions Daisy at lunchtime, showing no hesitation as she pulls up a chair on the trendy terrace overlooking the Boulevard de la Croisette and the beautiful vista of the Baie de Cannes, with its yachts and islands shimmering in the midday heat.

Not me, he thinks, but John Smith and American Express can. "Sure thing," he drawls.

"You really must have the *salade niçoise* on the *terrasse* of the Grand Bleu in Cannes," Samantha insisted before he left England, her face warming in memory of a university soiree some years earlier.

Now seems like an ideal opportunity, and if the *salade niçoise* is taking its time neither of them notice, laughing at the French idioms Daisy is using in answer to Bliss's apparently light-hearted suggestion that, perhaps, not everything in paradise is as straightforward as it appears on the surface — hoping that by touching on the point he may get her to leak something about Johnson and his investments.

"All Frenchmen are very honest," she starts, straight-faced, then cracks a little as she goes on. "Everything is, like you English say, on zhe straight and narrow — just like our roads."

"But your roads are as crooked as ... Oh. I get it."

"No — not crooked, *Monsieur*, just a little twisty, perhaps. Now zhe roads of Corse, zhey are crooked."

"So I understand," he says, having studied a map of Corsica left by a previous tenant.

"Here we *roulons le fisc un peu*, but beating zhe taxman is just a sport. Everyone likes to cheat zhe system a little — don't you?"

Bliss is staying clear as he queries, "And ... Morgan Johnson. Does he like to cheat the system?"

"*Bof*," she says, shrugging. "*Peut-être* — perhaps. Most of zhe roads zhat lead foreigners here are more zhan a little kinky."

It's a start, he thinks, checking his watch, wondering how long it takes to make a salad. Even lazy lunches have their limits and time is running out on theirs. Finally, more in concern than annoyance, he calls the waitress.

"*Pardon, Monsieur*," she says with a drawn face. "Zhere has been a *catastrophe* in zhe kitchen."

Thinking they may have run out of anchovies or some other ingredient, he queries, "A catastrophe?"

"*Oui*," she says, then her face crumples as she admits, "It is zhe chef. He is *mort*."

"I wonder if she means dead or murdered ..." Bliss breathes aloud, then leaps to his feet.

With the St. John Ambulance first aid manual running through his mind he rushes to the kitchen, with Daisy in his wake, and finds a moribund scene as waiters, porters, and sous-chefs stand in rigor, surrounding the huge body of the chef, flat on his back like a beached white whale. A bright crimson stain surrounds the spot where a large kitchen knife juts out of his chest, and Bliss's face sinks.

"Not again," he groans, annoyed his prediction to Samantha could be coming true. People did keep getting murdered whenever he was involved, but this has nothing to do with him, or the Johnson case — or does it?

Mentally putting on his policeman's cap he quickly runs through the sudden death procedures: protect the scene, preserve evidence — especially any possible weapon — detain potential witnesses and suspects ... but he's overlooked something. He racks his brain for just a second before seizing on the missing task — the first task: establish death has occurred. Has anyone checked, he wonders, and asks Daisy to enquire of the surrounding crowd. The way the worried-faced workers inch away from the body is enough of an answer, and Bliss leaps to grab one of the big man's wrists.

Consternation turns to confusion as he drops the wrist and rips open the man's jacket. The knife falls away and clatters onto the ceramic floor, making several of the minions leap, and Bliss runs his eyes over the exposed blubbery chest but finds little more than a flesh wound.

"What the —" he starts, then his frown turns to the start of a smile as he raises his head to the adjacent stainless steel work table. "Can somebody help?" he calls, as he puts a hand over the barely bleeding nick, but they hang back in reverence of the great man. "It's all right," he says, nodding to the table. "It's just beetroot juice."

"He must've fainted and stabbed himself on the way to the floor," he explains to Daisy as they take their seats on the terrace a few minutes later, the old chef on his way to the hospital for observation. "I can't believe no one checked his pulse."

"Zhey were scared," explains Daisy. "He is a very big man."

"Enormous," agrees Bliss.

But she laughs. "I mean important — big."

"Oh. That too," he sniggers, as a smart-suited man delivers their salads.

Their waiter turned out to be the general manager and embarrassed Bliss by the effusiveness of his attention. It wasn't as if he'd saved the chef's life. The man would have come around eventually, although, as Bliss joked to Daisy, his concern was that had he not stepped in, the staff would have had the old guy in a box and on his way to the cemetery.

"He would have lived," she explained, detailing the French custom of attaching a graveside bell to a cord in a buried person's hand, but Bliss, laughing, wouldn't let her off the hook. "Maybe they would have cremated him in his own oven."

Following lunch — on the house, *naturellement* — the manager pumps Bliss's hand furiously and insists that he and his beautiful wife — a *faux pas* Daisy doesn't feel obliged to rectify as she clings to Bliss's arm in admiration — should be his guests for dinner in the hotel's elegant dining room, La Scala.

"*C'est le coup de fusil*," mutters Daisy, making it clear the price of dinner at La Scala is way out of her league.

"You must come on Sunday evening," he commands, and Bliss doesn't argue.

Daisy, still holding tight, thanks him profusely on Bliss's behalf and assures him that Sunday will be absolutely "*parfait*."

"*Oh là là*," she says, mentally working on her outfit as the manager leaves them to their lunch. "It will be *magnifique — le tralala*," she enthuses, then, catching

Bliss's critical eye, disarms him with a cheeky smile. "So — who else were you going to take?"

"My wife," he starts, then sees her frown and gives in. "I'd be delighted to invite you, Daisy," he says, bringing back the smile, though it is fairly obvious from her victorious look that the subject of etchings is going to come up, and he starts mentally preparing excuses.

The *salade niçoise* is everything Samantha cracked it up to be, and Bliss eats in anticipation of dinner.

"So," he prods Daisy between bites, "what can you tell me about the Johnsons?"

It seems Daisy's knowledge of Johnson and his wife is limited to rumour, but, weighing off her allegiance to someone who can command a table at La Scala with a man who indirectly pays her wages, Bliss wins, and she sketches an image of a rake who has his fingers in any number of pies — and people.

"And he was in your office yesterday morning?" Bliss notes.

"*Oui, avec sa pépée.*"

"With his what?" he asks, thinking it sounds crude.

"His *pépée* … his *poule* … his *petite* girlfriend," she sneers.

Daisy's obviously not a fan of Mr. Johnson, he deduces, but how far can he trust her? How can she help him?

"When Morgan Johnson is with his little *pépée*," he asks, "what does Mrs. Johnson do?"

Daisy gives him a quizzical look. "Why you want to know?"

His first thought is to tell her he's writing an exposé of deviant sexual behaviour, but, worrying she might take it the wrong way and insist on a personal demonstration, he hesitates. Now what? Tell her about the man in the cage, perhaps. Why not? She seems to enjoy a little gossip. It'll make her day.

Daisy doesn't take him seriously at first. Raising her eyebrows in a smirk. "I zhink that is good idea. I zhink I might like also."

"You might?" he exclaims.

"*Oui*," she agrees, half-seriously. "Perhaps it will make him a good lover."

In answer, Bliss puts on an accent. "But I zhought zhe French men were all Casanovas."

"Casanovas," she scoffs. "Zhe problem wiz zhe French men is zhey only want zhe one zhing."

He hated asking, but did anyway.

"Food, of course," she spits, in all seriousness, then gives him a quizzical look. "Oh. I see what you zhink. You zhink sex."

"Sex," he echoes, refusing to be drawn.

"*Bof!* You are like all men — '*Cocorico*,' you cry, 'I am zhe big cock.' You zhink of sex; you talk of sex, but, *crac!* Always you would prefer *le beefsteak*."

"*Crac!*" he laughs. "What is *crac*?"

"It is *rien* — nothing — it is just an expression we use, like *bof*," she says, coming down a notch.

"*Bof*," mocks Bliss lightly, but he's getting nowhere on the subject of the Johnsons, so he switches to Grimes and his disappearing act of the previous night.

Describing the property, though not the reason for his interest, Bliss asks Daisy what is, and who owns, the Château Roger. He can see by the look on her face that she has a pretty good idea, but she clams up, claiming, "*Ce château est un panier de crabes.*"

"A basket of crabs?" he queries.

"*Oui*. And if you are wise you will keep your fingers out."

An uncharacteristic sternness in her generally jovial tone warns him there is little point pushing his enquiry. Maybe she'll be more amenable after dinner at La Scala on Sunday evening, he decides, and at least it will keep her mind off etchings.

Jacques is back in his regular place at L'Escale Thursday evening, apparently feeling forty-eight hours is sufficient to clear up a case of obstinate wind, and Bliss has no interest in bringing up the controversial subject, but Jacques insists. "We are very lucky," he explains. "Tomorrow will start zhe good winds."

"I hadn't noticed the bad ones," muses Bliss, but Jacques prefers not to hear as he continues, proudly, as if it were his doing. "Tomorrow, zhe wind will go northeast and zhe *gargali* will bring zhe warm airs and zhe sweet scent of zhe Tuscan olive groves."

Daisy saves Bliss from comment by, just coincidentally, strolling along the promenade at that precise moment and catching his eye.

"Daisy — Jacques; Jacques — Daisy," Bliss introduces, although from the wary eye they give each other, he assumes they've met. Then he orders drinks for all from Angeline, who has just skirted death for the third time since his arrival.

"*Les Anglais débarquent*," mutters Jacques, making Daisy snigger, as Hugh, Mavis, Jennifer, and John arrive, then squabble over the seats. "I wonder if zhey went to zhe beach today?"

"Did you get to the beach, Hugh?" pipes up Bliss, guessing by their continued pallidness that it's unlikely.

"The beach, old chap?" he responds as if giving himself thinking space. "Good Lord, no. Bit too hot, wasn't it, dear," he adds, looking to Mavis for support. But Mavis has conveniently spotted something of great importance somewhere in the middle distance.

"We did think about it," continues Hugh, realizing he's been abandoned by his stooge. "Didn't want to risk it. Cancer," he mouths, nodding to Mavis, who is trying to point out the slightly unusual hue of an all-white seagull to Jennifer.

"Oh. I'm sorry. I'd no idea," whispers Bliss.

Hugh's face screws in confusion for a second, then he catches on. "Oh no, dear boy. She hasn't got it. Well, not as far as we know. She just worries about getting it."

"Yeah," Bliss says, tongue in cheek. "I can understand that."

The sarcasm flies over Hugh as he continues, "John and Jennifer went."

"I can see that," says Bliss.

"Oh well, there's always next year."

"Good idea. Maybe the weather'll be more favourable then."

"Possibly, dear boy," says Hugh, studiously searching the clear moonlit sky for a clue. "Possibly."

"So, why did you laugh when Jacques said the English have arrived?" he asks Daisy seriously after Jacques has left, telling them, in a manner of speaking, that he had other fish to fry. "*J'ai d'autres chats à fouetter*," he explained.

"*Les Anglais débarquent* — the Engleesh have arrived — is what we say," she giggles, "at zhe special time in zhe month for a woman." Then she leans conspiratorially closer and adds, "Also, we call a condom an Engleesh cap — *une capote anglaise;* and *le vice anglais* is zhe homosexuality."

"Thanks a lot," says Bliss, facetiously, "I really needed to know all that."

"Why you want to know about zhe château?" Daisy questions. The seriousness of her tone gives him the feeling that she may have tracked him down specifically to question him about his interest, but, he reasons, she is an estate agent — maybe the place is for sale.

"Researching for my book," he tells her, guessing he won't earn enough in his lifetime to even put a deposit on such an enormous estate in its prestigious neighbourhood.

"You are writing a book?"

"Yes. That is what I do. I told you."

Daisy softens in relief. She's evidently forgotten, and he's been so caught up in the Johnson case that he's written little during the week.

"So zhat is why you spy on Johnson's wife and zhe boy," she says, laughing.

"I didn't spy," he cuts in. "I just happened to be in the garden early one morning and saw him."

"And zhen you stare into his window?"

"All right. I know it sounds bad, but he was behaving strangely."

With his apparent interest in the château out in the open, Daisy's face clouds again as she solemnly warns him. "People who go zhere disappear."

"Seriously?" he asks. "What people? When?"

It is only a rumour, apparently, but, as Daisy puts it, "Zhere is no evidence against it."

That's the obstinate nature of rumours, he explains. The supporting facts may be filmier than plastic wrapping, but, without contradictory evidence, some folks will believe it. And, like most rumours, there seems little to prove that the old château is some sort of black hole.

"So," he pushes on, still waiting for an answer, "how many have disappeared? When? Who?"

Her vacant look gives him the answer.

"Sounds like a good way to keep trespassers out, as far as I can see," he continues dismissively, thinking the rumour is probably fostered by the uniformed goons whispering menacingly to curious children: "D'ye wann'a know what happens to kids who go in there?" And he certainly knows what the guards in the vicinity of the estate are like. He met a few the previous afternoon.

After leaving Daisy in Cannes ("I have zhe little business," she explained), he tried the library and the tourist information office for particulars about the Château Roger. There's more than one way to handle a snappy crustacean, he thought, but the reaction from the attendant in the tourist information office, on the promenade of St-Juan, was so alarming that Daisy's warning about a basket of crabs seemed mild.

"It is private," the bald-headed, beaky-nosed man snapped, scowling at Bliss's off-hand enquiry.

"Yes, I'm aware of that —" he started conciliatorily, but he was rudely cut off as, with colour and voice rising, the little man laid into him. "I said private. Private ... don't you understand?"

"Yes. I —"

"Listen to me," he ordered, teacherly. "You cannot go there." Then, almost pushing Bliss out the door, he raised a finger angrily, shouting, "It is private.... Private.... Private. Why don't you listen to me? It is not for tourists."

Feeling he might have got a friendlier reception had he asked for directions to the municipal brothel, he slunk off to the local library. "*Fermé*," declared the sign on the bolted door, so he sought the museum instead.

The female curator, uncharacteristically frothy with her bouncy blond curls and laughing eyes, was gushingly unhelpful. "I'm sorry. I wish I could help you. But zhis museum is dedicated entirely to Napoleon Bonaparte," she explained, adding proudly, "He landed here in 1815, you know."

"I know," Bliss said, though he doubted the locals take the event so significantly, considering the trivial commemoration stone, on the promenade, that he'd seen several tourists trip over, not to mention the memorial in the town park: a soaring fluted stone column with solid pedestal and elaborate capital, surmounted by a pathetically small bust of the Emperor looking more like a plaster-cast "mantelpiece model" of Elvis.

The curator must have caught the look of disappointment on his face, and, fearing it to be an expression of distaste for one of England's greatest bugbears, she pursed her lips and whispered disdainfully, "He wasn't really French. His name was Napoleone Buonoparte. He was actually a Corsican."

No further ahead, but still determined, Bliss spent the afternoon under the glare of security men, walking around the perimeter of the château's estate looking for some other entry, and exhausted himself in the sweltering heat. But many stretches of the fence hide behind the walls and surveillance cameras of villas that abut the grounds, so that he couldn't be sure he hadn't missed some gateway more modest than the main portal. There had to be a tradesman's entrance somewhere, he assumed, retracing his steps. He eventually concluded that it had to be in the leg of the fence where a uniformed, and conspicuously armed, guard sternly warned him that the entire street was "*privée.*"

"Bloody nerve," mused Bliss, moving off. "So much for *liberté, egalité, et fraternité*. I wonder what the *prolétaires* of the revolution would think of that?" But, knowing the uselessness of arguing with any security guard, let alone a foreign one, he skulked away. Behind him, the guard made a point of pulling out his radio to loudly broadcast that a *crétin* was in the area.

Forced to take to the hills, well away from the château's grounds, he climbed a steep, twisting road into an area where the view alone would fetch more than the average 4 bed. suburban Des. Res., and he began to understand the guards' concern. Who but a *crétin* would walk here?

chapter six

Another week is slipping by, but at least he's making progress. With Marcia exposed, though God knows where she is, and the *Sea-Quester* identified, even if he had only caught a glimpse of Johnson and young Miss Grimes as they scrambled aboard, Friday dawns with the bright promise of another glorious day.

From his balcony Bliss looks down on the garden and the lemon tree. The fallen lemon still sits on the grass, but it has lost some of its attraction as it wilts in the relentless sun and he decides that, until he figures out a plan to deal with the man in the cage and Morgan Johnson resurfaces, he may as well concentrate on the perplexing case of the Château Roger.

Although not ideally situated, his apartment's balcony gives him a view across the thickly wooded promontory at the other end of the bay, and he scours the lush hillsides with his binoculars, knowing that obscured somewhere deep inside the jungle of eucalyptus and palm trees should be a mansion. Defeated by distance, and a feathery drape of early morning mist, he gives up for awhile and spends time tweaking grey hairs out of his moustache, but then, returning to the binoculars as the warmth of the sun burns away the haze, his eye catches the glint of metal amongst the trees, and he realizes he's been deceived. The château is there — has been there all along — an imposing edifice, lost in the tangled greenery, with only the multitude of steeply angled roofs jutting skyward, marking its spot. Camouflaged by centuries of verdigris, which has taken the sheen off the copper and blended with the surrounding verdure, the roofs hint of the enormity and grandeur of the building beneath, but, try as he might, he cannot even glimpse the structure through the dense woodland.

The ancient château, hidden deep in the forest, has a certain fairytale quality that sets him daydreaming about enchanted castles — though he doesn't picture himself as the handsome prince coming to rescue an imprisoned damsel. And, despite his long blond hair, the young man in the cage downstairs would never count as sleeping beauty — not in Bliss's mind, anyway.

With the château's existence and location now established, Bliss leaves his balcony, heads for the *boulangerie*, then sits in his usual place on the seawall, hoping that Marcia will show up with news of Johnson's whereabouts. Then, peering out over the bay through his binoculars, seeking the *Sea-Quester*, he is suddenly struck by a way to get a better view of the château.

"Stupid," he chides himself, for not realizing sooner that, whilst the building may be obscured from the prying eyes of landlubbers, it was obviously built to take advantage of the expansive vista of the bay and the offshore islands.

With two croissants, a baguette, and a bottle of Perrier, Bliss heads to the marina, where numerous signs dot the quayside offering boats for hire, but he is quickly disappointed and his plan starts to unravel. Without proof of his maritime skills, and an accompanying certificate, nobody will rent him anything more seaworthy than a kiddie's *pédalo*, unless he also hires the service of a duly qualified skipper.

He could — it's not that his credit card won't take the strain — but he doesn't want anyone standing over his shoulder demanding, "Why you look at zhe château all day? *Regarde les bateaux*, zhe fish, zhe sea, zhe sky, and zhe beautiful islands."

The thought of the islands gives him an idea, and he races to the far end of the quay in time to catch the passenger ferry that chugs its way across the bay, three or four times a day, with happy boatloads of paraphernalia-wielding picnickers heading for the beaches and crystal clear waters of Île Sainte-Marguerite.

As they steam out of the harbour and head for the cobalt of deeper water, Bliss turns back and is rewarded with an ever-expanding view of the Château Roger. Though still deeply nestled in the thick tangle of undergrowth, its shape and grandeur is unmistakable — like a maharajah's palace rising majestically out of the Bengal jungle. Bliss turns to his fellow passengers, wanting to sing out, "Quick — look at the château," but they have their faces and minds turned to the island ahead.

Realizing that no one else sees the château, he momentarily, and quite seriously, questions himself. Maybe it is a fairytale. What if I'm imagining it? What if it's an apparition, a hallucination, a mirage? What if it's the ghost of a château long demolished?

Is that possible? Do razed buildings leave ghosts?

Maybe.

What if it's a ghost in my mind — a remnant of memory from a past life?

You don't believe that garbage ...

I didn't before!

A slight jolt as the little ferry trips over the wake of a passing speedboat jump-starts his brain, and he swings the binoculars back to shore.

It is definitely real, he tells himself, though now he's farther out in the bay, and as more of the facade becomes exposed, the individual aspects become more indistinct. By the time the top floors, with their swooping balconies and sculpted canopies have been exposed, even through his binoculars the features are melting, and when the grand entranceway, with its colonnade of Corinthian pillars, has risen to view, the château is just a smudge in the landscape. The monumental building, raised on a giant plinth to give the aristocratic occupiers the most spectacular view in the world, is absorbed into the surrounding foliage and disappears from sight as they reach their destination on the island.

With time to kill before the ferry's return, Bliss tacks onto the mule-train of holidaymakers as they hump hampers, inflated toys, beach mats, picnic tables, and kids up the steep paths and head for secluded bays with hundreds of others. At least cars and motorbikes aren't allowed, he is thinking, as he idles along a sandy path, his mind still on the château, when he's almost run down by a speeding forestry truck.

"*Putain*," he swears at the fleeing vehicle, emerging from the dust cloud with a fleck of grit in his eye.

He wanders through the groves of giant eucalyptus, almost deafened by the screeching cicadas, until he comes out on a headland and is surprised to find himself almost on top of a fortress.

Like the Château Roger, the imposing cliff-top castle appeared insignificant from a distance. It is only when he has crossed the stone bridge, entered the archway where the portcullis once dropped, along with buckets of boiling oil and burning pitch, and walked up the cobblestone road into the main courtyard that he comprehends its size and significance.

Typically French, he thinks immediately, surveying the construction of le Fort Royal and its buildings. The thick walls are just a jumble of rough rocks slapped together with powdery mortar and stuccoed with sandy plaster — none of the accurately milled stone blocks with cushioned facings and paper thin joints of their uptight English counterparts. The seventeenth-century buildings appear as slapdash as the *pétanque* courts to Bliss, though he has to admit they seem to stand, and inside the fortress he finds an entire town, with houses, barracks, a church, and even a primitive laundromat — a giant stone wash basin fed from a well. A dusty parade square, overlooking the mainland, takes him back to his marching drills at police college, and he wonders how many *légionnaires* wished they'd never signed up for the crossing over the narrow straights from Cannes as he winces in memory of the blisters and sore knees.

Signs point him to the water cisterns — essential on an arid Mediterranean island — built by the first inhabitants, the Romans, two thousand years earlier. Displayed inside the roman cisterns are enormous hand-wrought terracotta amphorae. Some are streaked with iron oxide, and all are partially encrusted with barnacles.

"Amphorae from the wreck of the *Tradeliere* discovered in 1971," proclaims the legend, and, despite the ubiquitous *"Ne pas toucher"* signs, Bliss reaches over the electronic tripwire and transports himself backwards through two millennia. Lightly stroking a finger across the sandpapery surface of a giant double-handed wine pot, he feels a tingle of consanguinity as he connects with the Roman potter — a man, Bliss senses, probably not unlike Greg Grimes, with ambitions of creating award-winning ceramic pieces, who was forced by the economics of the time, or a slave-master's whip, to knock out practical pots. At least his were fired and used, Bliss is thinking, when an Australian woman catches her husband's arm and exclaims, "Geez, Bruce! Just look at the size of that."

"Yeah," Bliss mutters in all seriousness, "I wouldn't wanna try stuffing one of those babies down a toilet."

But Bliss has only a few moments to absorb this potter's work. As he looks around the relatively modern building that houses the antique amphorae, everything suddenly slots into place in his mind. This was a prison — a feared prison in the time of Louis XIV — but this is also a place of legend, a place that has housed the spirit of one of the world's greatest unsolved mysteries for more than three hundred years, and, as a modern-day detective, Bliss walks the corridors and cells with an incredible feeling of déjà vu.

Then, "*Crac!*" he exclaims, the plot and characters of his novel falling into place in his mind with such clarity that he can hardly constrain his pen.

Rushing through the building, noting every feature with fervour while frantically scribbling page after page in his journal, he emerges back onto the parade square and takes the deepest, most satisfying breath of his life, knowing that he has the makings of one of the greatest literary mysteries of all time.

Now, looking back over the blue waters to Cannes and St-Juan, Bliss stands on the castle ramparts, his mind dancing with ideas for his book. Then, "*Crac!*" he exclaims even louder, as he realizes that not only has he found the plot for his novel, but, incredibly, he has simultaneously solved the ancient mystery of the citadel's most famous prisoner, a conundrum that has teased the minds of historians, researchers, chroniclers, writers, and philosophers for over three hundred years. Because this is the infamous prison that once housed the man in the iron mask — a man whose identity was such a closely guarded secret that even trusted jailers could never look on his face, or know his name, a man known only as "*l'homme au masque de fer.*"

It takes a few minutes for the answer to sink in, as he runs it around his mind checking for flaws, but no, it is so obvious as to defy logic that no one should have considered it before, although he can easily see why, realizing that every luminary who'd ever turned their mind to the identity of the man in the iron mask had failed simply because they had asked the wrong question. It takes a detective (with a little help from a daughter who happens to be a lawyer, he concedes) to know the right question, and, although he has yet to name the prisoner, he gazes shoreward with the sagacious belief that he knows exactly where the answer lies.

Bliss savours the moment and takes a celebratory swig of Perrier as he looks out over the blue bay, knowing that not only has he solved this great mystery, but he has the means at his fingertips, and the time, to lay out his thesis in the form of a mystery novel to end mystery novels — a mystery novel that will take the publishing world and stand it on its head. And he opens a new page in his notebook and starts afresh.

It was July 13th in the year 1687. King William and Queen Mary of Orange sat on the throne of England, in place of the disgraced King James II. The Grand Alliance was forming for war with King Louis XIV, and the combined armies were moving against France in the north. But no fighting had reached the quiet Mediterranean village of St-Juan-sur-Mer, and, for the peasants tending a handful of scabby sheep in the olive groves and scavenging oysters and mussels from the beach, life had changed little from the time their parents and grandparents struggled to survive along the same shore. Kings, popes, famines, and wars had, for the most part, bypassed this quiet backwater of Provence.

Galleys, bargues, and fat-bellied fluyts, trading among the bustling ports of Marseilles, Toulon, and Genova, filled the bay with sails and shouts of encouragement to men at oars, but none put ashore at sleepy St-Juan.

In the heat of the midday sun, a man in knee-breeches and commoners' garb, calling himself François Couperin (a name he'd taken from a manuscript of harpsichord music he had found in the vil-

lage's tiny church), sat on the rocks thinking that, one day, when the war was over, this would be a good place to build a harbour.

Angélique, the buxom serving wench from the nearby hostelry, dodged the donkey carts trundling along the beachside track, her modest woollen skirt brushing the ground, whilst her maidenly corsage barely concealed her assets, and delivered a goblet of wine to Couperin.

"Zhat is a bon télescope you 'ave," said Angélique, struggling with her English.

"Oui," the man agreed, though added nothing as he paid her a few centimes for the wine, angry that she had so easily identified him as a foreigner.

As Angélique fought her way back to the inn, dodging a speeding musketeer on his charger, Fredrick Chapel — for that was his true name — took out a quill and pad and wrote in his journal:

> The shiny façade of the Côte d'Azur is painted gaily across the skyline, and the set is finished with a spectacular backdrop of snow-capped peaks. Across the bay, a cluster of green islands swim in the perfectly blue sea. King Louis' fortress on the Île Sainte-Marguerite is now completed, and stands firm against invasion. A garrison of légionnaires are making their newly built home more comfortable, and in one of the prison cells languishes the man they call only "l'homme au masque de fer."

Glancing at his watch, Bliss is horrified to realize he's been so absorbed that he is within minutes of missing the day's last ferry sailing and risks spending the night on a beach under the stars. Momentarily, he is tempted, but then his stomach sends him rushing headlong down the winding path from the fort to the jetty.

The trip back across the bay is full of excitement and expectation for Bliss as he mentally works on his book. The *vent de midi* has kicked up a chop that stops him from writing, even spraying an occasional shower of warm sea over the passengers on the open bow, where he sits, eagerly looking forward to St-Juan. With his mind still on his amazing discovery, he focuses on the patch of headland where the Château Roger is slowly, and indistinctly, taking shape out of the greenery. Now that he knows where to look, his eyes easily find the roofs and even a trace of the great doorway, when, "*Crac!* Of course," he cries, having solved yet another great mystery: the mystery of the missing entrance to the château's grounds.

The reason he could not find another entrance to the château was that, at the time it was built, the aristocratic owners and their noble guests wouldn't risk the dangers of the road; they would come by ship and anchor in the sheltered bay, while a *pinasse* would ferry them and their personal staff ashore. Then, carried from the beach in sedan chairs, they would process up through the ornamental gardens, full of statuary, fountains, peacocks, and swans — the air scented with orange and lemon blossoms — and finally on up the magnificent flight of white marble steps to the gigantic front door. Only the outdoor staff and local tradespeople would use the steep, dusty hillside tracks that were the haunts of robbers, thieves, and common criminals. (That's interesting, Bliss thinks, realizing how little has changed over the centuries.) But the giant gates, as grandiose as they might have been, were simply the château's back entrance where the riff-raff came and went.

Now, looking shoreward, all becomes clear, and Bliss realizes he's overlooked the obvious in his search for an entrance because of the simple detail that, at sometime in the past century, a strip of land lying just off the beach was appropriated by the government for the construction of the railway line and a modern road linking Cannes with Nice. Separated from the beach by the demands of mechanized transportation, with its most charming and practical feature throttled by pollution and noise, the château had died, and even the ostentatious back gate had become obsolete.

Arriving back at the apartment, with a hurriedly grabbed pizza, Bliss is bursting with excitement over his discoveries and phones Samantha.

"You'll never guess —" he starts, but she cuts him off and her voice falls.

"Oh shit! Don't tell me you've seen Edwards again."

"No," he begins, then brightens himself with the realization that he hasn't given Edwards a moment's thought all day. "No. I don't care about him anymore."

"Good for you, Dad," she says. "Getting out of that old cage at last."

"I'm not ..." he protests, then lets it drop to ask her if she knows of the legend of Île Sainte-Marguerite.

"Sure," she replies, "*l'homme au masque de fer*. I went there on a school trip — remember?"

He doesn't remember, but plays along and says, "That's right," and goes on to explain that, in addition to finding Johnson, releasing Grimes's daughter from his clutches, uncovering the secret of the château, and dealing with the young man in the cage, he is now working on solving the mystery of the man in the iron mask.

Samantha laughs. "Dad, that's five different cases."

"I know," he says. "The Dave Burbeck five."

"Dave Burbeck?" she queries, unaware of his *nom de guerre*.

Putting down the phone, Bliss foregoes his usual evening stroll to L'Escale and concentrates on his book while the ideas are still fresh. In any case, Jacques is likely to be as capricious as the *gargali* turned out to be, and the thought of Hugh and Mavis expostulating on the reason for their failure to make the beach yet again irks him. This is their last night, he realizes, with a certain relief. It is also the last night for many others, as a raw batch arrive tomorrow for the weekend changeover. Saturday's crowd — pale, excited, even a little apprehensive — will pour into town loaded with cash and burdened with credit, and will be an easy target for the thieves and rip-off merchants who wait, like bears at a waterfall — though most will avoid the villains and rob themselves by overspending.

Every Saturday evening, Bliss sat on the promenade watching them — the first-timers and northerners, clutching sweaters and anoraks as they explore the promenade, wary of the balminess of the night air, unwilling to accept the reassurance of travel agents, and especially distrustful of tour operator's brochures. "Remember that dung heap they sent us to in ..." they say, in bitter memory of a five-star hellhole that prompted them thereafter to cart umbrellas, sweaters, laxatives, purgatives, diuretics, and rolls of toilet paper wherever they go.

As for Marcia, her daughter, Morgan Johnson, and the man in the cage, they can wait. He has more important plans; he has *"d'autres chats à fouetter,"* as Jacques would say, though whipped cats are not exactly what he has in mind.

Opening a fresh bottle of Côtes de Provence, he picks up his binoculars and confirms that neither the château nor the island's fortress has evaporated into the realms of castles in the air, and he sets his mind to work as he recalls his visit to the prison.

Stepping into the notorious cell, Bliss found himself in the mantle of a modern-day Doctor Watson. "Well, Holmes, what do you make of it?" he imagined himself saying, as he peered out of the triple-barred window, but, not expecting to uncover any evidence in the indigo waters of the Mediterranean, he turned back to the room.

For a cell, the room was expansive by any prison's standard, more like a spacious drawing room with a pleasantly situated window and proportionately high ceiling. Opposite the window, on a stretch of wall pierced only by the door, were the faded remains of several murals. The central and most dominant fresco depicted a lineup of shadowy figures, across a stage perhaps, with one figure kneeling and the suggestion of an audience in the foreground. Another picture, showing a furnished room with a single man standing in the light of the chandelier, had a window not unlike the window of the room in which Bliss stood, and he found himself drawn questioningly back to the large aperture, with the feeling that it looked out on more than just the sea — imagining that it was some kind of window into the past. Maybe the artist had left a clue to his identity, he mused, as he again looked out over the bay and saw St-Juan-sur-Mer in the far distance.

Spying nothing of interest, he returned to the room itself, but the floor, ceiling, and other walls bore no clues that he could find without the aid of a magnifying glass, and, though Holmes might have chided him for the oversight, he didn't possess one.

A laminated notice board screwed to one wall informed him that, despite three hundred years of investigation, the identity of the prisoner remained a shadowy enigma, and that more than sixty names had been proposed for the unfortunate who'd been imprisoned in the room for eleven years, from 1687 to 1698. However, it was the accompanying list of possibles that Bliss found most intriguing. Headed by the usual suspects of disassociated royalty, the king's brother and half-brother, various dowagers, dukes, and counts, the list also included the enigmatically vague suggestion, *"une femme."*

"A woman," Bliss mused with a smile, figuring that whoever came up with that solution had hit a pretty wide target.

"Nabo the Negro" also caught his eye, but it was the unnamed "Son of Cromwell," that intrigued him most and set his plot in motion.

"Come on, Watson," he said to himself in the guise of Holmes. "Give me your thoughts. What can you deduce?"

"Well ... the first thing is the size. This isn't a cell — this is more like a hotel room — and one with a better view than most. And look at the murals — this was a man who knew luxury. I wouldn't mind wagering this room was stuffed with furniture and draperies."

"And from that, you deduce what, my dear Watson?"

At that point, he was stumped. What did that prove? Nothing. Only that the proponents of the excommunicated royalty theory were probably correct. "But what about you, Holmes," he asked, turning the tables in his mind. "What would you look for?"

"Simple, my dear Watson — the one fragment of evidence overlooked by everyone else, of course."

"But this room has been pored over by thousands of intrepid investigators for three hundred years in search of clues. What could possibly have been overlooked? And who knows what evidence has been removed, lost, contaminated, or destroyed in three centuries?"

"But you, Watson, are yourself overlooking one critical fact."

"And what is that, Holmes?"

"It is elementary, my dear Watson. You've had a wealth of experience in dealing with prisoners, have you not?"

"Indeed I have — even my own daughter accuses me of being such."

"Quite — so what does that tell you about the man who resided here?"

The answer exploded through Bliss's mind with the force of a hurricane, and he couldn't help but blurt out, "He wasn't a prisoner."

"Precisely, my dear Doctor," the voice in his mind said, but Bliss was already racing ahead as he surveyed in the scene.

Everything extant in the room spoke of grandeur and opulence: the size, the proportionate dimensions, the enormous window overlooking the bay, the murals. This was no dungeon; neither was it a cell designed for a single prisoner. An equally capacious adjacent cell had housed twelve dissident Huguenots for many years, and an entire rank of more modest cells were cramped into a second corridor.

So what manner of prisoner could command, not just a cell, but a prince among cells? he questioned, then understood where every previous investigator and chronicler had been deceived. They had ignored the fundamental tenet of criminal investigation: that a detective should never assume or dismiss anything. Most, if not all, had erred in both respects — assumption and dismissal.

Firstly — because of the relative sumptuousness of the cell — it had been universally accepted that the occupant, male or female, was either a member of the monarchy or in some way connected to the aristocracy. And secondly, everyone had dismissed, without consideration, the notion that the tenant could have been anything but a prisoner.

With the distant castle now fading in the dying rays of the sun, Bliss puts his binoculars down on the balcony, takes a swig of wine, picks up his pen, and returns to his journal, taking up the story of Frederick Chapel, alias François Couperin, where he left off.

Frederick Chapel was still sitting on the beach at St-Juan-sur-Mer as the sun faded over the humble fishermen's hovels, across the headland, in the paltry settlement of Cannes-sur-Mer.

"Jean le Pêcheur," a local sardine fisherman introduced himself, as he slumped to the sand and bellowed across the cart track for Angélique to bring him a "goblet" of wine.

"I would like to cross to Île Sainte-Marguerite," said Chapel, once he had gained the other man's confidence.

"Zhen you will cross alone," Jean scoffed. "And if you cross, you will never return," he warned, then added, expressively, "Zip, boum, you will have zhe raccourci."

"What is raccourci?"

"It is, as you say, zhe shortcut." He laughed, slicing a hand expressively across his throat.

Chapel didn't give up. He couldn't afford to give up. Whilst the guillotine might chop short his life in France, if he failed, the English hangman was readying to stretch his neck.

"If I cannot be transported to the island with a warranty of safe passage, perhaps you would tell me of some person who might bring me knowledge of what I seek there. It is very important," he pleaded, giving Jean a despairing look.

The silence, brokered by Jean as he stared resolutely across the azure bay towards the offshore island, as if in a trance, was broken by the yelp of a carriage driver as he yanked the reins to veer his stallions clear of Angélique, who was dashing across the cart track with another flagon for the two men on the beach.

"Putain," swore the driver, and Angélique gave him a friendly wave.

"Perhaps I can help," Jean relented, as Angélique slipped back to the inn under the nose of a cartload of manure hauled by a plodding ox. "Merde," the fisherman muttered, and began, "It will not be easy, but I have a friend ..." then explained that, for a substantial fee — "The finest gold, naturellement" — his friend might be able to obtain the desired information. "But what exactly is zhat you wish to know, Monsieur Couperin?"

The merest mention of the man in the iron mask had the Frenchman struggling to his feet. "You are *crazy, Engleesh. I go before we are both* raccourcis.*"*

"Sit down and keep quiet, man," ordered Chapel. "No one must know that I am English — we are at war."

"Bof." Jean shrugged, flopping back to the sand. "We are not at war — our crazy kings and zheir crazy generals are at war. Me — my war is out zhere with zhe sea and zhe sardines. And you, Monsieur Couperin — if zhat is your real name — where is your war? Who is your enemy?"

Frederick Chapel had only one enemy. A man who had clawed his way to power and left barbs in many of his victims, so that, when the need arose, he need only twist the hook. And now the need had arisen, because, though he had no ambition of divulging it to Jean, there were certain people in the loftiest echelons of English aristocracy and commerce who were looking for their pound of flesh. And the pound they sought was borne on the person of the miscreant Richard Cromwell, elder son of the deceased Lord Protector of England, Oliver Cromwell, whose relatives, proving themselves more insidious and less pious than he, had not only inveigled themselves into important government circles during his period of royal usurpatory, but had also inveigled themselves into other men's pockets.

Richard Cromwell, more commonly branded "Tumble Down Dick," in recognition of his celebrated ability to repeatedly fall flat on his face, was chief amongst these rogue relatives, and his ability to plunder purses had been improved by a short, though ill-conceived, spell in his father's seat — if not in his shoes — following the old Roundhead's death in 1658.

Richard Cromwell's impecuniousness had grown proportionately to his unpopularity, so that, when he *finally plummeted into the mire, his hands were so deeply pocketed that he had no hope of saving himself, and he scarpered to Paris and lived it up under the name of John Clarke.*

However, the downfall of inveigling in other men's pockets is that when they catch on to the ruse, they tend to develop very long arms. And now that there was a new king on the English throne and war had been declared on France, some of those long arms were reaching out to recover that which was inveigled — either in hard cash or in "Dirty Dick's" hide.

Doesn't anybody ever use their real name? questions Bliss, as he takes a breather from writing to follow the spectacular sunset that has smeared the colour of his wine from horizon to horizon in a heavenly display.

A knock on the apartment's door brings him down to earth. Still engrossed in the past, he has a fleeting vision of a troop of *légionnaires*, with a guillotine erected under the lemon tree, but then he pulls himself up smartly. No one knows I'm here, he reminds himself. And there's a security lock on the street door.

He vacillates as he recalls Commander Richards's warning that precipitous action in the Johnson case could prove fatal — advice he'd sloughed off at the time, before he knew he was dealing with a big wheel.

Realizing that drug bosses can get pretty antsy about people sniffing in their cesspools, he stands well away from the door and wonders if they have someone in the garden lest he should go for the roof or fire escape. The big boys usually play for keeps, he is worrying as the knock is repeated, and, judging by the size of his yacht, Johnson is certainly in the biggest league.

"Monsieur Bliss," demands the visitor.

He deflates in relief. "Daisy — I might have guessed," he says, opening the door.

"Is it a ghost you have seen?" she questions, peering concernedly into his pallid face.

"No," he says, though feels she may be more on the mark than he's willing to admit.

"I am sorry to shake you up, but zhere is a woman at *le bar*. She asks everyone for you."

"For me?" he queries, knowing that Daisy is the only person who uses his real name.

"She doesn't give your name, but she says, 'Zhe tall handsome Engleesh who comes here each night.' And I know it must be you."

"Zhank you." He smiles, flattered and relieved.

"'I know him,' I says. And I come fetch you."

It has to be Marcia, he thinks, as Daisy catches his hand and bounces him along the promenade like a five-year-old who's found a seaside pal.

"Are the four English people there?" he asks, hoping not.

"Zhey were, but zhey have gone now. Zhey were like zhe lobsters, zhe poor zhings — zhey were at zhe beach today, I zhink."

He can't help laughing, though he stops abruptly as Marcia rushes along the seafront to greet him.

"They're in Corsica," she blurts. "Hurry or you'll miss them."

chapter seven

Daisy listens intently to the conversation between Bliss and Marcia, though she picks up little as Marcia circumspectly explains to Bliss that her daughter, Natalia, has decided to leave her boyfriend in Corsica. "And I was wondering," she asks with an eye on Daisy, "if you'd care to go over to make sure she is all right. Only I remember you saying you were interested in visiting the island."

So, Bliss thinks, Natalia Grimes has seemingly seen the light at last — or has she? Although he listens pokerfaced to Marcia enthusing on the prospects of her daughter's expected return, he knows the stated aims of drug addicts are generally as capricious as Jacques's wind.

Daisy, completely in the dark, is ecstatic. "Your little girl comes home, yes? Zhat is good, no?" But on the subject of Bliss taking off for Corsica she is more taciturn. "Why you go?" she bemoans, still in the dark, after Marcia leaves.

"My book ..." he explains, feeling that is explanation enough, but Daisy rebounds. "I come with you. I translate."

Although he tries to quash the idea with a flat, "No," she reels off a dozen reasons in favour, until eventually he pulls her plug by announcing he will probably be away for weeks. "That's the trouble with literary research," he notes. "It's boundless."

Her face falls sharply. "You have forgotten?"

"No," he protests, then is forced to surrender. "Forgotten what?"

Dinner at La Scala — Sunday evening — as guests of the general manager, or *"une grosse légume,"* as Daisy described him. Amidst his excitement over his book, the masked man, and now Johnson's re-emergence, he's put everything else on the back burner.

"Sorry," he says, promising to make it up to her on his return.

The early morning ferry from Nice to the northern Corsican port of Calvi leaves gulls floundering as it zips across the 150-kilometre gap. This is fast, thinks Bliss, as he reclines in the aircraft-like cabin of the super-sleek, jet-powered craft, which skates over the silky surface at seventy kilometres per hour.

With less than three hours to Calvi, the current haven of the *Sea-Quester* according to Natalia, who phoned her mother the previous day, Bliss takes advantage of the smooth ride and settles down with a meaty writing block to transcribe his notes into a manuscript.

The coastline of France is rapidly shrinking as he begins, then, with barely a word written, he stops in momentary concern.

"I've forgotten my passport," he explains to the smart-suited purser a few minute later.

"*Bof. Ben quoi?* So what?" says the dark-skinned, cow-eyed beauty as she explains, "Corsica is French — for zhe moment."

The smugness of her tone as she adds "for zhe moment" leaves him thinking she knows something others have yet to discover, but, with his mind at ease, he heads to the bar for coffee and a croissant.

With the plot of his novel finally fleshing out, he sits in the lounge surveying his surroundings, his mind full of seventeenth-century intrigue, thinking how, at a time of sail and oar, Frederick Chapel would have put the wind up the *légionnaires* on the island of Sainte-Marguerite if he'd screamed into the bay at the helm of a snorting sea monster like this one. He would have had no difficulty strolling ashore and demanding they hand over the jailed man, he decides, then pauses, questioning where his storyline is headed. No, he concludes, that wasn't Chapel's mandate. To save his neck, all he had to do was conclusively identify the prisoner as Dirty Dick Cromwell, then leave it to the masked man's aggrieved victims to winkle him out of jail and spirit him back to England to recoup their pounds — of one kind or the other.

A couple of hours later, with several pages under his belt, Bliss breaks off to view the fast-approaching peaks and orients himself with the aid of the map he's brought from the apartment. The jutting pinnacles, glowing golden in the morning sun, cut into the royal blue sky like spikes of a coronet, and he realizes Corsica isn't so much an island as one big mountain plopped into the sweeping corner of the Mediterranean, where France leaps past Monaco and rounds the bend into Italy.

The mountainous nature of the isle really impresses itself on him when, a short time later, he struggles up flight after flight of steep stone steps, heading for the summit of the castle overlooking the small harbour of Calvi.

"You must take zhe donkey on Corsica," Daisy burbled as she dropped him in Nice earlier, and he looks around before he starts his climb. BMWs and Ferraris dot the quayside, but there are no donkeys as far as he can see, so he makes do with Shank's pony.

Bliss reaches the castle's battlements and uses his binoculars to check the rugged coastline and wide ocean — to no avail. There is no trace of the *Sea-Quester* in the town's port or anchored off the beach on the other side of the inlet, leaving him to conclude that either Natalia Grimes lied to her mother or they've sailed on.

Jogging back down to the port, he is tempted to simply put up his feet in one of the bright quayside cafés and concentrate on his book, then realizes he's only one step away from his plan to disappear. This looks a neat little place to live, he thinks, assessing the tiny terraces of medieval houses and the colourful displays of touristy stores, but he shrugs off the notion, knowing it has a fatal flaw — Daisy. Already disappointed at missing dinner at La Scala, it wouldn't be long before she'd panic and phone Richards, or whoever made the apartment's reservation, and set the hounds on him. In any case, he decides, eyeing the scores of holidaymakers in the popular spot, someone's bound to recognize me.

The harbourmaster's office, *la capitainerie,* is the only place that might have information about Johnson, he figures, and he stands at the public enquiry counter with an innocent face. "I was supposed to be picked up by a friend," he explains, having established that the squat, scruffily shaved assistant speaks English.

"His name?" the man demands, with a degree of hostility that catches Bliss off balance, and he nearly replies, "Morgan Johnson," but holds back, wondering how well connected his quarry might be. The harbourmaster's assistant, with nicotine teeth and an eighth-month gut, looks to Bliss like a man with greasy palms and sticky fingers and, on an island where the provincial flag is a bandit's profile complete with spotted bandana, he decides to be prudent. What if the grubby little man picks up the radio microphone on the desk in front of him and announces, "Monsieur Johnson, on board zhe *Sea-Quester,* I have a friend here for you," then adds, "Hold please," and shoves it under his nose? So he resorts to the cover of vagueness. "I think the boat is the *Sea-Quest* or something like that."

"He's gone."

"Gone," echoes Bliss, but gets no response as the man turns his back with a noisy fart and lights a cigarette.

For a moment he seriously considers breaking rank by pulling out his Scotland Yard ID, but quickly shakes off the idea. His interest in Johnson may already have jangled an alarm bell in the Corsican's mind. Also, he realizes, it is not helpful that he's left the card inside his passport, under the mattress, in his apartment in St-Juan.

Plan B sees Bliss catching the same ferry for a return run. But ten minutes later he exclaims, "Wow!" watching from the dock as she picks herself out of the water and flies, then he takes a look behind him and heads for Plan C, the mountains and the wide sweep of coastline he judges he'll view from up there — but he needs transport.

The notion of tracking down a donkey is amusing, though clearly impractical. Not only would the climb take too long, but he's yet to see a trace of one. There certainly haven't been any donkeys trundling tourists up and down the castle's steep ramparts in dinky wooden carts, and, as far as he can see, there are none trotting the kids along the beach. So he makes for a car hire establishment that is shutting shop just as he arrives. It's midday Saturday, and he withers under the glare of the scraggy teenager dragging on the complaining gate. Then he wangles his way into the showroom by feigning global deafness. How many languages does the office girl speak? he wonders, ducking the word "Closed" in at least six, but he has a trump card and he flashes it with the magic words, "I would like your most expensive car please."

"Phew! Thank God the Rolls Royce Corniche was out," he breathes later, checking the hire company's price list, but the rugged open-topped Jeep he's driving wasn't cheap, either. No matter, he thinks, as he rides the beast, with its baritone growl, up into the high passes and soars over the mountains with the sun on his face and the wind in his hair, purring, "This is the American Express life."

Startlingly white sandy coves and deeply gouged natural harbours make themselves camera-ready as he crests jagged headlands. As each spectacular vista opens, another primes itself beyond the next bluff and tantalizingly reveals a brilliant splash of blue sea or an ancient slate of red-tiled roofs.

Then, as the narrow carriageway plunges him into the intervening ravine, he snakes along the tortuously knitted road, skirting gorges and precipices that drop a thousand feet or more without even a line of paint for protection, his humming tires sending gravel and pebbles singing off into the chasms.

Four sweltering hours, and forty sandy bays and sheltered havens later, he chooses a remote cove carved into the cliffs and swims naked in the translucent water that runs over his desiccated body like a cool, clear salve. Swimming out into the emerald bay from the deserted white sand beach he delights in watching his bronzed arms and hands gliding effortlessly through the soft water, as opaque as liquid glass. A school of flying fish startle him, as they take to the air ahead, and he quickly scouts around for signs of a predator before realizing it is he who has scared the skittish fish.

This really is the life, he tells himself, and he lays back with his eyes on the crags above, watching gulls riding the wind, thinking this is the place where he should take flight. Forget it, he goes on. You stitched yourself up by using the credit card in Calvi. Even if Daisy kept quiet they'd soon track down the rented motor. You should have cleaned out a cash machine or two before you left the mainland if you were going to do that.

Thought of cash reminds him he has very little, although he has his credit card. I need some food, he thinks, realizing that he's eaten nothing since the croissants on the ferry. Drink has not been a problem; natural springs gush straight out of the rock at regular intervals along the roadside and he's stopped at several. I'll give it another half an hour, he decides, climbing back into the Jeep, then I'll head for the nearest town and dinner.

The *Sea-Quester,* when Bliss finds the yacht ten minutes later, is easily identified by the luminous yellow submarine on deck. As it floats quietly in a narrow sound, two crewmen manhandle a large container into the aft hold. What's in that box? wonders Bliss, as he watches from a rocky peninsula above the peaceful cove. Then he does a mental take on an atlas and puts everything into perspective. The island of Corsica — slap bang in the midst of the trading routes between the Orient and ancient capitals like Genoa and Marseilles — must be a wreck diver's dream.

"Sunken treasure," he muses knowingly, guessing that many sailing ships were driven aground — lured in with false lights set by entrepreneurial locals on stormy nights, like the West Country wreckers back home. Sounds like Samantha was right, he admits to himself, remembering the Roman amphorae in the museum on Île Sainte-Marguerite and thinking that many Roman galleys must litter the Mediterranean.

But would the French let an English privateer plunder a valuable wreck? Bliss questions as he watches Johnson's yacht. Then he shakes his head. No, this wouldn't interest Johnson — too much hard work — too much risk for the return — too much red tape. A ship the size of the *Sea-Quester* must cost a couple million a year just to keep afloat, what with fuel, fees, crew, and refits — and, from what he's seen in the shipbroker's windows in St-Juan, she must be worth ten million, at least. I wonder if that's where the investors' money has been sunk, he thinks.

Bliss focusses his binoculars and finds Morgan Johnson in his crosshairs. "Bingo," he breathes. "Got you — and I bet I know what's in that container."

The place Bliss rolls into several hours later is undeserving of the epithet "town," but, no matter, he has found the *Sea-Quester.* Now all he needs is a good meal and a place to sleep, then first thing Sunday morning he can start his homebound journey.

A young girl, saying, "I speeka Engleesh," puts herself forward as Bliss looks around the dismal antechamber of a cramped terraced house overlooking the quaint harbour of the small town. With eyes screwed in skepticism, he asks, "Is this a hotel?"

"*Si, Signore,*" says the smiling six-year-old with a rascally face. "Zhis hotel."

The only comforting thing about the place is the American Express sign on the counter. The only other hotel in town, in the whole district, apparently, took "cash money only" according to the woman who guarded the front desk.

Smiling back at the young girl, as her father hovers watchfully — extraordinarily watchfully, half-concealed by a thick door curtain — Bliss enquires if they have a room.

"*Si, Signore.* "

"With a bath?"

Her face clouds, but he doesn't know whether he's overstepped her linguistic capability or the hotel's plumbing, so he turns to the father.

The man's rigid stare and straight face say only one thing, "One false move on my little girl and ..." And what? wonders Bliss, but has a fairly good idea the fierce-faced Corsican is not holding a loofah behind the curtain.

"Forget the bath," he says, realizing there's a crystal lagoon just steps away from the front door. "I'll take the room."

"*Si, Signore.*"

Ten minutes later he's still at the desk. His credit card has apparently lost its lustre no matter which way the young girl swipes it.

"This doesn't make sense," he fumes, taking back the card. "It worked when I hired the Jeep." Perhaps I've blown the limit, he thinks, puzzling over the barely scratched card, but there was no limit when he'd checked. Maybe Commander Richards has cancelled it. But why? He hasn't been extravagant — the ferry and car hire were the only big items, and the rest were essentials: groceries and the odd restaurant meal. "Never mind," he says, reaching for his personal MasterCard, then he pales. His own card is hiding in the apartment with his passport.

Nudging the little girl aside and feeling her father's face darkening as the curtain twitches, he desperately tries the card himself. "Insufficient Funds," the electronic wizard repeatedly claims, and he curses technology, wishing they'd stuck to the old-fashioned manual swipers and the subsequent paper trail that would take longer to trek back to his bank than he.

But his encroachment on the young girl brings the old man into the open and, without taking his eyes off Bliss, he stealthily tucks his daughter behind him, from where she peeps, now smileless, as though sheltering from a potential explosion. Bliss considers offering her a few coins as mollification, but fears he'll be misunderstood, so he smiles solicitously and uses sign language to indicate that he wants to use the phone.

The 1-800 enquiry number on the card works perfectly, and the cheerful attendant speaks English perfectly. The only thing that doesn't work is the card.

"It has no limit," he explains, and she agrees. The problem appears to be the fact he's overstepped his daily threshold of fifty thousand euros. "Purely for your own protection," she adds.

He doesn't need protection, he agitatedly explains, he needs a bed, bath, food, fuel, and a stiff drink.

"Did you buy a car?" she soothingly enquires, calming him with her charm school manner.

"No — I rented —" he starts, but is cut off.

"Then, it is simple — I see the problem."

Apparently, in her haste to close shop, and still struggling with the switch from francs to the European currency, the girl in the car rental office mistakenly took a security deposit of fifty thousand euros, instead of a measly five thousand.

"It is easy to see how it happened," says the pleasant girl on the phone.

Bliss blows out a sigh. "Thank God. So, can you straighten it out?"

"Certainly — of course. As soon as the garage opens on Monday we will confirm the mistake and voilà — your card will be freed."

"Monday!" he bristles, then calms. "It's OK. I'll just wait 'til midnight."

"Aah ..." Her hesitation warns him of a technical hitch. "When I say a limit of fifty thousand a day, it is twenty-four hours of which I speak."

"That's preposterous," he retorts.

"It is for your own protection, Mr. Smith."

"If you say that one more time," he breathes, with the mouthpiece partially covered. He then keeps her hanging while working out how to make the best of the situation. Checking his watch, he solves the problem. With a slap-up dinner, drinks at the bar, and a soft bed in mind, he realizes he hired the Jeep at roughly twelve o'clock that day.

"If I put the hotelier on the phone will you explain the card will be good at midday tomorrow?" he asks.

It is foolproof — almost.

"What?" he explodes when she refuses, explaining that, purely for his own protection, she has now put a hold on all transactions until the dispute with the car rental company has been resolved on Monday.

He tries — entreaties, pleas, demands, and threats — but Miss Charm School coolly rebuffs all suggestions, repeatedly reassuring him that it is entirely for his own protection. "If the card is stolen," she purrs, "and the thief has already taken fifty thousand euros, you would not want him to steal another fifty thousand tomorrow, would you?"

"The card is not stolen."

"Then there will be no problem, Mr. Smith. Monday —"

"But surely there is some way."

Apparently there is a way, she agrees, after a consultation with her supervisor. All he needs to do to get a temporary release of a few hundred euros is correctly answer a number of very personal questions, beginning with his mother's maiden name and date of birth.

He slams down the phone in disgust. How the hell is he supposed to know what Richards dreamt up to procure his alter ego's card?

Any thought Bliss may of had of sleeping on the beach is squelched by the hostile stares of locals as he sits on the rustic stone harbour wall waiting for nightfall, so he heads back into the mountains.

Now, parked on a terrace of an apparently abandoned olive grove, he tots up his cash, then fumbles under the seats and rummages through the glovebox.

With the two euros he finds under the carpet, he has enough money to buy a meal, providing he's willing to physically push the Jeep two hundred kilometres over the mountains back to Calvi. Alternatively, he could spend a second day and another night in the open and hope his card is cleared Monday morning. Plumping for a speedy return to civilization he chooses to starve, although finding fuel on Sunday might be a problem. He would have filled up in the small town, but the only filling station had already closed for the day. Was it too much to pray that the Corsican owner would be an atheist?

Pulling out his manuscript, he decides to use the failing light to advantage and writes of his protagonist, Frederick Chapel, alias harpsichordist François Couperin, wandering the beach of St-Juan, day after day, with his eyes on the island's fortress across the bay, and his mind on his seemingly impossible task.

He must have dreamed of simply running away, Bliss decides, as he constructs his character and delves into his mind, envisioning him escaping to some paradise island with sweeping white sand beaches and distant horizons — but the plot compels him to continue his mission. Fear, sense of duty, loyalty to his homeland, or, perhaps more plausibly, a simple refusal to be defeated, appear to be valid motives. Chapel is a man, Bliss notes, with the strength of character to stand up and be counted, a man who refuses to be bowed by a bully. Here was someone who would expose the identity of the man in the iron mask whatever it took. And if he failed, whether he offered his neck perpendicularly or horizontally, his spine would remain upright.

The practical difficulty of a lone seventeenth-century buccaneer storming the *castel* is a problem that concerns Bliss in his desire for authenticity, especially as Frederick Chapel is clearly more a pressed man than a hard-bitten swashbuckler of his time. What, then, if Chapel were to assault the island by stealth? But sailing under cover of night would be risky, with uncertain winds and uncharted shoals, and the noise of oars from a heavy wooden rowboat would draw the guard's attention — and fire.

The sun settling over the Mediterranean hovers briefly on the surface, as if reluctant to end another picture-perfect day, and Bliss stops writing to watch the celestial firework slowly fizzle out. Then, in the twilight he continues his story, writing:

Frederick Chapel sat on the beach at St-Juan as Angélique risked her pretty neck in a race with a mounted légionnaire, *delivered him his customary* gobelet, *surveyed his dishevelled appearance and demanded, "Hey Engleesh. Where you sleep?"*

With only a modest settlement from his patron he had precious little for lodgings, and had slept under a tree in an olive grove since his arrival.

"I 'ave zhe friend," went on Angélique with a lecherous wink. And, for a humble fee, Dorothée provided him a straw paillasse and all the comforts of home in a converted pigsty.

With little prospect of stealthily fetching up on the island by boat, Chapel decided to swim the reach on a moonless night, though the remainder of his escapade was yet to be resolved. In preparation for the swim, he took to the sea each daybreak, along with the disabled and disfigured who bathed their wounds in the salt water, and he strengthened his stroke until he judged he was ready.

The execution of the principal part of his plan required him to identify a suitable departure point, and, as he sat in his usual place one eve, he turned with innocent casualness to Jean le pêcheur and enquired, "What is afoot on the spit of land extending into the bay over there?"

Jean turned to glance, then scoffed, "Zhey are building zhe château."

"Whose château?" asked Chapel, puzzled by Jean's apparent scorn.

"Merde!" exclaimed the wily fisherman. "I know not. But zhey are crazy to build a château here." Then he spat, "Zhis place stinks of goat shit — c'est de la crotte de bique. Zhe sand is bleached under a sun zhat scorches from morn to night. Zhe plainness of zhe sea and sky will offend your eyes, and zhe plainness of zhe food, your gut. And zhe women here zhink only of sex."

"Ah ... the food is poor," agreed Chapel, surviving chiefly on the oysters, lobsters, olives, and figs bought from scavengers, but he persisted in his enquiry about the château, whose grounds seemingly extended to the beach.

"I have heard it is a panier de crabes," said Jean, pulling Chapel towards him with a conspirator's tone.

"It is rumoured zhat zhe watchguards have zhe orders to shoot trespassers on sight. Indeed, I know of three such men personally, and two others who have been savaged to death by zhe guard's dogs."

Chapel sat back with a skeptical eye. He had known Jean for only a short while, but, in one or two other matters, had found him a trifle wanting.

A snorting sound brings Bliss's head up, and he is surprised to find he's been so engrossed in his work that the light has gone completely. Switching on the Jeep's headlamps he jumps. He is surrounded by a herd of long-snouted, lean-bodied wild pigs warily inching towards him. What would Frederick Chapel have done? he wonders, and considers posing the problem to his fictional character at some point, though now, as the animals edge closer, he jokingly muses, "Dinner at last," and light-heartedly considers leaping out with a tire iron and hammering one to death. But as they become bolder, snuffling and snorting right up to the car, he realizes the shoe is on the other foot, and he turns on the ignition. Whatever possessed me to hire an open-topped vehicle? he is thinking, as one or two of the animals buffet the big car. How vicious are they? he worries, and what would happen if they ganged up and attacked, taking a chunk out of one of the tires — or out of me? How high can they jump — or scramble?

Dropping the Jeep into gear, he gently nudges a few of the big animals aside and hits the road at a run.

The lights of the small fishing port glow on the coast beneath him, but otherwise there is no sign of life. No one knows I'm here, he realizes, as he heads back to civilization, deciding that even the fierce-faced locals are less threatening than wild boars. But what would have happened had the pigs got me? he ponders. The unidentified body of John Smith of no fixed abode, with only a fraudulently obtained credit card in his possession, would be buried in an unmarked Corsican grave, and David Anthony Bliss, Police Inspector of London, England, would become a missing person without even trying — just like the rattan beach mat's owner.

But he has to go back — now wants to go back. He has a novel to finish and the riddle of the Château Roger to solve. It is certainly strange, he thinks, that people who'd lived in St-Juan-sur-Mer for years, maybe even for life, either never noticed it or, like Daisy, clammed up at its mention.

Concentrating fiercely on the twisting mountain road, fearful that one of the many untethered goats or cows he'd seen on the narrow rocky verge earlier will leap out and force him over the precipice, he makes his way to the small port to wait for the filling station to open in the morning.

A boat launch ramp leading to the beach makes an ideal parking spot, and he drifts to sleep in the moonlight, listening to the gentle sigh of waves on sand in the warm Mediterranean air, smiling to himself in childhood memory of Brighton beach and the stout little donkeys with gaily ribboned tack that had trotted him past the winning post of The Derby on so many occasions.

chapter eight

Bliss's second day on Corsica starts early. His stomach wakes him at dawn to a strawberry and champagne world, with feathery pink sky and gently fizzing surf. In the soft, calm Sunday air, he eyes the ranks of medieval terraces crowded around the little stone-walled harbour with a feeling of guilt that he and his snorting monster have intruded into a historical montage.

What if I've been spun back three centuries? he momentarily ponders, and pictures the locals awakening in awe to a fair-skinned Jeep driver on the harbour's boat ramp. For a few seconds he imagines the intrigue of some, the terror of others, and the certain condemnation of the parish priest — or would the cleric be theologically astute enough to turn it to his advantage and quickly pronounce the second coming? He could then gleefully anticipate the pontiff decreeing his sainthood and the elevation of his

measly church to the second holiest place in the world —
surely the dream of every priest.

"*Allez, ouste!*" shouts an arm-waving fisherman,
wanting to launch his three-hundred-horsepower supercharged sardine hunter down the ramp occupied by Bliss.

So much for historical quaintness and ecclesiastical
musings, Bliss thinks, startled from his reverie.

Fortunately Bliss has enough cash for fuel and the
filling station in the small port opens early this Sunday
morning to service the fishermen's thirsty machines.
With sufficient fuel in the tank to take him back to
Calvi, he is pleasantly surprised to find some money left
for food. A few freshly made sandwiches lie baited at
the garage for late-rising fishermen, and Bliss checks
them out carefully. One whiff of the cheese confirms his
suspicion. "*Brebis*," he snorts, already acquainted with
the black sheep of the cheese world and its ability to
decapitate an unwary eater, so he plumps for the meat.

"*Bon* — is good?" he asks.

"*Si*," replies the old man enthusiastically. "It is *la
spécialité de la Corse*."

Ah — ah! The Corsican speciality, he thinks. Why not?

Having poked a snotty note, together with the
Jeep's ignition key, through the rental car office letter-
box, he catches the first ferry, grateful he bought a
return ticket, and treats himself to a coffee with his last
few coins. With dinner at La Scala in her sights, he correctly guesses Daisy will happily take his collect call and
meet him in Nice.

He tries phoning Richards the moment he arrives
back at the apartment, muttering, "Bugger security. I'm
not going to Antibes to use a public pay phone. I'm on
my way out of here."

"It's Sunday," the duty officer at Scotland Yard stresses in a puzzled tone when he asks for Commander Richards.

"Sorry. Should have thought ..." he says, putting down the phone and looking over the balcony. The decaying lemon, dissolving slowly into the ground, bitterly accuses him of neglecting the boy in the cage, but the château has also dissolved, and he picks up his binoculars and stares in disbelief. Was it a mirage after all? he wonders, then chastises himself. You saw it from the ferryboat. It has to be there.

It is a trick of the light — the green copper roofs and creeper-entwined stonework are so deeply ingrained in the landscape that it is almost as if the building were a natural feature. Probably the reason the locals don't even acknowledge its existence, he reasons, finally getting it in focus. I really have to have a good look in there before I leave, he resolves, knowing how critical the château is to the solution of the masked man case.

The suddenness of the street lights going out at ten o'clock has Bliss musing, "Power cut," and raising himself inquisitively. Then all the remaining lights follow suit and he sits back, his suspicion confirmed, when *bang!* a violent explosion cracks the air with such force that the moment is held and seems incapable of moving forward. Then the second and third explosions hit with equal power, rocketing across the bay, sending seagulls and small children running for cover. With the blasts still reverberating around the hillsides, a mega-speaker rocks to life with a pop version of the national anthem,

"La Marseillaise." Bliss gives himself a shake and leans across the restaurant table to Daisy. "What the hell ...?"

"It's Bastille Day," she explodes. "Did you not know?"

He'd forgotten.

"*Mesdames et messieurs*; ladies and gentlemen," booms a giant voice from the water, "welcome to the Bastille Day festival of fireworks of Cannes."

"*Youpi!*" the crowd exclaims, as three luminescent balloons burst overhead and expand in a giant tricolour of patriotism. Then the sky fills with friendly fire as starbursts, grenades, and mortars explode in joyful release. Eye-blinking flashes, choreographed to a musical maelstrom, light the sky with a billion flashbulbs. A flotilla of ships, yachts, and ferries ringing the bay are lit in the sun-bright burst of radiance, and half a million uplifted faces on the promenade, quays, and jetties are warmed in the glow.

Above the jostle, from his perch on the balcony of La Scala restaurant, Bliss watches, mesmerized, as the sky is repeatedly shredded by exuberant colour and pierced by lightning-bright flashes. The floating city ahead of him, poured from every port along the coast, is picked out in the brilliance like the D-Day armada, the vessels seemingly so numerous and close that, from shore, he imagines being able to clamber across the bay, dry-footed.

"This is amazing," he exclaims, as rockets and shells of all kinds rip repeatedly into the sky in perfect rhythm and the deafening blasts rock in time to the music.

Daisy's face is alight with joy as she grasps his hand over the table and says, "You like — no?"

"I like." He smiles and feels that this is a fitting end to a perfect — well, almost perfect — weekend, but at least he is now free.

"Look at zhat," Daisy cries, as multicoloured fireballs explode one after another, pushing out balls of iridescent starlets that grow to fill the entire sky over the bay of Cannes.

"You didn't tell me about the fireworks," he exclaims, his face lit in delight.

Her mischievous smirk says she'd deliberately kept him in the dark to add to the moment. "You like — *Daavid*?" she questions, pronouncing his name with the long "aah," like the Welsh, while squeezing his hand.

"Yes. I like," he replies, and realizes that after three weeks on tenterhooks, this is the first time he's been able to relax with a clear mind. With Johnson in the bag, all he needs to do is call Commander Richards first thing Monday, then he'll be on his way.

Not so fast, he thinks. There are a couple of loose ends, including sorting out the mix-up with the Corsican car hire company over the credit card. Plus, the caged boy situation still has to be resolved.

"*Daavid — Daavid*!" Daisy calls through his musings. "Are you all right?"

"Oh! Sorry," he says, "I was miles away."

"It's OK," says Daisy as another bomb bursts overhead. "I ask if you will take some more wine."

"*Merci* — thanks."

"By zhe way," she asks, "did you take zhe donkey in Corsica?"

"I didn't find any," he admits.

"Oh zhat is zhe shame," she says. "It is zhe *spécialité de la Corse.*"

A momentary groan from Bliss as his stomach heaves is stifled by the *finale spectaculaire*. A hundred gigantic fireworks simultaneously take to the air from three separate barges, drown the music in a thunderous blitz, and set the sky afire. Then the applause of the crowd and the blaring sirens of every ship in the bay pick up the deafening chant and carry it on and on in a spontaneous joyous outburst that leaves Bliss slumped in his chair with barely controlled tears.

"Wow! That was *incroyable*," he murmurs.

Daisy's face sinks when Bliss excuses himself on arrival in St-Juan. It is barely midnight, but he needs to find Marcia Grimes as soon as possible.

"I come," Daisy says, but he is firm.

Natalia did not surface on the deck of the *Sea-Quester*, and he kept watch until the vessel took off from the bay with its cargo. Has she already returned to her mother?

"Why you see that woman?" demands Daisy, and he pulls her up harshly, annoyed at her presumptuousness.

"Daisy, I've had a very nice time, but now I have to go."

That was a bit rough, he scolds himself as he walks along the promenade. She's really very nice; why did you do that? But he knows why — it isn't her fault. It's him. With too many impossible relationships under his belt, too many painful memories, he is determined to keep his hands in his pockets. In any case, he only has another day or two — three at the most.

The promenade at St-Juan-sur-Mer is alive with Bastille Day revellers, but L'Escale has lost some of its sport without Hugh and his followers. Hopefully Jacques will be back. He's probably giving the *gargali* a little more time to show up, thinks Bliss, as he sits and signals Angeline for his usual tipple. In the meantime he will just have to make do with the *vent de midi*, which still arrives unfailingly at around eleven o'clock daily, ruffling the warm water and starching the beachside flags.

A giant "Happy Bastille Day" balloon escaped from a kid at eleven-thirty and he's still screaming half an hour later. What would the eighteenth-century French *aristos* have thought of that? Bliss wonders, as three lardy English women, looking tarty in their skin-tight skirts and T-shirts, hobble past in stilettos.

"Watch your purse, dear," says one. "You can't trust these bloody foreigners."

Bliss looks around, observing, "Half of these foreigners are English."

Grimes must be in his usual spot, he realizes, seeing a particularly pretty girl pass, proudly displaying a very large and elaborate pot in both hands, as if she had thrown it herself.

"*Merde!* A double blocker," he mumbles, and watches to see which seafront hotel is going to suffer. She could do a whole sewer with that one, he is thinking, when she trips on the corner of the Napoleon memorial, falls, and splats the wet pot across the promenade.

"Probably for the best, luv," he mutters, as her face crumples.

"David Bliss, I presume," says a voice at his shoulder, and he cracks his neck, with Edwards on his mind and "Burbeck" on his lips.

"Peter Marshall, Chief Inspector at the Yard," the voice introduces itself.

"Ah ..."

"Commander Richards said I'd find you here," continues the voice, as Bliss is still trying to sort out his mind. Richards has sent someone to check up on me, he guesses, and flies off angrily, "He could've phoned."

"What are you bleating about, Dave?" Marshall starts, but Bliss lays into him.

"How dare you spy —"

"Hey, Dave — cool it," soothes the chief inspector, easing himself into a chair. "No one's spying. I just happened to be on my way down here with the wife and kiddies for a week and he pulled me aside and said you were here convalescing — that's all."

Bliss sinks back, now fearful his outburst has blown his cover. "Convalescing. Is that all he said?"

Marshall's face suggests he knows more, but he answers, "Yes."

"Guv. Level with me, please," says Bliss, looking over the other man's shoulder, wondering just how much he knows of Johnson or Edwards, still hoping to find out whether or not the case is genuine or just an excuse to keep him out of the way.

Marshall pulls his chair closer and admits sheepishly, "OK. He told me you'd had a really rough time in that Canadian affair. But everyone knows that. Edwards really did a number on you." What he doesn't say is that Commander Richards's face blanched at the prospect of Bliss's presence in St-Juan being uncovered by another officer.

Bliss tones himself down and drops the other man's rank. "Sorry, Peter, I just thought he might have phoned, that's all."

"Probably didn't have a chance. I was just clearing up a few things in the office yesterday, and I bumped into him and Edwards chatting in the mess."

Bliss's brain shoots back into overdrive. "Does Edwards know I'm here?"

Marshall shrugs. "I couldn't say. Like I said, Richards sort of pulled me to one side. Maybe — I don't know. Is that a problem?"

Why am I worried? thinks Bliss, I'm going home in a day or so. "No — no problem.... So, Richards didn't send any message or anything?"

"No — not really. Just said I should keep mum about you being here. Wouldn't want the troops getting uppity if they thought one of the officers was getting a special deal — you know what they're like. But that's not a problem for me. It's about time us officers got a bit of gravy."

However, there is a problem — a big problem, in Bliss's mind. Edwards is suspended. What would he be doing at the Yard, especially on a Saturday, talking to Richards? And he's still trying to decide what to say when Marshall leaps out of his seat, breathing, "Oh my God!"

Then Angeline appears, unscathed as always, from behind a fleeing bus and nonchalantly delivers drinks to a nearby table.

"I thought she'd been swatted," Marshall admits, taking a breath and sitting down.

"You need a few tips," says Bliss, orders the chief inspector a double Scotch, then fills him in on the local customs, ending with a warning about the shiftiness of Jacques's wind, finally adding, "Always tip well or you'll get a sneezer next time."

"I'll remember," he says with a hard swallow.

"So where is your missus?" asks Bliss.

"Down the other end trying to charm a free pot off a bloke," Marshall scoffs, rising to leave, and Bliss resists the temptation to say she's wasting her time — unless she's got a six-hundred-degree kiln in her suitcase.

Grimes is a right charmer, thinks Bliss a few minutes later, as a bright little girl offers him a view of her newly struck potpourri dish. "*C'est très joli,*" he says, and she beams a toothy smile before lumbering her father with the wet pot.

Women — always women. Women and girls. He checks out each one and draws them in like the Pied Piper, Bliss decides, then wonders how many of them might end up dancing the night away with him. That would certainly explain his wife's attitude. But where the hell do they live? And where is Marcia? he is thinking as Jacques slips unseen into the seat opposite. "You are waiting for someone. A woman, perhaps?"

"*Bonsoir*, Jacques," he says, pretending not to be startled. "No — no one, not a woman," he says, just a touch too vehemently.

"You watch like zhis," Jacques says, raising himself and sticking his head in the air as he parodies Bliss.

Am I that obvious? he thinks, sinking lower as people passing stare at Jacques.

"So," demands Jacques, "who is she?"

Hugh and Mavis save him answering.

"I don't believe it," Bliss says, rising with a genuine smile and waving them to the adjacent seats. "I thought you'd gone home."

Hugh is not smiling. "This is your fault, Brubeck. Mavis and I aren't stopping, thank you. We just wanted you to know that, thanks to you, we're still here."

"Still here," trills Mavis.

"It's Burbeck," corrects Bliss, but then he's lost for words. "Um ... I'm not with you."

"I thought you'd deny it," says Hugh sternly, and turns to Jacques for support. "Fortunately we have a witness." Then he pauses to put emphasis behind his words. "Sunstroke," he declares, adding accusingly, "Your fault, Brubeck. Keeping on about the beach all the time. You should be more careful about what you say."

Bliss shouldn't have guffawed. It was Jacques's fault — creased in laughter under the table.

"You might laugh," complains Hugh, "but now we're stuck in this pestiferous hole for another two weeks."

"Why two?" enquires Bliss, straightening his face a notch.

"We couldn't move on Saturday — had to call the doctor — the only thing to do was to take the next booking. Now we've paid we might as well stay."

"You're in luck." Jacques smirks. "The pesky winds of zhe last few weeks have blown away completely. Now zhe easterly wind, *la levantade,* will bring us zhe peaceful weather and sunny skies."

"I thought he was going to thump you," says Bliss, after Hugh and Mavis have stormed away.

"He is *un couillon*," laughs Jacques.

"A what?"

"No matter," he says. "Buy yourself a dictionary."

Bliss's attempt to follow Grimes again fails at the first hurdle. Taking the same path to the edge of town has been easy, with the Bastille Day drunks still thick on the ground, but the guards of the hillside villas are on high alert. The first hulking shadow steps straight out in front of Bliss, demanding a light for his cigarette. Feigning deafness, Bliss sidesteps and walks into a roadblock. "What you want?" demands the second man.

"This is a public road —" he starts, but the first man cuts him off.

"You live here?"

"No," he admits under the weight of the demand.

"Then go."

Heavily outweighed, he turns, but at least he now knows the potter must live there. The guards obviously recognized him, he reasons, as he slinks back to the promenade on his way home, and Grimes would never be able to buy these guys off with a gooey look and a wet clay pot.

The Monday morning blues for Bliss are the azure sea and the navy sky, and he dances around the apartment with Brubeck blaring "Blue Rondo a la Turk" while tossing his dirty laundry straight into his suitcase — marking time until England catches up.

At ten o'clock precisely, though still only nine in London, he phones New Scotland Yard and gushes while Richards struggles out of his raincoat. "That's him, Guv. I've nailed him positively. He's on his yacht the *Sea-Quester*." Then he relaxes, home clear and free, thinking, I'll probably stay on for a day or two to finish research for the book; I've definitely got to take a peek into the château, one way or another, and probably fit in another trip to Île Ste-Marguerite, just to confirm the viability of my theory — Frederick Chapel's theory — of the identity of the masked prisoner.

"So that's it, Sir," he says, thinking: And any devious plan you and Edwards hatched to keep me quiet has just come unstuck, because I shall tuck myself away at home and write my novel. And, apart from an occasional trip to a good library — the British Library, probably — to confirm a few things my schoolboy history could be a bit wobbly on, I'll keep my head down until Edwards's disciplinary hearing in September.

"OK," says Richards. "Stay with him. I've gotta call a few people. See what we're going to do."

What's this, "Stay with him?" Bliss is wondering when the vagueness in the commander's voice begins ringing bells. "I thought you said you'd get a warrant," he starts.

"We will, Inspector ... probably. Just takes time, that's all."

"This is not on, Guv," he complains. "I've been here three bloody weeks. I've got black rings around my eyes."

"Not enough sleep, Dave. You wanna watch that."

"No," he spits, close to insubordination, "peering through effin' binoculars trying to spot bloody Johnson."

Richards's voice rises warningly. "You're getting paid, aren't you? Don't go all girlie on me, Dave. I told you it's a delicate job. You'll just have to hang on for a bit."

"A day or so."

"All right.... Now where exactly is he?"

"I've no idea."

The strangled, "What the fu —?" is in response to the steaming coffee Richards has accidentally dumped in his lap, but Bliss, unaware, remonstrates tetchily, "My job was to confirm his identity — that's all you said."

"Don't be a bloody idiot, man," shouts Richards, and then reigns back. "Sorry, Dave, but use your loaf. We need to know where he is now — where to send the troops."

Bliss's monosyllabic explanation is intended to be as rude as it sounds. "Sir. This guy is on a boat in the sea.

But I don't have a boat, Sir, so I can't keep up with him 'cos I can't walk on water."

"All right, Dave, you've made your point. But surely he's not always on the move?"

"Ninety percent of the yachts here never go anywhere, as far as I can tell," he explains, calming. "They're just floating gin palaces. But Johnson is on the go all the time. I thought you'd know that. That's what drug smugglers do."

"Who said anything about drugs?" enquires Richards, throwing Bliss completely off balance.

"Ah —" he starts, but Richards saves him. "You're just going to have to stay there and call me the minute he hits port."

"Bugger," swears Bliss as he drops the phone. "They don't even know what Johnson's up to, and all that wishy-washy stuff about having to talk to people. If this was a genuine job they'd already have a warrant sworn out."

"That was a waste of bloody time," he mutters, dragging his laundry back out of his suitcase and shoving it in the washing machine. Then he stands in the sun on the balcony, letting the warmth and the breathtaking panorama pacify him. A few more days won't hurt, he concedes, especially as he still has work to do, and a glance into the garden reminds him he meant to tell Richards about Johnson's ownership of the apartment, and that his wife was downstairs with some kinky guy in a cage. He also intended to challenge Richards on the tête-à-tête he'd been having with Edwards, though now realizes it would have been pointless. However, he never intended to reveal that he has solved the case of the prisoner of Île Sainte-Marguerite. That will be his secret — and his swansong from the police force — and he smiles, imagining the look on Edwards's and Richards's faces when they discover that in their effort to silence him they've given him not only the tools to solve the *cause célèbre* of the seventeenth century but also the time to write the book.

"If Commander Richards wants me to stay," he says to the air, "then I'll stay. As long as he doesn't expect me to waste my time running after Johnson and his whacko entourage, I'll play their game — put my feet up and write my book."

The public library in Cannes, unlike the one in St-Juan, is open, but is still a disappointment. After three hours he gives up trying to find information about the Château Roger and turns his attention to English history. But this is no British Library, and the only reference he finds of Richard Cromwell seemingly dismisses him as the likely wearer of the iron mask. According to the chronicler, rumour placed Tumble Down Dick back in England at the time in question, keeping a very low profile on his Chesham estate lest his creditors should lynch him or have him thrown in debtor's prison. The age-old undependability of rumour, thinks Bliss, absorbing the information, though still preferring to believe it possible Louis XIV had the maladroit man welded into an iron mask, perhaps to use as a bargaining chip in the war with the Grand Alliance under King William and Queen Mary.

Leaving the library, itself housed in an impressive château, Bliss suddenly stops with an idea and rushes back. Ten minutes later he emerges with a complete inventory of the works of François Couperin — at least now Frederick Chapel will have an idea of the man whose name he's taken.

Manuscript in hand, Bliss heads along the seafront of Cannes, seeking lunch and a quiet place to write — but it's now the middle of July, and he's hit the Parisian holiday season. The packed beaches heave with the constant flux of occupation, and seaside paraphernalia remorselessly shifts to dominate the space available as the city savvy hordes take tenure. Here, an abandoned mat risks being swept aside by a northern tide of newcomers, swamping the beach with inflated plastic toys and mattresses as they struggle along the sand, bare breasts to the left, bare bums to the right. "Mind that kid," shouts the wife.

"I didn't see the kid."

"You weren't looking."

"Why would I?"

Lost kids scream for parents, while parents of un-lost kids scream, "Get lost," and, like Patagonian penguins, the welter of new arrivals continually disturbs the colony until, mid-morning, with territory secured, everyone settles.

With a quick check to make sure the *Sea-Quester* hasn't returned to its berth, Bliss sits on the seafront with a wedge of Camembert and a baguette. Pulling out his manuscript he attempts to place himself in Frederick Chapel's mind and tries to picture Cannes before mass mobility, and the movie industry, turned it into a tourist mecca. With his pen poised, he tries to wash away three centuries of development and dig back to the sand dunes and dehydrated seagrass, but the constant bustle of trendy tourists, with chattering cellphones and flashy cameras, get in the way, so he gives up and watches the masses drift back and forth, while others snooze in the seafront bars, allowing the tide of life to drift past as they absorb the local wine, musing, "*Ah! c'est la vie en rouge.*"

A skinny woman with an overstuffed poodle sits beside him and articulately lights a cigarette as lingua franca. "Hi," she puffs as the cigarette says, "Watch the lips."

"What you write?" she asks, using it as a pointer.

"A novel."

The powerful word demands a meditatively lengthy pull.

"What your name?" escapes amid a puff of smoke.

"Dave Burbeck."

"I have read," she replies, takes a quick drag, and blows a smoke ring as punctuation before adding, "Gates of wrath."

"Close," he coughs, snaps his book shut and heads for the quiet of his apartment.

He walks the coast road back to St-Juan, knowing it will take him past the château's grounds and perhaps afford him a glimpse of the great house through the trees. Spurred on by natural inquisitiveness, and led by a detective's nose that smells sardines when something as innocuous as the presence of an old château make peoples' asses twitch, he is more than ever determined to find a way in. He wants to bury himself in its character, to absorb its ambience, to slide his hands over the walls and feel the vibes of the builders and occupants, perhaps even meet a ghost or two, but, more than anything, he wants to establish whether or not the crux of his theory will hold water. There has to be a way in, he thinks, as he passes the southern boundary of the château's grounds and considers a pre-dawn raid — although the signs on the twelve-foot-high steel fence make him pause. "*Chiens méchants*," they warn — vicious dogs.

Maybe it's a conspiracy, he briefly wonders. What if the locals all know who the man in the mask was, and that the château might house a clue to his identity, but want it to remain a secret to preserve the tourist trade?

The gentle onshore breeze, the *vent de midi,* dies with the sun, but will return tomorrow, as constant and dependable as the clear blue sea and sky. But, as Bliss takes his seat at L'Escale this evening and Angeline cheats the Grim Reaper with a deft feint that sends a Citroën into a spin, he feels a change in the air. Maybe Jacques's forecast is right at last, he is thinking, feeling a distinct lightness and freshness, although looking about him he realizes nothing has changed — only him.

"Here is your friend," says Angeline, spotting a familiar face as she places his wine on the table.

"Brubeck, old chap," says Hugh, offering a sheepish hand. "Can't stop. Just wanted to say that I think I might have been a bit hasty last night. Sorry about that."

"It's Burbeck," reminds Bliss, adding with a smile, "No problem, Hugh. No harm done." Although he's itching to say, "I guess you're worried you'll show up in my book as a caricature."

Then Daisy springs along the promenade, and he leaps to apologize for dumping her the previous night, saying, "It's only fair to warn you I'll probably be leaving in a few days."

"Why you go?"

"Back to work — get my book finished."

"But I don't understand," she says, crestfallen. "Your apartment is booked until zhe end of September."

"OK, Commander Richards, and your bosom pal Chief Superintendent Edwards," Bliss seethes under his breath, "this is war."

chapter nine

It is the last Saturday in July. The long cloudless days stretch into warm moonlit nights as Bliss whiles away his weeks in the sun. The real Dave Brubeck has played "How High the Moon" on his headphones a hundred times and more, and similarly his character, Frederick Chapel, has wandered the beaches and bays, humming snippets of François Couperin's harpsichord composition "La Visionnaire" while looking for ways to unmask the enigmatic prisoner on Île Sainte-Marguerite. Frederick Chapel has also struggled, along with his creator, with the problem of entering the Château Roger's grounds without being murdered or mauled, though Bliss has virtually given up hope of ever finding a way into the ancient building. Even Jacques, though seemingly interested, proved unhelpful.

"What château?" he asked at its mention, apparently as blind as the rest of the inhabitants. "But why do you want to know?" he wondered after Bliss described its location.

The temptation to disclose his amazing revelation regarding the man in the iron mask was considerable, especially in view of the fact that Jacques's piscatorial predecessor, Jean, was playing a significant role in his novel.

"I know the château's secret," he started, but left it at that, realizing that the less people knew the better. The chance, however slight, that the locals were conspiring to keep the prisoner's identity under wraps was enough to keep him quiet.

"What secret?" Jacques scoffed and tried to worm the reason out of him, but he closed his manuscript and refused to be drawn.

Summer Saturday evenings on the promenade at St-Juan-sur-Mer are usually quieter than other evenings. The Saturday arrivals, dragging suitcases, kids, and granny halfway across Europe, have collapsed comatose into lumpy beds to dream of Sunday — being comatose with a bottle of cheap plonk on the beach. This Saturday is no exception, as Hugh and Mavis pull up chairs at Bliss's table outside the bar L'Escale.

"How's the old book coming on?" asks Hugh.

"Evening, Hugh … Mavis," Bliss acknowledges with a nod. "Nicely, thanks. I guess this is your last night."

Mavis spies a seagull in the distance as Hugh leans forward. "Thought we might stay on for a bit actually, old chap. That's the nice thing about being retired; you can blow with the wind." Then he whispers, "Mavis wants to work on her tan a little more."

"Oh.... Good." Bliss smiles.

"I thought you were in a rush to get back, though," says Hugh, as Angeline sends a motor scooter skidding into the path of a speeding Toyota.

"Close one," breathes Bliss, as the scooter driver escapes by mounting the curb, swerving through three tables of tourists, skimming the Napoleon monument, and driving off without a backward glance.

"Not me," he says, realizing that, to all intents and purposes, he has disappeared.

In the past two weeks Samantha called once, and he phoned Richards just to tell him there was nothing to report. Richards seemed relieved. Why wouldn't he be? Bliss thought, but his problem will come September 1, when I turn up at the Yard, bronzed as a button, to testify against Edwards.

"It's been a nice day again," Bliss adds to Hugh, as Angeline delivers their drinks, but every day has been nice — brilliantly clear skies and turquoise seas rucked only by the *vent de midi. La levantade* proved as shifty as the other winds forecast by Jacques, and its absence was followed by that of *la bech* — a very nasty southeasterly, according to Jacques, which would most assuredly sweep up the full length of the Mediterranean and storm head on to the beach of St-Juan. The *vent de midi* breezed its way ashore the following day as usual, and Jacques, true to form, ducked under the parapet for awhile.

Bliss has met Daisy for dinner several times since their night at La Scala and, while she sloughed off his attempts to discuss the Château Roger, he vigorously avoided a show of her etchings.

"It is a very bad place," she insisted one evening, when he pushed her on the building's disposition.

"I was thinking of buying it," he lied, hoping the prospect of a juicy commission might soften her stance.

"You cannot," she shot back without consideration.

"Why not?"

Pausing with a deeply calculating look, her eyes held a glimmer of interest as she asked, "Do you have a lot of money?"

So — what is your price, Madame? he wondered, answering, "Maybe."

"It is not possible — is not for sale," she said, quickly backtracking.

But everything here is for sale, he told her. "*À vendre*" signs are everywhere: on villas, houses, apartments, yachts, and even that most coveted possession — a parking space for a car.

Daisy wouldn't budge, huffily insisting, "Zhe château is not for sale."

Pinky and Perky have formed a trio with a dulcimer-playing shrew who pecks away on his instrument with little hammers and dances as he keeps time with both feet. "Guantanamera" sounds good on a dulcimer — but only the first time, Bliss decides, as a sour-faced group of hoteliers start pulling chairs into a forum.

"It is *l'association* again," confirms Angeline, and Bliss doesn't need her to explain the agenda. The nightly procession of beaming pot carriers has continued unabated since their previous meeting three weeks earlier, but this time the chairman starts the proceedings without the blessing of the priest. He probably wants to stay in close communion with the spirits, Bliss wryly guesses, having spied the black robe slipping into the back entrance of the bar across the road.

The hoteliers' discussion is too heated for Bliss to follow, though the pesky potter is clearly the only topic, and, from their tone, he figures some would like to get hold of Grimes and stuff him down his own toilet. But where is his toilet? Bliss still wonders.

He tried following Grimes a couple of times, but was headed off at the pass on both occasions. Another time he waylaid the potter at L'Offshore Club, but, hampered by the confidential nature of his connection to the other man's wife and his knowledge of his daughter, Natalia, he learnt little.

Marcia showed up at L'Escale one evening after Bliss's Corsican excursion, tearfully informing him Natalia hadn't come back as promised, and she had no idea where she and Johnson were.

Surprise, surprise, he said to himself, then shrugged his unconcern on both counts and carried on writing as he listened to Brubeck's jazzy version of "These Foolish Things."

The case of Johnson's wife and the man in the cage was resolved in a way — they disappeared. It wasn't a particularly satisfactory resolution and left Bliss with a bad taste and Daisy with a headache.

Daisy had agreed to knock on the ground-floor apartment door one day, fawning, "Just want to make sure everything is all right, *Madame*," while Bliss skulked behind the lemon tree, then slipped in the kitchen from the back garden, excusing himself. "Sorry — my mistake — wrong door. Are you OK?"

The young man, cradling the dog in terror, leapt into his cage, screamed, and continued screaming until

Johnson's wife broke away from Daisy, crashed into the kitchen, and bundled Bliss out of the back door, shouting, "Get out — get out."

"What will Morgan Johnson say?" worried Daisy, as they held an inquest in a nearby coffee house, but Bliss calmed her. "It was nothing to do with you; I was the one in the kitchen."

An hour later, Johnson's wife and the strange man cleared out, and Morgan Johnson was on the phone to Daisy, bullying her to reveal the identity of the person who'd broken into his wife's kitchen.

The hastily convened extraordinary meeting of L'association des hôteliers de St-Juan-sur-Mer falls apart fairly soon after the chairman advises the eight attendees that both the town's mayor — *le maire* — and *l'inspecteur de police* have refused to take action against Grimes, stating that whilst his soggy pots might cause offence, he himself did not.

"I wish Jacques was here," Bliss confides to Hugh. "I'd love to know what they're going to do."

But Jacques's interpretation becomes superfluous as one of the hoteliers reaches out, snatches a passing pot from the hand of a startled nymphet, and pancakes it onto the table with a fist.

"Punch-up," mutters Bliss, as the young girl's father hurtles across the promenade and, in a single movement, scrapes the clay into a ball and thwacks it into the offender's face.

The fracas turns into a debacle and ends in a general melee, with other pot recipients getting dragged into the fray as their treasures are snatched and trampled. Bliss is rising with the word "Police" on his lips, when Angeline pries the priest out of the bar to restore order.

"Disgraceful," mutters Hugh, but Bliss sits back, relieved he hasn't revealed his true vocation.

Sunday morning sees Bliss back at L'Escale for coffee and croissant, as Angeline mops away the last traces of clay from the pot fight.

A chic young woman, in Sunday skirt and a flouncy red hat, sashays along the promenade with everything in perfect rhythm — makeup, clothes, handbag, shoes, and attitude all in tune. Snubbing Bliss, she sidesteps Angeline's mop and stubs her toe on a corner of the Napoleon memorial.

"Napoleon landed there in 1815," Bliss explains, but her scowl says "Leave me alone," and she scurries into a nearby laneway.

"Just trying to be friendly," he mutters, as a female turtledove alights on the seawall, eyeing his plate, and he quickly tears a small hunk off his patisserie. Then, while his mind darkens in memory of the drowned duck, a male dove lands on the hen's back and has his way with the surprised bird. "At least that won't kill you," Bliss muses, eating the croissant himself.

Relaxing on the promenade, shaded by one of L'Escale's giant parasols, Bliss casually glances over the seawall into the still harbour, and his eye is taken by a spooky aberration. Amid the fringe of flotsam drawn to the harbour wall is what appears to be an industrial-strength latex glove, with the ochre fingers clawing upwards as if Neptune is reaching out to grasp an unwary fisherman and drag him to a watery grave. With an involuntary shudder Bliss returns to his writing, but a few moments later he is drawn back to the glove with the nagging feeling he's seen movement. Probably just the current or wavelets, he tells himself, staring intently, but ends up grappling with the fact that the only ripples are those caused by the glove's movement. "It is moving," he breathes.

Wondering if it could be the hand of a diver carrying out underwater maintenance on the seawall, he saunters inquisitively down the short flight of steps to the quay, peers deeply, and realizes it is the frenzied attack of small fry giving the glove life, jiggling it around in the water as they scythe, piranha-like, in silvery waves. But these Mediterranean midgets are no piranhas, and, satisfied there is no partially stripped skeleton attached to the glove, Bliss lets it go and returns to his writing. Thirty seconds later, he looks back at the water, the words: "Why would fish attack an old glove?" playing on his mind. Rushing back down the steps he confirms his worst fears, then heads to the bar for assistance.

Ten minutes later, in answer to Angeline's call, a minibus of *la gendarmerie* screams down the bustling main street and heads west on the promenade.

"Where are they going?" Bliss demands in disbelief, but gets no answer from the small crowd of rubberneckers craning for a peek at the dismembered hand in the water. Thirty seconds later the police chief in his Renault takes the same route to the promenade, but turns east.

"Christ!" swears Bliss as the minibus roars back along the promenade, screaming *pin-pon, pin-pon*, overshoots, and heads east in pursuit of the chief.

"I don't believe this," he mutters incredulously, watching as a minute later the chief and his braves head west once more and screech up outside the bar. He's still trying to work out the French for "Keystone Cops" when Jacques pulls up on his shoulder and immediately catches on. "*Les flics sont cons*," he complains, giving Bliss his answer.

Bliss drops back into the shadows and waits as the policemen shoo away the small crowd, share cigarettes, and, he judges by their laughter, joke about the appendage in the water coming in handy.

The delicate task of retrieving the hand from the harbour is discussed and debated for nearly fifteen minutes before a passing fisherman, who's wandered unconcernedly through the invisible cordon, scoops it out with one sweep of his net and plonks it at the policemen's feet with a wet thud.

"Oy — you can't do that," screams one of the policeman in French, but the old fisherman throws up his hands and moseys off, as if saying, "If you don't want it — chuck it back."

A flurry of silvery fish wriggle home across the quay as Bliss wanders forward to take a peek. One of the gendarmes glowers in professional disapproval, but is at a loss to explain why a solitary severed hand should require a fifty-metre exclusion zone.

"Oh God," Bliss breathes to himself, immediately recognizing the hand. It is the potter's right hand — no glove, just ruddy brown clay ingrained in the pores and caked around the nails. There is no doubt. He'd recognize Greg Grimes's hands anywhere. Even the shape is still evident — the cupped palm and the crooked index finger from years of moulding and crimping the delicate pots.

L'association des hôteliers immediately springs to Bliss's mind, but this surely is an exceptionally draconian method of keeping their plumbing unclogged. Then darker thoughts drag him down. This wasn't the hoteliers' doing. This is a warning. This is somebody's very unsubtle way of saying, "Keep your hands off." But a warning from whom? And — more importantly — for whom?

It takes a few moments for him to get his mind in gear and he stands, immobile, until he's jerked into action by the realization that he's been so concerned about the hand, and who may be responsible, he's overlooked the rest of the man. "Oh my God! Where is Grimes and what sort of shape is he in?" he breathes with his hand to his mouth.

Jacques appears undisturbed as he sips espresso on the promenade and reads the Sunday paper.

"It's the potter's hand," Bliss enlightens him breathlessly as he sits.

"Zhat'll please zhe *hôteliers*."

"Yes — but where's the rest of him?" he asks, and gets the nonchalant shrug and the indifferent "*bof!*" he expected in response.

Peering thoughtfully towards the enclave of nosebleed villas stretching up the hillside behind the town, Bliss muses, "He lives up there somewhere."

"I don't zhink so," Jacques replies, checking out the paper's weather forecast.

"Yes — I know he does."

With a thoughtful glance, Jacques takes in a sweep of some of the world's most expensive real estate, asking, "How do you know?"

Quelling a temptation to admit following Grimes, Bliss lies, "He told me."

"And you believed him?"

"Why not?"

The reason is simple, claims Jacques, dismissing the idea of a mere potter like Grimes affording even a dog kennel in the lofty heights above the town. "Up zhere lives *la crème de la crème*," he says, then he reels off a star-studded cast of musicians, film stars, and mega-rich sports personalities.

What happened to the gangsters, fraudsters, and corporate raiders? wonders Bliss, thinking Jacques should get a PR job with the tourist board. But Jacques is still proselytizing. "We have an expression for zhese people," he says, his tone resolute with admiration. "It is '*la grande servitude.*' It means zhose who have great wealth also have great slavery. *Oh là là!* how *le gratin* suffer."

"*Le gratin?*"

"*Oui* — zhe top crust," he says with great solemnity. "Zhe responsibility of such wealth weighs heavily upon zhem."

Looks like it, thinks Bliss, sweeping his gaze across the flotilla of multi-million-dollar yachts and up into the hills, to the hideouts of the seriously rich and the laundries of the seriously naughty.

The gendarmes, backed up by a posse of *police nationale,* still stand perplexed around the severed hand, and Bliss is itching to put them in the picture, but realizes that as a foreign novelist he would have little credibility.

Should he break cover? he wonders, and considers calling Richards for guidance. But it's Sunday morning. He checks his watch — a little before ten; still not nine in England. The duty officer at the Yard would give him the commander's emergency contact number if pushed, although he would take some convincing — but the image of Richards grumpily reaching from beneath the duvet is enough to dissuade him. Jacques still has his head in the paper, so, using his inadequate grasp of French as an excuse, Bliss primes Angeline to fill the police in on the hand's provenance and slips away in search of Daisy.

I'll get her to check the hospitals first, he's planning as he heads towards her office. She should be in, he hopes, remembering her complaining that summer Sundays were always crowded with Saturday's new arrivals, carping about their apartments' noisy neighbours or blocked plumbing. At least Grimes can't get the blame for that in future, he thinks, and then stops with the realization that the promenade will be a duller place without the nightly convoy of happy pot carriers. As useless as the little pots might have been, St-Juan-sur-Mer will be a poorer place without them, he decides, then muses, "What if Grimes is not in hospital? What will you do then?"

Step back, he tells himself. This isn't your problem. Let the local police deal with this. It has nothing to do with you.

Are you sure? What was it you said to Samantha about people having a habit of getting killed when you become involved?

Greg Grimes isn't in hospital — any hospital. Even as far away as Cannes, Nice, and Antibes. No one has heard of Greg Grimes.

"You don't know he is dead. His hand could have been chopped off by accident," suggests Daisy after she has foisted off a few complainers with promises of immediate action and phoned all of the medical institutes she can think of.

"He's a potter, Daisy, not a lumberjack," Bliss tells her. "The sharpest tools he uses are a wet rag and a wooden spatula. But there are other ways."

"How?"

"It could have been chopped off by a propeller in a boating accident."

"OK," says Daisy, "zhen why is he not in zhe hospital?"

"Let's get some lunch," suggests Bliss, rather than admitting that he has no palatable answer.

"*Moules et frites*," says Daisy, ordering the local favourite on the quayside patio of one of the fish restaurants a few minutes later.

"Mussels and chips," mutters Bliss, preoccupied with concern over Grimes. "I'll have the same," he says, unable to escape a pinprick of guilt that he really invited her to pump her for information, but the necessity of quickly tracking down Grimes, or his wife, overrides the self-reproach, and he has to admit he quite enjoys her company. He needs someone to confide in, particularly someone in the real estate business who might have access to all kinds of confidential information about the ownership and tenancy of local properties.

He tried looking up Grimes in the local telephone directory while waiting for Daisy to deal with a particularly vociferous complainant, though he wasn't surprised to come up blank, guessing that the names of few, if any, of the owners of the villas on the hill would appear in any phonebook, anywhere. In fact, he would be willing to bet his pension that most of the property ownerships would be buried in companies registered in islands so far offshore they wouldn't appear in any other kind of book, either.

If Daisy knows or has guessed his credentials she certainly doesn't give any indication. "So what you do here?" she asks, when he finally confesses to being a British policeman.

"I am writing a book," he admits. "But I'm also here secretly to investigate a very important case. But I can't tell you any more."

"I know what it is," she says, taking him completely unawares.

"You do?"

"Yes — I guessed. Zhat is why you want to get into Mrs. Johnson's apartment."

"No," he protests, "I was worried about the man in the cage, that's all."

"I wonder where zhéy have gone," muses Daisy — a thought that has been preying on his mind as well since finding the hand. As remote as the possibility might be, he can't help thinking there could be a link between the two incidents. Morgan Johnson is certainly connected to both his wife and the father of his girlfriend — but what could Grimes have done to deserve this?

"So. Why you keep asking about zhe château?" Daisy continues.

"It's for the book ..." he starts, and then stops in thought. The security guards protecting the villas surrounding the château's estate must know where Grimes lives. They let the potter pass unquestionally each night before they stepped out of the shadows and confronted him.

Following a hasty lunch, Daisy happily escorts Bliss to the hill, and, explaining they are worried about a friend, describes Grimes to a couple of the heavies guarding the gates of a mansion.

"*Oui*," they admit. He has sometimes walked that way at night — always alone.

But as for exactly where he lives — "*Bof!*" they say, shrugging.

"Does that mean they don't know, or won't tell?" Bliss asks her.

"*Bof!*" She shrugs, still leaving him in the dark.

Out in the open, with Daisy in tow, he climbs the tortuously twisted section of road over and over as he tries to recall precisely when he lost the sound of Grimes's footfalls the first night he tailed him. Finally, isolating a short segment between two hairpin bends, he digs in and insists, "This must be it."

But just as he previously discovered, there are no doorways or gates in the fortress-like wall on one side, and the château's steel barricade on the other rules out any possibility of ... But there he stops and starts tugging at the undergrowth sprouting around the railing's roots.

"What are you doing?" demands Daisy worriedly.

"Grimes disappeared here somewhere," he explains, pausing. "He couldn't have climbed the wall or the fence, but what if he went through?" Then he points. "Start looking at that end, will you? See if any of these posts are loose."

Daisy shies away. "Zhat is zhe château."

"I know," he says, continuing to rip seedlings and grass aside. "But maybe Grimes found a shortcut through the grounds."

Daisy pales at the prospect. "*Non.* Zhat is not possible."

"Why?"

"Zhe *chiens de garde* — zhe dogs."

Her words stop Bliss with a curious awareness. "That's funny," he mutters. "What dogs?" Where are the fearsome hounds the signs warn about? And where are the dog handlers and security guards? None of the heavyweight wrestlers who accosted him on the hill were connected with the château, as far as he could tell. If they were, they certainly weren't guarding any doors or gates. This is at least the fourth time he's been close to the fence, and he walked the southern perimeter on his return from Cannes one day, yet there has been no sign of a guard or dog.

"Here boy, here boy," he starts shouting through the fence, and immediately Daisy is on his arm, dragging him away, her voice rising in terror. "*Non, non. Arrête, Daavid.* Stop. Stop — please. You must stop."

Freeing himself with a sharp tug, he stands back. "What's the matter?" he asks. "They can't get at us through the fence." But he fails to mollify her as she stands, trembling.

"Don't, *Daavid*, please," she whimpers, and he's forced to comfort her with a hug.

"Sorry," he says, deciding to abandon the fence, and he escorts her back down the hill, past the guards, to the town.

After her paroxysm at the château's fence, Daisy excuses herself, promising to make discreet enquiries of one of her tenants, a local gendarme. Then Bliss spends the rest of the afternoon and early evening walking the beaches, quays, and jetties, desperately seeking any sign of Greg

Grimes, worried he might have been murdered, chopped into pieces, and scattered at sea. And it doesn't escape his notice that the marine unit of the local police has spent the afternoon sweeping up and down the bay with a couple of men hanging over the sides of a patrol boat.

The pathetic sight of a procession of empty-handed promenaders saddens Bliss as he sits at L'Escale Sunday evening, desperately hoping Marcia Grimes will show up. He's not overly hopeful and has fostered a growing concern that Marcia Grimes had a better reason to handicap her husband than anyone else, but he has run out of other ideas. Earlier he checked the cupboard Grimes used to store his wheel and supplies. The padlock was firmly in place — not surprisingly, he thought, considering that the hand that would normally turn the key had been permanently detached from its owner.

Daisy's violent aversion to anything connected with the Château Roger continues to puzzle him, but so does everything about the building. The realist in him wants to believe it is simply an abandoned structure with no more heart than an empty garbage bin, yet the negative passion its presence generates in the community shakes his logic. I must be going soft, he thinks, wondering what his colleagues might say if he suggested the grand old house was a major source of malodorous vibes. But he knows what their reaction would be. "Show me the evidence," they'd demand pragmatically, highly suspicious of anything metaphysical or unconventional, and equally skeptical of anyone promulgating such ideas or other wacky notions such as alternative punishments, remedies, religions, or lifestyles.

Time weighs heavily as Bliss, completely frustrated by his inability to find either of the Grimeses or to do anything about an apparently serious crime, waits at L'Escale, watching the sun slip over the rim of the world. With nothing else to do he rereads his growing manuscript and realizes Frederick Chapel is in a similar quandary over the château. He too is chary of the mystique being developed around the nascent building, but he has to get into the grounds some way or another. Now with two reasons for wanting to infiltrate the well-protected property, Bliss takes up his pen and gives his three-hundred-year-old character the task of finding a solution.

The days stretched from weeks into months as Frederick Chapel paced the hot dunes of St-Juan in constant fear of his true identity being exposed. France's war with England raged ever closer as the summer progressed, until he had become almost entirely cut off from his mother country. Although his chances of successfully completing his mission were remote, his determination to swim the strait to Île Sainte-Marguerite from the beach at the foot of the Château Roger's grounds was unwavering.

Every day the château had grown in size and splendour. The materials, craftsmen, and labourers arrived in tall-masted ships that lay at anchor in the wide blue bay. Fine Italian marbles, exotic timbers from Mozambique, Chinese silks, drapes, and Persian carpets were all barged ashore from traders' barks and fluyts. And every day Frederick Chapel puzzled over the motivation for constructing such an impressive and exquisite building where the occupants would be plagued by heat, mos-

quitoes, and the notorious gangs of blackguards who roamed the hills, cutlasses at the ready.

"Bonsoir, Jean," said Chapel to the fisherman, as he sat on the sand one evening, eyeing the developing edifice. "I see the château is almost completed."

"Ah! Mon Dieu. Mon ami," Jean said, throwing up his hands in horror, "I have warned you. You should not talk of zhe château. If you are overheard you will most surely get le raccourci."

It matters little, Chapel thought to himself. I can no longer return to England. I may as well risk my neck here as risk my neck in war.

"Jean," he said, "you are a wily character. I see it in your eyes. You must see therefore that I have a good reason for wanting to get into the château's grounds."

Leaning forward, Jean replied, "I have not told you zhis, but I know many of zhe guards. Zhey fish for sardines all day and zhey keep watch at night. But when can zhey sleep?"

"I understand," said Chapel, "but what of the dogs?"

"Aha," said Jean. "Zhe dogs are so hungry they would kill each other for a morsel. Zhey would certainly take off your hand. But, perhaps — and it is only perhaps — perhaps if you offer le beefsteak you will save your hand.

Some things never change, thinks Bliss, his eye taken by the lighthouse on the promontory of Cap D'Antibes as it pulses out its warning. Then his gaze falls to the harbour and he watches the moon diamonds sparkling off a gently rippling sea as Dave Brubeck jazzes up his version of "Look for the Silver Lining" in his ears.

"I wonder if Grimes, the poor bastard, is out there somewhere," he muses as he falls under a shadow, and it takes him a few seconds to catch onto the fact that someone is standing over him, demanding, "Have you seen him?"

It's Marcia Grimes, and he rips off his headphones and pulls himself out of his seat. "No — where is he?"

Slumping as her face drains, she sighs, "He's gone again."

"Gone where?" he queries.

"I don't know," she spits. "Back to Corsica, probably."

Angeline has braved the great divide and recognizes Marcia. "Oh. Your friend comes back," she says to Bliss, but his mind is elsewhere as he explains to Marcia, "I thought you meant your husband."

"Where is he?" she asks, eyes screwed in puzzlement as she searches passing hands for signs of wet clay pots.

Angeline scurries away as Bliss describes the morning's grisly discovery, and Marcia rises in alarm, repeatedly questioning, "What's happened? ... What's happened?" as she scours the promenade and dark harbour.

"I was hoping you'd be able to tell me," he says, keeping a carefully trained eye on her reaction.

"I've no idea," she answers clearly, her face taut in consternation and concern.

Could she have done it? he asks himself, but draws a blank. She certainly had good reason. Jealousy is a potent motivator, he knows from previous cases, and judging by the venomous way she spoke of the clique of women who nightly swarmed her husband, she was certainly motivated.

"He's obviously not at home, then."

The reply is almost swallowed in the tears as she mumbles, "We don't have a home, Inspector. Thanks to Morgan Johnson."

Bliss urges Marcia to report her husband's disappearance to the local police, but she shrinks away with more fear than Daisy showed at the château's fence, and he is sorely tempted to disobey his commander and approach the gendarmerie himself. But Marcia persuades him to wait until Monday morning.

"He'll turn up, I'm certain," she blubbers.

"I'm not so sure," he mumbles, but he has been vacillating on the notion of putting the police in the picture all Sunday afternoon. It isn't as if he has any concrete evidence to offer, other than the possibility that Grimes might use the château's grounds as a shortcut.

"And where exactly is zhis potter — zhis Monsieur Grimes — going?" he imagines the desk sergeant demanding. He'd have no answer, but the trickier question would be: "And who, precisely, authorized you to carry out zhis surveillance?" Even at home, a detective straying from his patch into an adjacent jurisdiction could get his knuckles severely rapped.

"Where has your husband been living?" Bliss asks, but Marcia Grimes is of little assistance.

"Do you think he would have told me?" she shoots back angrily, immediately confirming his suspicion that there is some other woman in Grimes's life.

Trying diplomacy, he responds, "Not to put too fine a point on it, Marcia, it seems as though he was popular with the ladies."

"Inspector —" she starts, but he quickly cuts her off.

"Please call me Dave."

"I'd rather use your rank, if you don't mind," she responds coolly, and he understands. Spilling the embarrassing minutiae of your partner's sexual peccadilloes is easier if there is a shield of professionalism. Calling him by his first name would be like calling her doctor John or Billy, then trying not to cringe as he slips on a glove for an internal exam.

"It was me," she continues, breaking down. "It was my fault. He's a good man. He worked as hard as he could. He never messed around — not as far as I know. And it wasn't as though he didn't have offers. You saw the way women watch ..." She pauses, unable to talk through the tears, and then corrects herself. "You saw how they couldn't take their eyes off him."

Trying to soften the blow Bliss suggests an alternative. "People just like to see others working — makes them feel good when they're on holiday. If some bloke stood on the quayside sandpapering his nails some people would watch."

The cynical look she gives him borders on incredulity.

"OK. I noticed it," he admits. "He had something special — warmth. It was as if he gave part of his heart away with every pot."

"He did. But you're wrong if you're thinking he wanted something in return."

"So, why always women then?"

"Oh, come on, Inspector. How many men are going to hold out their hands for a prissy pot? Anyway — it wasn't just women."

Daisy's bustling arrival at L'Escale prevents Bliss from asking what she means, and they sit glumly as the newcomer explains that, according to her source, the police don't have a clue.

"OK," he says, making up his mind. "If he hasn't shown up by the morning, I'm going to contact my office for advice."

chapter ten

The restaurants and bars on the promenade of St-Juan are winding down Sunday night as Bliss makes his way towards his apartment, but black thoughts turn him around at the door. You can't just leave the poor devil, he tells himself, you are a policeman. Then he spends the next hour prowling the promenade and beaches until finally, around one o'clock in the morning, he takes the potter's usual route out of town and up the hill towards the château.

A guard he doesn't recognize steps out of the shadows and silently challenges him. "This is a public road and I'm just going for a walk," Bliss calls out with innocent panache as he keeps up a firm pace. The guard and his partner back away from a confrontation, and once out of their sight Bliss quickly finds the loosened post in the fence.

"Good night, lads," he calls cheerily on his return,

and shrugs off their hostile scowls as he works on his plan for the following night if the missing potter should fail to materialize.

Rather than risk missing Commander Richards Monday morning, Bliss puts in a call to the duty officer at Scotland Yard in the early hours, stressing the importance of the commander calling him as soon as he reports for work, not after the Monday morning prayers. "It's critical," he insists, knowing nobody will want to disturb Richards once he is in communion with other senior officers over the weekend's statistics, shaking their heads in disgust at the number of crimes; bellyaching about the inefficiency of junior ranks; complaining about politicians, activists, apologists, and civil libertarians; then debating at length the relative merits of various golf courses, hotels, and restaurants, before setting the agenda for the next freemasonry meeting.

Richards phones back at ten-thirty, indignant about Bliss using traceable phones. Dismissing the criticism without comment, Bliss fills him in, emphasizing the link between Grimes and Johnson as his reason for wanting to take action, though carefully avoiding the use of names.

Richards is unconvinced. "It's probably safer if you stay out of it, Dave," he says, his mind clearly spinning to come up with a good reason. "I should let the locals deal with it."

The equivocation in the commander's reply gives Bliss encouragement to push his point that the locals are working completely in the dark. Stopping short of divulging his identity, can't he point them in the right direction?

"Well, don't do anything hasty," Richards replies, and Bliss has to laugh at the typical cop-out clause, guessing the conversation is being taped and knowing that, should anything go wrong, Richards will stand back and say, "I ordered him not to do anything risky," and if medals are being doled out, he'll be there glad-handing, saying, "He took my advice and went ahead with care."

"Do you need anything?" Richards adds, and Bliss moans about the inadequacy of one pair of grotty binoculars and a cellphone that is so insecure he is expected to use telephone booths.

"How come I didn't get any Superman gadgets?" he says, half-jokingly.

"Let me know if there's anything serious you need, Inspector," ripostes Richards, clearly for the benefit of the tape recording, and Bliss catches on and calls his bluff for sport.

"Actually, Sir, there is. I'm going to need a million-dollar power boat."

"Dave — I said serious," laughs Richards.

"I am, Guv. This guy gets away with gawd-knows-how-much and you expect me to catch him with a boy scout survival kit. I'm surprised you didn't give me one of those things for getting stones out of horses' hooves. The only way I'll ever keep up with him is with a yacht."

"You must be out of your mind," Richards starts, then questions, "Who told you about the missing investments?"

"I have my sources, Guv."

"Be careful, Dave. If he's caught on, you could have serious problems. Maybe you should leave this Grimes thing alone. This is not the reason you're there."

"Look, Guv. I know exactly why I'm here," Bliss says. "This is a load of baloney. It's just a make-work project to keep me out of the way while Edwards slips the noose."

"Dave that's —" Richards starts to protest.

"How come I'm not allowed to tell anyone where I am or what I'm doing, then?" Bliss cuts in. "It's all a bit too bloody convenient as far as I can see."

"Dave, believe me. It's not like that," Richards insists, but Bliss is unconvinced.

"OK. Well, if you're serious, what about the yacht?"

Richards ducks the question again, asking, "Have you any idea where the target is now?" being careful not to mention Johnson by name.

An alarm bell rings in Bliss's mind. He's missed something important, something Marcia Grimes said Sunday evening at L'Escale, and he quickly replays the meeting as he catches on to the fact that when she said, "Have you seen him — he's gone again," she was talking about Johnson. He was so preoccupied with her husband's fate he'd completely forgotten.

"He must have been here at the weekend, Guv," he tells Richards, adding with growing awareness, "And, from the way she spoke, probably Saturday night — the night Grimes lost his hand."

"Dave ... this sounds very iffy," Richards warns.

The cranky sound of a reluctant engine gives Bliss his signal, and the rusted iron railing leaps free under his gloved hand. With a deep breath, he slips through the gap, repairs the fence, and edges warily forward. At least he isn't facing the death penalty, like Frederick Chapel — he hopes.

Daisy's stalled car engine bursts into life at the fifth try, and, with a wave of thanks to the hoodwinked security guards, she heads back to keep Marcia company on the promenade and await Bliss's return — she hopes. Earlier, her obstinate reluctance to participate in the plan to distract the guards while Bliss slipped past in the darkness and found the loosened stake was only overcome by his gruesome description of a severely wounded man bleeding to death. Marcia's tearful pleadings finally persuaded her, though her hands shook as she dropped him at the bottom of the hill. "Be careful, *Daavid* — please," she implored. "Zhat is a very bad place."

The path is obvious as soon as Bliss folds back the curtain of undergrowth. A worn track with cracked twigs and bent foliage stands out in the sickly green light of his night vision goggles. The goggles — high-end Soviet military specifications — were smuggled, he guessed, by one of the Moscow Mafia with a villa on the hills above St-Juan, together with the odd MiG fighter or Scud missile. He picked them up in a specialist spy store in the heart of Cannes, together with a couple of miniature flashlights and several aerosols of pepper spray. Then he headed to the supermarket for a five-kilo family pack of the best rump steak. The hounds of the Château Roger, if they existed, were to have a juicy alternative to a gloved hand.

The light-intensifying goggles leave both his hands free for wielding the carrot and the stick as he heads deeper into the undergrowth, southwest towards the château, according to the luminous wrist compass obtained from the same source as the glasses, although the likelihood of finding Grimes alive, anywhere, is becoming remote. It is now more than thirty-six hours since Bliss's gruesome find. It is three o'clock Tuesday morning and there have been no developments. The gendarmes are stumped, according to Daisy's source. With only a cleanly severed hand — nothing chewed, no shark or propeller attack — and with no personal details beyond the fact that they suspect the loser to be the promenade potter, they've shoved the hand in a cooler at the morgue to await the discovery of the rest of the body.

Now inside the grounds he's safe from the heavies on the hill, but he inches ahead cagily, worried about not only guards and dogs, but also the possibility of tripwires and booby traps. He saw graphic signs warning of high-voltage security devices prominently displayed around the perimeters of several of the nearby villas, and, whilst he only noticed the "Guard Dogs" signs on the château's fencing, he is taking no chances.

Strands of bright moonlight filtering through the heavy foliage turn night to day through the lenses of his goggles, but the greenish tinge of the intensifiers adds to the creepiness of the petrified forest. Unkempt and overgrown, with straggly vines hanging like tentacles and decaying trees lying drunkenly against the living as if their downfall has been frozen in time, the woodland has a darkness deeper than that of night. And Bliss's mind isn't made any easier by the nerve-racking nature of his quest. If Greg Grimes is still alive he might be a ghastly sight. But Bliss has had his share of stomach-turners in his career, and he tries to put the chilling thoughts behind him as he forges through the undergrowth, wondering where the path will lead.

Progress along the trail is sluggish as Bliss treads warily, musing, "If Grimes comes this way every night, he's got more guts than me."

Slowly moving shadows in the moonlight keep his adrenalin pumping unnecessarily as palm fronds waft in the light airs, and every so often he leaps at the sound of a tiny nocturnal creature scampering for its life. More than once the deafening sound of a dead leaf crashing through the branches in the silence stops him in his tracks, and a rabbit, panicked to the earth at his approach, kicks to life just two feet ahead and sends him hurtling to the ground.

"Little bastard," he swears, brushing himself down, then he pushes on until he suddenly finds his path blocked. Looking up, he discovers that he stands in the moon-shadow of the giant building, and realizes the path he's followed is not a shortcut but a direct lead to the château. A thin mist of cloud has frosted the moon, but the eerie light only enhances the awesomeness of the structure. Like an ancient temple swallowed by the rampages of a steamy rainforest, the ghostly ruin still struggles to maintain dignity. But once-proud columns buckle under the strain of age and weight, canopied balconies with ornate stone balustrades droop wearily, and wounded statues lie where they fell. It's not so much decaying as melting, he concludes, surveying the sagging facade, although it has retained sufficient pride to keep its roof above the surrounding trees. The only things missing are a troupe of chattering monkeys and a flock of squawking parrots, he thinks as he takes off his goggles, surveys the monolith through the eyes of an intrepid explorer, and breathes, "*Merde* — this is creepy."

Apprehensive at the prospect of entering the crumbling edifice, though heartened by the apparent absence of guards or dogs, he climbs the flagging marble steps, keeping tight to the edge, gingerly testing each slab first. Lizards scurry into crevices and snakes slither aside as the flight of steps opens onto a wide tiled apron surrounding the building, and he nervously eyes the château's enormous entrance doors, ominously shadowed under a heavy canopy perched on a colonnade of fluted pillars.

Maybe I should call in the local boys, he thinks, reaching for his cellphone, then pulls back, realizing nothing has changed. If the Johnson case isn't strictly above-board, and he blows it by causing an international incident, Richards will have him for breakfast. Neither Interpol nor the Sûreté will be satisfied with anything short of major bloodletting at such a blatant breach of protocol. But how can it be above-board? he thinks. There are no written reports, no orders on paper, nothing incontrovertible. I'm not even supposed to use the cellphone in case someone traces the number.

"Oh well. Nothing ventured ..." he breathes and steps towards the doors, his mind made up.

The main doors are bolted and barred with a "Danger!" sign stapled across the central joint. A side door looks more inviting and gives easily — too easily — so easily that he falls through the opening and stumbles across the floor. But at least there is a floor. The solid marble floor of the cathedral-vaulted main entrance hall takes his weight as his footfalls echo around the cavernous chamber.

"Wow," he breathes, awed by the enormity of the room with its twin staircases curling off into the distance.

"Hello! ... Anyone here?" he calls, and is annoyed at the crack in his voice. His weak entreaty echoes eerily around the enormous cavity and elicits no response, yet he senses someone's presence as certainly as he has sensed an evil ambiance from the moment he entered the grounds. "No wonder Daisy is scared to death of the place," he says to himself, but tries to rationalize the ghostly atmosphere by blaming it on the phosphorous green aura his goggles give to everything.

Realizing he is invisible in the darkness, he lays down the lump of steak, takes off his goggles, and switches to a flashlight. The piercing shaft of white light brings everything into sharp focus and makes it scarier than ever. At least the goggles gave everything an appearance of unreality — like watching a grainy old movie.

"I should get out of here," he says to himself. Then what? Go back and tell Marcia Grimes I don't know if Greg's here because I crapped myself at the front door? OK. But if he is here, he's probably in hiding — worried to death that whoever lopped off his right hand might come back for the other.

The slender beam of light reveals jagged cracks and dislodged chunks of stucco, but he judges the inside is in better shape than the outside.

Now what? he says to himself as he stands in the vast hall staring at the giant staircases, his resolve draining at the enormity of the problem. Up there must be at least a dozen bedrooms, with bathrooms, dressing rooms, and numerous closets and hidey-holes, then, above that, the servants' quarters in the dormers and attics under the numerous gables and roofs — scary at the best of times. On this floor there must be any number of kitchens, studies, sitting rooms, and smaller rooms, and …

But he doesn't want to think about the cellars. Yet, judging by the way the château has been built up on a plinth to give the best possible view across the bay, there is at least one level of basement beneath him.

A team of men with dogs would take the best part of a day to search this place properly, he is thinking, when his already frazzled nerves take a severe jolt as the door swings shut behind him with a loud *click*.

Run, says his inner voice, but nothing happens as he waits for his legs to get the message. "Who's there?" he calls weakly once his mouth thaws.

I should have brought Marcia with me, he tells himself, and, gripping the can of pepper spray firmly in one hand and the flashlight in the other, he starts towards one of the movie-set staircases.

He begins up the stairs, then balks. Three very creaky steps snap his nerve, and he scuttles out to the patio to calm himself in the moonlight, while he paces and seeks a new strategy. The lights of the castle across the strait on Île Sainte-Marguerite flicker indistinctly through the trees, and he finds himself thinking of the man who'd spent eleven years of his life in a cell there, with his head caged in a heavy iron helmet, and how Frederick Chapel could have got to him. It's like a Houdini escapology illusion in reverse, he concludes. Instead of Houdini getting out, Frederick Chapel has to figure a way to get in — to invade the island, break into the prison, divert some guards, immobilize others, crack open the cell, and unmask the prisoner.

Now is not a time to be thinking of abstracts, he reproaches himself, then freezes in thought. The abstract is the answer. "Thank you, Frederick Chapel," he mouths in relief, quickly plays it over in his mind a second time to iron out any flaws, then goes on the offensive.

Ten minutes later he's ready; everything is in place. Now he's backed up with an entire division of men. He's got a man ready at the back door, others to go upstairs, some to go down; then there are the dog teams — specialist cadaver sniffers as well as tracker dogs; and, finally, a group of officers for general searching duties.

He starts with a battering against the back door, shouting, "Police! Open up. Police." Then he dashes around the side, up the steps, and through the front, stomping across the floor, slamming open doors and shutting others, shouting and prattling on in nonsensical French, dropping lumps of wood and flopping hunks of steak. Then, swivelling both flashlights furiously around the huge hall, he shouts, "Right — you two. Get the dogs ready. Those of you ..." he starts, then loudly shuffles his feet before shouting, "Stand still at the back. That's better. Now those of you who speak English translate for the others. Remember — the man we're looking for is English. We know he's hurt. We must find him quickly."

"Yes, you — what is it?" he demands loudly in response to his own mumbling. "Yes, we've got lots more officers coming. But you twelve are going to make a start. I want you to bring in the dogs and check everywhere. Wait a minute!" he hollers at the top of his lungs. "Before we start ..." Then he pauses to shuffle his feet noisily and shriek, "Stand still that man! Before we start I want everyone to stay perfectly quiet and listen for any sounds Mr. Grimes might make."

An hour later, with Greg Grimes in intensive care in Cannes General Hospital, Bliss slumps over a Scotch in an all-night bar, wondering if the concept of a phantom invasion force would fly in his novel to uncover the identity of the masked man. Daisy doesn't care. She's just happy to hold his hand.

chapter eleven

"Iwas worried about you," Commander Richards claims when Bliss answers his early morning telephone call.

Yeah, I bet you were, Bliss yawns to himself. "You needn't worry, Guv, I found him," he says aloud as he struggles out of bed.

"Is he all right?"

"I can't imagine there are many happy one-handed potters in the world, but he'll live. I found him slumped under a stoneware sink in a kitchen below the château's great hall."

"Who did it?"

"I thought you wanted me to stay out of it, Guv."

"Sounds as though you're already in it."

He is in it, but has no idea who might have amputated Grimes's hand. And any help in that direction that the potter himself may have given has been pre-empted by his wife. Marcia made a very solid point of warning her husband to keep quiet as she and Daisy manhandled the injured man through the gap in the fence. "Mr. Bliss is a police inspector from England, dear," she pointedly proclaimed, though whether or not the potter took it in, he couldn't know.

"He's not saying anything — not to me, anyway," Bliss tells Richards as he yanks the phone cord out to the balcony.

"Do you think it was our man?" asks Richards, with Johnson in mind.

"It could have been almost anyone," Bliss replies, stretching himself on the lounger in the sun "Though I'm pretty certain it wasn't his wife. The way she cried over him; even the way he looked at her. It was quite touching, really, considering what they've been through."

"Who else could it have been?" Richards wants to know, as Bliss picks up his binoculars and strains to pick out the château's roofs in the distance.

"I've no idea, to be honest. I don't know a lot about him, although he's certainly upset the local hoteliers pretty badly."

"Doing moonlight flits," suggests Richards.

"No," Bliss laughs before explaining the saga of the wet pots.

As for the question of Bliss's next step: "I'm not sure at the moment," he explains, though now with the château in his sights he knows his first priority is to get back inside. There's bound to be some evidence in there somewhere, he tells himself, though he is careful not to give Richards the impression he has plans.

"I don't even know where it actually happened, Guv," he adds, then complains about Grimes being uncooperative. "Anybody would think he was the villain the way he clammed up."

With nothing further to report, Bliss is about to hang up and return to bed when Richards takes him by surprise. "About that boat you wanted, Dave ..."

"You're kidding!" Bliss exclaims.

"No. I've had a word in the right place. I need you to get some quotes — nothing flashy, but big enough to do the job — then we'll have another meeting and take a look at it."

I might have guessed, Bliss thinks, quickly deflating as he recognizes the time-honoured stalling tactics. Start with meetings, requisition proposals, submissions, suggestions, estimates, and quotes, then have more meetings to discuss, etc., before asking for revised quotes, etc., then ... etc., etc., etc. He's been around that circle before.

"All right, Guv," he replies with little enthusiasm as he peers over the balcony at the shrivelled lemon in the garden below and is reminded he never told Richards about Johnson's wife. Who, he is certain, is back. The caged boy is back, at any rate. Bliss saw him at daybreak when he returned from Grimes's bedside. He spotted him in the garden, passionately kissing the dog — French kissing the dog, as far as he could tell.

"I've got to do something about that," he sniggered to himself, no longer dumbfounded. "That dog could get all sorts of germs."

That must mean Johnson's wife is back, he thought, and immediately jumped to the conclusion that her return was somehow related to the potter's injury. Maybe the hand was a warning to stop me from meddling, he thought.

Once he gets off the phone with Richards he deliberates the situation and concludes that, assuming Grimes didn't chopped off his own hand, whoever did it clearly meant it to be found — otherwise they would have left it in the château with the rest of the body. And with that thought, he goes back to bed, planning his next assault on the old building.

Wednesday morning broke as cleanly as every other morning, and as the sun picked itself out of the sea, Bliss was already on the château's grounds. A workman's tool bag and a frayed pair of plasterer's overalls he bought from a guy on the construction site just off the promenade walked him past the sleepy guards on the hill without question. The worker — the only one in his group approaching six feet — had been confused, then amused, at the strange Englishman who was willing to buy his clothes and bag of oldest tools for triple the price of new.

"*C'est un vrai cinglé, ce type,*" he laughed to his mates, accusing Bliss of being a real nutcase, but Bliss was steadfast, proffering a large wad of cash with an open expression.

In the warm light of the reborn sun the patina of centuries shadows the once-bright marble, and the elaborately carved waisted balusters surrounding the south-facing patio and balconies at the front of the building have split and spalled in the twin ravages of sun and salt air. The scrolled acanthus leaves on the capitals of the Corinthian columns that form the entrance portico and support the enormous canopy have not fared well either, though the massive pillars themselves appear firm as he stands on the patio taking a few deep breaths.

The continued absence of guards and dogs is a comfort, although the property owner — whoever that is — has done a great job of scare-mongering in the local community. Daisy was so alarmed by his intention to return that she refused to assist in any manner. In fact the mere suggestion had her jittery. "You no go back," she implored staunchly. But now that he knew the secret of the entrance he could risk it in broad daylight under the noses of the goons, he explained to her, appealing, "Just drop me off at the right spot and I'll be out of the car and through the fence in seconds."

"No. Zhe château is *dangereux*."

"Don't be silly," he retorted. "There's nothing to be scared of. It's just an abandoned old house." But he was quite unprepared for her emotional outburst.

"I no want you to go," she cried, and continued crying, despite every effort on his part to calm her.

"But why?" he asked repeatedly.

"Zhe dogs —" she blubbered eventually, but he cut her off sharply.

"There are no dogs or guards."

Nothing he said made any difference. She wouldn't help and she wanted him to promise not to go back.

"I promise," he said, fingers crossed.

Now, standing on the patio with its symmetrical octagonal tiles, he still worries there may be guard dogs. He knows that a properly trained dog will smell his anxiety and go for him despite the lump of steak and the canister of pepper spray he carries. He also knows that once inside the building he'll be easily cornered, and, even armed with a couple of battery-powered floodlights, a dozen candles, and a bagful of sharp tools, he still has to steel himself to re-enter.

Daisy's intuition rings true as he faces the door and the hairs on the back of his neck rise. "What the hell is it?" he asks, feeling a shiver, and then he talks himself forward, "It's just a decrepit old mansion — now get on with it."

Slender beams of early morning light, sieved through the thick wooden shutters and filthy windows, dance with midges and motes as he enters the great hall, and he shudders at the chill of the marble. Up or down, he deliberates, warily eyeing the jagged cracks in the twin sweep of stone staircases ahead. He'll need to venture upstairs eventually for the sake of his novel, although he was fairly satisfied on the basic viability of his theory during his previous visit. Standing on the patio of the château in the early hours of Tuesday morning, while drumming up the guts to search for Grimes, he saw the lights of the castle on Île Sainte-Marguerite and he knew that if he could see the lights, then an incarcerated person could have looked from the window of the cell of *l'homme au masque de fer* and seen him.

Frederick Chapel, alias François Couperin, would have been delighted to know that in 1687, he thought later, as he spent an hour updating his manuscript with a gripping description of the adventure of François Couperin the night he finally plucked up the courage to get into the château's grounds. In his novel, Bliss wrote of Couperin trailing a group of construction workers as they sneaked back into the grounds through a hole in the fence one dark night, having visited the village to satisfy themselves at the inn and at the various wells of Venus. Apparently Jean the fisherman had been right about the sleeping guards, and the steaks Couperin had hacked from a dead donkey he'd found on the roadside had easily quieted the dogs.

Leaving behind the dusty shafts of daylight, Bliss descends to the basement — to the kitchen where he found Grimes — but now his way is lighted by a powerful floodlight that throws ghostly shadows off the forest of stone pillars and sends creatures scurrying in all directions. The workman's bag is stuffed with builder's weapons, and he quickly pulls out a lethal-looking chisel when a couple of large rats challenge him, making him understand why Grimes scrunched himself into a protective ball under the sink with a lump of wood in his remaining hand.

The poor bastard must have been terrified, thinks Bliss as he lights candles, frightening himself silly as the flickering lights bring ghosts to life. But what the hell was Grimes doing down here?

"*Merde* — this is really scary," he mouths, as he systematically searches the vaulted dungeon. "You shouldn't have come alone." But neither Marcia nor Daisy would join him in the escapade, and he was reluctant to admit to Jacques or Hugh that he'd hoodwinked them for nearly a month. In any case, who would believe he couldn't simply take his suspicions to the local police?

Apart from an ancient iron stove and some heavy metal stacking chairs — circa 1940s, he guesses — the only furnishing of interest is a tatty mattress covered with stains he'd rather not dwell on. Then his light catches the edge of movement.

"Who's there?" he calls, whipping around.

A sinister rustling sound spins him as it echoes off the walls.

"Who is it?" he demands, and his own voice bounces back and shakes him.

"Shit," he exclaims, startled.

Get out, Dave! screams his inner voice, but he stands his ground.

No wonder the locals are petrified — no one mentioned ghosts. Though no one mentioned people having their limbs chopped off, either. What's moving? Something is definitely moving, he decides, and tries to remain rational as he listens to the ghostly dry whisper. Isolating the sound, he's drawn to the old mattress and gingerly edges forward to tap it with his foot, then he shrinks away as it comes to life. The ancient horse-hair mattress heaves and writhes for a few seconds, then slowly settles as the nest of lizards calms. "*Merde,*" he breathes. "Grimes obviously wasn't sleeping on that."

So what was the potter doing down here? Bliss asks himself, looking around the virtually bare cellar and wondering why Grimes risked the rats. He should have been able to walk, until the blood loss weakened him anyway, he thinks, then wonders: where is the blood?

Scouting for the precise crime scene doesn't take long. The blood-soaked wooden chopping block on a stone work table tells a nightmarish tale, but there's no sign of the knife — or did he use an axe?

He? Bliss's inner voice questions critically. Not making assumptions again, are we, Dave?

But the thought of a woman deliberately slicing off a living hand seems somehow more ghoulish. I might expect it of a man, he reasons. In any case, it would take considerable strength to hold a screaming man down while carving off his hand at the wrist.

Another rat scrabbles across the floor and he recoils again, thinking of Grimes with the stump of his arm leaking sticky fluid that would drive the shady creatures into a feeding frenzy. The cloying smell of blood is still in the air, and he retches at the image of the potter fighting off the vicious rodents day and night — though down here there is only night. So why stay here? Water, he realizes, as he turns the lime-encrusted tap and is amazed when it flows. That must be why Grimes stayed by the sink — to bathe the raw stump and replenish lost fluids.

Leaving the main chamber, Bliss has no idea what he's expecting as he follows a trail of candle stubs down a tunnelled passageway, the flagstone floor echoing each footstep. Doors leading off the tunnel beg to be opened — but every closed door is a plug on hell. What horror lurks behind? What gruesome sights might await? What skeleton might leap out and scare the daylights out of him? How many Greg Grimeses weren't fortunate enough to have someone searching for them?

Why the hell am I bothering to do this? he stops to demand of himself. Grimes obviously isn't going to name his attacker; Marcia clearly knows a lot more than she's letting on; Richards is playing footsy with Edwards; and I'm just the bloody ball. It's attempted procrastination and he knows it. Oh well. I'm here now.

The first dank, dark chamber laughs at his timidity, and he is about to shut the door on the empty dungeon when his hand freezes in shock. It isn't empty at all. The musty air is heavy with occupation — the room is crowded. His eye catches on the rusted chains and he feels his resolve sinking as he realizes the significance of what he sees. This is a torture chamber, and the tormented spirits of men are still hanging in the wicked shackles fastened to the walls with rusted steel bolts. He balks at entering; the chains and manacles tell him more than he wants to know. Grimes obviously wasn't the first man tortured here. And now that he's prised the lid off this particular hell he feels the anguish and hears the screams. This isn't a nicely sanitized historical recreation. This is authentic. This is where real men suffered and died.

A few shreds of old clothing are nestled in one corner, and, steeling himself against the expected rush of rodents, he uses a long screwdriver from his work bag to prod the small heap. "Snakes," he shudders, as he pulls out the remains of a shirt and sees the creatures slithering deeper into the pile. The tattered shirt puzzles him — it's old, though not old enough to have lost the memory of its owner.

Ten minutes later he's slammed open another six doors and uncapped six equally horrifying hellholes. Manacles, leg irons, and shackles speak so vividly of sickening horrors that his mind suddenly curdles and he flees back to the kitchen, up the stairs, and out to the patio with the shirt.

Outside, he hyperventilates on the clean air and feels his head swimming. Slumping on the top step of the grand entrance flight with his head between his knees, he stares into the past. If the images of a fully conscious man having his hand chopped off in the château are bad, the thought of what might have happened to the others is a thousand times worse. A rough calculation by his shell-shocked brain tells him that a hundred or more people could have been shackled to the walls at a time. But what people? At what time? And what happened to them eventually? If the stains on this shredded shirt could talk, he thinks, as he braces to examine the remains of the garment more closely, though its abandonment in the dungeon tells its own pitiful story.

Maybe that's why the locals don't talk about the place, he surmises. Maybe they don't want the world digging into their dirty laundry. But that doesn't make sense — this whole area is a tourist mecca. A Frankenstein house of horrors — particularly a genuine one, with spooky dungeons filled with real tormented souls — would delight L'association des hôteliers and have St-Juan-sur-Mer on every travel agent's tongue. Consider the popularity of the prison block over there, he thinks, eyeing the island's fortress in the distance, and just how many tourists flock to the torture chamber of the Tower of London each year?

Yet, as he turns the old shirt over on the end of the screwdriver, he begins to see a difference. Wide stripes and soft tones give the shirt a modern appearance, despite the fact that it is dirty, old, and worn. The cracked brown buttons seem old-fashioned. "Bakelite," he murmurs in memory of the brittle plastic of his childhood as one of the buttons falls in half under his fingers. Puzzled, he decides to brave the rats and other horrors and return to the cellars, but his nerves are in rags and he shelves the idea at the last moment. Firmly shutting the door to the basement he concentrates on the main floor. But no more horrors await as he sweeps through the lofty-ceilinged rooms. The entire floor, with its ornate baroque mouldings and extravagant fireplaces, boldly proclaims its innocence and is alive with joyful images of courtly *dames*, stiff with crinolines and coiffures, lightly bantering with flamboyantly costumed bewigged French aristocrats. Just twenty feet below, prisoners might have hung on the walls as lifeless as the sides of wild boar and venison in the well-stocked larders, but up here the seventeenth-century counter-reformation of Louis XIV was dancing with gay frivolity.

The bedrooms and dressing rooms upstairs are equally easy on his mind, once he's conquered the rotten thirty-foot staircase. And even the dingy attic rooms don't reflect the terrors of the basement. A few broken windows have let small birds and bats slip through cracks in the shutters, and the ledges are deep with dropping — the air acrid with ammonia. Many floorboards need attention, but otherwise the château is in remarkably good condition.

A door to the roof is what he seeks, and finds, and as he carefully steps out onto a rooftop balcony the view that rewards him virtually wipes out the horrors in the chambers below. The entire bay expands at his feet, and the Castle of Fort Royal on Île Sainte-Marguerite stands out like a beacon.

"Well, Sherlock Holmes, I guess you've solved yet another case," he says to the air with the realization that, as fictional as he may be, Frederick Chapel could have stood on this spot three centuries earlier and solved the riddle of the man in the iron mask.

I guess Grimes was just taking a shortcut through the grounds to wherever he's living, he thinks to himself a few minutes later, back on the patio, as he carefully packs the old shirt into his bag with his flashlights. And, with more than a sigh of relief, he heads for the fence.

chapter twelve

Guessing that Daisy will be furious with him if she
finds he's visited the château, Bliss gives her office
a wide berth as he walks back to his apartment mid-
morning, still in workman's garb. The shirt in his bag
torments him all the way. The assumption that the last
occupant of the vestment had not given it up willingly
plays on his mind to the point where he begins to regret
taking it, feeling he has somehow desecrated a grave.

"Where you been?" demands Daisy, skulking around
the apartment lobby and catching him by surprise. Then
her face screws in confusion. "What are you doing?"

"You'd better come up," he says, trying to usher her
into the elevator, readying to bite the bullet, but she
shies away.

"No — I must go. I have zhe work. But I come to
warn you zhat Monsieur Johnson telephoned again. He
is still crazy. He say you must leave his wife alone."

"I haven't touched her," he protests, reddening, but is thankful when she just shrugs it off. "I see you tonight at L'Escale."

"Phew," he breathes, then, with plenty of time to come up with an explanation, decides to pay a visit to Greg and Marcia Grimes before they start giving him the runaround again. A shower first, he thinks, fighting his way out of the dirty workman's overalls, then a quick phone call. He needs information and knows who can get it for him.

"I'm really busy, Dad," complains Samantha as soon as she answers.

"No. Seriously. I will pay," he says, but his offer of the standard rate for legal work brings only a sardonic laugh.

"All right. What do you need, Dad?"

Bliss gives her the gory details of Grimes's mutilation before asking her to drive out to the picturesque Suffolk village where his pottery had been located. "The locals must know something about them," he tells her. "They lived there long enough. Find out what you can about them, would you?"

"This sounds like an attempted murder case. Why don't you get the force to do it?"

"I've told you. I think Richards and Edwards have set me up."

"It doesn't sound so Machiavellian now, though, does it?" she says, making a good point.

"Machiavellian or not, I wasn't sent here to investigate the mutilation of an irritating potter."

"OK," she agrees. "If I can find the time."

At least Bliss knows where to find Grimes and his wife, and a little later he sits over a coffee with Marcia in the waiting room at the hospital in Cannes — but she's no more helpful than her husband when it comes to fingering the offender.

"What about Morgan Johnson?" he queries, and she flies at him.

"Morgan would never do anything like that."

That's rich, he thinks, taking up his policeman's baton and getting rough. "From what you tell me, Johnson had no qualms about getting into your knickers, then he dumped you to bonk your daughter and turn her into a junkie. Now you're protecting him."

"It wasn't like that," she protests.

"That's what it looks like from here."

"OK," she concedes, her indignation cooling. "But he had no reason to do this to Greg."

"But he was here Saturday night when it happened, wasn't he?"

"Maybe."

"Don't 'maybe' me," he barks. "I'm fed up with this crap, Marcia. This isn't a bloody game. Greg would've been dead by now if I hadn't stuck my neck out. You told me Johnson was here at the weekend. Was he?"

Visibly startled, she stutters, "I ... I think so. But even if he was, he wouldn't have done this. He didn't need to."

That's an interesting perspective, he thinks. He's already wrenched out the man's heart; therefore, he no longer needs to lop off his hand? "Well, who did it then?"

"Greg has upset a few people ..." she admits.

"Not the hoteliers," says Bliss, cutting in disbelievingly. "Surely they wouldn't go that far."

"No, not the hoteliers," she agrees.

"Who, then?"

Tight-lipped, she puts on a blank face.

"I'd better turn up the heat on Greg, then," he says, starting to rise, hoping to jog her conscience.

Marcia brightens visibly. "You can't. He's in the operating theatre. They say there's a chance they can reattach his hand. It'll never be the same, of course, but luckily the French are world leaders in the techniques."

Sitting down again, he takes on a softer tone. "Don't you want the offender caught, Marcia?"

"It's not that simple, Inspector," she says, leaving a distinct impression he's working on today's crossword with yesterday's clues, leading him to suggest, "This does involve Johnson in some way, though, doesn't it?"

With the feeling Marcia is jerking him around, Bliss heads off to the museum to solicit the aid of the friendly curator.

"Did you find out about zhe château?" She smiles, emerging from her cubicle behind the information desk, clearly remembering him and his quest.

"Not really," he replies, now even warier of divulging his interest since his discovery.

Ten minutes later, with the shirt laid out on a table in a backroom overstuffed with racks of military costumes and bundles of swords, the young woman inspects it with a professional eye and uses a magnifying glass on an ominously dark splotch. "Blood stays forever," she remarks, comparing the stain with those on some clothing taken from Napoleonic battlefield corpses. "See — it is *très similaire*," she says, offering him the glass. "Zhough zhe style of zhis shirt is much later. Early twentieth century, I would zhink. Where did it come from?"

"I think you're right," he says, concentrating on the stain and ignoring her question. "And these buttons look like Bakelite. What do you think?"

Shaking her head, she apologizes. Her expertise ends in the middle of the nineteenth century. "I'm fairly sure zhis is a twentieth-century shirt," she repeats. "Nineteen-twenties, maybe, but," she warns, "zhat's only a guess."

"Who would be able to say for sure?" he wants to know.

"My university *professeur*. He knows everything," she says with a sly wink.

The comforting warmth of the perfectly clear afternoon sun and the soothing breeze of the *vent de midi* fail to lift Bliss's spirits as he heads to L'Escale for a late lunch. The growing certainty that some monumental terror has occurred within spitting distance of the sparkling beach casts a pall over his mind. The château, hiding shamefacedly in the trees, is beyond his view, but visions of living scarecrows crucified in shackles in its dungeons continue to torment him.

Unaware of the role Bliss played in the potter's rescue, Angeline is bursting with news and miscalculates the speed of a taxi as she rushes the river of traffic, calling excitedly, "It is on zhe television and zhe radio, zhey say zhe poor man had a terrible accident."

"And there's another one," Bliss mumbles, as the diverted taxi topples a parked Harley, though doesn't stop. "So that's the official line, is it?" he muses as he orders a sandwich and beer. I wondered what story the Grimeses would dream up for the doctors and the police.

He has a few hours to kill before an after-class meeting with the *professeur d'histoire* at Nice University arranged by the helpful curator. Sitting on the promenade, waiting for the brouhaha that will follow when the owner of the mangled motorbike shows up, he tries to piece together scrappy snatches of schoolboy history. What could have happened here during the 1920s? he wonders, surveying the tall terraces of tightly packed houses that clearly predate the era. The upheaval of the revolution was long past. The manacles and shackles, redolent of the Bastille, had been reused by Napoleon and his mob — twice. The Victorians had bored themselves to extinction. The First World War and the great flu epidemic had wiped out a sizeable portion of Europe's population, though the ones left had made up for it in the jazzed-up era of the Roaring Twenties.

Would it have been a lot different back then? he ponders, scanning the seafront stores and hotels. Most had certainly been around a hundred years. Some even boasted their longevity with early sepia photos in their brochures and window displays. And what about the yachts? he wonders, looking out beyond the harbour to the procession of small private liners steaming in and out of the bay of Cannes. Memories of silent black-and-white media clips from the 1920s, with superstars like Mary Pickford and Douglas Fairbanks sunning themselves on yachts in the Med, convince him that whatever dreadful things were going on in the château at that time, they were not in accord with life in general.

The curator's *professeur* at Nice University greets him studiously, his critical stare clearly asking, "And what kind of eccentric Englishman do we have here?"

"*Entrez,* Monsieur Burbeck," he bids, waving Bliss into his study. "Sit please. I have 'eard much about you."

I doubt it, thinks Bliss, placing the old shirt on the corner of the professor's desk. "Thank you for seeing me so quickly."

"It is always zhe pleasure to meet an author," he replies, though has difficulty getting the appropriate expression on his face. Then he removes his wire-framed spectacles and places them, with thoughtful precision, on the table facing Bliss. "So," he demands, eyes down, addressing his glasses, seemingly using them as a prism into Bliss's mind, "why do you want to know about zhis shirt, Monsieur Burbeck?"

The old third degree, thinks Bliss, finding himself drawn to the glasses as he starts to reply, "I'm writing a book ..." Then he looks up and finds the other man fiercely focusing on the pair of bifocals as if they are a form of lie detector.

That's an interesting technique, considers Bliss, as the *professeur* continues, eyes down, bouncing questions off his spectacles, wanting to know precisely where, when, and under what circumstances the old shirt was found. Bliss parries the questions with a vague allusion to an old building he'd stumbled into the previous day. But when he declares his research revolves around the case of the man in the iron mask, the old *professeur* sits back in amusement.

"So that is your eccentricity, Monsieur Englishman," he says with smug satisfaction as he picks up the shirt. "Sorry to disappoint you," he laughs, putting on his glasses and poring over the cloth through a large magnifier, "but zhis shirt is not Louis-Quatorze. It is from zhe nineteen-twenties or thirties, I would say from zhe pattern and material. And take a good look at zhe buttons. I zhink zhey are Bakelite, although I am surprised zhey have survived so well. Bakelite usually becomes brittle after a while."

"In daylight?" queries Bliss.

"Yes, especially in daylight, as far as I remember from my school chemistry days. Sorry, I can't help," he says sarcastically, chuckling as he rises, "but *bonne chance* — good luck. I zhink your book will be very funny."

"You just wait," mouths Bliss, smiling his thanks.

Still baffled over the identity of the château's prisoners, Bliss returns to L'Escale in time to see the skin-headed Harley-Davidson owner sitting on the curb crying. He's only a kid — probably lives in a crummy basement and washes cars for a living, thinks Bliss, wondering whether or not to get involved, when Daisy bounds up, her earlier crustiness forgotten.

"Hello, *Daavid*," she sings, kissing him on both cheeks. "Would you like to see more fireworks?"

"I —" is as far as he gets.

"*Formidable*," she cries and kisses him again as Angeline shrugs past the motorcyclist with a "*bof*," and smiles in delight.

"Ah, Monsieur. Now you 'ave zhe friend."

"What fireworks?" he wants to know as Angeline sidesteps the crestfallen rider to return to the bar for their drinks.

"It is in two weeks, August twenty-four, but we must book early," she enthuses. "Everyone will be at La Scala. It will be super, *fantastique*. You will like very much."

"You haven't told me what it's for."

"It is zhe Liberation Day, of course. Many, many big fireworks."

"I thought June sixth was Liberation Day," he queries.

"*Non. Non,* zhat was D-Day in Normandie in zhe *nord* of France. It was another two months before zhe allies came ashore here," she says, and carries on prattling about the fabulous firework display and the wonderful food at La Scala, unaware that Bliss has paled, and his face numbed, as nightmarish memories of the château's cellars invade his mind.

"The Germans were here?" his disembodied voice asks, but he already knows the answer.

"Of course," replies Daisy, feeling herself being dragged down by his darkened mood.

The speed the entire picture falls into place in his mind leaves him staring blankly ahead.

"What is zhe matter, *Daavid*?" Daisy queries softly, but he doesn't answer. He is walking back though the château's underground chambers, checking out his dreadful discoveries. The old metal stacking chairs in the kitchen were typical utilitarian government issue — almost any government. The shackles and chains in the dungeons weren't medieval torture implements. They were certainly rusty — but not the deeply pitted flaky wrought iron of pre-industrialized Europe. They'd been sharp and bright just sixty years earlier. They were steel — wartime German steel. And the bloodstained clothing ...?

Shaking himself clear of the nightmare, he turns on Daisy and gives her a broadside. "Enough of the games,

Daisy. This is serious. I don't want to hear any more nonsense about the château being a basket of crabs. I know it is. One of them clawed off Grimes's hand. Now I want some straight answers."

She doesn't have the answers, she claims.

"Let me tell you what I think, then —" he starts angrily, but she stops him.

"*Daavid.* Please don't shout. You are right. Zhe château does have a terrible secret. But I cannot tell."

"I'm going to find out," he warns, but holds himself back at the sight of an interloper.

"Hah!" says Jacques, pulling up a chair. "*Oh là là!* look at your faces. I zhink zhere is a very cold wind, *n'est-ce pas?*"

"*Ferme-la!*" Daisy spits, grabs Bliss's hand, and drags him away.

"That sounded rude," says Bliss, as she hurries him along the promenade.

"*Bof!*" She shrugs furiously. "I tell him ... shut up. Zhat man is *un cochon* — a pig."

"So ... where are we going?" he asks, as she pulls him into a cramped back alley where flights of narrow stone steps lead to neat apartments above the old Main Street stores.

"I show you," she says, turning up one of the whitewashed staircases and ushering him through a tight doorway.

"*Maman,*" she calls, waving Bliss to a small wooden settle just inside the door as she pushes on through a heavy curtain.

The virtual darkness between curtain and door keeps him in limbo as his nose tells him he's about to walk into the past. The dusty smell of the thick woollen curtain mixes with the aromas of age: the mustiness of old furniture, old carpets, old clothes, and old people. He hears only one voice, besides Daisy's, but the gentle mews of a familiar sibling's greetings are soon swamped by harsher tones, which quickly rise in intensity to a full-scale shouting match. Disconcerted at being the cause of such a heated family row, he is seriously considering creeping out and slamming the door behind him when the curtain is flung aside by Daisy.

"Please come in, *Daavid*," she says, as if nothing has happened. "You will have to excuse my mother. Sometimes she can have *une tête de mule* — how you say?"

"Mule-headed," he suggests.

"*Oui*, zhat is right. But now she is happy to tell you of zhe château."

You call that happy? thinks Bliss, shrinking under the weight of the elderly woman's dark glare, as she braces herself into her well-worn armchair as if waiting for lift-off.

Trying to unfreeze the frightened old woman with a smile, he offers her a cheery "hello," but Daisy touches his arm.

"She doesn't speak Engleesh. I will translate. But first she asks zhat you promise to keep zhe secret."

"Of course I will," Bliss replies, and, conscious of the enormous impact his presence has in the small room, he shrivels into a corner while Daisy's mother equivocates over what to reveal.

"It was a long time ago," explains Daisy finally as her mother weeps in memory, but the images she conjures are neither misted by time nor tears. It could have happened yesterday; in Daisy's mother's mind, it had.

Through thin wan lips the old lady paints a Monet portrait of herself as a happy young schoolgirl who, with her brothers and friends, had danced on the lawns, splashed in the fountains and lily ponds, and swung from trees in the grounds of the beautiful old château.

"Sometimes zhe children who lived at zhe château would take zhem down into zhe dungeons," interprets Daisy as her mother talks. "Zhey would play ghosts and *fantômes* until zhe cook chase zhem out — zhen she give zhem warm biscuits from zhe oven, or sometimes special zhings like chocolate cake and ice cream."

Daisy's mother's eyes light with bygone excitement as she recounts the fun of running through a tunnel under the château, and how she and the other children stamped and shouted as they tried to out-echo each other until they emerged breathless on the soft sand beach of a little private cove to swim and play in the clear, warm water.

"Zhen, one day, my mother's mother has fire in her eyes and she say to zhem, 'You must not go to zhe château again. It is very *dangereux*,'" continues Daisy.

"But we were only children," Daisy's mother explains through her daughter. "We did not listen. And when we went to zhe château we found soldiers in a wooden sentry house."

Bliss smiles in irony at the old lady's memory — nothing changes, he thinks. But everything has changed for Daisy's mother. Her childhood friends and their family and servants in the château simply vanished. In their place were the Nazis.

"That makes sense," Bliss suggests, as he listens to the account and sees the light dying in the old woman's eyes. "The château overlooks the straits and would obviously make a good observation post."

"It wasn't a lookout," Daisy's mother continues through her daughter. The château had been transformed into a ghastly portal to purgatory, where everyone suspected of being involved in *la Résistance*, or in helping allies escape through the underground, had disappeared without trace.

"But it was not just zhe freedom fighters who disappeared zhrough zhe château's gates," Daisy carries on, straining to keep her voice level as she explains that many old scores were settled, that disagreeable neighbours would be whisked off in a dawn raid, and that inconvenient business partnerships, even marriages, dissolved with a whisper in the right place. A *lettre de cachet* — the notorious anonymous correspondence from a venomous pen — or even a malicious rumour was all it took to buy an adversary an entry pass. And there were no exit passes. Risk of *la dénonciation* pitted neighbour against neighbour, even friend against friend. Divide and conquer was the invader's mantra, and everyone cowered in the dark shadow of the château.

Now the shackles and the shirt make sense to Bliss, as he listens to the old woman's emotional tales of men, young and old, being dragged from their beds or off the streets; of terrified wives, mothers, and children, tearfully clinging to their menfolk until they were roughly butted away with rifle stocks — if they were lucky; and of the portico of the Château Roger becoming the gates of St. Peter.

Daisy's mother breaks into inconsolable sobs as the bitter memories bite, but finally she brightens a little as the war reaches its end, and Daisy translates, "It was twenty-four August, 1944, *la Libération*. Zhe American Sixth Army came and zhe Nazis run like *poules mouil-*

lées — like wet chickens — and zhe mayor, zhe *chef de police*, and some other men, zhey find some guns and go to zhe château."

The town's men returned stone-faced and with vomit-splashed shoes, she explains. The Germans had gone, but the horrors that confronted the men were too dreadful to retell. There were no survivors, and for weeks afterwards a small group of sad men spent their days digging in the grounds. And although nobody in the small town truthfully expected a happier outcome, everyone prayerfully retained a hope. Silence gave them strength. During the war no one spoke of the château — it was a malignant tumour in the heart of the community for which there was no cure, and by general unspoken consensus it was never mentioned.

Nothing changed with the war's end. When the advance party returned to the town hall, families clamouring for information were gently taken aside and told they should forget, that they would gain nothing by seeing the sights in the château. So they silently went home, carried on with their lives, and, by continuing to ignore the château, kept their hopes alive.

Listening to the horrifying story, Bliss realizes that the selective amnesia of the townsfolk is more than a simple reaction to indescribable visions of torture and terror. It is a shared and pervasive sense of remorse. In Daisy's mother's tone he hears a note of guilt and shame that the malignancy had been allowed to fester amongst them when radical surgery may have saved some of the men, if not all. And, as his comprehension grows, he can't help feeling that, in a way, little has changed over the years. Everything on the surface in sleepy St-Juan-sur-Mer is still normal and above-board. But no one looks beneath the surface. No one peeks under the beds of some of the inhabitants of the villas on the hillsides. No one will challenge their guards and check to see if they have skeletons in their basements.

"Who were the owners?" Bliss enquires of Daisy, when it seems her mother is running out of nightmares.

"Zhey were Jewish," Daisy interprets, and doesn't need to explain.

"Auschwitz or Dachau," he muses, guessing they would have been prime furnace fuel, being not only Jewish but rich property owners. They might have got away, he momentarily thinks, with a degree of hope — some did. Then why didn't they come back after the war to reclaim their home? OK. They didn't get away.

Now, with the château's ugly history exposed, the painted advertisements on the sides of old shops in the town have meaning. The badly faded signs proclaiming *Charcuterie*, *Traiteur*, and *Boulangerie* had obviously been left deliberately. The butchers, caterers, and bakers who'd owned the family stores hadn't simply gone out of business — they'd gone, though not in the minds of the locals. An entire generation had accepted a code of silence that kept men alive, in many cases well beyond their natural lifespans. Wives, once young and vibrant, and even a few surviving mothers, still waited for the day when the front door would burst open and a strapping young man would walk in and throw out his arms in joyous greeting.

The bright moon has replaced the sun by the time Bliss and Daisy leave the apartment and descend the narrow steps, but the balmy evening air does nothing to take the chill off Bliss's mind. Daisy's mother has levered herself out of her chair and stands at the top of the stairs in her long, black dress and gives them a parting wave. Waving back, Daisy whispers to Bliss, "She has not been so happy for a long time."

Turning for a final look at the diminutive old lady in her widow's weeds, Bliss reflects on the depths of melancholy she has surfaced from. And if she has found happiness it has come at a gruelling cost. Daisy did not translate her mother's tears — those needed no translation.

Bliss's promise to become part of the conspiracy cheered the old lady somewhat. It was an easy decision, knowing that should he, or anyone else, reveal the secret of the château, the place would swarm with neo-Nazi nutcases and other bloodthirsty freaks bent on snatching a genuine torture instrument or a few shreds of bloodsoaked clothing. For the world's weirdos such a find would be Atlantis. In any case, he doesn't want to be the one to rip the rug out from under an entire community.

As he and Daisy sit over a carafe of wine in a nearby bar, he ponders returning to the château, explaining to her that the ghosts in the basement are less frightful than those in her mother's mind, though he has difficulty with the words.

"You must not go back," Daisy protests.

"Look, I'm not the only one who knows about the château. I promised your mother I wouldn't tell anyone — but what about Grimes? He's got no reason to keep quiet.... Wait a minute," he pauses thoughtfully. "Why has he kept quiet? Why did he tell the police it was an accident?"

Staring out across the harbour towards the promontory it occurs to him that the potter would have stayed in the château only if he had nowhere else to go. People have walked miles with whole arms ripped off in battles, he realizes, then swears to the wind. "Bugger! I'll have to go back. I must have missed a room — maybe even a wing."

"Please don't go back. It is *dangereux*," whines Daisy.

"Don't start that again," he says, putting his arms round her. "It isn't dangerous — it's just scary."

She won't be comforted and, holding her firmly, he says, "There's absolutely nothing to fear there," although he can't believe he's saying it. Neither is he certain he can face the building for a third time, particularly as the ghosts have taken on much more substance. One ghost had particular significance for Daisy's mother — her father, whom she'd referred to in the present tense.

"What happened to your grandmother?" Bliss asks Daisy, and is bowled over when she says, "She was zhere, but she wouldn't listen to me. She put her hands over her ears and went to her room."

"Oh my God," he breathes, realizing the magnitude of the problem.

"She is ninety-three years old," explains Daisy, which, Bliss guesses, would put her mother in her early seventies — probably ten or twelve years old when her innocent childhood was trampled.

"Did your mother see her father hauled away?" he wonders aloud, but Daisy doesn't know.

"Zhey never speak. Zhey zhink by not speaking maybe it did not happen."

Bliss sits back with a jaundiced eye, finding it inconceivable that there hadn't been periods of lucidity, although he can see a certain rationale. Without a body and a marked grave wasn't it just possible he'd survived, if not actually in the château, perhaps in some remote concentration camp yet to be unearthed? Enduring the years of silent hopefulness had clearly strengthened the memories, and if dealing with the horror in 1944 had been too much for them, with each anniversary it would have become more and more difficult. The unexpected discovery of Japanese soldiers still holding out in the jungle on a Pacific island in 1974 must have given them a real lift.

How many of them had parcelled the happy memories of their pre-war lives into brightly coloured packages in their mind and blocked out any dark images? he wonders as he looks over the moonlit bay, guessing that taking the lid off now will blow the packages to smithereens. Their hopes, however illogical, will be blown to the wind, and, subconsciously knowing that, many must have lived in fear of the day some loose-lipped drunk stumbled across the mausoleum or some Nosy Parker dug up the past and let their demons escape. But as Bliss watched the frail woman recount the tragedy it became apparent that continued concealment was more than just a refusal to accept the inevitable. As the years progressed another factor crept into the equation — embarrassment. The longer the concealment continued, the more important it became to maintain it, not just to preserve the memories and the hopes, but to avoid the world's focus, and even a degree of humiliation. Thinking of this, Bliss finds himself imagining a TV camera stuck in Daisy's mother's face and a pushy reporter asking incredulously, "So tell me, Madame ... I understand you've known about the château over there for more than fifty years," etc.

"Oh, yes.... Sorry. I forgot," would hardly cut it, especially if the reporter were to add with a smarmy tone, "So what exactly did you think had happened to your husband — late at the office, *peut-être?*"

chapter thirteen

Thoughts of Daisy's mother and grandmother holed up in their apartment for decades, waiting for her grandfather's return, play on Bliss's mind as he tries to chart his next steps. Daisy puts him in the picture about her grandfather.

"I assumed your mother lost someone in the war," he says to her as they sit in the bar after leaving the apartment. "I noticed her black clothes."

"*Maman* likes black," she explains. "When I was young all women wore black. I didn't know it zhen, but it was because zhey had lost zheir husbands or sons to zhe château."

The use of the euphemism doesn't escape him. Her mother did the same, saying, "Zhe château took our men," as if their disappearance could be blamed on the defenceless old building, rather than on war or the Nazis.

Now that Bliss has been swept into the conspiracy he's discovered just how easily it could have happened. While everybody probably accepted the truth at some level, no individual wanted to speak out and be responsible for destroying the hopes of others. It's a reciprocating cycle of self-deceit, he decides: an authentic saga of the emperor's new clothes. Yet in nearly sixty years no little boy has dashed from the crowd to point out the naked reality. By hiding deep in the woods, behind the high fence and locked gates, the mansion hasn't pompously paraded its nudity, but rather has made the task of sustaining the charade easier. Keeping its head bowed it has spent the decades slowly melting into the ground, although it still has a very long way to go.

After he leaves Daisy, Bliss walks alone along the beach listening to Brubeck playing "Blues in the Dark" as he tries to pick out the château's roofs in the moonlight. "I wonder if the grand old dame will take her sombre secret to the grave," he muses. "Or will some insensitive, money-grubbing historian realize the potential of revealing her presence and write a book ..." At this point he chokes. Until now, it hasn't crossed his mind that his book — Frederick Chapel's revelation of the identity of the man in the iron mask — will blow the lid off the château just as explosively as any historian's account. His deductions and eventual solution only hold water because of the château and its location. Once his book hits the bookstores and he gets on a few radio talk shows, the *merde* will certainly hit the *ventilateur*.

Once exposed, the attention of the whole world will focus on the previously neglected building. Millions will flock, led by teams of skeptical historians, nonplussed at the possibility that after three hundred years of vain research by some of the world's finest in academia, a lowly London copper could figure it out in ten minutes flat.

Bliss's manuscript, now swollen to more than a hundred pages with insightful imagery of the local landscapes, reports of the weather, historical anecdotes, and depictions of local characters, sits on his kitchen table and torments him like a bunch of Tantalus's grapes. The revelation in the final few pages plagues him most, and he picks it up and rereads it as he wanders to the balcony.

The days passed slowly for Frederick Chapel. The relentless sun and continual concern sapped his energy as he idled on the beach of St-Juan-sur-Mer, feeling his neck being stretched inexorably 'twixt the blade and the rope.

In her haste to serve him, Angélique misjudged the speed of a gentleman's carriage and sent the shying horse careering into the sleek chariot of a young cavalier. "Bof!" she said, and shrugged, delivering Chapel's gobelet with an unconcerned smile. "Bonjour, Monsieur Couperin."

"Bonjour, Angélique."

The war between France and Britain's northern alliance crept ever closer, and he became more and more despairing of his chances of solving the riddle and returning safely to his home in England. During the warm Provençal nights he had turned to Dorothée, his landlady, for comfort, although he was well aware that he was not the only one supping at that particular Venusian well.

When Dorothée revealed one night that she had been to the château to provide her fulsome service to the chief of security, Frederick Chapel could hardly contain his excitement. Whilst his clandestine visit to the site a few weeks earlier had confirmed his belief that it would be possible to swim the straits to the island from the château's beach, he was still doubtful of his plan to invade the fortress. His strategy to divert the guards by the creation of a phantom invasion force had, on closer examination, become untenable.

"It is zhe big secret, François," Dorothée had said, "but I know for whom zhe château is built."

"I do not believe you," he had said.

"Oui. It is true," she had protested, sitting up fiercely on his straw paillasse. "Zhere is a letter zhat zhe chef de sécurité showed me. It is from zhe man zhey call only 'l'homme au masque de fer.'"

Frederick Chapel could not believe his luck. For nearly two months he had paced the beaches and dunes of St-Juan searching for a way to identify the masked man, and now he lay with the woman who has the answer.

But she held the secret to ransom. "What will you give me if I tell?"

A little pressure applied in the right spot forced her hand.

"It is zhe billet doux," she claimed, as she rose theatrically and clasped her hands to her naked bosom. "He writes of his love for zhe woman and says, 'I shall wear zhis mask until you release me by your love. Every day I watch from my cell and see zhe château rise on zhe promontory, and, when it is finished, it will be my gift to you as a symbol of my love. You will be its mistress

*and you will raise a white flag which will signal an end
to my torment. Flying on the sirocco wind I will haste
across the bay and claim my prize. Until zhat day, zhis
mask, zhis cell, zhis fortress, will keep me from all eyes.
My body shall remain as pure and unsullied as my heart,
and only you — my sweet love — will ever look upon
me again. I am forever your prisoner.'"*

*Curling herself back into Frederick Chapel's clutches,
Dorothée had said, "It is very romantic, n'est-ce pas?"*

*"Very." He laughed, barely able to conceal his
incredulity at the thought of all the time and money that
had been wasted searching for Richard Cromwell when
all along the* prisonnier au masque de fer *had been nothing more than a lovesick romantic. "But who is this
man? What is his name?"*

"Roger."

"Roger who?"

Rereading the entry as he sits on his lounger looking
over the distant island, Bliss worries about its soppiness.
Will anyone believe that a seventeenth-century aristo-
crat would volunteer to be incarcerated out there, with
his head encased in iron, just to prove how much he
loved a woman? Is it far-fetched for a man in an era of
great romanticism to declare, "No one will look upon
my face until you agree to be mine — I will build you a
dream château and wait"?

Is it bizarre? he asks himself, re-evaluating the
whole scenario.

No — this is not bizarre, he responds. Pop songs,
literature, and history are full of parallels: I'll climb
the highest mountain, swim the widest ocean, throw

myself to the waves, build you the Taj Mahal. It was the exuberant era of Louis-Quatorze — long before the base barbarism of the revolution. For those rich enough, or corrupt enough, to afford it, it was a period of grandiose architecture and lavish design; clothes and footwear so elaborate and ostentatious that women couldn't move in them; outrageous food like lark's tongue pie and roast peacock. And, above all, it was a time of great romanticism.

My theory is just as valid as every other, he protests to himself. And more valid than most. It certainly carries more weight than the one proposed by the idiot who came up with "*une femme*." And what the hell did Nabo the Negro do to warrant inclusion on the list of the sixty most likely candidates?

Go back to basics, he tells himself. Consider the hard facts.

And he starts working through a mental reconstruction of the evidence. The Château Roger was built in 1687, according to the inscription on the gate pillar — the same year as the masked man's incarceration; the geographic location puts it directly across the strait from the fortress; the size and luxuriousness of his cell are more redolent of a premier hotel than a prison; the murals on the wall suggest a joyous gathering — a wedding, perhaps. And, as Daisy would say, "Zhere is no evidence against it." The fact that everyone has always believed him to be a prisoner does not make it so: everyone believes I'm on convalescent leave; widows here believe their menfolk are still in the château; women believed that Grimes gave them a free pot.

A buzz on the apartment's intercom interrupts his musings. Marcia Grimes, dishevelled, tear-stained, and distraught, falls through his doorway and crumples, snivelling, "Daisy told me where to find you."

"The damn woman," he mutters lightly, but is not ungrateful. He has some choice words readied for Marcia Grimes, but has been stalling until her husband was out of danger.

"They couldn't reattach Greg's hand," Marcia manages to tell him through the tears, but he shows her little sympathy.

"If you thought that much about your husband why did you go off with Johnson?"

Her tone drops as she confesses, "I guess it was money …"

But Bliss knows that. He already got that from his daughter. Samantha phoned back a couple of days earlier, bitching about being used, as usual.

"I said I'd pay," he told her.

"This is the last time, Dad."

"The last time on this case, or …" he said, but she talked over him. "It was quite strange, really. I did the village store and the post office. Everyone knew them. Telling me about them playing the happy family: church — sometimes, village fetes, and jumble sales, etcetera, though often they were selling their pots. 'Typical artsy couple,' most people said, which probably means they wore weird clothes, smoked a bit of dope, and ate funny grub — sprouty stuff and spinach, I expect. Anyway, the only really strange thing was that they disappeared without trace over a year ago."

"That's interesting," Bliss said, wondering what his neighbours would say about him.

"Their place is all boarded up, but it's next door to the pub so I thought I'd get some lunch. But when I asked the barman if he knew Greg Grimes the whole place suddenly went dead. It was like I'd stood in the middle of a funeral and shouted, 'Who farted?'"

"Samantha," he laughed. "So what's their problem?"

"Money — isn't that everybody's problem?"

It was certainly Marcia Grimes's problem. "I'd gone without for years for Greg and the business," she whimpers as she sits on his balcony seeking sympathy in a large cognac, "but we never got anywhere."

"I think I can understand," Bliss says, with a touch of malice. "Greg didn't have a yacht and a limousine."

Marcia finds the yellow smudge of disintegrated lemon on the lawn in the garden below and sticks to it. "The truth is a rich man's bed may be more comfortable than a poor man's, but there's no such thing as a free fuck."

"Is that what Johnson was hoping for?"

"Not him," she cries. "Me."

"Oh," he says, taken aback, not sure how to respond. "You mean, he wanted more than just sex?"

"He didn't want sex — he wanted power. That's the problem with being rich. When you can buy whatever you want, you don't want anything you can buy. Cars, boats, houses, and people lose all their value. You only want what you can't have."

"And what does Johnson want that he can't have?" But he already knows the answer. Samantha told him that also.

"What did they say about Grimes and money?" he asked Samantha, referring to the customers in their local pub.

"From what I can gather almost everyone in the village invested money in the venture."

"So they're all cogs in a major drug ring, then?"

"No — not drugs, Dad."

"What then?"

"The treasure hunt."

"Do you mean Johnson and Greg Grimes were both hunting for treasure?"

"No — not Greg Grimes. Everybody thinks the world of him. She's the one everybody's pissed off with. She gave them a line about her partner having found a Roman galley — that it was all a bit dodgy because he didn't have permission to —"

"Aha, the classic con," he cut in knowingly. "Tell the mark the venture isn't strictly above-board, maybe even downright illegal, and they fall for it every time. Apart from adding a touch of spice, it also explains how the deal can offer astronomical dividends. But the great thing is that the poor sucker can't complain to the authorities without admitting to being a co-conspirator in a crooked deal."

"Correct, Dad. So when I started asking questions, they probably figured I was a cop and kept quiet. Then, in the pub, I sort of disillusioned them."

"How?"

"Dad," she hesitated, "this has nothing to do with you — I just made a few uncomplimentary remarks about cops."

"Why?"

"'Cos I got a fuckin' parking ticket, if you must know. I mean — what a prick the cop was ..."

"Yes, all right."

"No, I mean it. I'd call him a moron, but he's not that bright. So there I was in the pub letting off steam, and when I brought up Marcia's name — well, you know the rest."

"Any idea how much?"

"No — and they don't know, either. In fact I got the distinct impression most of them didn't know the guy standing next to him had been suckered into doling out some cash."

"Another beauty of the scam," he replied, knowing the con man warns everyone to keep it quiet. "So could any of the investors have hired someone to chop off his hand?"

"Hardly likely, Dad. They still don't know their money's gone."

"The eternal triumph of hope over expectation," Bliss replied, wondering if he was talking about the investors or the widows of St-Juan.

"Anyway," Samantha carried on, "they've got no gripes against Greg Grimes — only her. I get the impression she's a bit of a slag — always carping about him not working hard enough, not keeping her in a standard to which she wanted to become accustomed. And I got the distinct feeling quite a few of the men had got some return on their investment already, if you get my drift."

"I can see that," he said, realizing that if Greg Grimes could have captivated a bevy of women with his sensuous hands, Marcia had body parts that would have a similarly devastating effect on men.

"She'd been stringing them along for over a year before they disappeared," Samantha continued, "but what could they do? They're not likely to have receipts, and who would be willing to stand up in court and admit they'd invested in a seriously dodgy treasure hunt? It seems pretty obvious to me their money's gone, but they're still planning early retirements. There's none so olfactorially challenged as those who don't want to smell."

"They should get together with a bunch of widows I know," he replied.

"Widows?" she asked.

Respecting his promise to Daisy's mother he did not elaborate, though he put Samantha in the picture about the cache Johnson took aboard the *Sea-Quester* off the coast of Corsica.

"Maybe it was treasure," she agreed. "Maybe they will get their reward after all."

Sitting back now to take a good look at the dark-haired Marcia, Bliss doesn't find it difficult to believe she persuaded most of the men in the village to invest in a treasure hunt — Morgan Johnson's treasure hunt. She has an attractive cockiness about her, a prick-teaser's hip-sway capable of keeping many guys within sniffing distance, even if there is a hint of fishiness in the air.

"So," he asks, "what's Johnson's interest in Roman pottery?"

"How do you know ..." she starts, and then gives up the struggle. "He isn't interested, really," she snorts. "He's only interested in what he can sell it for. He's addicted to money."

And like every addict, Bliss thinks to himself, he can never get enough; the next Scotch, next snort, or next spin of the wheel is going to make everything right — but it never does. Another few million will buy another yacht or another villa, but with it comes another round of responsibilities and headaches — *la grande servitude*. "If money brings misery, more money just brings more misery," he muses aloud, adding, "Strikes me if anybody should have something chopped off, it should have been Johnson. And I know what. But what about Greg? If anyone has an eye for the women it seems Greg wasn't far behind."

"It wasn't women," she tells him. "I told you. Didn't you listen? He always tried to choose pretty young women."

"That's what I mean —" he starts, but she angrily cuts him short.

"No. You don't understand," she cries. "It was Natalia he was looking for, not some bird for a quick shag. When I left him he coped, but when Johnson turned Natalia against him he went to pieces."

"What do you expect me to do?" he asks, for Greg's sake — not hers.

"Find out who did it, of course — who cut Greg's …" She stops, unable to complete the horrific sentence.

"But why now?" he starts, and then pauses. "Oh. I get it. You've spoken to Johnson, haven't you?"

Taking a drink as an excuse, she doesn't answer immediately, and he weighs up her mind. She obviously blamed her ex-lover initially — that's why she warned her husband to keep quiet — so what changed her mind?

"Morgan Johnson says he didn't do it," she admits finally.

"And you believe him."

"He's terrified. He thinks he's next."

Four days sitting on his balcony picking at his nails hasn't brought Bliss any closer to solving his dilemma over the château, and the problem is exacerbated by his inability to discuss his predicament with anyone without giving the game away.

Feeling like a 1945 bomber pilot with a map of Hiroshima in his pocket, he tries to convince himself his revelation isn't going to kill anyone who isn't already dead. Then he envisions trainloads of grief counsellors and psychologists being shipped in from all over the country to stem the flow of suicides caused by his exposé of the château's past. Where were they when they were needed? he wonders, but the question is six decades too late.

Since figuring out the true reason for the presence of the masked man in the fortress, and the part the château played in his scheme, Bliss fondly imagined being welcomed as a hero, and saw himself shepherding a new era of tourism and prosperity to the quaint little resort that cowers in the shadow of its more publicized neighbours. But now he realizes the effect on the community could be catastrophic. Once he opens the cage and lets the dark genie out no amount of stuffing will get it back in. Maybe it's time, he thinks, maybe they'll thank me — but maybe they won't. And, as preposterous as it seems, he worries many of the château's widows have spent the remainder of their lives in celibacy, mindful of the possibility of their husbands' return — what a let-down when they discover the truth.

But he brightens with the realization that he's cleared up two of his original five conundrums. He now knows the secret of the château and, although he doesn't yet have a name, he has the means to discover the identity of the man in the iron mask. However, he'll have to go back to the château — eventually. He has to do something about the boy in the cage — eventually. He's got to find Johnson eventually, and he would still like to see Natalia Grimes released from the man's evil clutches.

The potter's wheel has not thrown off a pot for nearly a week, yet women are still drawn by an invisible residue of magnetism that causes them to dither at the spot, just for a second. Bliss and Daisy pause to watch them as they take an evening stroll on the promenade.

"Zhey look very sad," Daisy says, but Bliss's mind is still wrestling with the château's history. If the building's original secret could be maintained for three hundred years, is it so preposterous to believe people would keep the secret of the Nazi terrors for another sixty?

"You don't believe it, do you, Daisy?" he asks, sensing she'll know he's talking about the missing *résistance* fighters.

"No — of course not," she replies, "but you must understand, it is real to zhe women of my grandmother's age because zhey have zhe faith."

"It sounds like religion," he says, nodding knowingly. "Idolizing someone who died a long time ago and devoting the rest of your life in prayer for their resurrection."

"But zhey believe zhe men are still alive. As long as no one goes to zhe château zhere's no evidence against it."

"That sounds more like a rumour than a religion," he says, still shaking his head in disbelief as he spots Hugh and Mavis at L'Escale.

"Was that Jacques?" he asks, thinking he recognized the back of the distant figure.

"Yes," says Hugh, looking confused. "He was just telling us about the different winds when he saw you and Daisy coming and said he had an appointment."

"That's strange," Bliss says, seating Daisy as he gives Angeline a wave. "He hasn't forecast an ill wind for over a week now."

"Actually he was just saying that tomorrow we can expect a bit of a nasty blow. What did he call it, Mavis?"

"Louis Armstrong."

"No," he sneers, muttering "Stupid woman" under his breath. "It is the *lou marin* — or something like that."

"How long are you staying?" asks Daisy as Bliss orders their drinks.

"This is our last few days," says Hugh. "It's nearly the fifteenth of August."

"So?" queries Bliss.

"End of summer, old boy. Didn't you know?"

"It can't be," he says, eyeing the star-filled sky that still preserves a strong memory of the day's blue.

"Oh yes," continues Hugh. "Everyone will tell you. Regular as clockwork the weather goes to pot here on the fifteenth."

"Sounds like one of Jacques's winds," Bliss mutters disbelievingly, but Daisy steps in. "No. It is right. August fifteen is zhe end."

That's only two days, Bliss realizes with a quick calculation, and suddenly sees an opportunity to enlist an aid. "You strike me as a man with a military background, Hugh," he says, his tone heavy with bullshit.

Hugh straightens himself and exhales, "Army."

"I thought so," says Bliss. "I can usually spot a good Sandhurst man."

Hugh deflates a touch. "To be honest, I didn't quite make Sandhurst, old boy."

That's the same as being not quite pregnant, thinks Bliss, though he'd never pegged Hugh as a graduate of the elite officer training college — guessing he'd probably done a couple of years compulsory national service, most of it spent on a parade ground, square-bashing or pushing a pen in the Pay Corps. Leaning forward to cut Mavis out of earshot, he adds a dose of flattery, "I bet you're still game for a bit of excitement, though."

"Naturally, old boy," replies Hugh, though adds diffidently, "What did you have in mind?"

A bold assault on the château is his plan. He and Hugh marching assertively past the guards on the hill, slipping through the fence, and carrying out a full daylight recce. The prospect of entering the decaying structure alone for a third time, particularly with its growing legion of ghosts, has held him back for days, but the building possesses no ghosts for Hugh. "Tomorrow morning," whispers Bliss. "Be here at nine and I'll fill you in."

"What you ask zhat man?" Daisy wants to know as soon as they leave the L'Escale.

"I told you. I have to go back to the château to look for evidence. Whoever cut off Grimes's hand needs catching and I need someone to help me."

Daisy flies at him. "You can't take Hugh. He will tell."

"I need someone to hold the lights," he protests. Someone to hold his hand, he means, though would never admit it.

"I come," she whispers.

"Really."

"Yes. I not scared."

"You certainly sound it."

"If you go — I go."

chapter fourteen

While Bliss might have preferred the stouter company of Hugh, he acceded to Daisy's pleas, and now he holds aside the broken fence for her as they enter the château's grounds. But his motive in bringing Daisy has more to do with his novel than his quest for clues in the maiming case. If she sees for herself that the château is not an underground community of octogenarian resistance fighters and is able to convince her mother and grandmother and the other siblings and widows, then he will be able to publish his book without fear.

Although he's dispensed with the workman's plaster-caked overalls, the workman's bag carried them past the heavies on the hill, and as soon as he's replaced the fence post he extracts two cans of pepper spray and a couple of steaks.

Daisy's eyes go wild. "You said no guards. No dogs."

"There aren't," he soothes. "These are just to make you feel safe."

Her voice quivers. "I don't feel safe now."

"It's just a precaution," he says, taking her hand and drawing her away from the fence along the path to the château.

The mid-morning sun bathes the old stone building in a sepia warmth that touches on gold in places, and Daisy stands at the foot of the expansive flight of marble steps with her mouth open.

"Scared?" he asks, but she doesn't answer and he concludes it is awe: the Forbidden City, the Holy Grail, and the Pearly Gates all rolled into one. What's going through her mind? he wonders, as he gives her time to acclimatize while sorting out floodlights and his camera, but her rigid expression and clamped fists suggest she's holding on somewhere between dread and wonder.

The small door to the side of the giant aediculated entranceway is still open, and, buoyed by Daisy's presence, Bliss bustles through into the massive hall, dragging her in his wake. But he has no illusions. All the ghosts up here on the main floor are smiling and dancing — seventeenth-century merrymakers and twentieth-century Jewish revellers alike. It is in the eternal darkness below that the torment lies.

"Are you all right?" he asks as she hovers near the door, close to backing out.

Her mouth opens, though her voice won't work.

"Don't worry. There's no one here," he says, gently pulling her in, but he feels the weight of evil just as much as she.

His primary goal is to find the place where Grimes had set up camp. "He won't tell me where he's been living," Marcia admitted after Bliss agreed to try to find her husband's mutilator, "but I think he's been going to the old château for some time." The only additional information she could offer was that he'd been pounced on in the darkness and had absolutely no idea who his attacker was; he knew only that he reeked of cigarette smoke and garlic.

"That narrows it down to about ninety percent of French males," Bliss intoned sarcastically, but it was all she could offer.

"You said he'd upset people," he continued, seeking a motive. "Who?"

"We owe some money ..." she started sheepishly, though didn't need to elaborate and didn't try.

The sins of the wife shall be visited on the husband, he thought, and couldn't help wondering how many other men had been mutilated, one way or another, by the extravagance of their wives.

The inspection of the main floor and upper stories takes twenty minutes, including a five-minute stop on the rooftop balcony from where they gaze at the fortress on the island and watch yachts steaming through the treetops in the bay below. Finding no trace of Grimes's living quarters, Bliss takes a deep breath and heads for the basement.

"I no go," says Daisy, paling at the top of the dark staircase.

"Oh *merde!*" he mutters, fearing this was likely to happen. What now? He could happily have done the upstairs without someone riding shotgun, but downstairs isn't just a *panier de crabes*, it's a claw-filled mine-field. In any case, he can't have her going back to her mother and shrugging as she says, "*Bof!* Perhaps the men were downstairs. I did not look."

Does it really matter what her mother believes? he wonders, deliberating whether or not to force her. Why not just publish and be damned? But does he want to be damned by an entire community?

"Daisy, I really need you to come with me," he pleads.

"I scared," she confesses, though the tautness of her face and the coldness of her hand suggest "terrified" might be more appropriate. "You scared too?" she asks.

"A little," he admits. "But it's very important."

"OK," she says, arming herself with a hammer and a can of pepper spray. "I go."

Physically, nothing has changed in the basement. Rats and lizards scurry from the light in the ancient kitchen, the nauseating smell of blood is still in the musty air, and the atmosphere is still charged with fear, but in the dark torture chambers the souls hanging in the chains now have shadowy forms. One of the shadows is Daisy's grandfather, and tears stream down her face as she eyes the pathetic bundle of old clothes dumped in the corner. Some of the rags might have been the clothes he was wearing when he was wrested from her mother's grasp, and their presence brings the past into frighteningly painful focus as she pictures her mother, as a twelve-year-old, watching her grandfather broken, beaten, and dragged away in chains.

Bliss has no words to help her. It isn't her pain; it's her mother's pain. No wonder they couldn't accept the finality of the situation. They are devout Christians. They and their forebears had piously carried the Cross up the Chemin du Calvaire in nearby Antibes every Easter for more than a thousand years. And every year, without fail, there was a resurrection. So, as they trudged the rocky path to the war's end after years of hopeful prayer there had to be some salvation — some reward. The notion that they might have been cheated by the insufferable cruelty of their God, as well as that of their invaders, had been too much.

"*C'est horrible,*" mumbles Daisy succinctly, perfectly encapsulating the suffering of thousands — men and women alike.

Returning to the kitchen, with all the rooms checked, Bliss is stumped. "I was sure he was living here."

"Maybe zhe man who cut off his hand took his zhings."

"How?"

"Zhe tunnel to zhe beach," she says, then stops with a confused expression.

"That's a point," he says. "Where is the tunnel your mother spoke about?"

Daisy's shrug of denial is the most unconvincing he's ever seen, and the fact that it isn't accompanied by a "*bof*" alerts him immediately. The body language of the lie transcends national boundaries, he decides, and pushes her. "Where is the entrance to the tunnel, Daisy?"

Seeking refuge in tears, and his shoulder, she evades the question for several minutes, but he persists. "You obviously know where it is. We're not leaving 'til you show me."

Wiping her nose on his shirt, she snivels, "Why you want to know?"

"So you do know where it is."

"No."

"Daisy ... if Greg Grimes was living here perhaps he was in the tunnel. I need to know."

Breaking away, her eyes scour the basement as if she's preparing to run, then Bliss catches on. "You thought the tunnel was here, didn't you?"

Her refusal to answer is answer enough. "Where is it?" he demands, then pulls back. "Did your mother tell you it started in the basement?"

Her nod is another lie. He sees it, but lets it go. "We must've missed the entrance. Grab that light.... Wait a minute," he breathes, and bends to pick up the remnants of a cigarette stub that has been ground into the dirty wooden floor.

"Here's another," she cries, brightening at the discovery.

"Well, these haven't been here for sixty years," he says, carefully dropping them into the finger of a rubber glove from the workman's bag and stuffing it into his pocket.

The door to the sub-basement takes them both by surprise. It isn't concealed; it just doesn't look like a door. A couple of ring handles recessed into the floorboards at one end of the kitchen, next to the huge range, give it away.

"They must have brought the wood and coal up this way," he says, struggling with the weighty trap door. Daisy steps in to help, and together they uncover a steep flight of stone steps. The anomaly of a white plastic light switch at the top of the steps doesn't immediately register in Bliss's mind as he gives it a flick. Mild surprise at the flood of light in the room below turns to alarm as they are jolted rigid by the rattle of a generator firing up in the distance.

"What a nerve," whistles Bliss a few minutes later, stunned at the magnitude of their discovery. "This isn't squatting — this is a full-scale occupation."

The potter's studio, complete with electric wheel, walk-in kiln, giant steel drying racks, and stacks of bagged clay, sand, gravel, and other ingredients, has the appearance of a full commercial set-up. And in a curtained alcove to one side is a neat little bedroom.

"Why did he stay up there?" Bliss puzzles briefly, looking back up the steps and recalling Grimes cowering under the old stone sink, before realizing the weakened, disabled potter wouldn't have had the strength to lift the trap door.

"He must've shipped his entire studio out here," Bliss says, as he and Daisy inspect the equipment and supplies. "I wonder why he didn't just rent a proper space?"

"It is very expensive," she replies, though he doubts that was the reason as he muses, "How did he get all this stuff in here?"

The thrum of the generator provides the answer as it draws them from the chamber down an illuminated brick-lined tunnel, and Daisy recovers a little of her bounce. "Zhis goes to zhe beach," she tells him.

Bliss stops dead. "How do you know?"

A momentary hesitation warns him she's trying to come up with the correct answer. "*Maman* told me," she says, but her tone isn't convincing.

"She told me as well," he agrees, though can't get past the feeling Daisy is hiding something.

The noise of the powerful generator beats into their eardrums as they approach, and Bliss is surprised to discover the engine in a concrete-lined bunker the size of subway station, complete with narrow gauge sidings and tracks that lead down another tunnel — to the beach, he surmises. "The Germans must have dug this," he breathes, amazed by its size, and he puts it into context. The original brick-lined tunnel must have been built to allow supplies to be brought ashore and taken directly to the cellars of the château, without risk of offending the sensibilities of the gentry in the landscaped gardens above, but the concrete-lined cavern is obviously much more recent.

"I bet this is where the Germans stored their small craft," he calls, pointing out the rusted rail lines and the hand switches that would have allowed the boat-dollies to be shunted into sidings. "They could have even kept midget subs here."

Distracted by dark thoughts and seemingly uninterested, Daisy has wandered off and doesn't reply. There are pots — smashed pots — everywhere. Heaps of shattered stoneware. "It looks like someone's taken a wrecker's ball to the place," he says, picking through the shards of thick, rough terra cotta.

The darker recesses of the cavern attract him and he scouts around, looking for detritus of occupation. Some scraps of paper with German handwriting, and swastikas scratched into walls by bored sentries, are all he finds to confirm his suspicions.

"Somebody cleaned this place out pretty well after the war," he notes, finding nothing of value. Then the low rumble of a train overhead drowns out the generator and takes his eyes up a rusted steel ladder, which fades into the high ceiling. Shining a flashlight he finds a large steel trap door. "I bet that comes out by the side of the railway line."

Suddenly aware that he's been talking to himself for several minutes, he looks around for Daisy and finds her frozen in contemplation.

"What is it?" he calls, noticing some material in her hands.

"Just an old shirt," she says, dropping it back to the ground and heading down the tunnel towards the beach.

"They probably took prisoners out this way to the trains or boats," he chatters, catching her up as she emerges from the mouth of the tunnel onto a sunlit beach.

The charm and warmth of the perfect little cove contrasts so sharply with the cold tunnel and chilling images behind him that Bliss sinks to the sand and takes a deep breath as he surfaces from the nightmare to a dream.

"It's just like your mother described it," he mutters to himself, unaware Daisy has slunk out of earshot, head down, as she fights with demons and darkness.

Encircled by rocky peninsulas, the cove is entirely screened from the sea, and the serene surface could be that of an emerald lake in a hidden valley.

Whoever the man in the iron mask was trying to impress must have been blind to turn this down, he tells himself, as he lets warm rivulets of white sand slip through his fingers. Yet the lovesick man's romantic proposal was obviously rebuffed because, according to records, he waited eleven years in the fortress, earnestly seeking the white flag destined never to be raised over his beautiful château. Finally, in mourning for his lost love and feeling foolish at his failed scheme, he persuaded Louis XIV to let him spend the rest of his life in reflection and purgatory in the Bastille in Paris.

The ironic image of an entire town of masked women still waiting for the release of their loved ones drags Bliss's spirits down. There is no one to raise the white flag today any more than there was in Frederick Chapel's time, and the thought that such a beautiful building in such an idyllic setting has been the cause of misery to so many pains him.

Daisy sits contemplating the sea with such ferocity that he is wary of frightening her. Announcing his presence with a satisfied, "Aah," he sighs, "It is very pretty, isn't it?" But she's changed. Deep in thought she barely acknowledges him, and her customary shrug has none of the emphasis she usually manages to convey.

Sitting silently beside her for a few moments he feels a degree of animosity in the air and is saddened that, in a way, he's tricked her into facing the dark truth. Her hunched shoulders and downcast eyes tell him that, despite claiming not to believe in the myth of the missing men, she is struggling with the enormity of a destroyed faith. But he sees more. "You've been here before, haven't you?" he asks. Her confusion in the basement kitchen and hesitant replies have given her away, as has her certainty that the tunnel led to the beach.

"*Bof!*" She shrugs.

"*Bof?*" he questions.

"*Oui, bof!*"

"You *have* been here, haven't you?"

Her impassive face gives nothing away as she demands, "How you know?"

"I guessed."

"Don't guess, *Daavid*," she says, and her sudden coldness takes him aback, but before he can protest she shakes herself free of the sand. "Can we go now please? I no like it here."

"OK," he says, but she's already off, almost running back up the tunnel. Scrabbling to his feet he sets off in pursuit. "Wait a minute," he calls, but finds himself trailing as she storms through the wartime bunker.

Her footsteps are already clacking into the next tunnel as he quickly gathers some larger shards of broken pots, then he grabs the old shirt she'd been holding to use as a sling bag.

"Blasted woman," he curses, as he's forced to run to catch up, and she is already climbing the steps to the kitchen when he enters the underground studio. Quickly stuffing the hoard of pottery shards into his tool bag, he pulls out his camera and takes a few snapshots before racing after her.

Daisy, face drawn in anxiety, waits at the top of the steps, fearful of leaving the bright lights for the gloom of the basement. "Somebody really had it in for Grimes," Bliss says nonchalantly as he emerges from the trap door, trying to restore some normality to their relationship. "His wife said he'd upset someone — looks to me like he's upset a whole load of people."

The walk back to Daisy's car, in the parking lot at the bottom of the hill, is tortuously silent. Bliss tries to soften her a couple of times, but gives up when he realizes she is close to causing a scene.

"I'll walk home," he says, and feels the tension lift as she drives off.

Back in the apartment, he carefully transfers the crushed cigarette ends to a small plastic bag, spreads a newspaper over the kitchen table, and unfolds the shirt — but it's neither the pottery shards nor the stains of age on the shirt that cause him to catch his breath. It is the logo. "TAKE FIVE — The Dave Brubeck Quartet."

Either my doppelganger has lied about his age or this shirt did not belong in the château with the wartime relics, he decides, then puts it to one side as he picks through the pottery and phones Marcia. He has her number and address as part of a deal — *"If you expect me to find out who did it …"*

"Two questions, Marcia," he says. "Did Greg smoke?"

With her emphatic "No," he asks, "Who was he making pots for?"

"The young women …"

"No," says Bliss, "big pots — very big pots. Wait a minute," he cuts himself off, turning over a conical shard in his hand, thinking about treasure and pots and the Senegalese salesmen on the beaches flogging Rolex and Cartier knock-offs. "Johnson's treasure hunt wouldn't involve the search for Roman amphorae, would it?"

"Well done, Inspector."

"So, when you got people to invest in the deal they were actually investing in the search for pots that had never been anywhere near Rome or a galley. Is that right?"

"You said two questions."

"Do you want me to find Greg's attacker or not?"

"All right. Yes — if you must know, the amphorae may not be quite as old as they appear. Though I don't see what this has to do with Greg."

I bet they're roughly two thousand years newer than they look, Bliss guesses, then informs her, "Somebody's smashed all the pots."

"What pots?"

"The pots Greg made for Johnson."

"He didn't make any pots for Johnson. He wouldn't make them. He absolutely refused to get involved."

"Then I don't understand," says Bliss, and is preparing to put down the phone when he has a final thought. "Is Greg a Dave Brubeck fan?"

"Yes — why?"

August fifteenth breaks with all the fury of a feather cudgel. Good old Jacques, thinks Bliss, as he strolls to the warm balcony with his morning coffee, although he is mindful that Daisy was just as adamant about the imminent demise of summer.

Daisy has been keeping a low profile since yesterday morning, and he's purposefully avoided contacting her, figuring she needs time to digest the information and decide how to disenchant her mother and the other women. Or will she simply carry on as before? he wonders.

The manuscript of his novel, "The Truth Behind the Mask," nears completion as he adds descriptions of the château's basements and underground tunnels for colour. The only significant feature not yet clarified is the name of the jilted Romeo, but he is working on that when a muttered cry of annoyance from the garden below catches his attention.

"*Merde*," swears the old concierge, as he bends to scoop crap off the lawn, and Bliss is reminded that he's still done nothing about the young man in the cage. But what to do? In England it would be easy. Magistrate — swear out an affidavit alleging an arrestable offence and obtain a search warrant. But this is France. Who knows — the French might enjoy this kind of thing. There may be thousands of French kids living in cages with their dogs.

With Johnson complaining to Daisy about his interference and — whatever Marcia may claim — the strong possibility that Johnson had a hand in her husband's mutilation, he decides to leave it for the time being.

Hoping to catch Hugh and Mavis before their afternoon flight, he takes a stroll to L'Escale for an early lunch. A commotion in the road near the bar has attracted a small crowd, and an ambulance screeches to a halt as he arrives.

"What's happened?" he asks Hugh, peering along the promenade.

"Angeline," says Hugh, nodding to the waitress as she hobbles across the road to take their order, then details how she pirouetted neatly past a zooming white delivery van, squeezed through a gap between two racing Renaults, but miscalculated the speed of a sprinting cyclist and stabbed her foot through his front wheel. The bike stopped — but not the rider.

"*Bonjour, Monsieur*," sings Angeline, apparently unscathed.

"Are you all right?" he asks, concerned.

"*Oui, c'est rien* — no *problème*," she says, seemingly indifferent to the fate of the young man who screams in agony as he's loaded aboard the ambulance.

"Let me get your lunch, Dave," offers Hugh. "I feel we owe you something."

"Thanks," he says, ordering the oysters and chips in place of his usual mussels.

Angeline limps towards the bar, and Bliss resists the temptation to cry out as she plays chicken with the ambulance. For once the vehicle wins, but she leans on the sympathy of a bus driver in the medic's wake and hobbles across the road.

Hugh and Mavis are blushingly effusive in thanking him for persuading them to stay. "We've had a wonderful holiday," says Mavis, her deep bronze tan glowing golden in the midday sun. "We're coming for two months again next year." Then she adds slyly, "We've already booked."

"That's wonderful," he says, then asks, "With John and Jennifer?"

"Good grief. No," says Mavis, "they're a couple of old stick-in-the-muds."

Jacques pulls up a chair with a smile to Hugh. "You'll be thankful to have got out of here."

"Why is that, Jacques?" Bliss asks, knowing he'll regret it, knowing that some Beaufort blast is about to wreak havoc on the coast. "Are we expecting bad weather?"

"*Certainement*," he assures them. "By tonight zhe sirocco wind will scoop zhe red sands from zhe deserts of Africa and will scorch across zhe Mediterranean. By tomorrow zhe surf will pound our beaches and smash zhe boats."

"Sounds horrific," laughs Bliss. "Maybe I should leave as well."

"You would be very wise to consider it, Monsieur," says Jacques with a degree of seriousness that shakes Bliss. "Zhe summer is at an end," continues the Frenchman, forcefully. "It is time for everyone to go home."

Daisy is lying in ambush at the potter's old spot on the promenade, but Bliss's smile of greeting fades at the sight of her face.

"You've been crying," he says, as she takes his arm.

"I want to talk to you."

"Oh dear," he muses, sensing trouble, suspecting she bears a warning from the town's women not to upset the apple cart.

Ushering him into a dark corner of L'Offshore Club she sits stiffly, her eyes hunting the room. For what, he wonders, eavesdroppers or a way out? He waits patiently — this is her party.

"Cognac," she orders urgently, when an eagle-eyed, bandy-legged waiter swoops out of nowhere. And then she turns to Bliss with a question that seems determined to get out despite her best efforts to keep it in.

"You are a policeman. Yes?"

"Yes."

"You won't laugh zhen?"

"I promise," he says, but then she wins a short reprieve as the waiter delivers their drinks.

"I been to zhe château before," she admits after a momentary check for the emergency exit.

"I knew it," he replies with a degree of triumph. "But why didn't you tell me?"

Searching for an answer in her glass of liquid gold, she finds the sunshine of a warm summer's day in 1970. The last day of that year's summer — the fifteenth of August. A bubbly fifteen-year-old schoolgirl, tanned and toned from a summer on the beach of St-Juan, taunts a clean-bodied teenaged holidaymaker; Roland is *un Parisien*. Eighteen and a half — a city-sophisticate with savoir-faire and Daddy's souped-up British Mini.

"What is zhat château?" he asks while they lazily swim out into the bay and catch a glimpse of the building as they look back over the hills of St-Juan.

"It is a secret," she tells him, then dives through the shimmering blue in pursuit of a shoal of sardines. He dives, pursuing another variety of fish, and strikes. Kissing and fondling they play in the soft water bed until Roland seeks to land his catch.

"Let's go to zhe château," he suggests, but her face darkens.

"No. If we go zhere we will die."

"Zhat is crazy," he says, laughing. "It is a silly story to frighten *les enfants*. It is zhe ghost under zhe bed. Are you *une enfant, peut-être*? Do you still 'ave zhe ghost under zhe bed?"

"No," she protests, "I am no kid."

"OK. Zhen we go."

"Roland was from Paris — *un Parigot* — he knew everything," Daisy explains to Bliss as she looks up from her drink and describes how they swam around the rocky promontory and found the entrance to the hidden cove.

"Roland had been there before," she continues, then seeks consolation in her drink as she admits to being teased into submission.

"Are you scared, my little *poule*?" he calls, swimming through the narrow straits into the deserted emerald basin.

"I am not a chicken," she protests, and to prove her point she swims into his clutches.

Roland has slipped out of his trunks and T-shirt by the time she catches up.

"Roland!" she cries.

"I am James Bond — double-oh seven," he says in movie-learnt English. "Take off your clothes, Pussy Galore, and I will show you my weapon."

"I already see your weapon," she giggles.

Daisy's memories, shrouded in shame, dwell on the psychological hurt as she explains the few moments of Roland's sexual release. "I scared and say '*Non, non,*' but he laugh and call me chicken. Zhen I cry when I zhink I am not *une pucelle* — a virgin — anymore." Reliving the moment, she shuts her eyes as the reminiscence continues.

"*Cocorico!*" cries Roland one minute and thirty seconds later, as he dresses and strides off in search of another adventure, leaving her to weep into the sand.

The cave-like entrance to the dark tunnel takes his eye and he heads for it.

"If we go to zhe château we will die," she calls, as he beckons her to tag along.

"*Co-co-co-co,*" he clucks.

"I am no chicken," she says, following.

"I swim back on my own and never see Roland again," she tells Bliss in conclusion. "But I cry a lot. My *maman,* she says, 'Why you cry?' I say nothing, but I zhink maybe I 'ave zhe *ballon.*"

Bliss cocks his head, enquiring, "The *ballon*?"

"*Oui* — zhe *bébé,*" she replies, pointing to her stomach and starting to cry again.

"You thought you were pregnant."

"Perhaps. It is possible," she sniffles through the tears. "I did not know. But I could not tell *Maman* because it is a crime — she would kill me."

Bewildered by the depth of her concern over a teenager's thirty-year-old misjudgement, Bliss struggles to reassure her. "It doesn't matter now. Nobody worries today about things like that."

She shook him off. "It does matter."

"Why?"

"Because Roland is dead," she cries, her olive-black pupils holding him rigid as the import of her words sink in.

"When? Where?" he asks, but has guessed the answer.

"Zhe château."

The words of her mother, "Zhe château has taken our men," run through his mind as he pulls her into his arms while she sobs.

chapter fifteen

The phone is buzzing as Bliss lets himself into his apartment. "Somebody wants *me* for a change," he mumbles.

"We're still waiting for that quote for a yacht, Inspector," Commander Richards complains, seriously pissed off.

Methinks he doth demand too much, thinks Bliss, saying, "Sorry, Guv. I've been busy. I think I've got a murder on my hands."

"Oh God ... not Johnson. Please tell me it's not Johnson."

"No. Not Johnson. But why did you ask?"

"Dave. I warned you. Some people might want something to happen to him. But who's been murdered?"

He sloughs it off. "It's just an old case. But how come no one wants to tell me what Johnson's supposed to have done?"

The heavy silence suggests Richards is weighing his options. Bliss gives him a nudge. "Let me guess. Some prat in the pension department has invested my future in a seriously iffy treasure hunt and —"

"No," explodes Richards. "It's not a Force matter — not directly."

I guess I'm half-right then, he thinks, and pushes harder. "So ... what if someone with sunshine coming out his bum has ..." Then he stops. "You said, 'we are still waiting.' Who's 'we'?"

"Dave. I'll personally wring your bloody neck if this ever gets out, but you might as well know the Force Widows' and Orphans' Fund administrator has topped himself."

"Oh, shit."

"Quite. So stop messing about and find out where Johnson is. The bastard is swanning around the fuckin' Med in a yacht unofficially financed by the university fees of dozens of dead coppers' kids."

It was the usual thing, he explains — gambling debts. The administrator had dug himself a grave with his own money, then burrowed deeper and deeper into the charity's funds. And, just when he needed an undertaker, his sister-in-law popped up like an angel saying her boss was seeking investors who wanted to quadruple their money overnight.

"Marcia Grimes?" queries Bliss, quickly catching on. "Oh no! Not Greg Grimes's brother?"

"The very same. He's been under suspicion for a couple of months. Arrested in his office yesterday, five million quid short. We gave him bail and he decided to skip — permanently."

"Oh my God!" breathes Bliss, thinking of the potter.

"That poor bloke. First his wife. Then his daughter and his hand in quick succession. Now his brother. Has anyone told him?"

"I don't think so," replies Richards. "Officially no one knows where he and his wife are. Perhaps you would do the honours."

"That's not an honour. I was hoping to get away from that down here," he moans, thinking: Marcia Grimes, you have a lot to answer for.

Putting down the handset he finally realizes why Richards had been so concerned about him giving away his location, or information, over the phone. The digital recording of all calls to Scotland Yard is a godsend to snoopy coppers and admin clerks, and if Grimes had got wind someone was chasing Johnson and the missing money, he could have run.

Drifting thoughtfully to the balcony he notes that the complexion of everything has changed. The sky has changed. Though still cloudless, the blue has lost its softness and has taken on a dark intensity. The atmosphere has sharpened and bristles with an electric dryness. Île Sainte-Marguerite stands out so crisply in the crackly clear air that it has sprung into the foreground and now sits just off the château's promontory. The beach-front flags salute stiffly, palm fronds wave frenetically, and there is a vibrancy in the water as the tops of waves are whipped into an invigorating spray that enlivens the beachcombers.

So it wasn't a put-up job, he laughs to himself. And all the time you thought you were just an inconvenient pimple on Richards's backside. No wonder he wouldn't tell you why they wanted Johnson tracked. The media and the loony left would have a field day if they discovered someone had picked the purses of the widows of Her

Majesty's Grand Metropolitan Police Force — purveyors of policing to the royal personage, and the nation's capital, since 1827.

Wandering to the kitchen table, where the pot shards still lay scattered, he procrastinates by piecing fragments together as he puzzles over why Greg Grimes might have made a haul of pseudo-Romano amphorae, and why someone had wrecked them. But a bigger picture starts to come together in his mind as he picks at the shards, and Marcia Grimes's mug shot is front and centre. Disenchanted with her husband, she skips off to Johnson with a huge dowry collected from friends, family, and the grieving widows of Scotland Yard. No wonder she claimed there was no such thing as a free fuck. But if she had paid dearly for sex, most of the money had come from the pockets and purses of others.

None of the pottery shards appear to fit, either together or into the bigger picture, so he drops them and thoughtfully examines the grubby Brubeck T-shirt. How the hell am I going to break the news about his brother to him? he worries, as he stares at the old shirt and imagines Grimes wearing it in the underground bunker as he sweated over the large wine jars.

"Take Five" was recorded in 1959, his CD cover tells him, and he listens to the classic tune over and over as he peers at the faded logo and tries to fit it into the picture. "More than forty years," he muses, unsurprised, knowing that lurking in the bottom of his own wardrobe are similarly washed-out garments screaming "Beatles" and "Stones."

The dampness and dirt of the château's underground have left their mark, he realizes, but so has something darker — much darker.

Ten minutes later he's in Daisy's office with the door shut and the outline of a sketch in his mind as he holds the shirt accusingly in front of her face. "You recognized it," he says, gloves off.

"No."

"Daisy — please don't lie."

"I no lie —" she starts, but he stops her with a policeman's cautionary look and a tone of admonishment. "Daisy ..."

Cornered, she blabs, "OK. I tell you. I zhink maybe it was zhe shirt Roland was wearing the day we went to zhe château — but it is thirty years." Then she bursts into tears at the memory.

Whether it is pain or relief, Bliss has no way of knowing, and he waits until she has calmed before showing her the large semicircular stain of dried blood on the shirt's hem. "Do you know what this is?"

Her fear-filled eyes suggest she has a fairly good idea.

"So how did he die? Do you know?"

Nodding, she explains the little she knows. That she followed Roland into the tunnel and they found candles and matches amid some junk left by squatters near the entrance. Reluctantly, and petrified, she was dragged by peer pressure through the German bunker and on to the château's sub-basement, but when Roland mounted the steps towards the trap door she stalled. To go further, into the building itself, was sacrilegious and questioned the very canons of her mother's and grandmother's faith. She was already agnostic in her beliefs of the château's legend, but she knew in her heart that raising the trap door would reveal the unpalatable truth. Unwilling to deal with the ramifications of atheism in a deeply religious household, she ran. Two days later Roland's body washed ashore further along the beach.

"He was dead," she says, her eyes fixed darkly on the shirt, then she cheers herself a touch as she explains, "In France we say zhat he *bouffe les pissenlits par la racine.* Zhat means he is eating dandelions, roots first."

"That makes sense," agrees Bliss. "But do you know what had happened to him?"

"Zhey say he'd been stabbed to death," she says, adding quietly, "Some people say his *zizi* was cut off."

"His *zizi*," Bliss echoes, but doesn't bother to solicit a translation, asking instead, "And you never told anyone what happened that day?"

"No — never. You are zhe only person who knows. But I did tell one person zhat maybe I saw Roland swimming out to zhe *promontoire* zhat day. Zhat perhaps he go to zhe château."

"Who did you tell?"

"Jacques."

"Jacques the fisherman at L'Escale?"

"He is not *un pêcheur*," she laughs. "He is *un flic* — a detective like you. Zhat is why I zhink you talk to him."

"No. I had no idea he was a cop. And he thinks I'm a writer."

"He is under zhe covers like you. Zhat is why he says he is *un pêcheur*."

"Oh, I see," he says, adding, "But I thought you didn't like him."

"I don't. He is *un phallocrate* — a dirty chauvinist pig. He always wanted me to go with him when we were at school, but I say no. Zhen, when he becomes a policeman, I zhink I should tell him about Roland swimming to zhe château."

"What did he do?"

"He say he find nothing at zhe château. But it is perhaps two years after it happened zhat I tell him."

"But you didn't tell anyone you'd been in the château with him."

"No. I never tell," she says, and for more than thirty years the château had kept the secret with her.

"I still don't understand why you didn't tell anyone at the time it happened."

"I was young. I was scared," she replies, though doesn't distinguish between the fear of pregnancy, the risk of bringing down an entire religion, or even apprehension of being accused of killing the boy.

It's August the sixteenth. Summer has officially ended, though no one has told the sun. But the heat of excitement has gone, and Bliss slowly wanders along the harbour front, listening to his Walkman playing Brubeck's "All by Myself" as he summons the fortitude to inform Greg Grimes of his brother's death. The serious holidaymakers are winding down, although the less affluent, together with the physically and geographically challenged, will remain for a few more weeks. The stars of summer have moored their yachts, locked their villas, and jetted home for a few weeks of rest before hitting the ski slopes. Even the cut-rate backpackers are on the move — further south with the sun or north into the approaching snows.

The wind picks up a few notches as he walks the harbour side, catching a wheeled rack of wetsuits and water skis by surprise, threatening to dump the whole lot off the quay into the Mediterranean.

"*Merde*," shouts the rental equipment's owner, struggling to hang onto the wind-borne rack as it races to the edge. Rushing to his aid, Bliss grapples with the stand and wrestles it to the ground.

"*Merci. Merci, Monsieur*," mutters the puffed-out old man in thanks.

Boats and buoys bob furiously as they struggle against their moorings, and the sea darkens to indigo while a small powerboat drags its anchor across the bay. Cumulous clouds billow over the alps behind him, but the sun is in the south and still shines on the sea where sailboarders skim the surface like demented water-boat-men. A couple of kite-boarders soar off into the air and fly across the bay in the steady wind. The serious sail-boats are out today as well — enough wind for the first time in two months. The southwesterly sirocco playfully plucks out the gay spinnakers of a hundred yachts and sends them scooting off to Nice and Monte Carlo, and, with luck, will speed them back, close-hauled under a jib.

"It's a good day for a sail," says Bliss to a salty looking character sitting on the quay in front of L'Offshore Club reading *The Times*.

"Been a terrible summer," complains the wine-gutted greybeard in a captain's shirt. "Not enough wind to whip up a skirt," he adds, laughing wildly, then roars at what is, for him, another gem. "Blow the man down — ha, ha, ha."

A leaf, exhausted by the summer's heat and flogged by the wind, falls from a plane tree and lands on Bliss's table as he stops for a whisky at L'Escale, on his way to break the bad news to Grimes. He looks up in time to see Angeline miss her footing with a heavily laden tray, then slip off the edge of the curb into the path of a teenager's open-topped Mercedes. Saving her life with a desperate left-handed shove on the windshield, she is still off balance and ends up deftly passing her tray to the startled front-seat passenger as she fights to stay upright.

"*Espèce de salaud* — you bastard!" she screams as the driver slams his foot on the throttle and heads off with enough sundaes and cocktails for a beach party.

"*Merde*," she mutters, stomping back to the bar for replacements.

One whisky may not be enough, Bliss decides, with his mind on the hospital in Cannes where Grimes waits unsuspectingly, and he rattles through similarly taxing situations in his mind trying to figure out the easiest way of breaking the news. It only takes a minute or so to decide his best option is to pray a relative or friend may have already phoned. Telling a recovering amputee his brother is dead is one thing, but who wants to hear that his sibling popped open his skull with a shotgun because he'd been caught with his hand in a hundred widows' purses?

Maybe I should ask Daisy to come with me, he thinks, realizing Grimes might need comforting and is unlikely to want his wife sticking around once he knows she was the one who loaded his brother's gun. But Daisy has her own problems — twenty-four hours to tell the local police what she knows of the death of Roland or he'll do it for her.

"Oh well. Here goes," he says, slugging down the second Scotch as the taxi Angeline summoned for him pulls up outside the bar. The imprint of the Harley Davidson stands out clearly on the front wing of the cab, although the damage is unremarkable in a land where everyone drives by touch. "Tut-tut," says Bliss as he starts to climb in, then stops in surprise as he spots the *Sea-Quester* nosing its way into the harbour. "Thank Christ," he mutters, and heads off to the hospital with a packed agenda.

Marcia is at her husband's bedside, stroking his good hand and staring lovingly into his eyes, when Bliss arrives. "Hello, Inspector," she gabbles. "Greg's feeling a lot better today, aren't you, dear?"

He won't be in a moment, Bliss thinks, as he put on a funeral mien and asks Marcia if she would leave them for ten minutes.

"No. It's all right, Inspector. Anything you have to say to me, you can tell my wife," Grimes replies with a smile in her direction.

"Just give us a few minutes please," he repeats to Marcia forcefully.

"I'll stay," she starts, trying to hang on, when Bliss grasps her elbow and hisses in her ear, "I said, leave."

One look at Bliss's face warns her that whatever is coming is unlikely to bolster the relationship she's been rebuilding for the past few days, but she covers her apprehension with a parting smile. "Won't be long, dear."

Greg does not take the death of his brother Gordon any better than Bliss anticipated. The cause of the suicide, and the fact that Johnson seems to be bent on destroying his entire family, has him fighting to get out of bed. Holding him down, Bliss promises they are doing whatever they can — primarily recovering the widows' and orphans' five million pounds — although he acknowledges that anything he does won't help Grimes get his wife, daughter, brother, and livelihood back.

With Grimes bent on vengeance, Bliss seizes the opportunity to quiz him over the amphorae in the château and learns the potter has been fascinated with Roman ceramics from his childhood. Intrigued by the strength and sophistication of a design that enabled them to survive unscathed for two thousand years, he had spent most of his career toiling to emulate the work of the ancients until he could make exact replicas. It was then that Marcia told her employer, Morgan Johnson, whose eyes lit up at the prospect of a fortune. Marcia, seeing a way out of their continual impecuniousness, badgered and nagged him for months to make amphorae that Johnson could sell until one day she apparently gave up. Eventually he discovered she'd copied his research material and given it to Johnson. He threw her out and she threw herself at Johnson. Later he found that she was paying her rent by fundraising from friends and relatives, although he had no idea she'd got her hooks into his brother, Gordon.

"He was hardly likely to tell you he was investing the widows' mites in your wife's boyfriend's bent business," Bliss tells him, before enquiring about the amphorae in the château's tunnel.

"A man can only take so much, Inspector, and Morgan fucking Johnson had taken pretty much everything. So I was taking some of it back."

"And he caught you smashing the pots —"

"It was pitch black," Grimes cuts in, and Bliss's "You should go to the local police" has him shaking his head.

"Not until I can get Natalia away from him." Both men look at the bandaged stump and understand the implication.

"By the way," Bliss says, as he turns to open the door. "Have you ever owned a Dave Brubeck T-shirt?"

Catching Marcia in the hallway, Bliss drags her roughly outside and spins on her, pulling no punches as he tells her about her brother-in-law's brains being pulped.

"Morgan was going to give the money back — he promised," she protests.

"Yeah. Neatly parcelled with Greg's hand and the the remnants of Natalia."

"I told you. He had nothing to do with that."

"Who did, then?"

"I've no idea."

"Wait a minute," he calls, but she storms off.

Less than an hour later Bliss is on the phone to Richards, gaining permission to charter a yacht.

"Just don't go mad," Richards implores, limiting his personal liability.

Shopping for the boat is easier than Bliss expected.

"The season is finished," yawns the young Englishwoman in the shipbroker's office in St-Juan. "Take your pick," she says, uninterestedly sweeping her hand over a wall of flattering photos as she polishes a nail. "Most of them are available."

The sense of power is almost overwhelming as Bliss gapes at the array of yachts. In the pictures the vessels all frolic on a pancake sea and beam in the sun, but whether they can match Johnson's yacht, he has no clue. So, turning to face the harbour, he points to the *Sea-Quester* and puts his hand in his pocket for his credit card. "I'd like something similar to that — for a week to start?"

Tired of dealing with a summer season of fender kickers, the woman senses seriousness and smartens herself up. "Yes, Sir — I have exactly what you're looking for, and you've hit the market at precisely the right time."

You should be flogging real estate or cars, he thinks, watching her plump herself up and preen her face into a selling mode.

A few minutes later, after a couple of phone calls, she waltzes him down the quayside, past the *Sea-Quester,* to a similar-sized yacht.

"She's a little under forty metres," the familiar-faced captain explains, the three-day-old copy of *The Times* neatly stowed under his arm, as he straightens himself up and meets them on the gangway. "Come aboard, Mr. ...?"

"Smith," says Bliss, thinking, this is definitely going on the credit card. "John Smith."

"Nice to meet you again, Mr. Smith," greets the captain. "So. Let's show you around the *Mystère*."

"That's an interesting name," comments Bliss, stepping onto the teak deck.

"It's a mystery to me," the old man roars.

"It'll do nicely," says Bliss ten minutes later as they sit in the lounge over a cognac, but the sales pitch isn't quite over as Susan sums up, "She's a particularly fine vessel — a little snug for ten, perhaps."

"Snug," echoes Bliss, still reeling from the opulent sights of gold-plated staterooms and bathrooms that would accommodate fifty at a squeeze, and a hundred at a push. "And the price?" he asks, without particular concern.

"That's where you are in luck," Susan explains, as the captain tactfully excuses himself with the bottle of brandy. "The bare-boat charter is just twelve thousand dollars, American, plus expenses, of course."

"Sounds reasonable," he says, then asks, "Expenses?"

"Fuel, berthing fees, all the usual things, plus food, of course."

"Of course — but I won't need a lot of food."

She laughs, "You have to feed your crew, Mr. Smith. This isn't a slave ship."

"No. Right," he says, pulling out his credit card, "So, how much?"

Sitting at L'Escale a little later, he takes out his cell-phone, takes a deep breath, and calls Richards.

"I got that quote for you, Guv," he says, his eye on the *Sea-Quester* across the harbour.

"Just go ahead," Richards says, then senses something amiss. "How much?"

Bliss laughs; he can't help it. The twelve thousand dollars, which at first he thought was for the week, was per day. The captain and five crew would swallow another thousand, and the cost of fuel made him gag — thirty dollars a mile if he didn't push it. "I can probably do it on about a hundred and five thousand dollars a week, Guv."

"What's that in English?" asks Richards, not immediately concerned.

"About eighty thousand quid."

"Bloody hell! Bliss — I said rent it. Don't buy it."

"Quite, Sir," he chuckles. "That's what I thought."

"I'll get back to you," Richards says, telling him to do his best to keep tabs on Johnson in the meantime. "The commissioner's still deciding what to do in light of Gordon Grimes's death."

I bet he is, thinks Bliss, as he orders his usual glass of wine from Angeline. Since the theft of her tray, Angeline has adopted a more determined approach, and he watches, fascinated, as she steps smartly into the road, holding both hands high and walking like a hostage. It seems to work as confused motorists slide to a halt and look to see if someone's pointing a gun at her back.

The promenade is cheerless without the bustle of the high-season throngs, and the glum-faced trickle of hoteliers assembling for their end-of-season inquest seem even more dispirited than usual.

All twelve, together with the black-robed priest, show up by eight o'clock. But now they have time — the ten-week tornado of summer is winding down. Their rooms are half empty and toilets unblocked. Like the Provençal lavender farmers, their harvest is almost over for the year, and, just like the farmers, their crop will never fulfill their expectations: never enough clients, never enough staff, never enough ancillary sales. "*Merde* — they snacked all day in the snack bars and beach cafés and raided the supermarkets," they'll complain, running their eyes down the meagre restaurant takings.

Half expecting Hugh and Mavis to turn up, despite the fact that their plane left the previous day, Bliss is focussing on the empty-handed stragglers strolling by when his ears prick up.

"Are the hoteliers talking about the potter?" he asks Angeline as she bustles by.

"*Oui*," she says. "Some of them say they will buy special ovens next year and make money — to cook the pots."

"Typical," he mutters, having concluded from the general condition of the French houses that the only things that were ever fixed were those that weren't broken, and he shakes his head at a nation of techno-savvy people unable to unblock a toilet — "*Merde*."

Where's Jacques? he wonders, scanning the length of the promenade, expecting him to appear to gloat over the arrival of the sirocco — but Daisy has pleaded with Bliss to say nothing about Roland until she's had time to decide what to do. "Twenty-four hours," he told her, though he felt sorry for her, knowing how hard it would be for her to admit to Jacques, of all people, that she had lied by her silence.

Bliss looks up to find his fraternal brother approaching.

"Ah, Jacques," he greets warmly, "you were right about the sirocco."

"But of course, Monsieur. I am French. Being right is *mon forte*. And now *le pounant* — the warm westerly wind — will bring an end to zhe *tempêtes* of summer."

"I'm glad the tempests are over," laughs Bliss, going on to say, "But I understand we have something in common."

Jacques's reply falls somewhere between question and answer. "We do."

"*Oui*. I too am a fisherman," teases Bliss, but Jacques catches on immediately.

"But of course ... you are a policeman. The first time I saw you I say to myself, Jacques, zhat man Brubeck, he has *le nez fin* — zhe good nose — and *les écrase-merde* — zhe big feet — of a policeman. Zhen I say to you, zhe way you look, always watching, you see everyone and everything. I am right, *n'est-ce pas*?"

"*Oui*. You are right, Jacques," laughs Bliss, "but it's Burbeck, not Brubeck." Then he confides, "I'll tell you a secret, though. I don't usually work undercover."

"I can tell."

"But … the hand in the water?" enquires Bliss, suddenly remembering Jacques's apparent indifference to the event. "You said nothing to the gendarmes."

"*Oui.*"

"Why?"

"Zhat is how I know zhat you do not usually work under zhe covers like me. I watch, but it is not my case. *J'ai d'autres chats à fouetter,*" he carries on. "As you say … I have other cats to whip. And now, if you will excuse me, *Monsieur l'Inspecteur*, I have zhe little business to attend. *À bientôt, mon ami.*"

The question "How did you know my rank?" barely passes Bliss's lips as Jacques le Policier disappears from sight.

"Well, I'm damned," Bliss mutters, then casually dumps the contents of the table's glass ashtray into his pocket and heads for his apartment.

chapter sixteen

The black limousine in the driveway, driven by a sumo wrestler in chauffeur's uniform, warns Bliss something is happening in Johnson's ground-floor apartment. Hearing nothing at the door he races up to his balcony and looks over in time to see the caged boy's dog being used in a tug of war in the garden below.

"Give me the fucking thing, Nathaniel," hisses Johnson, tugging roughly at the Spaniel's hind-quarters, as his wife and the young man grapple with the yelping creature's front end.

"Leave him alone," cries the distraught owner, and Johnson's wife joins in, screaming, "Morgan, don't — please don't."

"Give it over," orders Johnson, yanking until the animal squeals. "I've had enough of this crap."

Oh, *merde*! thinks Bliss, but can't see what to do without becoming embroiled in the ruckus.

"I'm an effin' laughingstock," beefs Johnson as he keeps up the pressure. "What do you think people are saying? I hear your boy lives in a cage with an effin' dog. Look at him — long-haired fucking ponce."

"Morgan ... the neighbours," warns his wife.

"Bollocks to the neighbours. If they don't like it they can effin' move. Now give me the damn dog."

"Dad, don't," yells the young man, but Johnson tears the animal out of his son's hands, whips its head angrily against the trunk of the lemon tree, and tosses it onto the lawn, where it lands as limp as a wet rag.

Screaming hysterically, the young man scrabbles across the lawn, gathers up the lifeless animal, and curls into a sobbing ball. "Pooh-pooh," he cries. "What have you done to my Pooh-pooh?"

"Oh, shit," mutters Bliss.

"Stupid fucking kid," sneers Johnson, but his wife turns on him. "It was your fault. You abandoned him. All he needed was a proper father, not some piece of shit ..."

Johnson isn't listening. Shoving her forcefully to the ground he heads for the apartment's kitchen door and starts wrestling with the cage.

With the distraught young man still keening over his dog, his mother picks herself up and flies to the kitchen. The first slap sends Bliss running. Grabbing the workman's overall he is out of the apartment and down the hibiscus-lined lane to the port in seconds. I'll never get a better chance of catching Natalia on her own, he thinks, praying the dog will be the only fatality in the apartment.

The *Sea-Quester* sits grandly in the centre of the quay, lording it over less inflated craft on either side. The brilliant moonlight, along with the festive strings of quayside illuminations, picks out the impressive vessel and lights Bliss's way up the gangway. His workman's overalls give him some cover. *Just come to see if Mr. Johnson needs any painting done, mate*, he has on his lips, though it's not needed as he swings through the yacht's unguarded and deserted main deck from stern to stem. The darkness of the upper deck tells him not to bother, so he takes a companionway down from the bridge to the fore-cabins.

"Ahoy there," he calls hesitantly as he faces a number of cabin doors in the dim light. "Anybody aboard?"

A scuffling so slight it might have been imagined has him half-expecting one of the doors to crash open and the limousine driver's brother to flatten him for trespassing.

"Empty," he mouths, gingerly peeking into cabin after cabin before heading back up to the bridge. The tour of the charter boat earlier has turned into a godsend as he easily charts the ladder to the engine room and navigates his way past the giant powerhouses to the aft hold.

"Bingo!" he breathes, finding an Aladdin's cave of neo-Romano amphorae. Several of the giant double-handed wine jars with distinct, though clearly impractical, sharply pointed bottoms stand in specially constructed frames. A heavy fire extinguisher becomes a weapon, and in seconds Bliss shoves handfuls of shards into his pockets and sets off to search the rest of the vessel.

"Natalia," he calls, urgently tapping on one of the aft stateroom doors. "Come on," he murmurs, concerned Johnson and his gorilla may return at any moment.

"Natalia." He tries another door, but hears no answer. With a gentle shove he peeps in. The luxurious cabin, though well slept in, is empty, and he is about to close the door when he spies a soft light from an adjacent room.

"Hello," he calls, poking his head around the door, and finds a naked young woman flaked out in a gold-plated bathtub.

"Hello," she replies vacuously. "What's your name?"

The lack of water doesn't seem to concern her, but Bliss turns quickly and grabs a robe from the floor.

"I love to swim in gold," she croons, as she writhes sensuously and plays her hands over her body. "Do you?"

"I've never tried," he admits, offering her the robe. "But I guess you're Natalia Grimes."

Rising inquisitively to sit, she pushes the robe away, grasps his wrist and urges lasciviously, "Why don't you join me, then?"

Like mother, like daughter, he thinks, realizing Marcia had probably been just as stunning when she was eighteen. "Come on, get dressed. Your dad wants to see you," he says, keeping his eyes on her face.

"I don't think Morgan would like that," she mutters, climbing out and walking unashamedly to the bedroom.

"Please put some clothes on," he pleads, but she turns and poses statuesquely.

"What are you — a fag or something? Don't you think I've got a good body? Morgan does."

"Natalia, I don't have time for this," he says angrily. "Now put something on and come with me."

"I'd love to come with you," she drools, draping herself around him and reaching for his groin, "but Morgan would kill me."

Forcefully grabbing her wrists, he peels her off and holds her at arm's length. "You asked for it," he says, then puts her in the picture — straight — no mincing around: her father's disfigurement; her mother's involvement; her uncle's death. He finishes with a graphic account of Morgan splatting a little dog's head against a tree trunk.

"Oh! The poor dog," she whines, as if that's her biggest concern.

"Come on," he says, letting go of her wrists and holding out the bathrobe, but she shakes him off and slumps to the bed. "I can't.... Morgan will kill me."

"He'll kill you if you stay here."

"Why?" she asks. "I always give him what he wants."

A movement on the aft deck above them alerts Bliss to someone boarding.

"Quick," he implores. "Please come, Natalia."

Splaying herself provocatively across the bed she mocks, "Why don't you take me?"

The girl's not particularly heavy, he judges, and considers forcefully bundling her into the bedclothes and carrying her off. Will she scream or put up a fight? he is wondering, when the shuffling of heavy footsteps signifies some sort of struggle going on above them and he decides to retreat.

"Don't say I didn't warn you," he cautions, as he grabs a sharp-ended metal comb off the dressing table and makes for the companionway. But he's trapped. A full-scale war is raging on the main deck at the top of the stairs. Johnson and his gorilla are struggling with the young man while fighting off his mother.

Worrying that the bodyguard may be the surgeon who operated on Grimes, Bliss doesn't fancy being found anywhere near Johnson's naked girlfriend, but his only option is the escape hatch into the engine room. Squeezing himself into a dark corner behind a generator he waits for the commotion to die down.

The fleeting notion of snatching Natalia and carrying her ashore has him questioning his sanity, and he decides he'll be a winner if he manages to escape with his own life, let alone hers.

As the fuss in the passageway above subsides, Bliss stealthily arms himself with a heavy wrench and stands ready to pounce.

This is not fun, he thinks, and curses himself for getting caught up in something that is little more than a massive domestic debacle.

Approaching footsteps force him deep against the bulkhead, and he holds his breath as the hatch flies open.

"Where are you?" demands a distinctly English voice.

Natalia's told him, he thinks, as he readies to strike.

"I know you're there," the searcher claims, but he's playing a master and Bliss stays silent.

Apparently satisfied, Johnson shuts the hatch, and Bliss listens to the retreating footsteps with a deep breath and decreasing pulse, but, trapped below decks until Johnson and his goon are safely tucked in their bunks, he settles down to wait. Ten minutes later he's shaken rigid as the port engine bursts to life.

"Shit!" he swears, realizing what it means, and moments later the second engine fires up.

The engine room is alive with sound, and the air vibrates as the propeller shafts start to spin. "I've got to get out of here," he says to himself and heads for an escape ladder leading to a deck hatch. A swaying motion tells him the vessel is inching out of its berth as he struggles to unlatch the storm-proof catches, but the prospect of being taken for a one-way ride by a bunch of psychos urges him on. Fighting to undo the resilient fasteners he feels the bow starting to rise as the boat heads towards the port entrance. He doesn't relish the idea of swimming far in the dark waters, although he doesn't fancy swimming in the harbour, either. *You can't swim here — you can only go through the motions*, some enviro-activist had spray-painted along part of the harbour wall, and Bliss has seen hard evidence several times.

Caught by the wind, the hatch flies out of his hand, and he leaps onto the side deck just as the vessel rounds the harbour light and throttles out to sea. With barely a thought to the consequences he leaps over the rail, and as the boat rips through the narrow harbour entrance he is immediately swamped by the vessel's burgeoning wake. The wet clothes and pottery-filled pockets instantly drag him under. Disorientated in the dark water, he takes several seconds to reach the surface, and then the wind-whipped waves in the bay dunk him repeatedly as he fights to stay afloat. It's the weight of the workman's overall, he realizes, and, after struggling to free himself, he finally jettisons it in relief. A millisecond later, as he takes his first good breath, he remembers the amphorae shards and dives frantically to retrieve the sodden clothing and salvage his find.

Half an hour later he's back in the apartment's garden surveying the aftermath of Johnson's rampage. The carcass of the dead dog has taken the place of the fallen lemon, and the dull, sightless eyes accuse him of fatal procrastination. You should have done something to prevent this, the pathetic sight proclaims, and his spirits sink with the realization that if Natalia Grimes's naked body washes up on a beach one day soon he will be responsible for that, as well.

It's nearly midnight by the time he's tamped down the earth and re-turfed the mound under the lemon tree.

Stuffing the workman's trowel back in his tool bag, with the thought that the previous owner might have gagged at the uses to which his faithful servant has been put, he takes the elevator back to his apartment and phones Daisy as he pours himself another drink.

"I wasn't asleep," she assures him, though the background silence and drowsy huskiness in her voice suggest otherwise. "Would you like to come around and *voir mes estampes japonaises*?" she asks when he says he needs to see her.

"So that's what you call etchings, is it?" he laughs, having guessed one or other of them would bring the topic up eventually. "I'm sure your Japanese prints are lovely, Daisy, but I think L'Offshore Club would be more sensible."

"You no like me," she purrs.

"I like you very much," he starts, and is beginning to wonder why he's spent two months staving off a relationship. But he knows why, knows he's avoiding the inevitability of death by distance. Absence makes the heart grow crazy, he says to himself, in memory of recent scars, and can only repeat, "It wouldn't be sensible. I have to go home soon."

"OK, I come," Daisy concedes, and he puts down the phone, still wondering what's holding him back.

An attractive lone woman in a tight skirt sits quietly smoking on the quayside outside L'Offshore Club. Her eyes trail him hopefully as he passes, and she blows a message in a ring of smoke. He reads the message, answers "No thanks" with a subtle head shake, and saunters into the bar to wait for Daisy.

A sixty-year-old bopper with an eighteen-year-old's hairstyle, supercharged on Médoc or Merlot, dances with himself, hoping his Hawaiian shirt and glitter-framed Elton John glasses will attract attention. "Guantanamera, gua-ji-ra Guantanamera," he sings, grabbing a microphone and joining in with the animated keyboard player, and Bliss feels like strangling them both.

The captain of the charter yacht drunkenly waves him over, laughing. "Smith old son — come an' 'ave a tot."

Pretending not to hear, Bliss finds a quiet corner and watches a couple in their seventies swing into action as the music changes to that of their childhood. "In the mood," chants the keyboard player, but their bodies give out after a few turns. "Guantanamera" — again! Now everyone dances. The charter yacht captain grabs an unsuspecting sixty-year-old woman and grinds himself into her as he throws her around the floor. Three of her friends, all in their sixties, golden oldies with naturally white hair and unnaturally white teeth, twist and jive to the music of their youth, and an aged great-grandmother chats unconcernedly on her cellphone as she shuffles around the small dance floor.

One man in his nineties is eking out his last days, and his shoes, by dancing at quarter speed. Then a flouncy forty-year-old takes his hands and his limbs are juiced with adrenalin. "It'll kill him," worries one of the woman's friends. "At least he'll go out happy," says another.

Finding something bizarre about a bunch of white-haired French grannies twisting and jiving to the hits of the sixties, Bliss is wondering if headbangers and rappers will still be pounding to their music when they're retired, as Daisy arrives, head down, worrying, "I've haven't told Jacques about Roland yet."

Bliss lets her off with a *bof*. "It doesn't matter," he says, "I think you're probably right. It wouldn't make any difference. But what about your mother? Have you told her about the château?"

"I try," she says, perking up, though her reply suggests failure. "*Maman* says I must not tell *Grand-maman*. She says zhat I must believe."

"This is ridiculous," he starts, annoyed that so many otherwise sensible people could be caught up in the theological claptrap of blind faith — chanting in unison, "It must be true; zhere is no evidence against it."

"It doesn't matter," he says, winding himself back down. "I'm going to get my book published anyway."

"What book?" she enquires, assuming his scribbling had been purely for aesthetic purposes.

"This one," he declares, revealing his nearly completed manuscript, "'The Truth Behind the Mask.' But I still have to go back to the château again."

Her face falls. "Oh *non*."

"*Mais oui*," he says, then relates the heartrending story of the lovesick *amoureux* and his desperate plan to impress the object of his desire with his gift of the château and his masochistic immolation in the *castel*.

"Zhat is so romantic," she says with a catch in her voice, finding herself caught up in the tale. "But why you go back?"

"Because I have to find out who he was."

"Roger," she cries delightedly. "His name must be Roger. Zhat is why it is called Le Château Roger."

"That's what I suspect. But Roger who?" he questions, before explaining that whoever splashed out a fortune to build the love eyrie would want to make sure his paramour was in no doubt as to his identity. "Did you notice the coat of arms in each of the rooms, over the fireplaces?" he asks.

Daisy's blank face suggests she's in the dark, so he sketches an example.

"Ah, *les armoiries*," she exclaims in comprehension, though doesn't recall seeing any of the stuccoes.

"I didn't take much notice, either," he admits, recalling that they both had other things on their minds at the time, although he does picture rampant lions and other heraldic beasts. "But now I think the arms are probably the family crests, and I want to take photographs and make drawings. I know a historian who should be able to identify them."

"I come," says Daisy, suddenly energized by the prospect of being a party to the unearthing of history.

Thank God there's an hour's time difference, Bliss thinks, as he wakes just before ten the following morning to put Richards in the picture.

"He's gone again, Guv," he says, stretching in the stark sunlight on the balcony while checking the empty berth where the *Sea-Quester* was the night before.

"I don't know what to suggest," says Richards lamely, and Bliss imagines him and the rest of the senior brass moribund, sitting around with their metaphorical fingers up their bums, scared of pointing blame in case someone pulls out a finger to point back.

"Somebody's going to have to explain this to the Home Secretary and the Charities Commissioner," bleats Richards, well aware of the political discomfiture of admitting that more than thirty thousand policemen had apparently been asleep on the job when Gordon Grimes had robbed the graves of their fallen. "And I wouldn't mind betting questions will be asked in the House."

"Oops," says Bliss, smiling to himself.

"Technically Johnson hasn't broken any U.K. laws," Richards continues. "Apparently people flung their piggy banks at him 'cos he looked like a safe bet, and he's frittered it away without giving them any returns."

"He should have been a stockbroker," muses Bliss, getting a grunt of agreement from Richards, then continues half-heartedly, "The French could probably nick him for cruelty to animals."

"That won't do the widows a lot of good," gripes Richards.

"What about doing him for obtaining money by deception for the importation and sale of counterfeit Roman pottery?" queries Bliss, as if he's known the answer all along. "Presumably Grimes doled out the widows' funds on the assumption the investments were being used lawfully."

"Counterfeit pottery?"

"That's the treasure," he explains, then relates the story he's pieced together from Marcia and her husband.

"OK," says Richards, brightening, "but how can we prove it?"

I want a medal for this, thinks Bliss, gloating as he says, "I actually have some of the evidence in my hand right now."

Daisy, relieved of her thirty-year burden, is waiting for him in her office with bouncy anticipation, and it dawns on him that prior to their previous visit she may have attributed Roland's murder to the ghostly freedom fighters still inhabiting the Hades under the château.

"Courier first," he says, and he drops off a package addressed to Richards before they take the hill to the hole in the fence.

The custom's declaration stating "pottery" takes the eye of the FedEx clerk, a man well used to shipping priceless ceramics from the world's pottery capital. "*Fragile?*" he queries.

"*Non,*" laughs Bliss, but doesn't have the words to explain he is shipping a box of old earthenware chips. The value also confounds him, especially as some of the pieces nearly cost him his life.

The tangled undergrowth surrounding the old building no longer provides cover for snarling *chiens méchants*, although the risk of running into a patrolling security guard still exists.

"It looks so innocent, doesn't it?" Bliss sneers contemptuously as he photographs the château's sorry face, its windows shuttered in shame, pillars bowing under the weight of the oppressive canopies. "You have a lot to answer for," he adds, his thoughts turning to the man in the iron mask, the pre-war Jewish family, the *résistance* fighters, Roland, and Greg Grimes. And the fallen stone statues, burying their faces into the scrub of neglected lawns, take on greater significance as he scouts around for evidence. Then Daisy's anguished cry sends him running.

A line of mounds, bordered by sun-blanched beach pebbles, fills a clearing in the woods, and he bends over her as she kneels by one marked with her grandfather's name. "Someone must come here," he tells her, noting the graves are weed-free.

"*Grandmère*," she whispers, barely able to admit it to herself.

"What do you mean?" he starts, but she holds up a miniature picture frame with a photo of a white-haired woman. "*Bon anniversaire, mon cher Georges*," her grandmother had written across the print.

"She knows," Daisy breathes, holding back the tears.

From the condition of the frame Bliss guesses she's known for a while, and he now has a fairly good idea why she'd scuttled off to her room when the subject came up. "She just wanted to protect you and your mother," he suggests, comforting her with a gentle hand on her shoulder.

Sitting on the promenade as he waits for Daisy to return from her mothers', Bliss describes the château's heraldry in his manuscript with a feeling of relief that the revelations in his novel will not be as devastating as he'd worried. Although he can't help lamenting the fact that Daisy's mother was betrayed by her own mother — the High Priestess of her religion — and misled into carrying a cross for someone who would never be resurrected.

The days, though shorter, have an intensity about them. The hazy, lazy days were swept away with the scorching sirocco wind, leaving stark blue skies and searing sunlight that signal urgency to tardy beach-comers. But the beach has changed. Only the dregs remain. Society's leftovers — the fat and frumpy; single mothers with scruffy kids taking advantage of the bargain prices; single guys trolling the shoreline in one last desperate attempt to find some flotsam worth taking a run at.

Do you have to audition for peak season here, or is it only the beautiful who can afford the best holidays? Bliss muses, as he watches a woman with flabby cheeks bulging out of her swimsuit like a couple of saddlebags.

The beach café and *matelas* purveyors have packed up. Most of the holidaymakers have gone, but the weather has stayed. The tired summer blossoms have finally faded in the heat and shrivelled to fruit — *les fruits de la vendange* — grapevines weighed with bulging black and green bunches drooping from balconies and arbours. Oranges and lemons sharpen themselves up, as purple figs drop like hand grenades onto the pavement and turn to sticky puree underfoot. Cascades of golden palm fruit overhang sun-flushed pomegranates, and even tropical trespassers like bananas and coconuts ripen in the Mediterranean sun.

The old, the lame, and the locals have reclaimed the promenade, and a withered fisherman moans about the overbearing heat as he passes. "*Il fait trop chaud*," he complains, and Bliss nods in agreement. September may be approaching but the scorching sun-filled days continue — crisping the leaves of summer and bringing a glow to the fruits. But the young women are losing their lustre, and the waiters and store workers are tired and cranky. Ten weeks of fourteen-hour shifts, with headlights full on, have burnt them out. Now, with the end of the unremitting tornado of tourists in sight, many of them are coasting.

Dave Brubeck may still be playing "Summer Song" in his headphones, but Bliss realizes that summer is virtually at an end for him as well. As August slides rapidly downhill, his book is almost finished and the enigmas of the château and the boy in the cage are resolved.

L'homme au masque de fer will soon be unmasked and an international warrant will be issued for Johnson.

A short phone call gets him a booking to London, and he happily gives John Smith's credit card details.

"But you said your name was Bliss?" queries the pleasant-voiced travel agent.

"A friend's paying," he replies with a smile.

Now, with the flight confirmation number in his pocket, he has just over a week to pack and clear up a couple of loose ends. First, dinner with Daisy at La Scala — today is August 24th, Liberation Day.

chapter seventeen

Daisy has bounced back to her usual self by the time they arrive for the Libération dinner on the terrace of La Scala. Armed with the evidence from her grandfather's grave she confronted her grandmother, and was relieved to discover her revelation was greeted with no more alarm than if she'd announced St. Nicholas wasn't at the North Pole, either.

"Zhey all knew," she confesses sheepishly, and Bliss comes close to kissing her.

A busker playing "The Way You Look Tonight" à la Brubeck on the seafront beneath them leaves Bliss commenting, "You look very nice, Daisy."

Out in the Baie de Cannes, the azure sea and indigo sky are welded together with a darker seam of island green. Mackerel clouds redden progressively from carnation through carbuncle to claret and on to crimson as the sun sinks over L'Esterel mountains in the west, and just above the eastern horizon the con-trail of a jetliner streaks the sky like a flaming vermil-ion slash across blue velvet. In the warmth of the evening's light, Daisy's eyes take on a softness that gives Bliss the feeling that Japanese prints loom large in his future, but the ghosts of his past are already preparing an excuse in his mind.

A familiar figure approaching across the terrace has him slinking behind his menu. "Don't look —" he starts, but he's too late.

"*Bonsoir*, Monsieur Johnson," calls Daisy, then yelps as Bliss kicks her under the table.

"Don't forget — my name's Dave Burbeck," he hisses.

"Hello, Daisy," acknowledges Johnson, as he swings in their direction and Bliss rises with an out-stretched hand.

"Burbeck," he introduces himself, not trusting Daisy to get it right. "Dave Burbeck."

Johnson's eyes pinch questioningly as he's forced into a corner.

"Morgan Johnson," he responds, adding, "Nice to meet a fellow Brit." But his handshake is tentative, test-ing, probing: Do I know you?

Thank God he's never met me, thinks Bliss, but the intensity of Johnson's stare tells him he may be trying to match him against a collage of descriptions from his wife, his son, and Natalia.

"Monsieur Burbeck is an author," says Daisy, attempting to unfreeze the moment.

Johnson hesitates, looking for a way out. "Nice ..." he starts, then spots his dinner guests and ducks away. "Catch you later."

"Not if I catch you first," breathes Bliss, watching him go through a backslapping routine with a couple of barrel-chested primates at a nearby table. One of the gorillas looks his way, catches a rebuke from Johnson, and quickly inspects the sunset over Daisy's shoulder.

They're checking me out, thinks Bliss, pulling out his camera. "You look lovely Daisy," he says, and she beams as he frames her up. "Just a bit that way," he signals, keeping her on the fringe — Johnson and his cronies in shot.

"*Daavid* ..." she complains, realizing his aim is awry, but he gets off three good shots before Johnson's cohorts turn away.

"Sorry," he says, turning the spotlight back to her and speaking under the cover of the camera. "Don't look around. Just go to the *toilette* and see if you know the men Johnson is with."

"I zhink zhis is espionage," she whispers, touching his forearm conspiratorially as she rises.

The *Sea-Quester* must be out there somewhere, he thinks, straining unsuccessfully to pick out the yacht from the ring of navigation lights strung across the darkening bay. No wonder Johnson's ashore. I bet it's none too comfortable aboard with his lunatic son still pining over a dead cagemate, his frumpy wife bitching, and his air-headed floozie trying to squeeze him dry.

"Zhey are Corses," Daisy spits disdainfully as she returns to the table.

"You don't like them?"

"Zhey are *paysans* — peasants."

Peasantry is obviously not as poverty-stricken as it used to be, he thinks, eyeing Johnson's companions with their gold-plated suits, watches, and spectacles.

Although he admits to himself that the stocky characters have a certain ruddy earthiness in their features. "How do you know they're Corsican?"

"*L'accent*, of course. Zhey speak *français* —"

"I know," he says, cutting her off, "*comme une vache espagnole* — like a Spanish cow."

"How you know?" she asks with surprise.

"Jacques taught me."

Her face sours. "Oh."

"You don't like Jacques much either, do you?"

"*Bof!*" She shrugs, suggesting she can take him or leave him.

By the time Bliss checks in with Richards at ten the following morning, the package has arrived and is in the commander's hands.

A heavy package from the South of France was in itself sufficiently unusual to attract attention from the ordnance disposal officer stationed in the mailroom at the Yard, but it was the sender's name that really caught his eye. Bliss had considered using either of his aliases — Smith or Burbeck — but figured the parcel was more likely to be delivered to Richards intact if it bore his correct name.

"The bomb squad boys thought they'd got a live one," laughs Richards, "but it's on my desk now. It'll probably be a week or more before we get the results."

Bliss takes a deep breath. "That may be too late, Sir. I've booked my return flight."

The momentary silence heralds the obvious question. "When?"

Time enough to nail Edwards, thinks Bliss, with no intention of giving precise details. "Don't worry, Guv. I'll be back for the disciplinary hearing next Monday morning."

"You'd bloody better be."

"I don't care what you say ..." Bliss starts, already wound up, then pauses, exploring the back of his mind — what did he hear? "Pardon?"

"I said you'd better be back in time. You'll be on the carpet if you miss Chief Superintendent Edwards's disciplinary hearing."

Confusion makes Bliss wary. "I thought you were trying to keep me out of the way."

"We were. We were keeping you out of harm's way. Why? What did you think?"

Who's "we"? he wonders, but is still cagey. Richards has suddenly switched to a new script? "So. You're suggesting Edwards might have tried to nobble me."

"Don't put words in my mouth, Inspector," Richards warns, aware that the conversation is being recorded, though he adds with a laugh, "He's been frantic, pulling every string to find you. He even hired a PI to stake out your place."

"Why didn't you warn me?"

"I did. I told you a dozen times not to tell anyone where you were."

"No, I mean why didn't you warn me he was out to get me?"

"That'd be insubordination, Dave. You know that. Slagging off senior officers to their subordinates isn't good form."

"Yeah, Guv," he says, muttering *sotto voce*, "The bigger the lumps, the more they stick together."

"Anyway, we put a protection unit on your place, just to be on the safe side. That's who spotted the Dick."

"A protection team for an empty apartment ..." muses Bliss.

I'm obviously the monkey's paw in this, he thinks. They all want Edwards out of the job and if my evidence nails him everyone else is off the hook. But if I fail? Edwards will nail me and they'll all be standing around with hammers in hand to help him.

John Smith's credit card in his wallet tarnishes slightly as he realizes that his extended vacation is obviously being privately financed out of the pockets of a syndicate of Edwards's contemporaries — probably backing both sides — one financially, the other verbally, and he pictures Richards buddying up to Edwards with a consoling hand on his shoulder. "Don't worry, Michael. Everyone knows Bliss is a right shit disturber."

"Gordon Grimes dipping into the Widows' and Orphans' Fund was just a coincidence then — just luck I happened to be here."

"No, the auditors smelt a rat a couple of months ago and tipped us off. We needed someone on Johnson's tail so that when we made a move on Grimes we'd be ready to lift him. That's where you came in."

"Two birds with one stone," suggests Bliss, asking, "What went wrong?"

"When we lifted Grimes we tapped his phones. That's why we let him out on bail, thinking he'd rush home to tip off Johnson. Then we could have nicked Johnson for conspiracy to defraud."

"And he didn't try to call?"

"No — not unless he confused the risky end of a shotgun with a telephone mouthpiece."

"So where does that leave Johnson?"

"Free as a dicky-bird. He'll probably swear he had no idea where the money came from and put all the blame on Gordon Grimes. Unless we can prove the whole scheme was a fraud."

Bliss perks up. "We can. I'm sure Grimes and his wife will testify after what Johnson did to them, and the pieces of pot I sent you should corroborate it."

Some of the pot shards are already on their way to the British Museum for radiocarbon dating of the crustaceans embedded in the surface.

"They'll soon know if this stuff has been on the seabed for any length of time," Richards tells him. "We should have preliminary results in a couple of days."

"If my hunch is right," says Bliss, "Johnson used Greg Grimes's research to get someone to turn out the amphorae that'll be leaked onto the black market."

"What's the price tag?"

"Money means nothing to these guys from what I see," replies Bliss, recalling Marcia Grimes saying, "The rich only want what they can't buy."

"They're like shoplifters in a power failure, Guv," he adds, seeing in his mind's eye the inhabitants of the villas on the hills above St-Juan dipping into corporate funds and investors' pockets and then running when the lights come on.

"I'm hoping the other stuff will tell me who chopped off Grimes's hand," he goes on, and Richards confirms the T-shirt and cigarette butts are on their way to the Home Office's forensic science lab for DNA testing.

"Have you any idea where Johnson is now?"

"He was in Cannes last night, dining with a couple of shady-looking Corsicans," says Bliss, adding, "I was surprised to see him alive. Marcia Grimes must be ready to kill him — she was just easing herself back into her husband's bed — and his son and wife aren't exactly his biggest fans. Even Natalia Grimes might come to her senses when she sees what he's done."

"No shortage of suspects if he snuffs it then," says Richards.

"Five — with Greg Grimes, if he can shoot left-handed."

"The Dave Burbeck five," suggests Richards with a laugh.

"Not you as well," mumbles Bliss.

By Thursday he's taken on the attitude of the waiters and shop girls and is coasting. With three full days left he has only to fit together the heraldic puzzle to discover the name of the masked man, and then he can finish his novel and head home.

The golden beams streaming through the open window alert him to another brilliant dawn as he wakes to Brubeck playing "Balcony Rock."

I'm going to come back here to live when my book's published, he tells himself as he strolls out, naked, into the sun and stretches himself on the lounger with his eye on the Château Roger. The wind-thinned foliage of the surrounding trees and the clear air have given the château and its green roofs a lift, and he looks forward to the day when the old building's image has been restored. Maybe I could get a retirement job as a tourist guide, he ponders, thinking of the future when the château will attract visitors from around the world and students will enquire in awe: "Is it true, Monsieur

Bliss, that you are the one who unravelled the *mystère de l'homme au masque de fer*?"

"*Oui*," he will proudly admit, then sell them a translated copy of his famous novel, *The Truth Behind the Mask*.

The telephone bites into his thoughts. It's Daisy, with an invitation for coffee and, intriguingly, a chance to unearth some more information about the château.

"Eleven o'clock at L'Escale," he agrees.

With time speeding up as his summer sojourn nears its end, he spends an hour each morning swimming in the cyan depths of the bay of St-Juan. The few days of sirocco wind has churned the ocean, freshening the fouled water, and has stripped the summer staleness from the air. The sugar-coated alps in the background cut into the clean sky as if they've had a touch-up, and he floats on his back in the soft mattress of sea watching the mountains for some time before realizing they *have* been touched up; despite the burning sun at sea level the highest peaks are already nosing into winter.

A couple of hours later Daisy leads him from the bright sunlight of the promenade into the dusky interior of the parish church of St-Juan.

Anticipating the discovery of a relic or an archival reference to the Château Roger, he is expecting her to take him to the vault or sacristy, especially as there appears to be a service in progress, but she drags him straight through the chancel and up the aisle. By the time his eyes acclimatize, it is too late to run from the assemblage. "I think I've been ambushed," he breathes, halfway up the nave. The black-robed priest who officiated at the meetings of the hoteliers — *le cor-beau,* a crow, as Jacques calls him — stands ready at the altar, and the flock coughs itself to a wheezy silence. Faltering under the weight of eyes, Bliss momentarily considers lightening the atmosphere by asking Daisy to marry him, but worries she may take him seriously.

The red-nosed priest greets him with a welcoming hand and views him with a degree of wonderment — as if he is already famous — while the hostility on the austere faces of the remaining congregants burns into the back of his neck.

"Zhe ladies have heard of your interest in zhe château," intones the priest, and Bliss spins as the pressure of animosity raises his pulse. The audience, whom he judges from their uniform blackness to be a deputation of the château's relicts, stare malevolently from behind high-backed pews. Thirty ghostly white faces, seemingly unsupported as their age-withered bodies meld into the miasma of darkness, hold his gaze with as much contempt as if he were the Antichrist.

"I'm not the villain here," he wants to proclaim, but realizes that in a way the widows may see him as worse than the Nazis; the invaders took their menfolk — he is threatening to desecrate their souls. Perhaps the most disconcerting feature of the assembly is the fact that several women in the front row are knitting.

What has Daisy told them? he wonders, although there is no hiding his guilt. The manuscript of his novel is in his hand and he's half expecting a bunch of them to rush him, smack him in the face, and pinch it, when one old crone grips the pew in front of her, hauls herself as upright as she has been in years, and launches into a tirade. *"Espèce de salaud, je vais te casser la gueule."*

She's not happy, he guesses from her tone, and looks to Daisy for help.

"She's gaga," whispers Daisy, feeling that to be translation enough, and the priest warns the congregants to be careful with their words — God is listening.

Women, as spectral as their men, who have shied away from the glare of public pity for sixty years in an effort to preserve the fragile tenets of their belief, mutter behind clenched gums, hoping God will not hear. Bliss gets the message. The fierceness of the thirty-odd stares worries him, although he is relieved to see that at least a dozen look dazed, as though they've been dragged out of a home for the senile aged. If they'd ganged together as determinedly on the Nazis perhaps they would have got their men back, he is thinking, as another flies at him without ceremony.

"*Vous fourrez votre nez dans les affaires des autres.*"

"You should not put your nose into zhe affairs of others," Daisy translates unnecessarily, as another, with a silvery topknot, shouts, "*Occupe-toi de tes oignons.*"

Bliss holds up his hand to Daisy. "I get it: I should look after my own onions."

"*Oui.*"

The priest steps in with a sermon of tolerance as the women, all in their eighties and nineties, start to edge forward.

"*Ça va chauffer* — it is hotting up," warns Daisy, though Bliss doesn't need telling as he realizes that the passion may not simply be religious fervour, that there may be another dynamic. Thinking, this is worse than a bunch of civil libertarians trying to spring a freedom marcher after a riot, he wonders if they really know what they are trying to achieve. Then it dawns on him that they may have turned their misfortune into a lucrative profession, and now, as they come close to retirement, this big clumsy Englishman — *un casseur anglais* — threatens to dispel the château's mystique and end their careers. I wonder if the widows have survived on State sympathy since the château took their husbands, he thinks, surmising some may even have benefited from the guilt of the Judases who'd arranged for some of their men to be spirited away.

"If there is anything else you need, Madame ..." *boulangers, charcutiers,* and other purveyors may fawn, discreetly delivering sacraments of bread and meat in atonement, as they and their predecessors have done for nearly sixty years.

One old woman, described by Daisy as *"une vielle toupie,"* complains, *"Ça me donne une indigestion."*

"I got that," says Bliss, asking Daisy to tell her he is sorry he's upset her stomach, but perhaps it is time they move on with their lives.

"We will never *capituler,*" another shouts, with a smattering of English, confirming Bliss's suspicions that after sixty years of silence the embarrassment factor will deter any of them from publicly acknowledging the truth. This is not like exhuming the bodies; this is disinterring the past — their past — when they had manned the front lines while their men were picked off. Were they any different than the thousands of returning front line troops who'd taken their nightmares to the grave fifty years later with their widows crying, "He never talked about the war"?

"Les carottes sont cuites — all is lost," complains one woman when Bliss declines to hand over his manuscript, although he admits a certain empathy with the women. Rightly or wrongly, they'd protected the family graves for

six decades, and he wonders aloud if there is not some "*convention d'agrément*" that will satisfy everyone.

The priest, a *conciliateur* by trade, seeks conciliation. Perhaps Bliss would agree to *couper la poire en deux* — to cut the pear in half.

"But how?"

"You could change zhe name of zhe town and zhe château in your book."

"I could ..." Bliss gives ground willingly, and the priest speedily announces the resolution to his parishioners, thanks God, and heads to the bar L'Escale for lunch.

Leaving the church with Daisy, under the thankful smiles of thirty widows, Bliss feels a touch of guilt that he has permitted both the priest and the old women a degree of self-deception, realizing that anyone knowing the location of Île Sainte-Marguerite and the legend of the man in the iron mask will immediately work out the château's correct location even if he calls it Kathmandu or Kingdom Come.

"I'm sorry, *Daavid*," says Daisy. "I would have told you, but maybe you would not go."

"It's OK," he soothes. "Change can be scary for old people. I was only worried the priest was going to marry us."

"*Non*," she laughs, though did he detect disappointment? But hadn't she also lost a husband to the château in a way? Was the memory of Roland still blocking the aisle for her? Does she share the guilt of the widows — the guilt of doing nothing? And what about him? When will he come to terms with the truth and let go of past relationships? Is he scared of change as well?

chapter eighteen

By Thursday evening, with only two days to go, Bliss meanders along the promenade with the château's widows still on his back. They'll never let me live here in peace, he worries, and he can't avoid the feeling that without the novel's publication he has actually achieved nothing. Ten frenzied weeks have fizzled with as much furor as Jacques's winds. Johnson is still on the run with Natalia Grimes and the widows' mites; the potter's attacker is still free; and, though he may have released Nathaniel Johnson from his cage, the outcome was hardly satisfying.

Daisy, offering to take him somewhere special for dinner in atonement for setting him up with a hostile bunch of crones, has given him something to look forward to, and as he approaches the bar L'Escale, nearly an hour early, he watches Angeline hovering by the roadside as if she's picking her moment to cause motorized mayhem. But with the season winding down, she too is running out of steam, and awaits a break in the traffic before slipping inoffensively across the road. Jacques is back, thinks Bliss, as he spies his fellow officer in his customary spot and prepares to challenge him — his prophecy of *le pounant* has been as wayward as his other winds. But Jacques is not alone. Alarm bells in Bliss's mind force him to pull up behind a poster-plastered pillar as he takes a closer look. The sign, "*Festival du Jazz de la Côte d'Azur — avec Dave Brubeck*," now dog-eared, sun-faded, and more than two months out of date, rekindles warm memories of his first few weeks of summer. But the balding head of the man sitting opposite Jacques has an immediate and chilling effect.

The Shining Sands Hotel, a dismal back street *auberge* with a smoky snack bar infested with bikers and prostitutes, sits next to the railway tracks and is nowhere near a shiny grain of sand. Its only redeeming feature is the pay phone in the foyer.

"He's here," Bliss scowls as soon as he's connected to Richards at his home number.

"What?"

"Chief Superintendent Edwards is here, in St-Juan. I've just seen him. Someone has leaked."

Richards snorts his derision. "That's impossible. You must be imagining it. No one knows where you are."

"Peter Marshall does."

"He wouldn't grass on you," says Richards, and, without the electronic eavesdropper on his line, changes his tone. "He wants to see the skids under Edwards as much as anyone else."

"He's in Edwards's black book as well, then."

"You know about that?"

"Everybody knows about the black book," Bliss shouts. "Even the villains know about him and his dirty tricks. I've even heard old lags banged up in the slammer taking the piss. 'So — who's Edwards got the black on now?' they'd laugh."

"Shit," mutters Richards, though he knows that when it comes to black book diplomacy Edwards could be prime minister. Even the commissioner has joked that Edwards is more bilious than Napoleon.

"So. How did he find me?" Bliss asks Richards. "And what does he want?"

"He won't do anything. He just wants to put the frighteners on you. He's in a corner. Just lie low. He's got to be back here by Monday."

"So have I."

Edwards has staked out his apartment by the time he arrives home. Daisy dropped him in it. Jacques paid her a professional visit, saying Inspector Bliss's boss was looking for him.

Luckily, Bliss's defence strategy works. Since Grimes's disfigurement and his confrontation with Johnson's wife over her deranged son, he's been bothered by the possibility that his adversary knows where he lives, if not who he is. So, taking the elevator to the third floor, he stabs the button for the fourth, leaps out, and runs softly up the single flight of stairs. Edwards, focusing his attention on the arriving elevator, doesn't see the door open behind him, and by the time he turns Bliss is flying back down the stairs.

"*Merde*," mutters Bliss, returning to L'Escale and discovering that it is shuttered.

"*Fermé*," proclaims the hastily scribbled note taped to the front door.

His immediate concern that the unexpected closure of his favourite bar could somehow be related to Edwards's presence has him wondering if someone's paid off the landlord, and he peers thoughtfully through the slits in the shutters — is there movement? And where is Angeline? Every night for ten weeks. Now ... nothing.

"Jacques is a policeman — he is your friend, *n'est-ce pas?*" explains Daisy when he roots her out in her apartment, demanding to know how Edwards got his address.

"It's not your fault," he says, and she beams.

"You can stay here with me, *Daavid*."

The Japanese prints in her eyes bother him. "That is not a good idea, Daisy."

Her face drops.

"I can't stay with you because Jacques might bring Edwards to find me," he tells her, and she brightens. In any case, with only two days left he's already decided to cheer himself with a couple of nights in a swank hotel in Cannes. With Edwards standing guard at his front door he will also need some new clothes — thank you, John Smith. The apartment is paid for until the end of September; he'll come back and pick up his stuff later. All he needs is his passport, his plane ticket, and, most importantly, his manuscript.

"I go get for you," says Daisy, determined to make up for her mounting indiscretions.

Two backpackers seeking leftovers share a cut-price croissant over a couple of coffees in one of the beachside cafés as Bliss waits for Daisy. "Quiet little place," one muses, unaware of the maelstrom of humanity that passed just before them.

"Brilliant," says Bliss, as Daisy bustles in with a handful of documents. She has even put together a grab bag of toiletries and underwear and, as he rummages through the small case, he wonders aloud how long Edwards is likely to stay. Daisy leaps up, saying, "I 'ave zhe friend at zhe airport," and heads for the phone.

"He goes back to London Saturday afternoon," she smiles triumphantly a few minutes later.

"You're forgiven," he says, and offers, on John Smith's behalf, to buy her dinner in Cannes.

The sight of Johnson's yacht nudging into Cannes harbour doesn't faze him as he and Daisy pull up to the valet outside the Carlton Hotel. Until the forensic results are in and Richards has sworn out an arrest warrant, Morgan Johnson is just a greasy phantom who will constantly slip through his fingers. But even with an international warrant he knows he'll be sidelined. A couple of leather-jacketed *agents de la sûreté* from Paris, backed by a riot squad of *police nationale* CRS officers, will board the *Sea-Quester* one dawn and won't want anyone from Scotland Yard sticking his nose into their cesspit.

"John Smith is going out in style," he whispers, as Daisy flinches at the Carlton Hotel's prices.

"*Merde*," he mumbles, as the bellboy shows him into his room a few minutes later and he spots the Japanese prints on the walls.

"*Oh là là, les estampes japonaises*," Daisy coos, with an entirely different picture in mind as she slides in behind him.

"Time for dinner," says Bliss, turning her around and marching her back out.

Sunday morning dawns clearer and brighter than any day since his arrival and he is packed by nine o'clock. His three-thirty flight to London, allowing for a one-hour time difference, will get him in a little after four. First thing Monday morning he'll report to the Yard and Edwards's career will be over.

Still indecisive over whether or not to seek a publisher for his novel, he plumps for a final meditative visit to the beach and sits on the end of a wooden jetty looking over the château and the fort on Île Sainte-Marguerite, knowing that his revelation will forever change the relationship between the two buildings and their victims.

The winds have turned full circle, and the dreaded katabatic nor'wester, the mistral, which Jacques forecast with foreboding nearly three months earlier, has finally arrived. Sweeping powerfully down the valley of the Rhône the glacier of chilled air bites as sharply as sorbet on a cavity and drives many summer stragglers off the shore.

A spiked beach umbrella, snatched out of the sand by a ferocious gust, becomes a missile in the wind and hooks into the thigh of an angler. Rushing to the aid of the squealing victim at the shoreward end of the jetty, Bliss has taken a dozen steps when he stops, realizing he's left his manuscript and Walkman on the seaward end. He takes two steps back in concern when a second scream has him dancing in vacillation.

"Hold on," he shouts to the casualty and turns in time to witness a catastrophe. "Oh my God!" he yells, seeing the pages of his manuscript riffling in the wind, then a sudden blast plucks it off the jetty and dumps it into the sea.

"*Putain!*" he spits, and rushes back up the jetty. Tossing his wallet from his pocket onto the deck and struggling out of his shoes, he dives in. A silvery flash in the water beneath him catches his eye. It could be a sardine, he thinks, but it's not, and he finds himself staring at his apartment keys as they jink, like a lure, into thirty feet of water from his breast pocket. He surfaces for a breath, but the wind-driven waves are stronger than he anticipated, and by the time he looks back, the keys are gone. So is his manuscript — swamped under wave after wave. Torn between diving for his keys and retrieving his novel, he flounders for several long seconds before realizing that he is being towed out to sea and dragged down by his clothes. Letting go of the waterlogged pages he crawls to the beach and is washed ashore by the breakers. Sitting on the sand next to the injured fisherman, he watches forlornly as the manuscript is flopped around by the waves until it takes on water and sinks.

His socks squelch as he makes his way back up the jetty to retrieve his wallet and Walkman. "Three months' bloody work," he whines, facing into the mistral, and finds himself looking across the promontory.

Marcia Grimes, flying along the promenade in the gale, breaks into his melancholia. "Thank God I've found you," she cries, her words caught by the wind as she breathlessly tells of Johnson preparing to sail to pick up his haul. "You've got to stop him. He's going to get away."

But it's not Bliss's problem — he's on his way home. What do you want? he wonders, giving Marcia a sideways glance. "Help me," says her pleading look, and he sees her clinging to him to stop herself from drowning in guilt.

"You change your tune as often as your bed," he mocks, and she doesn't argue. In any case Morgan Johnson is passé, and, with his mind absorbed by his lost saga, he shrugs uninterestedly. "Where is this hoard?"

"Corsica, he reckons."

"That was fairly obvious," he snorts, letting her know where he stands. "And where does he go from there?"

"Who knows? North Africa, the Middle East — the world."

He is tempted to let her wallow, but the detective in him wants more, knowing that if the *Sea-Quester* makes it out of European waters with its shifty cargo no one will be particularly concerned about catching Johnson, and the widows of Scotland Yard will be five million out of purse. But he's suspicious of her motives. "How do you know?" he demands. "Did he tell you, or is this just another attempt to get me to rescue your stupid daughter?"

"She won't leave him. You know that."

"How do you know ..." he starts, and then catches on. "You were on-board," he breathes, recalling the slight scuffling he'd heard in the forward cabin the night he'd tried to get Natalia off the *Sea-Quester*.

Confessing by her silence, Marcia warns him, "Johnson knows who you are and what you're doing."

"That's interesting," he says, thinking, even I'm not sure of that anymore, then rounds on her angrily. "Whichever way I look at this shitty mess I see your face."

"It's my daughter ..."

"You don't deserve a daughter," he starts, but backs off at the sight of her face. "Crocodile tears, Marcia," he says, walking away with his own woes.

Commander Richards's dark tone alerts Bliss to the possibility that he's woken the senior officer. But why should he rest easy?

"Edwards is on his way back," says Bliss, recalling the previous afternoon, at Nice airport, when he and Daisy watched him go up the escalator and through the security gate from the safety of a surveillance monitor in her friend's office.

"It's still Chief Superintendent Edwards to you, Inspector, I've warned you about that before," cautions Richards, fearful of counting chickens.

"Not after tomorrow," replies Bliss, though doesn't know where to take the conversation. "There's something else ..." he starts.

Richards snorts, "Oh, what now?" and awakes in Bliss a mutineer. If he hadn't lost his manuscript he probably wouldn't have reacted, but, with the feeling that he has nothing further to lose, he bellows, "Get stuffed," and slams shut his cellphone.

"You need me more than I need you," he shouts to the phone and lumps Marcia, Richards, the commissioner, and even the force widows and orphans into one grovelling bundle. "What's in it for me? I'm not in Edwards's black book. I got my revenge — I broke his wrist. Fight your own battles."

His phone rings. It's Richards — boiling. "Make sure you get on that plane, Inspector. You will be back in my office at nine tomorrow. No ifs, buts, or maybes."

If the captain of the charter yacht had been sober he probably wouldn't have sailed. If Bliss had any sense he wouldn't have asked, but, as he insisted to Daisy,

"Johnson must be stopped." However, taking off to Corsica has nothing to do with catching Johnson, and he knows it. His war, he has decided, is against all the spectres of the Château Roger and the treacherous winds — especially the treacherous winds. Dispirited over the loss of the manuscript, he is determined to take at least one scalp back to England — Johnson's.

The sleek yacht is fully fuelled and ready to roll, according to Captain Jones, who is in a similar condition, but rounding up a crew will take time. With Johnson already two hours ahead Bliss can't wait. Can it be that difficult? he asks himself, surveying the controls and instruments on the bridge: ahead, astern, port, starboard. At least he won't have to worry about up and down, he thinks. If the old captain had been sober he probably wouldn't have agreed, but John Smith's gold weighs heavily in Bliss's favour.

"We'll need a cabin boy," the old man starts, and Daisy, still trying to atone, steps forward.

"Ah, ah. A frog Wren," he roars, as if it's the funniest thing anyone's ever said.

"I don't understand ..." says Daisy, but Bliss is anxious to get underway and studies the charts. Assuming the greybeard is steady enough to get them out of the harbour without ramming anything, he'll have plenty of searoom to practice while the old man sleeps it off, seeing that once past Île Sainte-Marguerite they have a straight run to Corsica.

The first hour is a training session and now, with the coast receding into a ragged line on the horizon, the captain slips beneath the radar into the watchkeeper's bunk, joking, "Call me when we hit land."

With his eyes glued to the blank horizon and his

hands fastened to the wheel, Bliss steers them on a course more drunkenly than the captain. Up and down appear to be the most predominant motions as the nor'westerly mistral, on the stern, drives the following waves that pick them up and corkscrew them through the water. It's fast — like a giant surfboard — and Bliss fights with the wheel as they come close to broaching time and again.

"It's a hundred and sixty kilometres, as the shite-hawks fly," the captain told them before taking to his bunk, but the seagulls are not flying today. The winterized wind has swept the sky clear of everything — clouds, birds, and haze — and whipped the wavetops into a blizzard of foam. Daisy opens the bridge door to throw up and is doused. Slamming the door, she stands dripping, like a contestant in a wet T-shirt contest, and laughs, "*Merde!*"

A school of bottlenosed dolphins leads the way, porpoising ahead of them and diving through the green waves. Daisy clings to Bliss's arm, fearful of the bow digging into a wave and spearing one of the playful mammals, but the fast-swimming creatures are always one leap ahead.

The compass arcs back and forth like a metronome as the wheel is wrenched one way and then the other, and Bliss's white fingers cramp numbly as he fights to hang on. "Should I stop?" he worries, but the thought of battling his way back, crashing head on into the waves, keeps him driving forward. But even at fifteen knots the yacht slams into walls of water that send reverberations rippling through the vessel. Fearful of submarining the bow beneath a wave, he slackens off.

"This'll take hours," he moans, feeling the boat relax as he brings the throttles back.

"Twelve — maybe more," the captain warned him before they took off.

"It took less than three on the ferry," he protested. But this isn't a colossal high-speed ferry — and this isn't a three-hour zip on a silk-smooth day. Even stabilized cruise liners will be passing out pills and plasticized paper bags today, he realizes, thinking it ironic that the only time Jacques didn't forecast a foul wind they were hit by a howler.

After a couple of hours, with his bladder straining, he sends Daisy to rouse the captain. She returns empty-handed. "He is *paf* — drunk."

"How the hell can anyone sleep through this?" he complains jovially, but is beginning to worry. The radar screen is as clear as the horizon, but what happens when it gets dark? What if it gets significantly rougher?

An hour later, ready to burst, he gives Daisy a quick lesson and dashes to the head.

"You're good," he says when he returns, and acknowledges that she has better control of the vessel than he.

The captain struggles to the surface late in the afternoon.

"Did anyone get the licence plate?" Bliss wonders aloud, as the old mariner hauls himself upright on the wheel. Bliss tries hanging on. His fingers and forearms ache, but there's a sense of achievement in navigating from A to B, even drunkenly. The captain is of the same opinion and insists on taking over. "This is nothing," he roars, swaying in rhythm.

"How about some late lunch?" Bliss suggests, realizing that neither he nor Daisy has eaten. But, in his haste to take off, it hadn't occurred to him that the vessel wouldn't have stores, that few charterers would simply jump aboard with a gold card saying, "Follow that yacht."

"Is there any food?" he asks the skipper, at which the old man gives him back the wheel. "Hang on," he says. He rummages through a bar fridge and comes up with a bottle. "Try this," he laughs. "It's a fairly hearty claret."

The only solid foods are cashews and condiments; they settle for the nuts while the captain gets his teeth into the Bordeaux.

Under the old skipper's hand the vessel straightens herself and lifts her prow towards the mountainous island coming at them over the horizon.

"Corsica," he pronounces, as if he'd discovered it.

The large blip of Johnson's yacht stands out brightly on the radar screen among a fleet of smaller vessels as they nudge into the shelter of the Golfe du Calvi a few hours later.

"Could that be the *Sea-Quester*?" Bliss enquires casually, pointing to the large dark shape silhouetted in the moonlight.

"*Bof!*" The skipper shrugs, unaware of Bliss's quest. "We'll get a berth in the harbour and go ashore," he adds, and gets no argument from either of them. The thought of bobbing around in the bay all night isn't appealing, and they need food — solid food.

Bliss's cellphone bursts to life as he readies to throw a line to the wharfinger in Calvi harbour, and he's tempted to ignore it.

"Catch," he shouts, tossing the line, and then flips open the phone.

It's Richards — apologetic. "Dave, we were cut off. I've been trying to get back to you all day," the commander says, blaming the unreliability of modern communications.

What a difference a day makes, thinks Bliss, playing along. "I've been all at sea."

"No sweat," says Richards, "I've got you now. Look, I've smoothed it over with the commissioner. We'll stall the hearing until two o'clock tomorrow afternoon. I've booked reservations for you on all three early flights."

"Sorry, Guv. No can do. I'm still convalescing," Bliss breaks in. "Anyway, I'm pretty sure I've got a cast-iron case."

"Don't give me that crap. Get your ass back here and be in my office —"

That didn't last long, thinks Bliss as he hits the off key, muttering, "Manners." Edwards will walk, but that's everyone else's problem. I'll be in his good books. Anyway, what will they do if I net Johnson and the missing money?

And what if you don't?

Maybe I won't go back. Maybe I'll just stretch Smith's credit card to the limit.

Bliss's credit snaps ten minutes later at the cash machine outside a main street bank. "*Putain*," he mutters, assuming that Richards has blocked the card, but Daisy steps in.

"It has no money," she explains, reading the screen, and they try three more banks without success. It's nearly midnight on Sunday, at the end of a busy weekend; the machines are exhausted.

"What is zhe plan?" asks Daisy once they've found a restaurant that takes credit cards. But he has no plan.

"I'm just fed up of being used," he confides, and realizes that he still has nothing to go on — only Marcia's word that Johnson is here to pick up the treasure. "All we can do is follow the *Sea-Quester* in the morning."

"If the captain is awake," says Daisy dubiously.

The captain is dining aboard — on a fairly filling Burgundy.

"We say he will 'ave *mal au cheveux* — zhe hairache — in zhe morning," she laughs, but Bliss doubts the well-practised old sailor will feel any effects.

"We'll just get out there first thing and follow Johnson before he has a chance to up anchor."

Bliss is saved the trouble. Gazing out of his cabin porthole at dawn, he is watching the India ink of night slowly bleed into sky blue at the start of yet another postcard day when he spots a commotion in the place where Johnson's yacht should be.

"He's gone," he blares in disbelief. Taking the *Sea-Quester*'s place in the bay is a flurry of small boats, and as he watches they break away and make for the port. Bliss grabs his shorts and heads them off at the harbour entrance. A sleek police launch escorts a couple of chugging sardine trawlers. On the deck of one of the trawlers a uniformed officer guards a tarpaulin that shrouds an ominous bulge. Throwing off his author's cloak as the boats come alongside, Bliss flashes his Scotland Yard ID card at the policeman.

"*C'est un macab*," says the cop with little concern, as he points to the concealed body. "*Un accident*," he explains with a shrug.

Bliss steels himself for a gruesome sight — he's seen bodies trawled from the depths before with chunks missing, crabs clawing their way out of mouths, eyeballs plucked out by seagulls — and sneaks a look under the tarpaulin.

"It's Morgan Johnson," he breathes, and sees that one of the man's feet is entangled in a rope attached to a hefty amphora. A blue bruise stands out on Johnson's pallid left temple and a flap of scalp hangs over his right ear. "You think this is an accident?" Bliss queries skeptically.

"*Oui — tragique*," replies the Corsican cop.

"Very tragic," agrees Bliss. But this is Corsica — accidental death is a way of life. More people stab themselves in the back here than anywhere else on earth, and Bliss doesn't need Sherlock Holmes to tell him that Johnson's demise is no unexpected mishap. Revenge, greed, anger, passion, and maybe all four, but no accident. The work of one of the Dave Burbeck five, he guesses, although he realizes that Grimes, the one-handed potter, would have needed an accompanist. It shouldn't be too difficult sorting out the guilty party from the *panier* of suspects on the *Sea-Quester*, he thinks, but where is the *Sea-Quester*?

"Tell your chief that this was murder," calls Bliss as he heads off at full speed to the harbourmaster's office.

Bliss recognizes the assistant by the stains on his bulging shirt. "Where's the *Sea-Quester*?" he demands.

"*Je ne parle pas anglais*," the scruffian claims, casually striking a match for his cigarette.

Bliss jumps on him. "Don't give me that crap. You spoke perfect English last month."

As a light flares in the assistant's dark eyes, Bliss yells, "Monsieur Johnson is dead. Where is his yacht?"

Taking three stubborn puffs, he picks up the radio microphone and tries calling. "*Bof!*" He shrugs with satisfaction at the whooshing of static, and Bliss races out the door and back to the *Mystère*.

"If Johnson's dead, who is at the helm of the *Sea-Quester*?" Bliss wants to know once he's assembled the crew and put them in the picture, but neither the captain nor Daisy has any suggestions.

"It's either the gorilla who drives his car, or the Corsicans he was with in Cannes," he muses, saying, "Let's have a look at the charts."

"What are we looking for?" asks the captain.

"Treasure," explains Bliss.

"And I s'pose you're Long John Silver," starts the old bacchanalian, then Bliss pulls out his ID card and straightens him out.

Half an hour later they're still tied up, when Bliss recalls Marcia saying that Johnson claimed to be following the winds.

"What winds?" asks the captain.

The mistral has been on their back with uncanny precision all the way from the mainland, heading them 135 degrees — directly southeast. The figures burned into his brain for more than ten hours as he fought with the wheel to keep the compass heading, even commenting to Daisy several times that the nor'wester would blow them directly from St-Juan-sur-Mer to Calvi if their engines failed.

"Maybe they went southwest," Bliss starts, seeing that to be the only direction that makes sense, then stops in surprise with his finger on an islet off the most westerly tip of Corsica. "This island's called 'Gargalo,'" he says, adding, "Isn't that the name of one of the winds?"

Before they can answer he picks up on another point of interest. "It's a job to tell on this map, but I'm pretty sure that's roughly where I saw the *Sea-Quester* before."

"This is silly," Bliss continues with his finger on the tiny island. "Don't take any notice of me — but look."

They look, but have no idea what he is talking about.

"It's the winds," he explains. "The Roman galleys would have been reliant on them, and a foul westerly or northwesterly might have driven them onto the rocks. If we knew the winds ..."

"You could phone Jacques," suggests Daisy, but he shakes off the idea as he recalls some of the names.

"I know *la tramontane* is north, and I'm sure the *gargali* came next."

"*La levantade* is an easterly," says Daisy, as the old captain unfolds an ancient diagram.

"Is this what you're looking for?" he asks.

"Yes," says Bliss, poring over the compass rose with each point named. "They must have meanings," he muses. "If you're going to name something, it must have some relevance." He turns to Daisy. "So what does *tramontane* mean?"

"*Bof!*" She shrugs. "It is not *français*."

"It sounds sort of Italian for three mountains," says Bliss. "But what about Gargali? Could that be a gargoyle?"

"Zhat is a *gargouille* in French," says Daisy.

"That's fairly close — it could be Corsican. And *Levantade*?"

"Zhat is easy. Zhe *levant* is zhe east."

"The southeast wind is *la bech*, according to this."

"*Une bêche* is what you call a spade for digging."

"Well, that doesn't make any kind of sense," says Bliss. "What's next?"

"*Lou marin*," says the captain.

"Are you sure it's not Louis Armstrong?" laughs Bliss, remembering Mavis's mispronunciation.

"No," replies the captain without humour. "Definitely *lou marin*."

"*Marin* means zhe sea," jumps in Daisy, beginning to enjoy the game, though "*lou*" has her stumped.

"A derivation of *la mer*, perhaps," suggests Bliss. "Though to me it sounds as if it should mean something like 'under the sea.'"

"Sirocco is a scorching hot sou'wester," says the captain from experience, though the westerly *pounant* stumps them all.

"Well, I'm damned," Bliss breathes as he studies the map. "It's obviously just a coincidence. I don't believe it."

"What?" Daisy and the captain demand simultaneously.

"Captain Morgan's treasure!" he shouts as he leaps up, saying, "Get ready to sail, Captain. I've just got to make one call."

Richards is hopping; Edwards is getting ready to walk. Bliss fully expects the charge of dereliction of duty. What he does not expect is the radiocarbon dating results on the shards of amphorae from the hold of Johnson's yacht.

"Two thousand years old," bleats Richards, "and that's how old you'll be before you set foot in my station again if you're not back here this afternoon."

"Do you mean the pottery is genuine?" asks Bliss, ignoring the rant.

"Yes. And boy are you in trouble if you smashed it. It's worth a bloody fortune, apparently — ten thousand quid or more."

"*Merde*," Bliss breathes, "it's a good job Johnson's dead then."

"What?"

I thought that would do it, thinks Bliss, and quickly brings his supervisor up to speed.

"So much for your cast-iron case," sneers Richards, adding, "Now you've got no excuse. Just get back here PDQ. You're booked on the ten-thirty and eleven-thirty flights from Nice. Just let the locals do their job."

Concluding that Richards will find out sooner or later, Bliss gives him the bad news.

"Corsica!" screams Richards, watching the case against Edwards crumbling, and Bliss is just about to slam the phone when he remembers why he phoned. "What about the DNA tests, Guv?"

"As it happens you were absolutely right. All three match. But it's not your —"

"Well, I'm damned," Bliss breathes, cutting Richards off as the *Mystère*'s engines fire up.

"Ready when you are, Sir," bellows the captain with nautical airiness, and they let go the ropes and inch slowly from the quayside.

"Where to?" asks the captain, as Bliss and Daisy join him on the bridge.

"Treasure Island, of course," says Bliss, smiling confidently.

chapter nineteen

"The Mediterranean island of Gargalo," trumpets Bliss as they round a headland near the most westerly tip of Corsica. The term is far too extravagant for the arid islet sitting just off the coast, and the old skipper is scornful. "That's not an island. I've had bigger hangovers than that."

Bliss checks the chart. "That's it, all right — just a rock, no roads or dock. I guess it's only about a mile square."

Standing out to sea they scan the steep cliffs, straining against the sun to peer into the few ragged coves.

"What are we looking for?" asks Daisy.

"Whoever sent Captain Morgan to Davy Jones's locker, I s'pose," mocks the skipper.

Bliss ignores the jibe as he sweeps the coastline with his binoculars. "My guess is that Johnson was on his way to pick up the treasure when his partner, or partners, got greedy and decided not to share."

"But why here?" asks Daisy.

"Because of this treasure map," Bliss explains, lowering his glasses to lay a finger on the chart.

"But that's just a standard navigation chart," scoffs the skipper.

With idling throttles, the *Mystère* lolls on the swell as Bliss lays out his suspicions that, while traditional pirates may have drawn up their own treasure maps, in this case it appeared someone had stashed their loot in accordance with an existing map — or two.

"Look," he says, laying the admiralty chart and a diagram of the Mediterranean's winds together and putting his finger on St-Juan-sur-Mer. "The trail began from the cove of the Château Roger."

"Why?" asks Daisy, still disconcerted by mention of the old building.

"I have my reasons," says Bliss, pushing on. "We came southeast — on the mistral — it's the only wind direction that misses both Île Sainte-Marguerite and the Cap d'Antibes."

"To Corse," says Daisy, her finger tracing a straight line to Calvi.

"Yes — Corsica. And from there *la tramontane* took us three mountains south; then the *gargali* brought us southwest to here — the island of Gargalo."

"But where next?"

Bliss's plan suddenly falls apart as he surveys the wide-open Mediterranean ahead to the west.

"That's Spain over there," the skipper points out. "But it's a bloody long way."

"No!" exclaims Bliss excitedly as he turns back to Gargalo. "Wait … it's an island. We haven't been all the way around. We are on the wrong side. If we were between Corsica and Gargalo, the next wind, the easterly *levantade*, would drive us into the east side of the island."

"That does it then," mutters the old captain as he leans on the throttles and swings the vessel out to sea.

"Hang on," says Bliss. "I said we had to go east, to the other side of the island. You're going west."

"And I shall keep going west," he replies as he pulls the chart from under Bliss's hands and points out the problem — the narrow sliver of sea separating the rocky outcrop of Gargalo from the stark mountains of Corsica.

"I wouldn't wanna squeeze a lemon through that," he explains. "My insurance wouldn't cover me, an' if I hit a rock I'd never get another command."

"OK," demurs Bliss, "but what will the insurance company say if they find out you were so pissed yesterday that you let a couple of rookies sail all the way from St-Juan to Calvi?"

"That's extortion."

"Blackmail, actually."

"All right — but you'll have to pay for any damage."

Something else for John Smith to worry about. "You can always claim a cop jumped aboard shouting 'follow that yacht,'" Bliss says, as they turn back to the island.

With the weight of the law on his tail the old sea dog noses the *Mystère* into the narrow strait. The late morning sun is still wheedling its way into the steep ravine as Bliss and Daisy keep watch on the foredeck, hanging over the bow looking for rocks in the clear indigo depths.

"If you are right about zhe winds," says Daisy, "what about *la bech* and *lou marin*? Where will zhey take us?"

"Let's just see what we can dig up under the sea, shall we?" he says with a wink.

The captain fortifies himself with a stiff tot as he nudges the *Mystère* through the steep-sided channel. Jagged peaks lurk beneath, like sharks waiting to rip out the vessel's underbelly and sink both him and his ship in minutes. With sweat pouring off his brow, he keeps his eyes glued to the echo sounder. The bubbling exhausts resounding off the rock walls have guided him along a central path, but a momentary change in tone alerts him to a cleft in the island's apparently impenetrable wall.

Bliss also spots the fissure as the *Mystère* steams slowly past and he frantically signals to the captain to cut the engines.

"Don't even ask," says the captain, as Bliss rushes to the bridge and points to the narrow break in the sheer cliffs.

"We'll need a dinghy then."

"I come," says Daisy.

Ten minutes later, an inflatable pushes off from the stern of the *Mystère*, Daisy at the helm and Bliss at the oars. Bliss would have preferred the ski boat with the double Johnson outboards, but the captain balked at winching it off the upper deck without a qualified crew.

The throb of the *Mystère*'s engines fade as they approach the vertical cliffs that stand sentinel to the channel. Only the gentle *plop* of the oars and the squeak of plastic rowlocks accompany them until they near the rock face, when the air suddenly comes alive with the screeching of panicked herring gulls. Dislodged pebbles drop like hailstones into the surrounding sea, and gulls swoop and wheel as they try to drive off the invaders.

"Zhere is nothing," says Daisy, as she fends off the birds and peers ahead through the gap to a solid rock wall.

Bliss is about to turn back when a new sound halts his rowing.

"Listen," he says, and under the shrieks of the gulls the unmistakable burble of powerful exhausts bounces off the rock face. They glide through the channel as the sound intensifies, then the rocks open into a sheltered cove where the *Sea-Quester* rides at anchor. There is activity on the aft deck and a bundle of cables snake over the side to feed the remote-controlled mini-sub below.

"Maybe we should call zhe police," whispers Daisy, shivering in the chill of the sunless ravine.

"I think they are already here," replies Bliss, spying a familiar figure.

Their approach is masked by the bobbling of the *Sea-Quester*'s diesels, and they are almost alongside before a head pops into view over the stern rail.

"Jacques," breathes Daisy.

"Aha. My dear Monsieur Burbeck and zhe charming Daisy. What brings you here?"

"A touch of wind," muses Bliss, as he leaps aboard the swimming platform at the vessel's stern.

Leaving Daisy to secure the inflatable, Bliss runs up the stairs to the aft deck and takes in the scene. Five giant amphorae lay at his feet and another is slowly rising from the depths in a crane's sling as two men prepare to bring it aboard. Bliss's sudden arrival sparks a hiatus as the men vacillate between their task, the newcomer, and Jacques.

After a moment's hesitation Jacques pulls out a pistol and lets it waver. "Ah, my dear *inspecteur*, enough of the charade. I have found Morgan Johnson's treasure."

"Are you pointing that gun at me?" queries Bliss.

Jacques glances at his gun as if he's surprised to find it in his hand, then swings it menacingly towards the two swarthy men.

"*Mais non, mon ami* — my dear friend. Of course not. It is zhese two villains who I arrest."

The Corsicans' confusion is obvious as they half-heartedly raise their hands on the end of Jacques's weapon. One steps forward as if to remonstrate, but Jacques forces him back with a vicious volley of French. The amphora swings gently — forgotten.

"Quick," shouts Jacques, turning back to Bliss, "take zheir guns."

By the time Daisy surfaces, the commotion is over. The two men are lying face down on the deck. Jacques is neatly trussing them, hands and feet, as Bliss stands guard with the French officer's pistol. The amphora still dangles from the davit mid-air, and the Corsicans' guns lay disarmed on a deck table.

"So — what's happening?" asks Bliss, as Jacques binds the wrist of the first man.

"I told you. I work under zhe covers." He gives the amphorae a nod. "Your Monsieur Johnson was trying to steal treasure from us. And zhese two — zhey are with him; zhey are pirates also."

They certainly look like pirates, thinks Bliss, recognizing the squat earthy Corsicans he'd seen with Johnson at La Scala.

"But surely you're not alone."

"*Oui* — yes. Zhere was no time. But now I will radio for assistance. A helicopter will arrive *tout de suite* and zhese villains will be —"

"But what about Johnson?"

Jacques shrugs as he works on the second man. "He is not here."

"I know. He's in the mortuary in Calvi."

"What you say? He is *disparu*?" asks Jacques with Gallic phlegmatism.

"If that means dead — yes."

Jacques stands with the neatly bundled Corsicans at his feet and holds out his hand for the gun, saying, "Zhat is good. It will save zhe *fisc* — zhe taxman."

"Oh!" exclaims Bliss, as an imperceptible movement of the vessel suddenly sends him lurching across the deck to crash into the table. As he reaches out to steady himself, he swipes the Corsicans' guns over the ship's side and flails wildly to keep himself upright. In a desperate move to save himself from falling overboard, he flings out his hand and drops Jacques's gun into the sea.

Daisy stands, completely unmoved, marvelling at the way she so easily maintained her balance. Jacques rushes to the rail. "*Mon Dieu!* What are you doing?"

Bliss looks mortified as he peers into the depths. "Oh. My dear chap — I can't believe it. I am so clumsy. Maybe we can use the sub —"

Jacques cuts him off. "*Non. Ce n'est pas possible.*" Then his stoicism returns with a "*bof!*" and he turns away. "It is no matter. I will radio for assistance from Calvi. Zhey will come very quickly. My prisoners cannot escape — all will be well."

Bliss gestures towards the bridge. "You go ahead and radio, Jacques. We'll wait until they arrive."

"Oh, *non*, Monsieur. Zhat will not be necessary. I would not wish you to change your plans and ruin your holiday — especially as you are spending it with such a delightful lady." His face puzzles. "But you did not row here from St-Juan."

Daisy is already flabbergasted by the scene, but she's bowled over when Bliss rustles up his phantom brigade again. "Oh no. There's a whole boatload of us." He throws his arm around her waist as he continues. "Thought we'd explore, get away from the crowd. They're just out there ..."

"In zhat case, my dear *collègue*, please, you must rejoin your friends. Everything is fine."

"I insist," says Bliss, adding, "In any case, Johnson was British. I have a duty to assist in your investigations."

"Zhere is no need," starts Jacques, but Bliss is adamant.

"Jacques — as a fellow officer it is the least I can do. You radio for help and I'll keep an eye on these two."

Jacques is clearly reluctant as he backs into the bridge. Daisy is still desperately trying to find her feet. "*Daavid*. I don't —"

Without taking his eyes off the bridge door, Bliss grabs her arm and starts dragging her aft. "Quick, Daisy. Get back to the boat. Tell the captain to call the police."

"But Jacques. He is un *flic* — a police —"

"Daisy, don't argue. Just call."

"But I don't understand."

Her confusion is instantly dispelled as Jacques reappears from the bridge with another gun in his hand. "I zhink Daisy should stay, *Monsieur l'Inspecteur*."

"My fingers, I zhink zhey are dead," moans Daisy as she struggles against the bindings on her wrist ten minutes later. Bliss has his ear stuck to the cabin door and shushes her as he tries to work out if anything is happening in the corridor outside. He checks the lock. It's not particularly strong — but is a maddened Corsican waiting with a Kalashnikov on the other side?

The background thrumming of the engines and the whine of a capstan raising another amphora make it impossible for him to hear, so he gives up and hobbles back to the bed. The police-issue plastic bindings cut deeply into his wrists and ankles, but knowing their strength he makes no effort to break free.

"How did you know it was Jacques?" asks Daisy, as Bliss slumps beside her.

"His DNA was on the cigarette ends we found in the château's basement after Grimes was attacked."

"Jacques's DNA?"

"*Oui. Certainement.* I sent them to London with some that he smoked at L'Escale. The saliva matched. And you remember the Brubeck T-shirt?"

Daisy's voice drops in painful memory. "Roland's?"

"*Oui*, Roland's. Well some of the blood on it was Jacques's. Roland must have put up a struggle — I certainly would if someone was trying to hack off my zizi."

"Jacques," she breathes. "But why? Zhat is terrible."

"My guess is the war widows aren't the only ones who want to keep secrets. When I asked Jacques about the château he said he'd never heard of it, but you told me that he'd searched it after Roland's death. And when he just *bof*'d at the potter's hand in the harbour, I thought, this is bizarre. Why would he lie? Unless he didn't want me to go there."

"So you zhink zhat is why he killed Roland — because he found zhe château?"

"Maybe.... And maybe the hand in the water was to warn me off. But why? That's what I don't understand."

"I zhink I know," says Daisy worriedly. "At school Jacques has no friends. Zhey spit at him, zhey hit him, zhey say he is *un cochon* — a pig. I am unhappy and tell my mother. 'Jacques is just a poor little *garçon*,' I say. Zhen she tells me zhat Jacques's father was in zhe château, but he was not like zhe other men. He would come home at night to his wife. Zhey were from Alsace."

Bliss's questioning expression invites an explanation.

"It is *français* now, but Alsace was German before zhe war. Jacques's father spoke German. He was a *traducteur* ... how you say ... a translateur for zhe Nazis, a *collaborateur*."

Bliss corrects Daisy's English as he echoes, "A translator." Then a horrific image springs to his mind as he pictures a terrified artisan chained to a steel bench in the château's torture chamber, with Jacques's father standing by with a scratch pad as he waits to catch the dying denunciation of yet another compatriot.

"What happened to Jacques's father after the war?" he asks Daisy

"*Bof*." She shrugs. "He is *disparu*. My mother says after *la Libération*, first zhey make him dig zhe graves for zhe others, zhen he dig for himself. But I did not see his name on zhe gravestones."

"That would explain why Jacques wouldn't want anyone going to the château," he reasons. "He didn't want people asking awkward questions."

"But I zhink everyone knew."

"Daisy — of course they all knew. They knew about their husbands, as well, but knowing it and admitting it are two different things. Although I doubt that any of the widows would have murdered and maimed to keep their secret. By the way, what is Jacques's family name?"

"Sauvage."

"Interesting ..." he muses. "Jacques Sauvage — Jack Wild."

Bliss lies back on the bed and closes his eyes as he desperately tries to piece together a convoluted jigsaw puzzle and comes up with a Picasso abstract.

"I don't get it," he says to Daisy, explaining how Johnson wasn't looking for treasure — he was creating it. Handcrafted copies of amphorae that needed a couple of years at the bottom of a sheltered cove to add a crust of barnacles, a few chips, and some ochreous stains. "But the amphora I found on his boat was genuine — the British Museum said so," he tells her. "He must have stumbled over a genuine hoard," he continues, "but it couldn't have been from the wreck of a passing galley. It was on the wrong side of the island."

"Maybe zhey were sheltering from a storm."

"It's possible," says Bliss, "but I still can't figure how the château or Jacques became involved."

Daisy interrupts his musing with the obvious. "*Daavid* ... do you think we should try to escape?"

The question has not left Bliss's mind from the moment Jacques and the Corsicans bundled him and Daisy into the cabin at gunpoint. It took little detective skill to conclude that, with two murders and a maiming to his credit, Jacques has little reason to ever voluntarily allow a nosy foreign cop and his sidekick to go free.

"It'll take something sharp to get these off," he says, examining the bindings, and searches for a knife-edged surface. But this is a luxury yacht — all life's dangerous edges have been neatly rounded or concealed. Then he slips off the bed, sinks to the cabin's sole, and starts working at the carpet.

"Daisy. Come and help," he says. "There may be a hatch to the engine room under here."

Fifteen minutes later, with the cabin in turmoil, he gives up and switches his attention to the bulkhead. "Maybe we can get into the next cabin." He taps lightly. "It's steel," he says, then jumps when his tapping echoes back with a five-second delay. "What the ..." he starts, then taps again.

The echo responds immediately, leaving him wishing he knew Morse code.

"Someone's there," he whispers unnecessarily, but who — a Kalashnikov killer? He cups his hand around his mouth and calls into the wall, "Can you hear me?"

Daisy has an ear to the bulkhead. "It is a woman, I zhink."

"Marcia," says Bliss, recognizing the faint voice calling for help. Then he looks to the ceiling and has an idea.

Two minutes later, Bliss bashes through the false ceiling of the adjoining cabin and finds three sets of frightened eyes staring up at him. Johnson's widow and son, together with Marcia, all similarly bound. Behind him, in the other cabin, Daisy is beginning to wobble as she buckles under his weight.

"*Daavid*," she pleads, but he has nowhere to go. With his hands tied he cannot break his fall.

"Quick," he shouts to Marcia, "pull the bed over here."

Marcia moves in slow motion and Daisy is beginning to fold, threatening to leave him stranded atop the bulkhead in the space carrying pipes and cables the length of the vessel, but the bed is fixed to the floor.

"Get the mattress," hisses Bliss, realizing that his stomach is balanced on the only sharp piece of steel that no one bothered to round off.

Johnson's widow helps finally, and with a kick off Daisy's shoulders he vaults the bulkhead, falls from the ceiling, and lands with a thud.

"How did you get here?" asks Marcia.

"We had the winds behind us," he answers cryptically as he looks around the cabin and sees that one of the Morgan Johnson quartet is missing. "Where's Natalia?"

Three pairs of eyes guide him to the bathroom door.

"Is she all right?"

The eyes drop. No one answers. Bliss knocks.

"She can't hear you," says Marcia with her head down. Bliss catches on and gingerly opens the door. Natalia is still naked, and the gold-plated tub is still waterless, but now she has another problem. Bliss checks her pulse, though wonders why he bothers. He's had a career built on similarly expressionless faces and staring eyes. An empty hypodermic on the floor tells him as much as he needs to know until he can get a pathologist's confirmation. He closes the door and looks to Marcia. Her cold, empty eyes suggest she has come unglued inside.

"Do you think I won't have to live with this?" she asks into the air.

"Do you think we don't all have to live with the aftermath of what we do?" he replies, with the château's widows uppermost in his mind.

Marcia shapes up and confesses. "I was going to kill him," she says, then realizes who she's talking to and stops herself. "Is that a crime — to want to kill someone?"

"If it was, the prisons would be overflowing."

"But I would have done it."

"Too late. You can't kill a dead man."

"Jacques ... dead?" queries Marcia.

"No. I thought you meant Morgan Johnson."

"Oh, I know he's dead," she says with little concern, and neither Johnson's widow nor his son seems particularly perturbed as she adds, "He went for a swim."

"I hit him," says Johnson's son, and his mother shouts, "Shuddup, Nathaniel," a moment too late.

"You hit him?" queries Bliss.

"He killed my Pooh-pooh," the boy starts, then begins sobbing.

"Don't take any notice. He doesn't know what he's saying," says his mother, but Bliss isn't convinced.

"Natalia killed him," says Marcia resolutely without looking up. "She stuck him with an overdose."

"I killed him," insists Nathaniel. "I hit him with a pot."

"Whoa ... wait a minute," says Bliss, seeing the Picasso morphing into a Salvador Dali. "I thought Jacques did it."

A heavy clunk reverberates through the vessel and announces the salvage of another amphora.

"We've got to get out of here," says Bliss, hoping that he will eventually see the whole picture in perspective. "But how?"

He inspects the lock. It's as flimsy as the one in the other cabin.

"It'll open," says Marcia, knowingly. "Safety ... so you can't get trapped if it sinks or there's a fire."

"A fire," breathes Bliss and looks to the ceiling with the germ of an idea.

"Daisy," he calls softy a few minutes later, "I'm coming back over."

On deck, yet another amphora is rising out of the depths and is manhandled aboard by Jacques and one of the Corsicans. The davit strains under the weight, and the vessel lurches as the giant pot is dropped onto the deck. Jacques wears a worried frown as he peers over the stern rail. With twelve giant amphorae jamming the aft deck the stern has dropped in the water, and the swimming platform is completely submerged.

"*Un,*" he calls to the Corsican as he holds up a single digit, and the man begins lowering the cradle for the final time. Jacques heads into the mini-sub's control cubicle and glues his eyes to the video screen as he prepares to operate the ROV's claws to snare another pot. The second Corsican sits on the stairs to the aft cabins, with his gun and a bottle of cognac by his side, and assumes that the crescendo of hissing sounds from below is somehow connected to the work going on above. No one is on the bridge or in the engine room to see the warning lights or hear the alarms.

Daisy has changed cabins and now sits alongside Marcia on the bed. Bliss easily shoved her up and over the partition wall, and his face now appears atop the bulkhead.

"You'll have to help me over," he calls, as he uses his elbows to lever himself up. A chair balanced on a table wobbles precariously beneath his hobbled feet. Daisy shuffles from the bed and reaches up to grab him. Her wrists are bleeding as the bindings cut into the flesh, but she doesn't flinch as she hauls at his hands. Squirming and heaving, he crests the barrier and Daisy breaks his fall.

"I hope you can all swim," says Bliss as he starts to dole out lifejackets.

"I hope we're doing the right thing," says Johnson's widow uncertainly.

"It'll take a while," replies Bliss, as he props a table against the bulkhead, clambers onto it, and inches himself up to peer back over into the other cabin.

On the stairs, at the end of the short corridor, the Corsican takes another swig from his bottle and listens to the growing crescendo of fizzing sounds with no more than a passing interest.

Bliss looks down at the pitiable trio in the cabin and whispers, "Now tell me again. What the hell is going on?"

Johnson's son and widow are searching for a galactic wormhole in the carpet and Marcia has suddenly contracted a dose of terminal dumbness.

"Marcia?" queries Bliss to break the silence before it builds into an explosion.

"Apparently Jacques was in it up to his neck with Morgan. Then you showed up," she says accusingly. "I told you not to talk to Greg, but you couldn't leave it, could you. Jacques saw you."

"In L'Offshore Club," mutters Bliss, recalling Jacques watching from the bar next door.

"Yeah. Greg had somehow found their place under the château and wrecked the pots, so when Jacques saw you two together —"

"He thought he was being fingered."

Now Marcia searches for a wormhole as she mutters, "So they chopped off ..." Her tears give Bliss a moment to add up his thoughts.

"So it wasn't Greg working in the château's basement. And I guess the hand in the harbour was directed at me."

"Me as well," says Marcia, looking up. "That's why it was hard for me to tell you things. I knew what they were like. Look what Morgan did to his kid."

"Brain damage," says Johnson's widow, stroking her son's tears away as she livens in anger. "He was all right as a baby, but if he cried or wet himself Morgan would get angry and shake him so hard his eyes would pop." Then she gives Marcia a scornful stare. "She was bloody welcome to him."

"Yeah, as long as he paid your bills," shoots back Marcia, and Bliss is thankful they're shackled.

"It was greed," explains Marcia. "Isn't it always greed? I mean, look at us — we're bloody pathetic. Got nothing left. She's lost her husband and his money. Her kid's lost his fucking dog and if I ever hear that stupid name again —"

Nathaniel keels over and bawls at the mere mention of the deceased animal. "Pooh-Pooh ... Pooh-Pooh," he cries.

"Oh, *merde*," mutters Bliss.

"If only I'd listened to Greg," Marcia snivels, then breaks down completely, sobbing, "I ruined my marriage, maimed my husband, and killed my daughter."

And your brother-in-law, thinks Bliss, but doesn't add to her misery as he protests, "You told me Johnson wouldn't have done that to Greg."

"Like I said, Inspector. It's amazing what greed does to you."

Outside the cabin, on the stairs, the Corsican reaches for his bottle and is surprised to discover it has slid away from him. He pulls himself upright, but he's listing and looks at the bottle for a cause. The hissing catches his ears and he picks up his gun and edges inquisitively down the stairs. The expensively piled carpet squelches under his feet as he steps into the corridor and his face screws in confusion as he feels the wetness.

Bliss has felt the steady shift to port as well and orchestrates his ensemble at the door, with Daisy taking the lead. "OK. Unlock it quietly and get ready to hop." Then he sticks his head over the parapet and waits.

On deck, Jacques scans the video image from the remotely operated vehicle, while the Corsican peers into the crystal water and watches as the luminously painted rover slowly snares the pot. But there's a touch of concern on his face. The surface of the water seems to be gradually creeping up the yacht's side. With the amphora hooked, Jacques pokes his head out of the cubicle and gestures for his cohort to start the davit's winch. The whining winch sends a shiver through the yacht as it strains to free the amphora from the rocks while, below deck, the watch-keeping Corsican throws his weight against the door of the empty cabin as he searches for the water source.

"Go! Go! Go!" shouts Bliss to the assault party and turns back in time to see the Corsican struggling into the room against a flood tide.

"Up here," yells Bliss, taunting the man. "I'm up here, look." The Corsican spins with his gun readied and is showered by an icy blast of water pouring out of the fire sprinkler system. "Here ... here," persists Bliss, keeping the man's attention off the corridor behind him. Water is flooding out of the bathroom, pouring from the ceiling and lapping at the opened window as the Corsican fights against the stream to get a bead on Bliss.

Bliss pops up and down like a fairground target, calling, "Hey ... hey ... hey ..." Then Daisy throws herself bodily at the gunman and bowls him over. Marcia and the others leap aboard and pin the big man to the sopping floor.

"Get his gun," yells Bliss from his perch, and Daisy kneels on his neck until Johnson's widow manages to wrestle the weapon free.

"Shoot him if you have to," Bliss calls as he flings himself off the table and hops to the door.

Two minutes later the amphora is nearing the surface. Jacques too has noticed the rising sea level on the port side and checks the horizon. Just the weight of the amphora, he assumes, and concentrates concernedly as the huge concretion breaks the surface. As the barnacle-encrusted pot swings inboard, Jacques turns to follow it and finds himself peering at a pistol.

"Put your hands up," says Bliss, and the winchman hits the wrong button in surprise and drops the amphora. The giant pot shatters on the deck, and Bliss and his posse stand with mouths agape.

Jacques shrugs. "*Bof*. So now you know."

But Bliss still hasn't caught on. The amphora's scattered contents glint golden in the midday sun. Treasure, certainly; gold and jewels, without a doubt; but this is so unexpected that he's beginning to wonder if he really has wandered into a movie. Then Marcia steps forward and picks up a glittering diamond necklace. "It is the missing Nazi treasure," she explains without a note of surprise.

"Nazi ..." breathes Bliss, but gets no further as he realizes that something is happening. "Quick, get off," he yells as the vessel slowly heels.

"Ahoy there, Captain Jones to the rescue," calls a welcome voice, as the *Mystère*'s skipper edges his ski boat into the cove and finds them floundering in the water. "What's this," he chuckles, "the John Smith five?"

"Not you ..." starts Bliss, then counts the bobbing heads as he looks around: Daisy, Marcia, Jacques, Nathanial Johnson, and his mother. But the Corsican crewmen are missing. "There should be a septet," he says, and seconds later the duo appear on deck, jump overboard, and head for the rocks, just as the yacht rolls. Bliss turns back to the *Mystère*'s launch. Jacques is trying to scramble aboard. He takes aim and calls, "Jacques ... women and children first."

"But I cannot swim."

"Good — now get off or I'll blast you off."

The Frenchman still clings on. Bliss takes two strokes and sticks the gun to his head. "I said off."

"I can't swim."

"You should have thought of that before you became a fisherman."

Jones is hauling Marcia aboard when the blast of Bliss's gun ricochets around the cove like a cannon. A thousand gulls take off with a communal shriek, Nathaniel Johnson lets out a yell that curdles the air, then Bliss lowers the gun a notch, back to Jacques's head, and counts. "*Un ... deux ... trois.*" Jacques lets go and dog-paddles frantically as Bliss passes the gun to

Jones, saying, "Keep him at bay, Captain, I'm coming aboard. Great timing, by the way."

"I was beginning to think you'd got lost. Anyway I was ready for lunch."

With the weight off its stern, the *Sea-Quester*'s upturned hull rides high in the water as the survivors skim back to the *Mystère*. Jacques slumps, deflated, in the retrieved dinghy that is being dragged behind the ski boat.

With the gun still trained on Jacques, Bliss questions Marcia.

"How do you know it's Nazi treasure?"

"Morgan told us yesterday — told us we'd all be rich if we kept quiet. He and Jacques had been working on the pot scam for a couple of years. He didn't know Jacques was a cop; just thought he'd got lucky when he found someone who knew a secret place where the pots could be made."

"But where did zhe *trésor* come from?" asks Daisy, still stunned by the multi-million-dollar hoard that is now back at the bottom of the cove.

"Everyone thought the Nazis dumped the stuff they stole from the Jews in some lake in Austria," Marcia explains, "but they didn't. They sent it by train to the château in St-Juan —"

"And packed it in Roman amphorae," concludes Bliss, as the Dali turns into a Monet and everything becomes clear. "Then they took them by subs or small boats to secluded offshore islands where they could dig them up after the fuss had died down."

"If the fuss did die down," says Johnson's widow.

"And if they survived," adds Marcia.

"I guess they didn't," continues Bliss. "But how was Jacques involved?"

"I zhink I know," says Daisy. "His father was in zhe château. Maybe he sees what zhey are doing. Maybe he tells Jacques.... *Non*, Jacques is just a *bébé.*"

"The winds!" exclaims Bliss. "Jacques knows all the winds." He turns to Daisy. "How many of the winds did you know?"

"Zhe mistral and sirocco," she says, then shrugs. "*Bof.*"

"Precisely," says Bliss. "But Jacques knew them all. I bet his father made sure he knew them — maybe he wrote them down for his son."

"He left a map," explains Marcia. "Morgan saw it, but all it showed was the names of the winds. They didn't understand it."

Daisy reaches out for Bliss's hand and beams at him. "But you did, *Daavid*. You understood it. You found zhe treasure from zhe map."

"It was fairly obvious," he says, shrugging off the compliment. "So, how did they find the treasure then?"

"Luck," pipes up Johnson's widow. "Just pure bloody luck. Typical of Morgan, that. He drops a dodgy pot in the sea, pulls out a real one, and then finds it's stuffed with gold."

"Won't do him any good now, though, will it?" scoffs Marcia.

"Easy come, easy go," says Bliss. Then, with the combined widows of the Holocaust, the Château Roger, and the London policemen in mind, he adds, "I suspect it'll make a lot of old women happy, though."

Mention of merry widows leaves Daisy questioning, "What about your book, *Daavid*?"

Twenty minutes later the small craft are stowed on the *Mystère*'s deck, Jacques is stowed in a secure locker, and Captain Jones has fired up the engines. Bliss and Daisy are back on the foredeck and looking out for rocks as the vessel slowly edges its way out of the channel and away from the island of Gargalo.

"What about 'Zhe Truth Behind zhe Mask,' *Daavid*. What will you do?" persists Daisy.

With the manuscript lost and the Château's victims still on his back, he's already decided to drop the idea. He'll stay in the police force — assuming Richards doesn't find a way to squeeze him out. The senior officer was so infused with anger when Bliss called him by ship's phone to tell him of Johnson's demise that he sounded close to breaking.

"Edwards bloody walked," Richards lamented. "You really screwed up, Bliss. The first time we've had anything concrete to lever the bastard out, and you —"

"Hang on, Guv," Bliss shouted. "Is this being recorded? I wouldn't want you slagging the chief superintendent off."

The line died with a *bang*.

"That wasn't so bad," he told Daisy with a smirk, following the call. "I've decided not to publish the book," he informs her disingenuously, reluctant to admit that he's been whipped by the mistral and a bunch of misguided faith-keepers.

"But who was the *l'homme au masque de fer?*" she wants to know.

"He is ... He is ..." He smiles. "He is just like the prisoners of St-Juan — immortal. And he will remain so unless some meddling historian or novelist discovers the château and makes public his name — but not me, Daisy. If your mother can keep a secret for sixty years, so can I."

"Zhank you, zhank you," she calls delightedly and kisses him on both cheeks — twice.

Policemen line the quayside in Calvi, and a small flotilla of commandeered craft ride their wake as Captain Jones, with a clean shirt and freshly combed hair, brings them alongside with the aplomb of a royal yacht commander.

Jacques isn't talking, but by the time Bliss and Daisy have outlined the evidence to the local police chief his future seems secure. Marcia Grimes and Petra Johnson share the same police car and are still bickering over which of their kids killed Johnson. Natalia went down with the *Sea-Quester*, and a doctor is peering into Nathaniel Johnson's eyes in the hope of finding something — anything. Captain Jones lunched on a particularly filling Côtes du Rhône and is examining the inside of his eyelids as Bliss gives final directions to a Police Nationale dive team on the quayside.

"We should be able to leave soon," he tells Daisy, as the officers pore over the map of Gargalo island.

"OK. I get some food."

"Hang on, Daisy," he calls as she heads to a quayside store. "Don't buy the *spécialité de la Corse* — I know what it is."

The sun is setting as the *Mystère* eases off the Calvi quayside and heads for the open sea.

"Phew ... what's that stink?" asks Bliss, nosing around in the galley as Daisy prepares supper.

"It is *fromage* — cheese," she says, as she takes the plate out on deck. Her face falls. "You no like?"

"Cheese, I like. But that smells like —"

"It is *brebis*."

"Oh, *merde*! Not the dreaded *brebis*?"

"Well you told me not to buy zhe donkey."

"But not zhat. Not *brebis*."

Daisy smiles. "You said, 'zhat.'"

"*Non*."

"*Oui*. You said, 'zhat.'"

"*Non. C'est ne pas possible.*"

"*Oui*."

"*Non. Moi, j'ne parler français pas.*"

"*Oui*," she laughs. "You speak French like zhe Spanish cows."

A flight of gulls and a school of dolphins escort them as they head northwest under a sapphire sky, towards home and the Côte d'Azur. The tempestuous winds of summer have abated and the soft balmy air brushes over them like billows of feathery down. The descending sun sets fire to the horizon and is slowly extinguished until only a warm memory remains. The adventurers stand on deck in awe as the heavens turn on the stars and light the moon. Venus — the evening star — shimmers so brilliantly above the western horizon that the slender shaft of its light touches them as they glide across the indigo sea.

"I'll be back," whispers Bliss, and he heads to the bridge to see if he can slip a bottle of liquid sunshine out from under the old sea dog's nose.

"An occasion like this demands champagne," says Captain Jones, digging a fine Krug out from his supply.

"Thanks," says Bliss, assuming that it'll go on the bill. "Would you like some?" he asks, as he selects some glasses from a fiddle rack.

"No thanks — already eaten," laughs Jones, adding, "We should be in St-Juan in about nine hours."

Bliss leans forward and eases the twin throttles back to the halfway mark. "I'm not in any rush — John Smith is paying."

Daisy is radiant in the glow of the moon as Bliss slips a CD in the player and emerges onto the aft deck with champagne and glasses. "Love walked in," starts Brubeck, as Bliss pops the cork and pours.

"*Daavid*," she queries, "why you no like me?"

"I do," he protests as he gives her a glass. "I like you very much, but my mind has been on so many other things."

"And now ... now zhose zhings are gone, maybe you will have zhe time for me ... *oui*?"

"Listen," he says, tenderly taking her hands and gazing into her eyes.

No one touches the volume control, but as the CD starts the next track the music slowly swells above the swish of the bow wave and the gentle burble of exhausts.

"It is beautiful," whispers Daisy. "What is it?"

"Dave Brubeck," he says, smiling as he gently pulls her towards him with a kiss readied on his lips. "It's Dave Brubeck playing 'When You Wish Upon a Star.'"

acknowledgements

With particular thanks to Mr. Dave Brubeck for his inspiration and for the five decades of listening pleasure he has given to the world. My thanks to you, Dave, and to Richard Jeweler, for your kind permission to centre this novel around your music.

My gratitude goes to Mme Beatrice Deroide of Provence for her tireless effort in straightening out my French. *Merci bien, Beatrice.*

Author's Website:
www.thefishkisser.com